KU-784-455

THE AUTHOR

Edward Frederic Benson was born at Wellington College, Berkshire in 1867. He was one of an extraordinary family. His father Edward White Benson – first headmaster of Wellington – later became Bishop at Lincoln, at Truro, and Archbishop of Canterbury. His mother, Mary Sidgwick, was described by Gladstone as 'the cleverest woman in Europe'. Two children died young but the other four, bachelors all, achieved distinction: Arthur Christopher as Master of Magdalene College, Cambridge and a prolific author; Maggie as an amateur egyptologist; Robert Hugh as a Catholic priest and propagandist novelist; and Fred.

Like his brothers and sisters, Fred was a precocious scribbler. He was still a student at Cambridge when he published his first book, *Sketches from Marlborough*. His first novel *Dodo* was published in 1893 to great success. Thereafter Benson devoted himself to writing, playing sports, watching birds, and gadding about. He mixed with the best and brightest of his day: Margot Asquith, Marie Corelli, his mother's friend Ethel Smyth and many other notables found their eccentricities exposed in the shrewd, hilarious world of his fiction.

Around 1918, E. F. Benson moved to Rye, Sussex. He was inaugurated mayor of the town in 1934. There in his garden room, the collie Taffy beside him, Benson wrote many of his comical novels, his sentimental fiction, ghost stories, informal biographies, and reminiscences like *As We Were* (1930) – almost one hundred books in all. Ten days before his death on 29 February 1940, E. F. Benson delivered to his publisher a last autobiography, *Final Edition*.

The Hogarth Press also publishes *Mrs Ames* and *Paying Guests*.

SECRET
LIVES

E. F. Benson

New Introduction by
Stephen Pile

THE HOGARTH PRESS
LONDON

Published in 1985 by

The Hogarth Press

40 William IV Street, London WC2N 4DF

First published in Great Britain by Hodder & Stoughton 1932
Hogarth edition offset from original British edition
Copyright the Executors of the Estate of the
Revd K. S. P. McDowall
Introduction copyright © Stephen Pile 1985

All rights reserved. No part of this publication may be reproduced, stored in a
retrieval system, or transmitted in any form, or by any means, electronic,
mechanical, photocopying, recording or otherwise, without the prior permission of the publisher.

British Library Cataloguing in Publication Data

Benson, E. F.
Secret Lives
I. Title
823′.8[F]   PR6063.E66
ISBN 0 7012 0565 2

Printed in Great Britain by
Cox & Wyman Ltd
Reading, Berkshire

INTRODUCTION

You would think, wouldn't you, that writing book introductions was a placid gentlemanly pastime? Not a bit of it. I wrote new ones to *Mrs Ames* and *Paying Guests*, published by The Hogarth Press in 1984, and now all hell and large parts of Rye in Sussex have broken loose. Since penning these vast essays – raving, as I thought, about the inimitable E. F. Benson – long, handwritten letters trembling with indignation have poured in by the sackload from the Tilling Society, his fan club. (It probably attracts its share of older members as I notice that it offers free life membership to anyone over a hundred.)

To list all the things that the Society (or, at least, this vociferous founder member who writes all the letters) did not like will take up more pages than *Secret Lives* itself, the wonderfully funny novel that you have so wisely bought, and now hold in your hands with rightful expectations of mirth. It might be easier to start with what they did like. They adored, in fact, lapped up my decision to include biographical details of their hero. So pleased am I to bask in the warmth of their approval that I have decided to stick it all in again.

Born in 1867, Edward Frederic Benson was the son of Queen Victoria's stern, unsmiling Archbishop of Canterbury. Benson *père* proposed to his cousin when she was eleven and he was twenty-five and seven years later the wedding took place. After producing six gifted and eccentric children, she deserted to Lesbos and spent the rest of her life co-habiting with Lucy Tait, daughter of the previous Archbishop of Canterbury.

After Marlborough and King's College, Cambridge, Fred, as the family called E. F., wrote almost one hundred books. In the midst of these biographies, memoirs and works of serious fiction were a dozen or so comic novels upon which his reputation rests. His subject matter was the snobbery of middle- to upper-middle-class England. His peculiar gift was to deflate it with affectionate, but deadly satire. While the Archbishop wrote his pious life of Saint Cyprian, E. F. produced this string of very funny, rather unforgiving, distinctly unepiscopal and decidedly camp comedies of manners . . . but here the skies darken, the boat rocks and we start running into trouble with the Tilling Society. I can bask no longer.

Since it seems most unlikely that I should have a monopoly on right thinking, it is only fair to give the opposition their say.

First, they did not like my clear, nasty, low, unpleasant and completely unnecessary suggestion, nay implication, nay bald, blatant statement that E. F. Benson was, like his mother and his brothers and sisters, 'more or less homosexual when he was anything'. OUTRAGE. In Rye, one imagines, such people are referred to, if at all, as mature bachelors and to have your local literary eminence proclaimed to all and sundry as a gay author is, I can quite see, galling in the extreme. One day the postman brought a copy of the Tilling newsletter which said by way of proof positive that 'Charlie Tomlin, E. F. B.'s manservant for many years, and also the maid Ivy Green (now Robbins) staunchly maintained that Benson was *not* homosexual, and the probability is that, although more attracted to men than to women, he didn't do anything about it.'

To such evidence I am forced to bow and I certainly agree with the Society in one thing: Fred's sexual preferences do not matter a hoot. However, I made the point then and do so again now merely to underline that his works have a prevailing campness of tone which places him closer not to Jane Austen, as the Tilling Society would dearly love to think, but to Ronald Firbank.

Second, and more importantly, the Society cries: 'You gave away the plot.' But how does one avoid it in, for example, *Secret Lives* when the whole marvel and miracle of the thing is its storyline? Not wishing to make the same mistake I wrote to the Tillingites seeking advice as to how much I could reasonably reveal, but no word was forthcoming. Criticism appears to be the local forte with constructive assistance coming a very long way behind.

Let us just say that in this novel, set in a London square, somebody has a secret life and the others do not find out until the very end after confusion, *faux pas* galore and much blushing. I shan't say a word more. My lips are sealed. (However, Benson himself gives away the plot on page 54 and thereafter applies his genius to unravelling the consequences of his central joke, the secret life.) None the less, it provides a classic opportunity for our author to apply distinctive irony to his favourite subject: the gaping difference between what we actually are and what we pretend to be.

His plot (whatever it is) gives Benson a chance to portray the very publishing world in which he lived. The portraits are timeless and unchanging. We have Mr Armstrong, the fearless and controversial critic, who takes time off when he should be doing his job as an MP, to bury literary reputations with the certainty of his journalistic trade. 'Next Sunday I shall speak of *The Brothers Karamazov*. There are many beautiful things in it. I shall point them out. But it is a book with which it is worthwhile finding serious fault. Most people regard it as a classic. My answer is monosyllabic. Rats.' Here also is Nunky Cartwright, the publisher, who has an unfailing eye for books that have 'all the atrocious qualities of a possible best seller'. He also prefers pretty women authors to any other known variety unless it be highly commercial ones. The gossip columnist, the literary snob, the writer who talks about writing books without the slightest ability to do so, the whole rogues' gallery of the publishing world is here. And all around them are the staple figures of Benson's England: Lady Eva Lowndes 'who was such a modern type, with her elbows on the table, eating chipped potatoes with her fingers' and her husband Captain Lowndes, who 'very likely had interesting things to say about Bombay if only he was allowed to say them'.

In a last-ditch attempt to ingratiate myself with the Tilling Society I next set about proving that P. G. Wodehouse pinched the idea of Jeeves, the all-seeing butler, from our own dear Benson in *Secret Lives*. Here Bosanquet resolves all dilemmas and knows how to handle every situation, being more adept than his employer in the intricacies of the English class system.

He even knows the correct way to address a guest who happens to be his nephew. 'Augustus said: "Good morning, Uncle Bob." Bosanquet completely grasped the situation and, doubling the character of the perfect uncle and perfect butler, said: "Good morning, Gus. Shall I take your coat, Sir?" "Thank you, Bosanquet," said Augustus, for he was now speaking to his friend's butler.' The ticklish situation was thus perfectly resolved. Sadly for me, Wodehouse first introduced Jeeves in 1911 which considerably predates the present novel and raises the chilling, never-to-be-mentioned possibility that Fred stole it from P.G., which I am sure is not the case and would not dream of suggesting. It would make matters with the Society even worse.

When once, exhausted and resting before renewed battle, I delayed a fortnight in my reply to the Society's latest assault, a postcard arrived gleefully inscribed: 'We must have annoyed you.' When they heard that I wished to refer to them in this very introduction my copious correspondent took prompt steps to censor the possibility. I don't see, she said, that it would help Benson.

Ah but, you see, it would. I relate this storm in a teacup mainly to show that England does not change and dear E.F. would have recognized us both and delighted in our absurdities: London smart-arse writes regrettably modern introduction making quite unnecessary suggestions about local author, whereupon good lady of Rye gathers her skirts about her and joins battle to perpetuate the myth that in provincial England all is sweetness and light. Oh, that Fred were alive at this hour to mock us as we deserve.

All of this brings me to the Tillingites' final objection: 'Your introductions were too long.' To this I have devised a swift, clear and total defence.

I answer the Society thus . . .

ends.

Stephen Pile, London 1984

MRS. MARGARET MANTRIP was undoubtedly the doyenne of the householders in the Square, if such establishments as the Swiss Convent and Norman's Hotel were regarded as being outside individual ownership. Those two corporations had existed there when Mrs. Mantrip's father bought the house which she still inhabited, but apart from them her title was undisputed, and she held that when matters concerning the collective interests of the Square were debated, it gave her opinion a greater weight than any two others. Though there was abundant evidence to show that nobody agreed with her, her conviction on this point remained unshaken. . . . There had been a brief interlude in her residence here, when, twenty years ago, she had married her late and unlamented husband, of whom the less said the better, and she had lived for eighteen months outside the precinct. At his death, which took place beneath the wheels of a traction engine (the driver being quite exonerated from blame in the accident), she had returned to her father's house in Durham Square, and had long ago succeeded in forgetting all about this unhappy experience. The only effect it had had on her was that since then she had never tasted intoxicating liquor.

Durham Square in those early days was very different, as regards its moral atmosphere, from the highly respectable quarter it had since become. In outward appearance its discreet and amiable dwellings were little altered, except for an occasional dining-room and kitchen built out at their backs, or an occasional

attic-story added at their tops, but inside, behind
those curtained windows, the change amounted to a
revolution.

" The Square was a moral slum, my dear, when
Papa first came to live here," said Mrs. Mantrip when,
with a short and sipping intake of her breath, as if it
was very hot tea, she alluded to those unregenerate
days. " Women, if you can call them such, quantities
of them, some mere girls, whom one does not like to
think about, far less to talk about, were the lessees of
many of the houses, and others lodged here. I fancy
the police were very remiss. Papa used to call the
Square an Augean stable, which always seemed to me
a very good description. Augeas, you know, that
dreadful man in the Greek mythology. It was Papa
who began buying up houses, as the leases expired,
and letting them only to thoroughly desirable tenants.
He retired from his parochial work—asthma—at the
age of forty, and came to live here, but I always
consider that he did his best and most effective Christian
ministry after that, in cleansing the Augean stable and
making our Square the sweet little place where we all
delight to live. He himself regarded it as his mission
till the end. Before very long I hope to publish a
memoir of him, and I think it will show many people
who perhaps have never heard of him, what a great
man he was. *The Life and Times of the Reverend
George Frederick Bondfield*. Two volumes. I cannot
possibly do justice to him in one. An immense
quantity of material. But a great responsibility, and
I must not hurry over it."

Mrs. Mantrip did not often speak of those unregenerate days when, night by night, quite late, so
many hansoms containing a single gentleman with a
lascivious face (or perhaps there was an attractive-
looking young lady with him) used to drive to the doors
of these houses and admit himself with a latch-key,
or whistle in a manner that suggested signalling. It

was pleasanter to contemplate changed conditions. To-day there was not a square in London of a more bland and blameless respectability: another mission in Durham Square would be mere waste of time. The missionary work, inaugurated by Mr. Bondfield, was over, and his efforts which had been productive of such admirable moral results, had been no less successful financially. He had bought half a dozen freeholds in the Square at a very small cost, since this was then so undesirable a neighbourhood for respectable tenants, and the cleansing had made them far more valuable. Then with the war had come a vast increase in taxes and the cost of living, and quite well-to-do folk, who proudly spoke of themselves as the new poor, had been eager to leave their houses in more palatial streets and squares and to settle down in these smaller abodes, which were much cheaper and easier to run and could be made exceedingly comfortable. They were a little old-fashioned, and many of their tenants had put in bathrooms and service-lifts which naturally increased the letting values of the houses. In a word, this property now belonging to Mrs. Mantrip had vastly appreciated, and her father proved to have served God and mammon with singular success. In spite of increased rents and large premiums, such houses were much sought after, and Mrs. Mantrip seldom had one on her hands that was vacant for long.

The Square itself was a lengthy oblong, the lower end of which opened into Durham Road: the top end, built on a curve, was a cul-de-sac. There was thus no through traffic, and they who inhabited houses at this top end where Mr. Bondfield had made his prudent purchases, enjoyed a quiet most unusual in London. No vehicles passed their front windows except those which had errands to the two or three residences beyond, while at the back, the houses on the west side of the Square looked, across an asphalted footway, on to the long disused graveyard attached to the parish

church. Tall elms and planes and chestnuts grew
there among crumbling, undecipherable tombstones,
and through their foliage, when the sun was low, pale
green-tinted light, as in forest aisles, glimmered on
the dinner-tables of these fortunate householders.
Scarcely a sound of traffic penetrated; the roar of
London was dim and distant and, as Mr. Bondfield had
often remarked, it was quite a *rus in urbe*. He
translated the phrase for those who had not had
a classical education.

Down the centre of the Square from end to end
ran a strip of garden, separated from the road on each
side by tall iron railings, and entered by half a dozen
gates, of which each householder had a key. Inside
were narrow lawns of grass, and trees yielding a desirable shade in summer-time, unless there was a plague
of caterpillars, in which case they shed on those who
sat under them more caterpillars than shadow. Mr.
Bondfield had planted half a dozen sumacs there, in
consequence of which Mrs. Mantrip invariably sat
under one of them when she visited the garden, and
regarded all the trees in it as a sort of family heirloom.
On the lawns were some curious erections, chalice-
shaped, made of crooked sections of gnarled boughs,
varnished and sturdily nailed together. These contained bowls of earth, in which, under favourable
circumstances and according to the season, there grew
daffodils or geraniums. There was also a summer-
house, built in the rustic style of the chalices, and a
few seats shaped like Victorian hip-baths of unparalleled hardness. A pair or two of wood-pigeons
annually nested here, and the cats of the Square annually succeeded in killing and eating the more succulent
parts of the families they reared. Mrs. Mantrip always
alluded to these wood-pigeons as " cushats," for Papa
had told her that such was their old English style; and
when she heard them cooing, she, with her strong
literary sense, was terribly liable to quote Tennyson's

pretty line " The moan of doves in immemorial elms,"
though they habitually nested in Papa's memorial
sumacs.

An attempt had once been made by the Garden
Committee to increase the population of cushats, by
keeping cats out of the garden. Rabbit-wire had been
affixed to the iron railings, and notices put up to say
that no cats were allowed there. But the cats never
heeded the notices, but jumped over the rabbit-wire
without the least difficulty and killed the young cushats
as usual. These notices had been taken down, but
there were others which forbade the presence of dogs
in the garden; they dated from early days when Mrs.
Mantrip's father had planted the sumacs and had been
President of the Garden Committee. Of late years
these anti-dog prohibitions had also failed to command
respect: there were usually more dogs in the garden
than flowers (though in consequence there were fewer
cats), and Mrs. Mantrip, coming out on to the balcony
of her drawing-room on this warm afternoon of June,
observed that her tenant and closest friend, Elizabeth
Conklin, was as usual taking her afternoon walk there
surrounded by a pack of the Pekinese dogs, which she
bred in hygienic kennels in her back yard and periodically sold at an outrageous profit. Mrs. Mantrip could
count eight of them scampering about the grass, and
there were one or two more in the bushes.

Something must be done about it, for the Pekinese
were really becoming a Chinese peril, not to speak of
the mess. She was on the Garden Committee herself,
and what is the use of a committee, she now reflected,
if nobody does what it tells them? She determined to
put down a motion at the forthcoming General Meeting
to the effect that the rule about dogs not being allowed
in the garden should be rigidly enforced. If Elizabeth
brought her dogs into the garden, why should not
Jimmie Mason take his bulldog there too? She was
a pleasant lady, called Atahualpa, but she detested

other dogs; and though her appearance in the garden
when there were so many Pekinese careering about
would doubtless diminish the acuteness of the Chinese
peril, nobody wanted a scene of carnage in front of their
drawing-room windows. " We are not gladiators,"
thought Mrs. Mantrip. Elizabeth, as well as she, was
a member of the Garden Committee, and if the matter
was brought up, Elizabeth would certainly oppose the
enforcement of the rule. But, as Mrs. Mantrip knew,
the Vicar, also on the Committee, was strongly anti-
dog. She would bring the question up at the General
Meeting next week. Papa, who planted the sumacs,
had said " No dogs in the garden," and had put up
the antique notices to that effect. Piety, as well as a
dislike of Pekinese, would amply justify a temporary
estrangement with Elizabeth.

The yapping swarm of dogs with their ineffective
mistress, to whose adjurations and whistlings and
commands they paid not the very slightest attention,
moved down out of sight in the direction of Durham
Road, and Mrs. Mantrip transferred her proprietary
gaze to the top end of the Square. Two doors away
vans from the neighbouring stores were unloading an
incredible number of small gilt chairs and hydrangeas
and smilax and flowers in pots at the house of Mr.
James Mason, who was giving a dinner and a musical
party that evening. He came fussing out of the
house, spreading his handkerchief over his shining
pink head to protect it from the sun, and began
talking genially and confidentially to the men who
were carrying in the apparatus for his party. " Just
as if he was their aunt," thought Mrs. Mantrip.
There was a young porter staggering under a colossal
hydrangea.

" You naughty boy," said Jimmie, patting him
on the arm. " Get one of your pals to help you.
You'll strain your inside and your mother will scold
me. Come on, another of you. There! Put it at

SECRET LIVES 11

the side of the steps leading to my music-room. My
servant will show you. Don't be frightened of Atahualpa. She won't bite you unless you're frightened.
She will only growl at your heels, which is her way of
showing that she approves. And all the gilt chairs to
go straight into the music-room. Good afternoon: are
you Mr. Foreman? Well, Mr. Foreman, I want all
the flowers in pots—what are they?—fuchsias or
lobelias? I never know their names—I want them all
put along the front of the platform in my music-room.
The smilax has to be wreathed round them. . . . Oh,
I forgot! The piano hasn't been brought in yet, so
you must wait to do that until it's been put in its place
on the platform. Why, if that isn't the piano-van
coming up the Square now! So you'll only have to
wait a minute. Go down to my basement, Mr. Foreman, and tell my servant to give you a nice glass of
beer, and by that time the piano will be in place and
you can begin.''

He caught sight of Mrs. Mantrip on her balcony
and went straight on without pause, for his tongue, so
the sarcastic Square believed, had discovered the secret
of perpetual motion.

'' *Ma chère*,'' he called out, wagging his hand to
her, '' do trot in and have a cup of tea with me.
Such horrible things have been happening. My new
refrigerator was put in this morning, and nobody
knows how to stop it making ice. It has made about
a ton already, and is still going on. I shall give a
skating-party to-morrow if it doesn't stop. Then that
tiresome Olga Premysirkovitch has got a sore throat
and can't sing. She was going to make her début
here to-night. So I got George Papadiamantopoulo
to come and play instead. I'm told he's marvellous,
and he looks like a Greek Faun, so all you ladies will
fall in love with him. But I've had to get a new piano
in, for he's under contract only to play on a Hippo-
crenides, or else he's fined a hundred pounds. It's

just arrived. . . . So do come in, and help me to arrange my dinner-table and tell me where to put everybody.''

Pride, curiosity, and good-nature wrestled together in Mrs. Mantrip's well-set-up bosom at this invitation. Pride suggested that Jimmie had only asked her to the musical party and not to dinner, and that therefore it would show a proper dignity not to take the least interest in the arrangement of his table. Curiosity suggested that she would very much like to know who was dining with him, and this was a good opportunity of learning that. Finally, good-nature suggested that it was kind of him to have asked her to any portion of his party, and, if he wanted her advice about the arrangement of his table, she ought to give it him. This last voice was not of the same volume as the others, but, such as it was, its counsel was the same as curiosity's. So she waggled her hand at him and called out that she would come at once, if he would undertake that Atahualpa should not meet her alone on the staircase. But before he could say more than that Atahualpa would be delighted to see her, and would say '' Woof ! '' and give her a paw, his telephone bell rang from inside the house and he hurried in, terrified that something had happened to George Papadiamantopoulo.

Familiar thoughts flitted through Mrs. Mantrip's mind, as, having been asleep on her sofa this hot afternoon, she refreshed her face with cold water before going out to tea. Jimmie Mason, she reflected, seemed to have no inner life at all : he was towed along on the crest of a smooth, elderly wave that would some day (and she sincerely hoped that day was far off) bump him down on the shore of the next world. When in London he dined out four or five nights a week, and on the others he entertained at home. There were his musical parties, and at each of them he produced some new and amazing genius of whom the world had never heard before and of whom it seldom heard again. This did not in the least discourage him; he found another young Russian singer who had escaped from a Bolshevist prison with or without a shirt on his back, or another Polish pianist who would certainly rival Paderewski. On other nights he had dinners for young people: for these he sent out cards with " Romps " written in the bottom right-hand corner, and when Romps were on, his style was that of the youngest of them all. He sat with one arm round a good-looking boy and the other round a pretty girl, while they were resting after a game of " Musical Chairs," and they tickled his ribs, and, between shrieks of falsetto laughter, he begged them to stop and hoped that they would go on. " A kind, Victorian old maid," thought Mrs. Mantrip, " who thinks she's modern. And no depth."

She mingled these moral reflections with a few business thoughts about him. He was the lease-holder of one of her most attractive houses and had greatly increased its desirability. He had built out a spacious music-room at the back with a parqueted floor, he had put in a couple of bathrooms, and a service-lift, and paved the hall in black and white marble. But he came to the end of his twenty years' lease next summer, and she felt sure that her business man would positively insist that she should raise the rent of the house, if he desired to renew it, because he had spent so much money on it and made it so much more valuable. As it now stood, he was getting it absurdly cheap. Evidently he had no real thought of turning out when his lease expired, for only the other day, so it had been credibly reported to Mrs. Mantrip, he had said that if the King made him a present of Buckingham Palace as a residence, he would thank His Majesty very warmly for his kind thought, but preferred to stop where he was. Jimmie had not, as yet, been actually called upon to make so momentous a decision, but

these sentiments indicated a very clear disinclination
to leave the Square. It was natural then that Mrs.
Mantrip should cursorily consider what increase of rent
her business man would insist that she should ask.
It would never do to lose him, for, shallow though his
nature might be, he and his parties were a feature of
social life here. Ulrica, who wrote the fashionable
column in the *Evening Chronicle*, invariably mentioned
them.

Atahualpa met Mrs. Mantrip in the marble-paved
hall. She was fussed with all these hydrangeas and
gilt chairs, and if she was delighted to see her, she concealed her joy so effectually that no one could have
suspected it. Instead of giving a paw, she gave an
ugly kind of grin which showed that her teeth were in
excellent order, and retreated to her basket with an
annoyed expression on her face; there were too many
strangers about. So Mrs. Mantrip decided not to go
upstairs by herself but to wait for Jimmie, whose voice,
in rather aggrieved tones, was talking to the telephone
in the room by the front door which he called his study.
It was there that he saw his cook every morning, and
read through her proposed commissariat for the day.
" And that's about all the reading he does," thought
Mrs. Mantrip, as, with an eye on Atahualpa and an ear
on the open door of the study, she listened with keen
attention to what he was saying.
" My dear, I wish you hadn't got it just now," he
complained. " Of course I don't mean that I wish
you'd get it at any time, but you couldn't have chosen
a more inconvenient time for me. Never mind, do as
they tell you, and go to bed and get better very soon,
and come to dinner another night when you're quite
normal again and there's no fear of infection. Such
a pity, for you'd have loved to hear George Papadiamantopoulo—no, Pa-pa-di-a-mant-o-poul-o; he plays
marvellously, and I should have put you next——"

Jimmie was practically incapable of stopping talking when he had got hold of somebody on the telephone, but at this moment there was a brisk click which undoubtedly denoted that his victim had hung up her receiver. So he came out into the hall where Mrs. Mantrip was awaiting his escort.

"My dear, sweet of you to come round, and we'll have tea," he said. "Look at my love-bird sitting in her basket if not as good as gold, as good as the best silver-gilt. My beautiful one, a little fussed, are you, with so many people about? Dear Margaret, I throw myself on your mercy. That tiresome Bessie Birmingham has got a temperature and has chucked me. Her name always sounds as if she was either a Gaiety Girl or the wife of a bishop. Too inconvenient; if she must have a temperature, she might have got it at some other time, not just a few hours before my party. So do be a kind good friend and take her place. I asked her specially so that she might sit next the Maharajah of Baracuta, and talk to him about tiger-hunting and diamonds, for Geoffrey Birmingham was Governor of the North West Province before he went mad. She would have made him feel at home, and warned him if there was any ham in anything. He came here once before and found that he had eaten some ham, just a little grated ham on his chicken. He's most strict in all his religious observances, and I had to send out for an emetic, and he was sick in my bedroom. Then of course he was hungry again, and we had to have the fish back. . . . That's too sweet of you, and there's a lump of sugar soaked in cream for my beautiful one. When you've had your tea you must help me to arrange the table, and see that I don't put next each other people who've been divorced and have then married somebody else. They're always doing that now, and then they marry each other again, like French farces. What is it, Figgis?"

"The piano's stuck in the hall, sir," said his butler,

" and they can't get it round the corner into the music-room anyways at all."

Jimmie hurried away with a piece of tea-cake in his hand to see to this fresh crisis. He had ordered in a concert-grand without considering its vast dimensions, and there it was on its side at this awkward corner, with its legs and its pedals off, like a stranded whale without any fins, incapable of progress.

" Nothing to be done but to take it away and bring a smaller one," he said. " Mr. Papadiamantopoulo would have to lie down on the floor and play it sideways and even then there wouldn't be any pedals. I couldn't ask a great artist to do that, for it would spoil his touch completely. And would you please be very quick, because we can't put the lobelias and things in their places till the piano is there. I'm sure none of you want to spoil my party."

He hastened back to Mrs. Mantrip, finishing his tea-cake on the way, walking with his feet turned very much out like a starling.

" And then there's another most important thing I want to tell you about," he said. " That new tenant of yours who has just moved into the house next me, that little woman with the big Alsatian. Either a gramophone with an extra-loud-speaker, or the wireless, and very often, I assure you, both together are going on the entire day, and I hear it as clearly as if it was in the room instead of next door. Jazz chiefly, and then a Beethoven symphony with somebody lecturing on modern English fiction mixed up with it. She doesn't seem to mind what it is as long as there's an appalling row. It begins at ten in the morning and goes on till lunch. Then there's a pause, for she goes out in her motor. As soon as she gets back it begins again, and practically doesn't stop till midnight. Something must be done, dear Margaret. Supposing she plays *Parsifal* to-night just when George Papadia-mantopoulo is going to begin his new minuet? The

noise is awful. And then there are the squeals and
barks of Elizabeth Conklin's Pekinese dogs, especially
when one of the ladies is having a family——''

'' Dear Jimmie ! I beg you ! '' said Mrs. Mantrip.

'' There, I suppose I've shocked you now ! You're
Victorian, Margaret. You know perfectly well that
lady-dogs do have families, but you don't like it spoken
of. Let's go back to your new tenant who only has
gramophones. Who is she ? What's her name ? ''

'' Miss Susan Leg,'' said Mrs. Mantrip.

'' Then can't you use your territorial influence with
her ? You've no idea how maddening it is, and after
all I'm your tenant too, and you should see fair
between us. It's becoming very uncomfortable.
I'm like the young lady from Banbury Cross, who
has music wherever she goes. And when I go out of
doors I am pounced upon by Elizabeth Conklin's eleven
thousand Pekinese dogs—she's like St. Ursula—all of
whom have a passion for my spats.''

'' I'll go and call on Miss Leg,'' said Mrs. Mantrip.
'' I'll see what I can do. One must be tactful, of
course, with a new tenant.''

'' And leave the old to take care of themselves,''
said Jimmie, with unwonted bitterness. '' You know
the Square isn't what it used to be. Less peaceful.
I shall go and live in an hotel, I think. Me and
Atahualpa. Shan't we, lovely one ? And you shall
eat a housemaid every night, and I shall get a neat black
wig to cover my bald head and grow some beautiful
whiskers, and then some nice Victorian girl like you,
Margaret, will want to marry me for my money, and
find there's none left. Or shall I propose to Susan Leg
on condition she has no more gramophones ? How
difficult life is, especially when you don't know whether
the piano will come in time or whether you'll have to
send round to the chemist's for another emetic for a
Maharajah. Now do let us arrange the table, instead
of chattering like this.''

Mrs. Mantrip gave him her best attention as to the disposition of his guests. That was soon done, for there appeared to be no couples recently divorced, at any rate, among them, and he ambled downstairs with her, having shut up Atahualpa in the drawing-room.

" Something has upset my beautiful one," he said, " and she wants to bite somebody. She must have her mutton chop in my dressing-room to-night, and be shut in there till all my party has gone. Ah, they've brought in the smaller piano. That's splendid. I shall help them to arrange the flowers and then get a good snooze to freshen me up. Oh, and the refrigerator has stopped making ice, has it, Figgis? Capital! Now things are beginning to get less tragic. But just hark to that gramophone next door! Do use your influence, dear Margaret."

II

TO-NIGHT Mrs. Conklin was among those who had been asked to come in after dinner for an hour's music, and as Mrs. Mantrip came out of Jimmie's house, leaving him to his Atahualpa and lobelias, she ran into her returning from her walk in the garden where she had been exercising her Pekinese dogs. Mrs. Conklin was large and round in figure: she had put all her dogs on leads to conduct them across the road, and with all these strings in her hand she vaguely resembled a balloon with a quantity of ropes attached to it. If all the Pekinese wanted to walk in the direction she was going, the combined pull of ten strong little animals wafted her briskly forward as if the balloon sailed on a fair wind; but if, as usually happened, there was no such unanimity and some wanted to investigate interesting smells or to do other things, it was as if the balloon drifted slowly in an almost windless air, or became quite stationary.

" A party at Jimmie's to-night," she said with a slightly superior air to Mrs. Mantrip. " Shall I see you there by any chance, Margaret ? "

Mrs. Mantrip was pleased she had said that.

" Yes, I'm dining there first," she said, as casually as she could. " I've been helping him to arrange the table."

Elizabeth Conklin's face fell.

" Indeed ? " she said. " Whom are you sitting next ? "

Mrs. Mantrip appeared to make an effort of memory.

" Let me think now," she said. " Oh, yes. A Maharajah. The Maharajah of Baracuta."

Elizabeth's interest in this extinguished all sense of jealousy.

" No ! Not really ! That was the one who was sick, wasn't it ? "

" I believe so. But he did it on purpose, dear."

" I don't see that that makes it any better," said Elizabeth. " Worse, in fact. Very unsocial. Dear me, I'm afraid you've got entangled in my dogs. They've got all wrapped round you. Stand still a moment and I'll free you. Oh, and another thing I wanted to ask you—Bully Boy, come this way, you silly creature, and darling Sabrina go the other way. That's it. Who is that Miss Leg who has come to live in the house between Jimmie and me ? Your tenant, I suppose. But incessant gramophones and wireless going on all day, sometimes together. What does it mean ? What is it all about ? Perfectly maddening for her neighbours."

Mrs. Mantrip stepped clear of the dogs.

" Jimmie was complaining of it too," she said.

" I know nothing about her, except that when she took the house I made the usual inquiries at the bank to which she gave me a reference. I must go and call on her: I haven't seen her yet."

" You can hear her though," said Elizabeth, for the gramophone was very audible; " and that goes on all day, I tell you. And it's monstrous that she should take that great dog into the Square garden with the notice staring her in the face that no dogs are allowed there."

" Quite scandalous," said Mrs. Mantrip, absently glancing at the canine swarm that surrounded her friend. She often said sharp, sarcastic things like that.

" My dear Margaret, it's quite different for me," said Elizabeth. " A Pekinese isn't an Alsatian. Where am I to take my little cherubs to except there? I can't exercise ten dogs in the streets, and exercise they must have. I'm bound to say that Miss Leg's Alsatian is harmless enough. He lets my dogs run in and out of his legs like chickens, and takes not the slightest notice of them, but it terrifies me to think what might happen if he took it into his head to lie down suddenly and roll. Can't you remind her when you call that dogs are not allowed in the garden? Large dogs, you know."

Mrs. Mantrip thought she would not tell Elizabeth that she intended to bring the question of dogs being taken into the garden before the General Meeting next week. She would have more time to get up a pro-dog movement. A feigned sympathy was the better way.

" Yes, I quite agree that that huge dog shouldn't be allowed in the garden," she said. " Au revoir, dear. We shall meet when you come in, after dinner, to Jimmie's. And I'll call on Miss Leg to-morrow."

Mrs. Mantrip let herself into her house two doors farther on, and went into the small sitting-room close to the front door, which was so properly known as the library. The books which had belonged to her father

lined the walls to within three feet of the ceiling, and on
the tops of the cases stood busts of eminent divines.
The library was devoted to ecclesiastical subjects:
there were volumes and volumes of sermons preached
by deans and bishops and published after their deaths
by the piety of their widows; there were biographies
of eminent churchmen; there were commentaries on
major and minor prophets; there were tomes of early
Christian fathers; there were the lives of an incredible
number of missionaries and the deaths of martyrs;
there were reports of Church conferences; there were
many collections of hymns. Her father had by his
will left them all to the Parish Library, but the
munificent legacy had been refused by its curators.
Before taking this extreme step, they had prudently
submitted a catalogue of these treasures to several
second-hand booksellers, who had declined to make
any offer at all for them. The curators had then
expressed themselves to Mrs. Mantrip as much touched
by the bequest, but they found that the space at their
disposal was wholly inadequate to hold so substantial
a collection. They would not indeed take the books
away at all, so they and the catalogue remained in her
possession, and it was here, inspired by their mute
presence and refreshed by the faint smell of Russian
leather in which many of these handsome volumes were
bound, that she sat every morning collecting and
arranging material for her father's life in two volumes,
about which she so often spoke to her friends.

It had not at present got very far in actual execution: indeed the bulk of her work consisted of the list
of the proposed headings for the chapters. These,
however, were complete:

    I. BIRTH AND PARENTAGE.
    II. EARLY BOYHOOD AND SCHOOL DAYS.
    III. UNIVERSITY CAREER AND PREPARATION
        FOR TAKING ORDERS.

But, as Mrs. Mantrip so justly felt, it was of the highest
importance to construct a good framework before
beginning to fill it in with the yet unwritten narrative,
and the framework was quite finished now. It could
hardly be bettered: it was chronological, it was
orderly, it was comprehensive and covered the ground.
These headings for chapters were spaced over five
pages of foolscap (two chapter-headings to a page),
and Mrs. Mantrip had lately been jotting down, in their
appropriate places, notes about asthma (Chapter VII),
the railway strike of 1911 (Chapter VIII) about which
her father held very strong views and to which he
alluded in an unfinished manuscript sermon, and the
hot summer of 1921 (Chapter IX). Soon, very soon,
now that the framework was ready she would be busy
over the actual writing of the book, but though as yet
she had not begun that, the sense that she had a definite
object ahead, a piece of solid serious literary work to
occupy her, caused her to contrast her own activities
very favourably with the aimless hedonistic drifting
of Jimmie and the narrow horizons of Elizabeth
Conklin's life which embraced little more than Pekinese
dogs. Merely to study music or distemper seemed to
her a very trifling and flippant way of filling the hours,
of which, as her father had once impressively remarked,

we should all have to render an account: *pereunt et imputantur*.

She turned to Chapter X of her framework, which dealt with " Summary of character," and made a note of this *obiter dictum*. It would be useful as a starting-point of a paragraph, and sentences began to form themselves in her brain. " My father," she murmured to herself, " had throughout his life a very strong sense of the value of time. As a little girl I can remember his finding me idling the hours away one morning, and playfully quoting ' Satan finds some mischief still for idle hands to do.' Though the words were spoken so lightly, they made a profound impression on me. It was not that he was a foe to timely recreation and innocent mirth, for no one had a keener sense of fun, but . . ."

Margaret seized a half-sheet of paper as these glib and rhythmical phrases flowed through her brain without any effort of conscious creation, and added them in minute handwriting to the note on Chapter X. Secretly, though she had hardly confessed it even to herself, occasional qualms had visited her as to whether she could write a book at all. She had perhaps talked a little prematurely about it to her friends, as if it was well on the way to completion, for she had only at present visualized herself covering page after page in her neat, legible hand with her interesting account of her father's asthma and of the cleansing of the Augean stable. She had long been a recognized leader of culture in the Square, and this well-won reputation of hers had undoubtedly been enhanced by the fact that she was strenuously occupied in writing her father's life. It was cheering, in respect of these secret qualms, to find that she could cast so shapely a sentence about his views on the value of time with such ease.

Her mind unbent itself after she had jotted this down and relaxed into more fugitive thoughts concern-

ing the entertainment this evening. Thanks to the
liberality of her early training, she had no conscientious
scruples whatever about sitting next to a man who was
undoubtedly not a Christian, even though he was a
Maharajah, and she felt sure that her father would have
agreed that she was right. He had not been of that
stern type of Christian that recited with relish the
inexorable clauses of the Athanasian Creed, and exult-
ingly proclaimed that anyone who did not believe them
would be damned, but distinctly stated, *ex pulpita*, in
one of his Screwby sermons, that even Jews, Turks and
infidels, should not be considered as altogether outside
the pale of a Christian's sympathy and brotherly love.
Consequently Margaret was quite prepared to be genial
to her distinguished neighbour at dinner to-night, for,
as the engaging story about the emetic proved, he was
a conscientious practitioner of his faith, such as it was,
and (*vide* the same sermon) a man who acted up to his
lights was doing the best he could. So in order to
render herself better equipped for intercourse with an
Indian, she got down from the shelves of the library
a volume of Bishop Heber's diary, and read about his
arrival at Calcutta.

The narrative failed to rivet her attention, and she
began to consider what she would wear that evening.
Her own chief article of jewellery was a pretty necklet
of seed-pearls, but she had heard that the Maharajah
had a string of larger ones about as big as marbles, and
if he wore them, the shine would be taken out of her
necklet. Pearls suggested jewels generally to her mind,
jewels led on to luxury and splendour, and these topics
set flowing within her the tide of her secret life. Highbrow though she was, well deserved as was her reputation as a devoted student of all that was best in
literature, author as she was known to be of a yet
unfinished work of a serious and clerical sort, there
was one writer of the present day for whom, though the
critics of the press took no notice whatever of his

books, Margaret secretly felt an admiration far more passionate than for any other master, dead or living. This creator of immortal stuff was Rudolph da Vinci, of whose novels up to date Margaret Mantrip owned the complete series. They fed her soul : they whisked her away as on a magic carpet from the commonplace though pleasant circumstances of life and even from her own high literary aims, and revealed to her how distinguished, how fiery and how lurid human existence might be. There were strong silent men (so unlike poor chattering Jimmie !) who loved deeply and purely and passionately. There was an exquisite girl, like a lily, who through the machinations of a worldly mother, had been mated to a perfect brute, and, after the fatal knot had been tied, met one of these Galahads who consecrated his life to her devoted service, and was rewarded towards the end of the book by the death, in circumstances of the utmost ignominy, of the perfect brute and by union with his beloved. There were little puny men with great hearts, there were plain women with golden ones, who brought happiness wherever they went; there were frail duchesses, and danger- ous diplomatists, politicians with tongues of golden eloquence and filthy minds. Almost best of all was a splendid bishop of aristocratic birth who gave up his princely income to the poor and needy, retaining for himself only £200 a year. He sold his jewel-encrusted pastoral staff, and got instead one made of deal; he turned his palace into a house of refuge for penitent prostitutes, and lived in a semi-detached villa with no carpet on the stairs. He smoked his pipe of an evening with tipsy fellows in the public-house, and said prayers before closing time. One day he saw a navvy beating his wife and, exclaiming " Damn it ! I can't stand it," took off his coat and gave the navvy what for. He was also the Lord-Lieutenant of his County. . . .

And in all these books there were sadic scenes. A Russian prince decoyed one of the lily-like girls to his house and, because she would not consent to his odious proposals, ordered a huge moujik with a beard to strip her stark and whip her. One desperate blow was about to fall on her shoulders, where it would have raised a livid weal, when the strong silent man leaped lightly through the window and flogged the Russian prince within an inch of his life. Plenty of weals. . . . There were scenes of reconciliation between splendid men and women just as the church bells broke out at midnight on Christmas Eve, and scenes of repentance for the fallen, and haughty marchionesses and diamond tiaras and drunken revels, but through all these splendours and debaucheries ran the unwavering certainty that in the end right would triumph. But before that consummation was reached, perilous seas had to be traversed, blood-hounds strangled, and cabin-boys turn out to be girls of high birth. Rudolph da Vinci never faltered. With the ruthlessness of the consummate artist he dragged his heroines through the most outrageous savageries and humiliations, yet kept them pure: he exposed his strong silent men to the wiles of the most accomplished Cleopatras, but the first time that any of these True Blues ever kissed a woman (except his mother) was when, in the last chapter (or possibly the last but one, for Rudolph was partial to an epilogue in which the heroic pair had raised a family of slim, golden-haired boys with their father's eyes, and of girls with their mother's nose), all came right and the woman he had worshipped was his.

Here, then, in the novels of Rudolph da Vinci (such a colourful name, thought Margaret Mantrip, though possibly a *nom de plume*) she found the joy of that secret life which no one suspected. These romances thrilled and entranced her, and not the less so because they had not the remotest resemblance to the routine of existence as she knew it. It was enough that their author had conceived such magnificent presences and souls of such fiery quality upon this dull earth dwelling.

The most authoritative critics never mentioned his works at all. Mr. S—— never wrote about them in the *Sunday Times*, nor Mr. P—— in the *Evening Standard*. Only once could Mrs. Mantrip remember seeing his name in such austere columns, and that was when Mr. G——, in some unusually severe strictures on another book, said that the characters in it resembled those in Rudolph da Vinci's novels, and made a very amusing pun about them, saying that they were "rude dolls." Probably there was a conspiracy in the press to be absolutely dumb about him, arising out of professional jealousy, for all the world knew that most of the critics had once tried to write novels and had dismally failed.

But how impotent was their malicious silence! Often with a thrill of vicarious pride Margaret read on the preliminary leaves of Rudolph's books the procession of printings that had followed the first issue. Often, too, Messrs. Cartwright, his publishers, inserted apologies in large type in the press, stating that the first printing of his new book, consisting of 50,000 copies had been exhausted so rapidly that, accustomed as they were to his prodigious popularity, they had been caught short of copies. A new printing, however, would be ready in a couple of days and all orders promptly attended to. The public, it was clear, was not in the critical conspiracy: it swarmed like bees round the flowers of Rudolph's imagination, and the flowers could not open fast enough for its desires. Margaret found in him her greatest intellectual pleasure, and indeed this was a joy that went deeper than that, for Rudolph da Vinci wrote for the aspiring heart of humanity.

Yet in spite of this, Margaret concealed, as if it had been a secret vice, her unbounded admiration for his works. Her friends knew her to be an ardent student of what was known as the best literature of the day, and she felt sure that she would compromise that enviable reputation if she declared herself in her true colours. Sometimes she was sorely tempted to do so, but she lacked the moral courage. Not long ago, for instance, she was lunching with that shallow hedonist two houses away. Jimmie had come across the book of Rudolph's in which the perfectly splendid bishop was so prominent a figure, and over their coffee he had read to them with cackles of falsetto laughter the magnificent scene in which that saintly prelate had laid the navvy out. Margaret knew she ought to have borne her testimony: she ought to have said that it hurt her to hear him laugh, as she thought this scene was the most moving and uplifting in all modern literature. But there were people (and she was afraid that he might be one) who simply had not got in their nature the power to appreciate the depths and the sublimities of great work, and so she was dumb. Possibly, when she thought it over afterwards, it was a technical error on Rudolph da Vinci's part to make the bishop the Lord-Lieutenant of the County, but was there not a play called *A Winter's Tale*, in which the dramatist spoke of the sea-board of Bohemia? And who wrote *A Winter's Tale*? Very likely Jimmie did not know, but she did. And did the theatre burst into cackles of laughter when in the performance of this sublime masterpiece there came that singular error in geography?

Though Rudolph da Vinci could never have sated the thirst of the fervent Margaret even if he had written two novels simultaneously, one with his right hand and one with his left, his books came out with very agreeable frequency; three during the course of a year might reasonably be expected. One was soon due; it had already been advertised, heading the list of Messrs. Cartwright's forthcoming publications, and Margaret had of course ordered a copy. During the week that followed its appearance, there would be no progress made with her filial memoirs, for she would have to read it through once with breathless speed, though without skipping anything, in the fury of ascertaining through what welter of tribulation and sadism the true lovers were united, and then she must read it through once again very slowly in order to taste in leisurely rapture the full flavour of that wonderful style, and pore over Rudolph's magical word-painting. He was surely a poet at heart, for in the more fiery scenes his emotional stress caused his prose actually to become poetry, the words falling into strict rhythm and scanning themselves into faultless blank verse for three or four lines at a time. These two readings of *Rosemary and Rue* (for such was the title of the forthcoming work) would take a week, and Margaret knew that during those days she would be absolutely incapable of working at her father's life at all. Deeply interesting to her as was the inner history of his soul-experience when, as curate (Chapter IV) to an Anglo-Catholic vicar, his conscience forbade him to perform certain gaudy ritualistic ceremonies which he knew were illegal in the English Church, it would be no use attempting to concentrate on the subtleties of that complicated business until she had finished the second reading of the new romance.

She must therefore be firm with herself now, and for the next few days, until *Rosemary and Rue* appeared, devote herself to ritualistic research. But it was too late to begin that this evening, for in half an hour she would have to be dressing for the hedonist's dinner-party. She went to the shelves below the window where, apart from the ecclesiastical library and veiled beneath a baize curtain, there stood the seventeen published volumes of Rudolph da Vinci's novels. She drew one out at random, and opened it at random. You couldn't go wrong.

III

DURHAM SQUARE had an atmosphere of its own, an air of self-contained tranquillity (though all the time it was purring with power like a dynamo) which presented a favourable contrast with the streets and squares of other residential quarters in London. This was largely due to the fact that it was a cul-de-sac and could not be used as a thoroughfare to other and alien places. Whatever taxis were proceeding along its road, whatever foot-passengers trod its pavements, it was certain that they were on the way to or from some house in the Square itself. Its inhabitants were accustomed to see the same figures issuing from the same doors, and these became quickly familiar, as they were not instantly swallowed up in the crowd of a hurrying street. All this conduced to a certain sense of expanded intimacy: the moment a householder came into the Square he felt he had come home, and all the folk he saw on the pavements had business in some corner of it.

Again, the kitchens for the most part were situated in the basements to the front of the houses, and thus if you returned, say, at 1 p.m., when the weather was warm, you passed a series of open windows from which came the suggestive savours of cookery, and a keen nose could augur what Nos. 20, 21, and 22 were about to partake of. By degrees such a nose with a retentive brain behind it could draw a sound logical inference that No. 20 was fond of Irish stew, and No. 26 of curry. Though you might never have met Mrs. Conklin of No. 26 in social intercourse, you had often seen her, balloon-like, with her ten Pekinese dogs daily defying the prohibition of the Garden Committee, and it was in your power to accost her, as she returned to her house of an afternoon, by a staggering demonstration of clairvoyance and express the hope that the curry had been satisfactory. But no one, of course, with any true respect for the privacy of domestic life would have thus violated it.

Apart from the adventitious aids to intimacy conferred by living in a cul-de-sac, the Durhamites cultivated a neighbourliness that was not common in cold-hearted London. In other squares, more magnificent perhaps but less friendly, it is not usual for older inhabitants to call upon a new-comer, simply because he has become part of the corporation of the place. Mere propinquity leads to nothing, and next-door neighbours may, and generally do, remain as unknown to each other as if one lived in Tooting and the other in Timbuctoo. Such aloofness was not the Durham use. A single female new-comer, her habit and appearance, would be scrutinized keenly, but not unkindly, for a week or two after she had settled in; then when she would no longer be embarrassed by the visit of a stranger, while pictures still lay in stacks upon the floor, and staircases were uncarpeted, one of the leaders of the social life in the Square, such as Mrs. Mantrip, would pay a call about tea-time. She, with her trained faculties, would make a quantity of valuable observations. If these were favourable, if the new-comer was, as Mrs. Mantrip said, " the sort of person we can know," one who might prove to be a welcome addition to the socialities of the Square, she would convene other leaders of local society, Mrs. Conklin, Captain and Lady Eva Lowndes, Jimmie, the Vicar, and others, and ask them to lunch to meet the candidate. The first scrutiny at tea-time would have already yielded useful information as to whether she played bridge, whether she had literary or artistic

tastes, whether she still had, or once had had, a
husband. It was important to know this for fear of
embarrassing topics being introduced when the candidate was passing her final examination at lunch, and
in these days, as Mrs. Mantrip said, there was no telling
from a woman's dress whether she was a widow or not,
since so many widows dressed like bridesmaids. But
with information on a few salient points like these,
conversation at the lunch-party would flow easily, and
could embrace a variety of topics by which the candidate's general style could be judged. No very high
standard was required, and if, when the candidate took
her departure afterwards, most of the other guests said,
" I hope we shall meet again before long," or something of the sort, it was as if they had said, " I con-
gratulate you on having passed."

This pleasant and neighbourly custom was now
traditional in the Square and dated from the days of
its regeneration, for Mr. Bondfield (after, it is unnecessary to state, the purging had taken place)
always called on the new and respectable tenants of
his freeholds. " Neighbours," he had once remarked,
" should be neighbourly," and when his first duty of
purging the Augean stable had been accomplished, he
was assiduous in putting into practice this fine Christian
principle, and rubbed noses with all the new horses.
" To make a friendly little focus of local life, in our
angulus terræ," he continued, " to cultivate friendly
relations with those whom propinquity has—has
brought near us, will be a sufficient social effort for
one like me, who has borne the burden and heat of the
day, and is now in the evening of life. Neighbours,"
he concluded (for he had got to repeat himself somewhat in the evening of life), " should be neighbourly."

This principle had taken root and flourished in the
Square, and it may safely be stated that more householders there knew each other and lunched and dined
with each other, than in any other square of the same

number of houses in London.   Mrs. Mantrip was on
visiting terms with twenty-two, and Captain and Lady
Eva Lowndes (between them) with thirty-seven.   Mr.
Jimmie Mason went to fewer, for the pleasures of the
table exercised an undue influence over him, and
though he made exceptions in favour of very old
friends, he would not dine twice at a house where
plain living was the rule, however high the thinking.
No amount of high thinking would make up for high
mutton. Besides, he was far smarter and more *répandu*
than most of his neighbours, and his smart Maharajah
parties and music opened to him circles about which
the rest of the Square only read in the doings of the
great world, as recorded in social columns of the press.
But his eagle flights certainly gave the Square distinction, and though he occasionally roused a malicious
pity when he alluded too often to countesses by their
Christian names, his friends forgave him for being such
a crashing snob, and hoped to be asked to his next
party.

But except for him, the majority of the householders
when they did not dine at home dined somewhere else
in the Square; it had become, as Mr. Bondfield had
planned, a little world to itself.   If it was a really wet
night, there would be a rapid interchange of messages
between Nos. 6, 19, 22, and 37, who were all dining
at No. 29, and one of them, the most distant from No.
29, would order a taxi at three minutes to eight, and
pick up the other guests.   This entailed agonizing sums
in mental arithmetic as to the sharing up of the expense
of a sixpenny taxi (for the rank was close at hand just
outside the Square) with the addition of extra payment
for extra passengers and a tip for the driver, but it was
far cheaper, even with that effort, than ordering four
taxis.   There was this advantage also, that the guests
all arrived simultaneously, and there was no waiting
for dinner.   Another taxi, if the rain still continued,
would convey the guests home.

It was then in the traditional neighbourly spirit that, on the day following Mr. Jimmie's musical party, Mrs. Mantrip, at precisely half-past four, rang the bell of Miss Leg's house. A butler, who looked all that a butler should be, left her for a moment to see if " Mademoiselle " (so he termed her) was at home; the gramophone was trumpeting away in the drawing-room upstairs, and this sounded as if she was. A tremendous volume of noise poured out as he opened the drawing-room door, and then it abruptly ceased. He returned with good news, and Mrs. Mantrip followed him up. She did not quite like the use of the word " mademoiselle ": there was something rather flashy about it, but after all, Julia's butler in Rudolph da Vinci's *Apples of Sodom* did the same. The house had evidently been decorated and furnished regardless of expense: the walls of the little hall were covered with stamped Spanish leather, an embossed Italian mirror faced her on the half landing, an immense gilded chandelier depended from the ceiling, the foot sank into the nap of a sapphire blue carpet, and some sweet heavy odour hung on the air. Smell is the most associative of all the senses, and instantly, under this illumination, a childish memory, long dim, flashed vividly into Mrs. Mantrip's mind. She had gone with her father to see a house in the Square lately vacated, at the termination of her lease, by one of those ladies who were now locally extinct. A dreadful swoony smell, an odour repulsive to the moral sense. Surely her opulent tenant . . .

A single glance at Miss Leg quite reassured her. She was a small woman of early middle age, and totally devoid of any meretricious attraction in face or figure. Her nose was slightly tip-tilted, giving her a look of inquisitive intelligence; her hair was of a dull brown, as innocent of dye as her cheeks and lips were of adventitious colouring matter; her eyes, set rather noticeably apart in a pale round face, blinked as she shook hands with her visitor. She was well dressed, and round her neck was a string of pearls about half-way in magnitude between Mrs. Mantrip's seeds and the Maharajah's marbles. Mrs. Mantrip first thought to herself, " Woolworth," and then, " I wonder? "

Miss Leg very genteelly touched her lips with the tip of her tongue before she spoke.

" Mrs. Mantrip, isn't it? " she said. " So kind of you to come and see me. Very friendly I call it. Bring up tea, Bosanquet. Bring cigarettes. Or a cocktail, Mrs. Mantrip? "

Mrs. Mantrip's eyes made a hasty circular excursion round the room, as she repudiated so sensational a refreshment. The opulent appointments of the hall and staircase she saw to be only the faintest adumbration of these larger splendours. There were Persian rugs on the floor; there was an alabaster fireplace with lapis lazuli plaques let into it; there was a mirror in a velvet frame, with lilies and butterflies painted on it. There was a boudoir grand piano with bright orange legs, the top of which was negligently draped with a crimson pall. There was an ormolu clock on a bracket, and the walls were panelled with rich and recent mahogany. The ceiling was painted blue with light clouds drifting over it, and curtains of blue brocade framed the windows. The gramophone, just silenced, stood on a mosaic-topped table, with a volume of records by it. Mrs. Mantrip's observant eye took in these more important features of the room in a moment, and came back to the plain, inquisitive, insignificant face which smiled at her.

" I should have called before, Miss Leg," she said, " but I thought you would not yet have settled in. So pleased to meet you now. You have indeed made a palace of my plain little house."

" On the contrary, a dear little house," said Miss Leg with great emphasis. " It suits me to perfection: so compact, so convenient. But as for your saying I

have made a palace of it—why, Mrs. Mantrip, I think
you are being very sarcastic. Just a few bits of things
to make a lining for my teeny nest."

Tea arrived instantly. There was a silver kettle
and silver teapot and sugar-basin, all heavily chased and
repoussé and of extraordinary ugliness. There was
a covered dish with something hot under it, cakes with
pink sugar, a dish of chocolates and another of strawberries; just such a tea as Jimmie provided when he
expected countesses. But none appeared now, and
Mrs. Mantrip was forced to suppose that her tenant had
a tea like this ready every day, in case somebody
dropped in.

"Sugar?" said Miss Leg. "And milk or cream?
Do you like your milk put in first? Some people have
a fancy for that. They say it mixes better, but for my
part I never find much difference. Dear me, I haven't
asked you if you prefer Indian tea. It will be ready
in a moment if you do."

Mrs. Mantrip declined Indian tea, and her milk was
added later. Her first impressions were not promising:
there was a personal insignificance and a complacency
and an opulence which did not go well together. Then
there was her suggestion of putting the milk first into
the tea-cup. Somehow Mrs. Mantrip associated such
a custom with the servants' hall. Not that there was
any harm in it, but just that . . .

"I wonder what my chef has sent me up under the
cover," continued Miss Leg. "Ah, yes, little scones
with caviare in them. He knows I am partial to them.
Try one, Mrs. Mantrip. They are not bad."

This dragging in of her chef seemed very disastrous:
Miss Leg must have known that her chef did not make
teacakes; she wanted to tell her visitor that she had one.
There was a careless ostentation about it. But there
was something rather pathetic about the plain little
woman with her blinking eyes and her eager, insignificant face, sitting all alone in the midst of her pearls

and her futility and her lapis lazuli plaques, and lugging in the fact that she had a chef. Perhaps she turned on the gramophone because she felt lonely. It would be impossible just now to tell her that her neighbours found it so trying. Obviously she was shy; obviously she desired to please. To encourage her, and at the same time to explore the quality of her mind, Mrs. Mantrip took another caviared scone, and introduced the subject of which she so often spoke.

"I spent a solitary but such a happy morning," she said, "reading over parts of my father's diary. I have volumes and volumes of it. All his life-work so faithfully and beautifully recorded."

"How wonderful! What a privilege to hear about it!" said Miss Leg enthusiastically. "All his life-work! Fancy! What was his life-work?"

That was better. This lonely little woman must have something in her, or she could not have been so interested. So Mrs. Mantrip spoke of her father's asthma and in a guarded way of the cleansing of the Square. Never had she had so appreciative a listener.

"But what a wonderful man he must have been," said Miss Leg. "And, as I say, such a privilege to be told about it. You ought to tell everybody about it, indeed you ought. Such a pattern for us all. Dear me, to think of all those naughty women living in our Square. What a change, Mrs. Mantrip! You ought to write a book about it all. I am sure you could if you tried. Such a beautiful book it would be, and I am so fond of reading."

At that moment Mrs. Mantrip resolved to get up a luncheon-party to scrutinize the new-comer. She might not be much to look at, she might have a streak of ostentation, she might talk with a slight accent, but she was trying her best. And she appreciated: there was surely something in her.

"I'm delighted that you are interested, Miss Leg," she said. "And as a matter of fact I am doing what

you tell me I ought to. I am busily engaged in writing
a memoir of my father. Two volumes——"

" Three: please make it three," cried Miss Leg.
" Well, that will be something to look forward to.
When may we expect it? "

" Not for a long time yet, I am afraid," said Mrs.
Mantrip, warming more and more to her. " It is a
great responsibility. I must not hurry over it."

" And are you fond of reading too? Have you
many books? " asked Miss Leg with a sort of candid
guilelessness.

" All my father's library," said Mrs. Mantrip. " I
have not sold a single volume. Ecclesiastical biographies, volumes of sermons, missionary journeys,
early Christian fathers. You must come and see them
some day before long."

The conversation, now proceeding swimmingly,
drifted away from these high topics to more local and
everyday interests: it almost verged on gossip, a
species of intercourse of which officially Mrs. Mantrip
strongly disapproved. But the occasion was special:
she thought the new-comer might be an asset to the
social life of the Square, and the sense that this was a
preliminary examination redeemed it from idle talk.
But Miss Leg seemed to care little about Elizabeth
Conklin and her horde of Pekinese: she was not thrilled
to hear that Mr. Salt bathed every morning in the
Serpentine, and that Mr. Gandish played Badminton
so beautifully, and that Lady Eva Lowndes (though the
title roused a gleam) was a student of the occult. But
when she heard about the party last night at her neighbour's house, and learned that her fortunate visitor had
sat next a Maharajah, once again, as on the subject
of Mrs. Mantrip's literary enterprise, her enthusiasm
kindled.

" Dear me, what a wonderful experience! " she
cried. " How useful—I mean how unique to sit next
a Maharajah. So interesting to meet a new type. Pray

tell me what he was like, and what you talked about.
Fancy there having been a Maharajah within a few
yards of me all yesterday evening! If I had known he
was there, I should certainly have hung about on my
balcony to catch a peep of him. How fashionable Mr.
Mason must be!"

Elizabeth Conklin dined alone that night with
Margaret Mantrip. They were such old friends that
it would have been ridiculous for either of them to
make a toilet for the other's benefit (especially as they
both knew all each other's toilets so well), or to be
at the trouble of doing their hair, which was neither
cropped nor shingled. Elizabeth therefore wore a hat,
and Margaret a boudoir cap. Their custom was to
play fierce games of piquet for love and hatred as soon
as dinner was over, but to-night it was long before they
got to the cards.

"I went to tea with Miss Leg this afternoon," said
Margaret, "and I can't entirely make up my mind
about her. She has nice points, but some rather
dreadful ones. I was puzzled."

"A good tea?" asked Elizabeth, who had observed
how very little Margaret had eaten at dinner.

It was one of Margaret's stunts to be wholly indiffer-
ent to the pleasures of the table. No one believed it,
though some colour was lent to her claim by the fact
that she had an execrable cook herself: Jimmie would
tell almost any lie to avoid dining with her. Besides,
her bad cook might only signify economy and not dis-
dain. But it was impossible for her to say that she did
not remember what there was for tea, since that formed
a clue as to the character of Miss Leg.

"A monstrous tea," she said. "Quite absurdly
extravagant. Split scones with caviare in between.
Hot. Cake with sugar icing. Chocolates. Strawberries. And she dragged in that she kept a chef.
Also she asked me if I would like my milk put in first."

" And did you ? " asked Elizabeth. Margaret was
sickeningly superior sometimes about the minutiæ of
good breeding, and it did her good to pretend not to
know what she meant. Besides, she was not impeccable herself if there happened to be a fishbone between
two teeth. Fingers every time.

Margaret took no notice of this question : that was
the best way.

" Then the house," she went on. " Feverish.
Evidently most expensive. Alabaster. Lapis lazuli.
Brocade. And perfume such as one associates . . .
It was reassuring to see how plain and undistinguished
she was, but as I went upstairs my heart sank. Then
tea, and very soon a great surprise. A really serious
nature, Elizabeth. She was intensely interested in the
little sketch I gave her of my life of Papa. I was quite
touched and encouraged about her. So sincere. I
could see how genuine and sincere she was. Then we
got on to other subjects such as—well, they seemed to
leave her cold. Then I told her about that pleasant
Maharajah I sat next last night at Jimmie's, and again
she was intensely keen to know about him. She seemed
to think it so marvellous that one should have sat next
him. All very contradictory. I hardly know what to
make of her."

" She sounds to me rather like a lunatic," remarked
Elizabeth, who had not succeeded in having a single
word with the Maharajah, and was embittered.

Margaret assumed her most judicial manner.

" I assure you it was not so," she said. " No
kind of confusion of thought. Not a trace. Merely I
couldn't classify her at all. I must certainly have a
lunch for her, and I shall be interested to see what Eva
Lowndes makes of her. I should not be in the least
surprised if she saw a very intellectual halo. But
never mind about that," she added hastily.

She was too late. The fatal subject had been mentioned, and no subsequent withdrawal of so dangerous

a topic could avert an explosion. Elizabeth's face began to turn red, as when the current is switched on to an electric heater.

" I don't mind about that," she said. " Who in their senses could mind the rubbish poor Eva talks about haloes? Anyone who could see a black halo round the head of my Bully Boy and tell me I must get rid of the dog because he has the heart of a murderer, must be merely colour-blind. All that nonsense about haloes! What a bore poor Eva is! Why, to my knowledge, she's seen three perfectly different haloes round Captain Lowndes's head. If she's annoyed with you she says you've got a black halo or a brown halo, which I understand is nearly as bad, but the moment afterwards, if you're her partner at bridge and hold four aces, she gives you a blue halo at once. What she sees is the reflection of her own mind, if indeed she sees anything at all. For my part I don't believe she does. Rubbish! She's mad."

" Very likely, dear," said Margaret soothingly, " and of course there is madness in the family. Lord Brosely, she told me herself, was convinced that one of his legs was a kleptomaniac, and if he mislaid anything he always thought his leg had stolen it, and took his trousers down to see where it had put it."

" There you are then! " said Elizabeth. " But go on about Miss Leg, not Lord Brosely's. Did you make any hints about her eternal gramophone? "

" No. I thought it would be wiser to establish friendly relations first. Now whom shall I have to meet her at my luncheon-party? I think I will find out on what day Jimmie can come. I shall give him several dates to choose from, for he is so often engaged if I only name one."

Mrs. Mantrip's maid came in with the last postal delivery, and instantly her thoughts were switched off from her Leg-party, for she saw that there was a parcel with Messrs. Cartwright's label on it. She had not

imagined that *Rosemary and Rue* would be published
for a couple of days yet, but there could be no doubt
that this parcel contained the sacred volume, and how
she longed to start on it! There would be a complete
stand-still in the progress of Papa's life for the next
week.

" Pray open your post, dear," said Elizabeth.

" There's nothing that looks interesting," said
Margaret, in a voice vibrant with perjury. " Just one
game of piquet? Or is it rather late? I see you feel
that it is."

This clear evidence that Margaret did not want to
play herself chimed with Elizabeth's inclination, for
Sabrina might be having a family at any moment, and
she went home.

She had but a few yards to traverse: only Mr. Salt's
house, Jimmie's and Miss Leg's intervened, and as soon
as she set foot on the pavement she heard loud and
clear the strident music of the gramophone pouring out
of the lit and open window of Miss Leg's drawing-room.
She crossed the road in order to get a better view of
the meretricious decorations she had heard about. She
could see the elaborate fireplace and the mahogany-
panelled walls, but the complete view was obstructed
because, close by the window, was drawn up a table
at which Miss Leg was sitting, busily writing. Immediately in front of her, with the loud speaker turned
towards her, was the great trumpet of the gramophone
bellowing out the overture to *Tannhäuser*. Instantly
Elizabeth forgot all about Sabrina.

" Most extraordinary," she thought to herself.
" It must be some form of lunacy, whatever Margaret
says. No sane person could write busily like that,
with that infernal din going on two inches away from
her ear. And now she is reading over what she has
written. Foolscap sheets."

Enthralled by this amazing sight, Elizabeth withdrew into the shadow of one of the sumacs, which Mrs.

Mantrip's father had planted, and watched. Miss Leg
evidently made a correction or two in what she had
written, and then, after putting a sheaf of foolscap sheets into a drawer of her writing-table, silenced
the gramophone in the very middle of a most exciting
bar. Surely that was strange conduct for so ardent a
lover of mechanical music, that she should switch it
off like that. But stranger still was the habit of writing, when it was bellowing full blast into her ear.
That would be a fresh puzzle for Margaret, who so
prided herself on the reading of character.

Elizabeth found Sabrina comfortable, though not
yet a mother, and went to bed. But long after the
rest of the Square had done the same, the light
in Margaret's chamber, conveniently placed for recum-
bent reading, burned steadfast, as she devoured the
pages of *Rosemary and Rue* in the first rapturous reading of it. Rudolph da Vinci had never given the world
anything finer.

Margaret found no difficulty in getting Jimmie to
name the day for his lunching with her to meet Miss
Leg, for he had often smelt the most sumptuous and
recondite odours coming from her kitchen, and had
observed her chef, without doubt a Frenchman, among
his pots and pans within. That was sufficient: anyone with a French chef was worth knowing even at
the mortification of a beastly lunch with Margaret.
Accordingly, a few days afterwards, a small company
of the local magnates of the Square were engaged to
meet at Mrs. Mantrip's house to make the acquaintance
of the new-comer. Captain and Lady Eva Lowndes
were the first to arrive; they looked as if they were
dressing up to impersonate each other, for he was slim
and wan and of a psychical aspect, while she was large
and robust and emphatic in manner, like a military
man in a farce, and wore a waistcoat with large checks
and a tall stiff collar and a skirt that just covered her

knees (which were a long way from the ground) and disclosed remarkably well-developed calves. She called her friends, male and female, by their surnames. Next arrived the Vicar, who both practised and preached about Yoga, and was a very good golfer. That health-giving game provided him with many vivid similes in his sermons. Prayer, he told his congregation, enabled the Christian soul to soar high over the traps and snares and pits that were so plentifully strewn over the course we had to traverse, making as few mistakes as possible, whereas the man who went scuffling along the ground ran into every bunker there was. Then came Elizabeth Conklin with the glad news that Sabrina had given birth to five puppies by Bully Boy, an unusual number, but all apparently healthy. Elizabeth was warmly congratulated, and they waited for the arrival of Jimmie and the candidate. Lady Eva was straddling in front of the fireplace, a full six feet high, smoking a cigarette, and describing a séance with the famous medium Corisande.

"And almost as soon as she went into trance," she said, "there came the direct voice, and I recognized it at once as my mother's. She asked if Little Doodleums was there. That was pretty good, because I always used to be called Little Doodleums, though there's nothing about me now that could have suggested that to Corisande. Could it? I ask you. Hullo, Mason!"

Jimmie shambled into the room.

"My dear, how sweet to see you, and I believe you've grown," said Jimmie. "Been raising spirits from the vasty deep as usual? I hope you've sent them all back and they've got drowned. And dear Hostess! And Liz-Liz Conklin. Congratulations on the addition to your family. I suppose you'll put it in *The Times*. And dear Padre, and gallant Captain! But Miss Leg not here yet? I was afraid I was late."

All this was very like Jimmie. He treated every party he went to as if it was his own, and had a kind word for all the other guests. Having welcomed them all he was kind to his hostess again.

" Just been seeing my Maharajah off at the station," he said, " and he wants me to go and stay with him at Baracuta. Nothing will induce me to, if I'm expected to shoot tigers. I should have to begin practising at haystacks at once, unless Liz-Liz wants to get rid of some of her new family. . . . Here she is."

Miss Leg entered, her small round face wreathed with the most fascinating society-smile, and her behaviour with the most finished company-manners. She apologized to her hostess for being late, saying how naughty it was of her. She bowed to the gentlemen; she shook hands with the ladies; she hung back when they went in to lunch, saying " After you, please," to Elizabeth, and then tripped forward with dainty little steps. She put her chin up and out when she was spoken to; she ate her grape-fruit with a little finger held in the air in an exclusive manner; she said " Pardon " with an engaging grimace when she failed to catch what the Vicar said to her; she called Lady Eva, " Lady Lowndes," as she did not yet know her well enough to use her Christian name. In five minutes Margaret was regretting that she had assembled this lunch-party to observe so unpromising a candidate. And there was Jimmie already concealing the greater part of his salmon mayonnaise under his fork, and Elizabeth smelling the dish, like one of her own dogs, and then declining it.

Mrs. Mantrip pulled herself together. She reminded herself that she was her father's daughter, and that such little annoyances were of no kind of consequence. Papa would never have noticed them at all; he would have launched forth into some subject of serious import, and held the table spell-bound till the salmon was taken away. She must firmly start a general conversation on a high theme to which everybody would contribute, though one hoped Miss Leg would only listen. What subject should she choose? India would do: there was Jimmie who had been asked to stay with a Maharajah; there was the Vicar who knew all about Yoga and other Oriental philosophies; there was Captain Lowndes who had been born in Bombay.

" Of all the Imperial problems which confront us," she said in a confident voice, " India is certainly the most pressing. The brightest jewel in the Crown of England——"

" Ah, that wonderful Koh-i-noor," said Miss Leg brightly. " Such a monster ! "

" I was speaking figuratively," said Margaret. " The Empire was what I was referring to. It was Kipling really who first awoke the nation, don't you think, dear Eva, to a sense of our responsibilities there? Papa used to say that Kipling discovered India for us."

" I entirely disagree, Mrs. Mantrip," said the Vicar. " The significance of India is purely spiritual. It doesn't matter two straws whether India is in the Imperial Crown or not. Its contribution towards the coming of the Kingdom of Heaven is its ancient philosophies which date from centuries before the Christian era. Yoga, for instance."

This was better: high talk was brewing thanks to Mrs. Mantrip's lead, and Miss Leg's little gentilities would soon be forgotten and would certainly never be seen again at her table. Jimmie made one of his futile and greedy observations, saying that the brightest jewel in the Crown of India was curry, but Mrs. Mantrip knew that the mention of Yoga would rouse Lady Eva. It did.

" Yoga ? " she said. " Yoga is magic, and black at that. I had a friend who studied Yoga and she went completely off her chump, such as it was. Most dangerous, and where does Yoga get you to at the best ? Only to a control of things which are much better left to themselves. Believe me, the only way in which we can approach the spiritual world is through mediums and the cultivation of the spiritual powers that lie dormant in ourselves, not through nerve-centres."

" I never liked Indian philosophy," said Elizabeth. " The Indians say that dogs are unclean. Wretches! Some of my dogs are the truest Christians. And then to tell me that I may be born again as a hyena! "

" My birthplace was Bombay," said Captain Lowndes in faint tones. " The first thing I can remember distinctly——"

The Vicar raised his voice, as if approaching the peroration of his sermon. What he said sounded like it, too.

" Reincarnation is the only solution for the manifold unfairnesses and injustices in this world," he said. " Why should one man be born to health and wealth and all the favours of good fortune, and another be from birth the victim of some gross hereditary taint, and start life in a slum? We all know that a Being infinitely just and tender is above all and through all and in all, and how can we reconcile it with our notion of justice that one man should have every chance and another none? Again, as to the evil we see in the world——"

" Dear Padre," interrupted Jimmie, " if you're going to talk about the origin of evil, I shan't listen. I'd sooner shoot a tiger. Nobody knows what it is, least of all such a lamb as you."

Jimmie always spoke with abundance of florid gesticulation, and upset a glass of reliable port procured that morning from the grocer's. A purple, tawny stain shot across Margaret's nice clean table-cloth.

" Oh, dear me! " cried Miss Leg. " Mop it up with your serviette, Mr. Mason, or the tablecloth will be soiled for ever. And pray let us hear more about

reincarnaton.   Most interesting.   I often wonder
what I was before I was me.''

She leaned forward with her chin out in an attitude
of rapt expectation, her face looking of incredible
insignificance underneath her spider-webbed hat which
was gorgeously trimmed with bunches of artificial
grapes in three colours, black, red and yellow, and
garnished with crimson vine leaves.   She wore her
string of pearls round her short, plump neck (and now
Mrs. Mantrip decided they were Woolworth); she wore
a bright green silk coat over a muslin dress in which
was pinned a cluster of malmaisons.   She was enjoying this party given in her honour quite immensely:
there was such lofty conversation to listen to, such
grand cosmic topics—India (though apparently not
the Koh-i-noor), reincarnation, mediumship, the infinite
beneficence of Providence, the origin of evil.   It was so
advanced of a clergyman of the Church of England to
believe in reincarnation and say so.   That was her
idea of a clergyman : bishops and deans should be like
that; they should bring religion home to the people,
make friends with sinners and publicans, pray with
them, drink a glass of beer with them, partake of their
joys and sorrows, tell them about reincarnation.   Then
on another plane of interest, but well worth observation, there was Lady Lowndes.   Such a modern type,
with her elbows on the table, eating chipped potatoes
with her fingers.   An aristocrat, too, of the bluest
blood, sister, as Susan Leg had already ascertained
from the pages of Debrett, of the Marquis of Brosely.
Then there was Lady Lowndes's husband, Captain
Lowndes apparently, though that was difficult to understand, who was most gentlemanly, not to say ladylike,
and very likely had interesting things to say about
Bombay, if he was only allowed to state them.   Her
hostess, she noticed, looked vexed : of course it was
annoying to have a glass of such highly coloured wine
upset over her clean tablecloth, but she ought not to

have minded that when there was such admirable talk
in progress, and everyone was so animated. . . .

There was a moment of dead silence when, having
given her napkin to Mr. Mason, Miss Leg said she
wondered who she had been before. No one had any
suggestion to make about that: they were all waiting
for her, no doubt, to tell them her own ideas on the
subject. Very gratifying.

"When I was last in Paris," she said—" I'm sure
you all know Paris—I drove over to Versailles and saw
Petty Trianon. And then an extraordinary feeling
came over me—was it not odd, for I had never been
there before—that I knew Petty Trianon quite well.
Like a conviction it was, something I felt sure about,
and I wondered if I had been poor Marie Antoinette."

"Very likely indeed," said Mrs. Mantrip, and then
there was another silence.

Jimmie broke it, and though nothing could have
been more irrelevant, any irrelevance was better than
nothing.

"I hear there's a new book by Rudolph da Vinci,"
he said. " I must get it at once. I hope there will be
another bishop in it who is a Lord-Lieutenant. I never
laughed so much in my life."

"Rudolph da Vinci?" asked the Vicar. "Who's
that?"

"The greatest treat of modern times," said Jimmie.
"Quite incredible. You can't believe it even when
you read it."

"Perfectly killing," said Mrs. Mantrip, feeling like
Judas. "How people can read him! Sells by the
hundred thousand I believe, too."

That finished with the silence and Lady Eva
resumed the subject of mediumship as an avenue leading into the spiritual world. The Vicar was not so
open-minded about that. He had doubts: he shook
his head.

"Dangerous to dabble in," he said. "The witch

of Endor, for instance; I regard the witch of Endor as
a medium."

"Yes, and a pretty successful one," said Lady Eva.
"She had Samuel up in a jiffy."

"But how do you know it was Samuel? " he asked.
"Far more likely that it was some spirit of evil impersonating him."

"I only know what the Bible says," said Eva.

Mrs. Mantrip seemed to have recovered from her
chagrin at the accident to her tablecloth.

"Without are dogs and sorcerers," she remarked,
as if she had put them there herself.

"No, not dogs, Margaret," cried Elizabeth. "I
won't have you couple dogs with sorcerers."

"I am not referring to your Pekinese, dear," said
Margaret. "Do not think that. I am only agreeing
with the Vicar, and I may say that my father also had
very strong views on the subject of mediums. He
regarded all spiritualism as witchcraft. Papa never
attended a séance: the idea horrified him, and he never
would listen to any talk about it, nor read anything
about it. He preached a wonderful sermon on the
subject."

"I'm sure, dear, it was quite wonderful," said
Eva, "if you tell us so. But as you also tell us that
he knew nothing about the subject, his conclusions
can't really be of much value to anybody."

"It was an instinctive feeling with Papa," said
Margaret. "How right it always is to trust an
instinct! His spirituality recoiled from spiritualism.
He turned with horror from it."

Lady Eva made a noise in her throat which might
be described as a snort. It betokened impatience.
Margaret was apt to endorse her own opinions by
saying that her father had shared them, and that he
had preached on this precise point.

"But be fair, Margaret," she said. "How can
your father's views about it, I repeat, matter to any-

body? I might as well have instincts about higher mathematics.''

"Or about Yoga, dear lady,'' said the Vicar. He had been waiting a long time to get in something sharp of that sort.

"Come, come, we shall all be quarrelling,'' said Jimmie in his comfortable voice, " and Miss Leg will be sorry she has come to live among such tiresome, argumentative people.''

"No, indeed: all so interesting,'' said Miss Leg. " I could listen for ever to such a discussion. There is always so much to be said on both sides.''

Lady Eva did not reply to this smart stroke of the Vicar's, but focussed her gaze in some far-away fashion on Miss Leg's hat, and an abstracted smile came on her lips. Miss Leg was delighted that her hat so evidently pleased Lady Eva—it was a remarkable hat—and she bent her head slightly to afford the Marquis's sister a better view. But all Eva's friends knew that she was not seeing the hat at all, nor the varieties of grapes that grew so abundantly there. "Eva's boiled look,'' was their description of that psychical gaze, and it betokened that Eva was seeing a halo. Margaret could never quite make up her mind whether she believed in her friend's visionary gifts. Sometimes if Eva saw a very unpleasant halo round the head of someone she herself disliked, she thought there was something in it, but if Eva saw a laudable emanation there, she was inclined to think it was all rubbish. If these powers were genuine there was something rather underhand about the exercise of them: it was like looking through a chink to which nobody else had access. But she would not go as far as Elizabeth and declare that Eva, if she saw anything at all, saw only a sort of coloured reflection of her own sentiments, for there had now and again been odd confirmations of her occult perception. It would be interesting to know what she was seeing round Miss Leg's head. Some tint, she now expected, that betrayed a common and undistinguished nature. She gave her time enough to have a good look, and rose.

" Let us have our coffee in the library," she said. " Miss Leg, I know, would like to see Papa's books."

Miss Leg softly clapped her fat little hands together to show her appreciation.

" Another treat for me ! " she cried. " Am I not lucky ? And may I have a peep at that sermon about spiritualism ? "

This boon was denied her. Mrs. Mantrip explained that a number of his sermons had gone to be bound, and that the counterblast to spiritualism was among them. No one believed that, and clearly there was no such sermon: Margaret had just invented it as a support to her own view. So Miss Leg was taken round the shelves to keep her quiet, and Margaret showed her the first edition of Bishop Heber's journal, and Law's *Serious Call*, and George Herbert's poems, and the complete works of St. Augustine, and Proctor on the Prayer Book, and the backs of thirty note-books containing Papa's diary. Susan would have liked to see what treasures there were on the book-shelf below the window where a curtain veiled the complete works of Rudolph da Vinci from the gaze of the profane, but Mrs. Mantrip stood firmly in front of it, and said there were only odds and ends. Before long the parlour-maid came in to say that Miss Leg's car was at the door. Miss Leg could not believe it was a quarter to three already; never had time passed so quickly, but she must tear herself away, for she was motoring down to Sussex for the week-end. She had told her chauffeur, she explained, to call for her here with her maid and her luggage, so that she could remain at her luncheon-party till the last possible moment. She fluttered off with all the bunches of grapes a-tremble on her hat, and kissed her hand to the watchers by the window as she got into her car.

Mrs. Mantrip's other guests, of course, went into committee about the candidate immediately she had left, with Mrs. Mantrip in the chair. The proceedings were very brief: her hat, her little finger, her " Lady Lowndes," her " serviette," her previous incarnation as Marie Antoinette, her extreme gentility had made an unfortunate impression, and she could not be seriously considered a social acquisition to the Square. Quite harmless, no doubt, but just that. . . . All this was deftly indicated by Mrs. Mantrip, and it was impossible to argue about it. Jimmie alone faintly dissented as he rose to go.

" Somehow I feel that there's something in her," he said, " though I'm sure I couldn't tell you what it is. I dare say intellect isn't her strong point, but then I haven't got any brains either. I shall ask her to dinner whatever anybody else does, and I hope she'll ask me. Delicious lunch, dear Margaret, and I'm so sorry about the port. I must go, for I'm off to a concert. Divine music. Two hours of bliss."

The Vicar went with him to get two hours of golf at the Mid-Surrey links, for it was possible to play a round before getting back for evensong at half-past six. Elizabeth returned home to see how Sabrina's family was taking nourishment, and to exercise the remaining Pekinese in the garden, and Captain Lowndes flitted out of sight like a moth in the dusk. He had elusive exits and entrances: sometimes you were aware that he was there, and then in a short while you saw that he wasn't. He had just gone away, like a vanishing lady in a conjuring-trick, without anybody noticing it. He could come back again in the same manner: you would find he was there.

There remained therefore in Mrs. Mantrip's library herself and Lady Eva. Had there been a plebiscite in the Square to choose two local ladies to represent mind and spirit in some international conference, a large majority would certainly have declared for them. Mrs.

Mantrip's literary labours and reputation entitled her
to one seat, Lady Eva's psychical gifts to the other.
But they did not hold such a high opinion of each
other's gifts as the Square. Eva's psychical perceptions
caused her to entertain grave private suspicions of
the quality and extent of Margaret's literary labours,
while Margaret's intellectual grasp told her that Eva's
psychical gifts were largely fudge. Consequently when
they were alone they often " strove together," the mind
warring against the spirit. These encounters aroused
no enmity between them : their blades only shone the
brighter with the application of each other's acids.

" Mantrip, it makes my heart bleed sometimes to
observe how superficial you are," said Eva, in order to
get to work at once. " Not your fault; I suppose you
can't help it. You have a real talent for observing
about people all that doesn't matter. You think you've
finished with Leg, added her up and found she amounts
to nothing, just because she calls me Lady Lowndes. I
wish you could learn to look below the surface."

Mantrip was ready for her.

" I suppose that means you have seen some marvellous halo coming out of the grapes in her hat," she
retorted. " Do take care of those delusions of yours,
or they will become real to you. I should think they
were chiefly liver. See a sensible doctor about them."

Eva gave a great hoarse laugh.

" A pretty answer," she said, " but I am being
serious. I can tell you more about her with that one
good look I had at her than you will ever learn by
yourself. My dear, she's got the most marvellous
gifts. You may laugh at me, but you'll find I'm
right. She has a power of imagination beyond anything I have ever seen. She has a golden-yellow
halo, the colour of a ripe harvest-field with the sun
on it. Dazzling and rich beyond words. I certainly
intend to see more of her, for she has some wonderful
secret life of which we know nothing. I am not

arguing with you, I am telling you. She has a colossal imaginative faculty.''

" The colossal imaginative faculty is your own,'' said Margaret.

" Not in the least; it's hers. It's a secret life.''

Eva gazed at her friend with that uncanny, far-away look.

" And I believe you've got one too,'' she said. " Several times in these last few days I have seen gleams and sparks in your halo which show that you are experiencing some intense inward joy of which you never speak. Something is making you happy inside: your soul is at a banquet. It makes no difference to me whether you deny it or not, for I know it's true. I wish you would confess: I won't tell anybody. Is there a man? ''

Margaret cast a hasty glance round the room at the mention of a secret life, though she felt sure that she had put *Rosemary and Rue* behind the small baize curtain. There was something strikingly true about Eva's pronouncement that for the last few days she had been in a state of inward bliss, for never had she been so profoundly affected by any previous book of her favourite author's. Even this suggestion that there was a man might have something in it, for she had begun to picture him with that inward eye which is the bane as well as the bliss of solitude, and his figure was becoming terribly vivid. A strong silent man with a mysterious smile and a horse-whip; he haunted her dreams last night, and her soul in a nightmare of agonized rapture had cried out to her that here was her perfect mate. No doubt this disturbing vision had been caused by a midnight indulgence in *Rosemary and Rue*, in which there was just such a figure as that which had haunted her dreams, but she had felt sure, as she read, that this splendid creature was the author's presentment of himself. Perhaps then there was in that uncomfortable region of the mind, which Eva alluded to as the subliminal, a man.

" That's an odd suggestion to make to me," she said, " and if you'll excuse my saying so, there's a coarseness about it. If you want my unequivocal denial of it, I shall be happy to give it you."

" I don't want your denial at all," said Eva. " I should be only too delighted to think that it was true. A love-affair, whether it ended in marriage or not, might deepen you. We all have our secret lives, I expect. Mine is the joy and the illumination that spiritualism gives me. I can tell you all about it, but it's secret all the same, since you can't imagine it. And I feel sure that you've had some secret joy in your life, for to-day I see those lights playing round you which are an infallible symptom. I can't believe that you find it in working at your papa's life, which you say is getting on so well. I see something more sensuous than writing the life of a clergyman could possibly give you. Besides, when you talk to me of your father's life, I see—well, never mind about that."

Eva strode about the room in her large, masculine manner as she made these observations which Margaret could not but feel to be very remarkable. But it was impossible to tell her, for the sake of her high-brow literary reputation, what was the source of that joy which she had so oddly divined, and she went back to the more impersonal subject of Miss Leg.

" You are at liberty, dear Eva," she said, " to see whatever you like anywhere, and to draw your own conclusions from it. But all that my poor blind eyes can see in Miss Leg is that she is a common, genteel little woman, and quite ridiculous. I was really ashamed of having asked you all to meet her. Cultivate her by all means if you like, and I sincerely hope that you will find in her the rich mental gifts that her corn-coloured halo betokens. When you do, I shall take it very kind in you, as I'm sure Miss

Leg would say, if you would call me, and I will acknowledge there's something in your haloes. Till then—well, leave it at that."

Margaret put as much finality into this conclusion as her uncompromising voice would carry, for she wanted Eva to go away, and let her get on with her second reading of *Rosemary and Rue*. But Eva's sensitiveness in the occult seemed to be balanced by a peculiar obtuseness in more superficial perceptions, and she continued to move about the room in a restless, disturbing manner. Then the telephone bell rang, and Margaret applied herself.

A voice hoarse with emotion and broken with sobs came to her ear.

" Is it Margaret? " it wailed. " I'm Elizabeth. And Bully Boy has killed two of Sabrina's litter."

" No! Dear me! How dreadful! " said Margaret. " I am sorry. What are you going to do? "

" Bury them or cremate them," said the broken voice.

" Yes, dear, quite so," said Margaret sympathetically. " Much the best thing to do with them. But about that dreadful Bully Boy? "

Eva looked sharply round.

" Eh? What has Bully Boy done? " she asked. "Killed two of Sabrina's litter. Good gracious, you did say that he had the halo of a murderer."

Certainly it was very odd.

Eva went off for a sitting with Corisande, and Mrs. Mantrip took *Rosemary and Rue* from behind the small baize curtain. There was Jimmie, greedy Jimmie, already hoping to dine with Miss Leg; there was Eva who, in a more spiritual manner, had seen a remarkable halo coming out of her absurd hat. But Mrs. Mantrip was not shaken in her conclusion: a silly, vulgar little woman. No good to the Square.

IV

SUSAN LEG, it may be remembered, had torn
herself away from Mrs. Mantrip's luncheon-party,
because she was motoring down to Sussex for the week-
end. That was a rich, vague statement; it suggested
a country-house visit, and sounded better than saying
that she was going to the Regency Palace Hotel on the
sea-front at Brighton. Breaking in on that high talk
and the privilege of examining (some of) the books
in Mrs. Mantrip's library, there would have been a
garishness and frivolity in such a disclosure. It was
better to say '' Sussex.''

She felt certain of enjoying herself. The air of
Brighton (Dr. Brighton, as she had heard it wittily
called) made her feel alert not in body only but in
mind. Moreover, the splendour of a great hotel
immensely appealed to a strain of childlike voluptuousness that was in her nature : it held magic for her.
Six years ago she had entered those august portals for
the first time, being bidden to meet there one whom
she now counted among her best friends. She had
never forgotten the impression that those soft carpeted
halls, those scagliola pillars, those gilded walls had
made on her; there were velvet chairs and palm-trees
and liveried men. It had seemed a fairyland, and fairy-
like were the folk who sat negligently at their little
tables, and at whose nod all the delicacies she had
heard of but never seen were brought by obsequious
attendants. Since then a sumptuous hotel had never
lost its glamour for her, even though now she could

stay in one as often as she liked, so romantic had
been her experience when first she set foot in one.

Susan dined by herself in the restaurant, getting
a table as near as possible to the band, for, as her
neighbours in the Square had already discovered, she
loved a loud noise close to her. In the restaurant one
ordered dinner *à la carte*, and after studying the *carte*
and composing her little speech in French, she said
to an English waiter: " *Consommé, s'il vous plait.
Poussin avec laitance. Asperges. Pêche Melba.
Café.*" The waiter, who, though English, understood
menu-French perfectly, looked rather astonished, and
inquired: " Will Madame take her herring-roe with
her bird?" Then, of course, Susan saw her mistake
and said: "I mean *laitue*." Rather annoying; for
the future she must insist on talking French to her
chef, Monsieur Rouen, in order to improve her knowledge of that elegant tongue, rather than allow him
to talk English to her in order to improve his.

The company was interesting: Susan always
studied people on all possible occasions. There was
a Cabinet Minister at a table close to her, dining with
his wife. She knew them from pictures in the
illustrated papers, and noticed that they both drank
water: not even bottled water, just Brighton water
that came from a tap. There was a young man with
a young lady who, Susan seemed to know at once,
was not his wife: they drank champagne. The
young lady had several long ropes of pearls; the kind
that swung lightly and gave the wrong sort of chink
when the wearer moved. A little querulous dog in a
coat sat on her knee, a Pekinese: that took Susan's
thoughts back for a moment to Durham Square and
Sabrina's babies. The two, she thought, must have
had a tiff, for they were eating their dinner in absolute
silence, he heavily frowning, and she breathing
through her nose. Then there was an elderly Jew
with a bald head and an immense shirt-front in which

gleamed a diamond stud. His wife, like an obese
cockatoo with a sulphur-coloured crest of hair, was
with him, and, obviously, a son and a daughter. They
all held their mouths slightly open even when they
were not putting things into them.

Close beside her was a table yet unoccupied, but
a single chair, cocked up over the edge of it, indicated
that it was engaged. Susan had just begun her
poussin when the head waiter conducted to it a man,
at the sight of whom her breath was momentarily
suspended, for this was none other than the great
Arthur Armstrong, whose features were so well known
to her from the illustrated press, and whose words,
even the lightest, copyright in all countries, had gone
out into the ends of the world, and probably farther
if all that people said about the wireless was true.
What a brain functioned beneath those permanently
waved locks! What genius beamed from that
prominent eye! Critic, poet, novelist, member of
Parliament, and giver of dinner-parties, duly recorded
by Ulrica and other social specialists, at the best
London restaurants, he represented to Susan Leg the
exemplar of a cultured and delectable existence.
Fervent loyalist though she was, she would scarcely
have been more thrilled if the King himself had come
to sit so near her.

Of course everyone knew him: the Cabinet Minister
whispered to his wife the reverend syllables of his name;
the father of the Semitic family said them out loud; the
head waiter, usually very upright, stood with his back
bent as if he had got severe lumbago, while he took his
order; the wine waiter came hurrying up, with his silver
chain of office jingling on his neck, to procure the next
audience, and the mixer of cocktails, knowing his
habits, busied himself among his bottles and his preserved cherries and his ice. He had brought in with
him, under his arm, a book which he laid on the table
as he gave his order, and now, sipping his accustomed

cocktail, he opened it, and, propping it up against the shade of the electric standard, he put on a pair of tortoiseshell spectacles. Susan longed to know what that book was, but the light cast a glare on to the page and she could not see.

She lingered over the asparagus that followed the *poussin*, and over the *Pêche Melba* that followed the asparagus. She felt it was good for her to be here, for the very presence of her neighbour seemed to diffuse, like some noble and subtle scent, the aroma of his glorious, his cultured existence. She hardly knew which facet of his gem-like life seemed the most brilliant. She always looked at the Parliamentary reports in the daily papers to see if he had spoken at Westminster the night before, and if he had she read aloud to herself those peremptory periods. He was of the Labour Party; he was also immensely wealthy, and how magnificently he justified his contention that the great landowners and capitalists of inherited fortunes ought to be taxed out of existence, their acres sequestrated by the State, and their capital divided among the workers! He himself had worked hard all his life for his money, and would continue to do so in order to secure as much more as possible. He might have been a recipient of the dole himself, so he asserted amid loud laughter, if he had not chosen to work, and while he would willingly give relief to the unemployed who could not get work, and even increase the dole at the expense of the holders of unearned increment, he would give periodical floggings to all who could get work and preferred to be lazy. Not a penny had he inherited: he had started life as an errand-boy in a book-shop, and labour had brought him capital. These admirable views, in which Susan whole-heartedly concurred, he often stated in those articles dealing chiefly with literary subjects, but by no means confined to them, which he wrote every week in the *Sunday Chronicle*.

Then there were his poems, those tonic and courage-

ous pieces, which told you that it was your duty to
banish from your soul all the annoyances and trials of
life, ill-health and penury and the rest, and march,
head up, on the journey of life, enraptured with all the
beautiful and interesting things that surrounded you.
Then there were his novels, soul-chronicles, as he so
aptly named them, of workers whose narrow and toil-
some lives were illuminated by their own astonishing
mental distinction. A foundry hand, he demonstrated,
or a lavatory attendant could be a gentleman of high
culture, and generally was. Then there were his great
luncheon-parties: with what vicarious rapture, as if she
had actually been a guest herself, Susan Leg read in the
papers that Mr. Arthur Armstrong had entertained the
following at Gascon's Restaurant! Often they began
with an ambassador; often they ended, in order of
precedence, with a baronet. Positively not one untitled
person present except himself, who was the greatest of
all. In the many dreams of her imaginative life the
vision that she might some day give parties like that
was among the brightest.

But most of all Susan revered his weekly articles in
the *Sunday Chronicle*. The wisdom and range of
them! The poise of his mind over the literature of the
world, like a hawk hovering, and then, like a hawk
stooping, the capture and dissection of the book he had
honoured by his choice! He spoke with authority, not
as other scribes, and against his decisions, clean-cut and
abrupt, there was no appeal. . . . He enjoyed this
book. He read it at a sitting. He meant to read it
again at another sitting. Powerful characterization.
Hitherto it had attracted no attention, but it was the
finest piece of imaginative fiction since George Bedford
wrote *Water Wagtails*. (Upon reading which, Susan
ordered *Water Wagtails* from the library and found
that it was out of print.) Sometimes he discussed
novels in general. There was too much sex-interest in
them. He was sick of that wearisome and trivial sub-

ject. There Susan could not find herself agreeing with
him: she could not imagine reading with any sort of
frenzy a novel in which love (a more delicate name for
sex-interest) with its endless vicissitudes, its savageries,
its softnesses, was not the main theme. But that
divergence did not detract from her reverence for his
illuminating articles. Often she had pictured him
dictating them, forehead on hand, to one of his typists
(for he had told the world that he kept three). He
would have glanced through the book he was to pro-
nounce on, and there he sat, occasionally referring to
pages he had noted, and minting between puffs at his
cigar, those golden coins of critical currency, all
stamped with his pontifical image. . . .

She rose, for her dinner had long been done, and
saw, as she passed his table, what book it was that he
had propped up there to read. It was *Rosemary and
Rue*.

Susan managed to articulate " *Café noir dans le
lounge*," to the English waiter as she passed out, but
her voice was trembling. Usually the lounge after
dinner supplied her with much entertainment and
interest, and she began to resume her observation of
her fellow-guests. The young couple who, she suspected, were not a couple in the best sense of the word,
seemed to have made their differences up, and were
sitting very close together in an obscure corner underneath a palm, and from it came the sound of giggles
and the chink of imitation pearls. The Semitic family
were playing bridge and cursing each other in Yiddish
(or so she took it to be): the Cabinet Minister and his
wife were reading. But to-night these and other groups
had no power to rivet her attention: her observation of
them was superficial, and she culled nothing from them,
for she was waiting in high and tingling suspense for
Mr. Armstrong to come out from his dinner. Presently
he arrived at the head of an imposing procession: one
waiter carried his coffee, another boxes and boxes of

cigars, from which he might make his choice, a third a
bottle of brandy and a glass as big as a football with
the top cut off. He sat down not far from her and
opened his book again. Susan took up an illustrated
paper and watched him over the top of it.

How she longed to know what thoughts marched
through the royal corridors of his brain as he read! It
seemed an infinite condescension that he should glance
at those unworthy pages. Perhaps it was a mere
relaxation, an unbending of the bow, a pastime for his
leisure, like a game of Patience or of noughts and
crosses. Though his face betrayed nothing, remaining
in majestic repose, he seemed interested, for he let his
coffee get cold, and his cigar burned sideways. Then
the delirious thought came to her that possibly he would
write about *Rosemary and Rue* in the *Sunday Chronicle*
next week.

Suddenly she could not bear to watch him any
longer: it would be unbearable if he fell asleep over it.
The night was hot, and she put on a light cloak and
stepped out of the hotel to stroll along the sea front and
tranquillize herself. Overhead and to the south was
spread a thick bank of cloud which obscured the moon,
so that the sea no more than glimmered uncertainly,
but far out there lay a band of glittering light, where
the moon, shrouded here, shone on to the water.
Romantic thoughts filled her brain: she saw her own
life portrayed there, with its early years of dim
obscurity and the dazzling brightness beyond. Susan
was sure that Nature, "the kind old nurse," as Mr.
Longfellow called her, was wonderfully sympathetic:
she had noticed that Nature often reflected her own
mood in the most flattering manner, and behaved
accordingly. If she felt the joy of life tingling in her,
Nature so often arranged that it should be a fine
morning; if she was depressed, it was as likely as not to
be wet. Her thoughts went back to the great critic,
novelist, M.P. and poet. What a wonderful novel he

might write about his own career, mingling, no doubt, fiction with fact in the fashion of true creators; the earlier chapters would concern the years when he was an errand-boy in a book-shop. But, great man though he was, had he the touch for it? Those early chapters would have to drip with pathos and sentimentality, the lack of which, Susan considered, was his only defect. She almost felt that she could write it for him better than he could write it for himself, and began idly to dwell on the lines of her narration. She thought she would describe how, instead of using his dinner hour to satisfy the claims of physical hunger, he lingered in the shop and fed his soul on the works of the great masters of literature. A dreamy boy who, when he was sent out to deliver books from the circulating library, sat down with his burden (say on this esplanade at Brighton) and read, instead of doing his errands. So absorbed was he in them that a subscriber, an old lady with a cold, who had selfishly looked forward to spending this afternoon sitting over the fire with the new book she had ordered, rang up the library and demanded to know why her book had not come. She would be told that the boy had started on his round two hours ago, and then he would be found on the sea front, oblivious to the rain that was falling heavily, soaking him and ruining the books. His master took him back to the shop, stripped off his coat and shirt, tied his hands above him, and covered his white shoulders with a criss-cross of cruel weals. Not a cry or a moan came from his lips, and he read more voraciously than ever. Then he fell in love with a young girl of patrician beauty, and they sat on the end of the pier together. This time the Earl, her father, whipped him. He was dismissed from the shop and wrote his first story on scraps of paper he picked up in the street, and spent his last penny in getting it typewritten. The Editor of *Tasty Bites* accepted it, and now his foot was on the ladder. The rest was easy.

Though such imaginations agreeably occupied her mind as she strolled along, there was something which subconsciously had been directing her steps, and now, automatically, she stopped opposite a block of bald buildings facing the sea. The upper stories were let as residential flats, but on three windows of the first floor was advertised in large white letters Ascham's Typewriting Agency. Well she knew the inside of that room, for she had spent there the working hours of fifteen years. There were half a dozen small tables, on each of which was a typewriter, and there all day (for the agency was famed far and wide for the neatness and accuracy of the work it turned out) used to sit six industrious spinsters, incessantly tapping the keys of their instruments. Click, clack, clack, click, a buzz at the end of a line, a rustle of paper, hour after hour in endless repetition. Susan could hear that noise in her head now, if she listened for the memories of old days. She herself had sat at a larger table with no typewriter on it, and her duty was to revise the sheets as they were finished and brought to her by the typists, to see that the order and the numbering of the pages were correct, to look through them for missing words and consult the manuscript to see if she could solve the conundrums, to estimate and note down in her ledger the number of words, and finally to enclose the copy in covers of thick red paper, to punch three holes on the near margin of it with a stamping machine, and thread it with ribbon. She had to keep her wits about her for those pagings and entries and calculations, and to attend very closely to her business, but before she had been there long the clatter of the typewriters round her assisted rather than inhibited attention, and noise became to her a most valuable aid to concentration.

Occasionally (and such days were indeed redlettered in Susan's memory) there came to the office a story by a really great writer. Mrs. Barclay had sent a full-length novel to be typed there, and Miss Marie

Corelli a short story. The checking of the pages and the computation of the number of words in the manuscript had then taken a long time, for Susan could not resist skimming through these mistress-pieces instead of confining herself to the cold work of correction and calculation. Once in the perusal of a very touching and painful passage, she lost control of herself altogether and a large tear-drop from one of her own eyes splashed on the page. She mopped it up, she dealt with the other tear, and followed the story to the end, keeping an iron hand on herself. It was therefore with the vividness of personal experience that she had been picturing Mr. Armstrong in his errand-boy days, which corresponded to her own typing-office days, sitting down on a bench in the rain, and reading the books from the lending library instead of delivering them.

It was only six years ago, thought Susan, as she now contemplated the windows of the flat behind which she had spent so many long hours, that she had been employed there at a salary of two pounds a week, and it was there that the impulse (or rather the compulsion) of writing herself had come to her. In the evening, when her work was done and she was alone in her room in the modest boarding-house where she lived, she had been accustomed to think out stories and scribble notes for them on the sheet or two of paper which she had secretly filched from the agency. But fertility of invention mostly came to her when she was at work in the middle of clacking typewriters: images and incidents swarmed into her mind then, the noise seemed to drive her into herself. Noise, not necessity, was to her the mother of invention. She saved up her money and bought a second-hand gramophone, and then her evening hours, when her official work was over, became really productive. She sat quite close to the braying machine, and under that strange psychological spur she began to write in

earnest. Half a dozen short stories of hers were taken
by a magazine, and then she started on a full-length
novel. It poured from her pen: she scribbled and
scribbled with the utmost facility, and was astonished
to find how soon it was done and how enormous its
length. She could not afford to have so substantial a
work typewritten, but she made a beautiful manuscript copy of it, almost without erasure, and sent
it to the publishing firm of Messrs. Cartwright.
Within a week she heard from him: he asked her to
lunch with him at the Regency Palace Hotel, where
he would be staying for the week-end. That was the
first time that she saw those marble halls, which, since
then, though now familiar to her, had never lost their
glamour.

On the ground floor below the windows of
Ascham's Typewriting Agency was a book-shop. It
was shut now, but there was no blind down, and by
the light of the street lamp just outside she could read
the titles of the books prominently displayed there.
There was half a shelf devoted to the novels of Mr.
Armstrong, but from the floor in front of the book-
case there rose a whole column, fifty copies at least,
of *Rosemary and Rue*.

She turned: the subconscious impulse had fulfilled
itself. The heavy bank of clouds which, half an hour
ago, had shrouded the moon had quite dispersed, and
a quivering silver path of reflected light led from her
to that admired luminary. Nature, as usual, had
done the sympathetic thing, and kept pace with
Susan's mood. She began to take notes in her mind.
The sky was velvet-blue (though Kipling had noticed
that already), and small ripples were breaking with a
hushing hiss along the shingle. Tenderly they kissed
the shingle with their white lips: Kipling had not
noticed that. There were still a good many people
strolling about, and their faces bleached by the moonlight looked refined and wistful. Susan pictured

them returning to their homes, and peeping into the nursery to see if the little ones were asleep. Or, equally well from another point of view, those faces might be blanched with unholy passions and the white lips of the ripples be giving Judas-kisses to the shore. The two would evidently, from the literary standpoint, go in pairs, thought Susan, thus:

(1) If the faces (blanched by the moonlight) were refined and wistful, the ripples would be kissing the shingle tenderly and wishing it good night.

(2) If the faces (blanched by the moonlight) were white with unholy passion, the ripples would be giving Judas-kisses.

Mr. Armstrong, she felt, did not look on nature and man with her own co-ordinating eye. He did not see more deeply—for what could be deeper than love and hate?—but he analysed more. He saw motives, conflictions, shades of character; he told you more about the everyday life of his people, and though for the most part they were not very remarkable, but in quite common walks of life, they had a reality about them. One perhaps made buns, and another boots, and though buns and boots were things to be taken for granted, bakers' ovens and cobblers' lasts were interesting when he told you about them in his analytical and authoritative manner. He gripped your attention: he had a power. Suddenly she saw him. He was sitting all by himself in one of the glass and cast-iron erections provided by the Corporation for the rest and shelter of passengers. He was gazing out to sea with a magisterial air as if he did not wholly approve of the moonlight. She longed to see with his eyes for a moment: perhaps he was memorizing his impression of the scene for future use, as she had been doing herself. Or was he thinking about *Rosemary and Rue*, perhaps even putting his thoughts into shape, in order to be ready for one of his typists?

Susan Leg drove back to London full of sea air and kindled aspirations. It was not that she had a low opinion of her own work, for none out of the thousands of adoring readers was more convinced than she of the transcendent quality of her genius; but she wanted something else as well, something with which Mr. Armstrong was brimming over, and in which, though to a vastly lesser degree, Mrs. Mantrip abounded. Mrs. Mantrip was devoting her days to a high emprise in writing that life of her father, for she could not think that she would make money out of it (or if she did, she would certainly experience a shocking disillusionment) nor could hope that it would be a best-seller. But her father, so she said, had done noble work at Screwby and in the Square, and her laborious days were spent in his library of ecclesiastical books, where she toiled, not for the sake of pelf, but in order to produce a serious literary work. Then there was her neighbour, Mr. Jimmie Mason, who devoted his life to music; there was the Vicar who knew so much about Indian philosophy; there was Lady Eva who lived in the spiritual world. The subjects of their various studies were widely different, but they were bound together by that mysterious quality called culture. Education and upbringing no doubt had much to do with it, but surely it wasn't too late to learn. At that luncheon-party at Mrs. Mantrip's, which she had so much enjoyed, they had all talked easily and naturally, though contradicting and interrupting each other, about their high subjects. Something, which she was aware she was deficient in, bound them together. " I want to be a lady," thought Susan, as her great car turned into Durham Square. " I want to give parties like Mr. Armstrong. . . ." And here she was again at her beautiful house.

She found several communications waiting for her return. The first was a notice from the Garden Com-

mittee, summoning a general meeting of the householders of the Square at the Vicarage on Wednesday.
Business: to lay the accounts of the upkeep of the
garden before them, and to discuss the question of
dogs being allowed therein. Certain members of the
Committee observed that though there was a rule,
which had been in existence for at least thirty years
and had never been repealed, to the effect that dogs
were definitely excluded from the garden, some householders habitually broke it. There would be a discussion as to whether the rule should be repealed, and a
vote taken. Should the vote be anti-dog, the Committee
intended to enforce the rule with the utmost strictness.

That sounded very reasonable, thought Susan.
The garden and the regulations concerning it were the
concern of the householders jointly, and if the anti-
dogs were in a majority she must take her Sigurd the
Alsatian for his walks elsewhere. It did not seem to
matter much. She was therefore astonished at the
impassioned tone of the next note she opened. It
was from her neighbour, Mrs. Conklin, and Mrs.
Conklin implored her, for the sake of her beautiful
dog, to put any other engagement aside and attend
the meeting as a pro-dog. If Miss Leg would look
in for a cup of tea this afternoon, she would unmask
to her what was neither more nor less than a base
conspiracy. Then there was a card from Mr. James
Mason, with the top left-hand corner turned down to
show he had paid a personal call, and another from
the Vicar, and an invitation from Lady Eva Lowndes
to lunch with her next day. All this was very
pleasant; the Square was getting neighbourly and she
saw her way before her like the clear shining of the
moon on the sea at Brighton.

Susan accepted these agreeable invitations, and as
there was a vacant hour in front of her, she took out
from the drawer of her writing-table the manuscript on
which she was engaged. She had stopped on Saturday

in the middle of a very rich and truculent scene between
some folk of the highest birth and the shadiest antecedents. It had been a great wrench to tear herself
away from it, for the situation was thrilling and the
word-painting of extraordinary vividness. Now, as
she read it through before starting again, it struck her
as a very powerful piece of work, but simultaneously
with that pleasant thought there came the sense that it
was more important than ever to preserve the secret of
her pseudonym. It had been mentioned with derision
at the luncheon-party which, otherwise, she had so
much enjoyed, by Mr. Jimmie; Mrs. Mantrip had
endorsed his scorn, while the Vicar had never heard of
the author in question. It would be fatal if, now that
she was getting a footing in cultured circles, it was
known who she was, since this was the collective verdict
of her neighbours on her work. Indeed, it was most
fortunate that no one suspected that there was incuba-
ting in their midst, and approaching the hatching days,
one of those books by the author whom no critic ever
mentioned and of whom an enlightened Vicar had
never heard.

Susan finished reading the scene on which she was
at work, and moved her wireless set, with its loud
speaker, close beside her. An organ recital was in
progress, and a great volume of sound poured forth.
That was sufficient: she would not need the gramophone as well, and she took up her pen. " Unhand
me," cried the Countess, as the fugue swept on its
majestic way. Simultaneously, three houses away, a
gush of tears came into Mrs. Mantrip's eyes as she
finished the second careful reading of *Rosemary and
Rue*. Round her stood the shelves containing all those
sermons and diaries of her father, to which again she
must turn her reluctant attention.

Below the seeming tranquillity of the Square surprising passions and secret lives were seething in
unsuspected cauldrons.

V

SUSAN found Mrs. Elizabeth Conklin alone in a gaunt room that smelt rather pleasantly of the soap in which she washed her dogs. Sabrina, in a capacious basket, was behaving as a mother should to her three surviving children, and on the chimney-piece was a small pseudo-alabaster bowl precisely similar to those which contain the best shaving soap, and make such suitable and comparatively inexpensive Christmas presents from wives to husbands who do not wear beards. Such indeed was its history. Elizabeth had given it to Mr. Conklin on the last Christmas morning that he had spent on earth, and though six Christmas mornings had elapsed since then, she knew it must be " somewhere." It was, and yesterday, finding a use for it, she had disinterred it from a cupboard where, in a stupor of camphor, lay the levée dress in which his Sovereign had decorated him with the order of the M.B.E. for war-services in connection with leather. There were a few other relics still there, for which she had not yet found employment. An ivory-backed hair-brush, rather bald in front, was among them. She had tried it on her dogs, but the bristles came out. . . .

She shook hands with Susan and pointed to the alabaster bowl with a trembling finger, and spoke in a trembling voice.

" I had them cremated," she said. " My innocents ! They came back yesterday. The baker did it."

Susan had left for Brighton before Saturday's double murder had been committed. But, with a flash of her corn-coloured halo, she guessed.

" Something dead? " she asked. " Not puppies, surely? Oh, I am sorry."

Elizabeth heaved a deep sigh and shook her head. It was surprising that anyone could be ignorant of this tragedy.

" Yes. Bully Boy killed them," she said. " Two of his own children. And would have eaten them, though he had just had his dinner. And him in the stud-book."

Elizabeth lifted the lid of the alabaster casket. There was a little ash inside as of a cigarette.

" There," she said, " two of them."

" Only fancy! " said Susan. " I should have thought it couldn't have been more than one."

Elizabeth replaced the lid on the funeral urn, and faced the world again.

" It's good of you to have come in to see me," she said, " at such short notice. It's about this base conspiracy, got up by the Vicar and Margaret Mantrip, and sprung on us all like this. For years now, morning and afternoon, except when the weather made it impossible, my dogs have had their exercise in the garden; and now those two are going to try to put in force an obsolete rule which I, for one, have always disregarded, and intend to go on doing so, whatever is the result of the meeting on Wednesday. Half an hour in the morning, and another half-hour in the afternoon is all I ask, and if any inhabitant of the Square objects to the ten best-bred Pekinese in England being in the garden when he is, aren't the remaining twenty-three hours of the day enough for him? The selfishness of such people is revolting."

" I've been taking my Sigurd there too," said Susan. " I always thought those notices on the railings were obsolete."

" Why, of course they are ! " cried Elizabeth,
pouring out tea. " The best preserved of them are so
weather-worn you can hardly read them, and one has
moss growing over it. A conspiracy, and Margaret
Mantrip is at the bottom of it. It's a cruel shock to me
—cruel—that she should trample on our old friendship
in that wanton manner. And she doesn't go into the
garden herself once a week."

" Then why——" began Susan.

" Because that's her nature," interrupted Elizabeth;
" meddling and managing. Of course she says it is
because the memory of her father is sacred to her.
He instituted the Garden Committee some time last
century, and then one day he was having a nap there,
and a dog barked at him and awoke him, so he got the
moss-covered notices put up. A tiresome old man if
ever there was one, and you could hear him breathing
all over the Square when he had an attack of asthma.
One was sorry for him, of course, but talk of nuisances !
Besides, when a man's been dead four years and more,
it's childish to prohibit dogs from going into the garden
because a dog once woke him up. That's the history
of those notices, and it's bunkum and rubbish."

Susan was astounded by the bitterness of these
expressions and the fire that flashed in Elizabeth's eye.
But it died down as she looked lovingly at the happy
though diminished family cuddling against Sabrina.

" And Margaret's such an old friend," she said;
" that's what cuts me to the heart. She has good
points too, plenty of them. Clean record : no secret
life of which she is ashamed. But managing. Wants
to be queen of the Square. She hasn't enough to do,
that's what ails her. She's always looking out for some
pie to get her fingers into."

" But surely she's very busy over her father's life,"
said Susan. " Two volumes."

Elizabeth gazed fixedly at her.

" On the day," she said, " when I have ocular

evidence that she has finished the first, I will promise to believe in the second. That's fair, I think, and quite without prejudice. Certainly she sits a great deal in that library of hers, where we had tepid coffee the other day, with missionaries and diaries up to the ceiling, but that doesn't prove she's written very much. If I spent my life in the Zoological Gardens it wouldn't turn me into a sea-lion, if you understand what I mean. But that's by the way, and pray don't quote me. What she has certainly done is to get up this conspiracy to put into force that ridiculous old obsolete rule about no dogs in the garden, and I hope you will make a point of coming to the General Meeting to vote against it. I shall be busy enough till then, whatever Margaret is, for I've made a list of all the people in the Square who keep dogs, and I shall make a personal call on every one to get their support."

"Certainly I will vote with you," said Susan. "So convenient to have the garden where I can take my Sigurd."

Elizabeth looked thoughtful.

"I am delighted to get your support," she said. "We'll make short work of the conspiracy, I hope. Then the question may arise about the size of the dogs to be allowed in the garden. If everyone kept bloodhounds, it wouldn't be pleasant to find fifty bloodhounds every morning in the garden. Its reposefulness would be quite gone."

"But then there's the question of numbers too," said Susan. "You see, you have ten dogs which you take there. Well, if everybody brought ten dogs into the garden, there would be five hundred of them. That wouldn't leave much reposefulness either."

Elizabeth found this a very absurd suggestion.

"I think, dear Miss Leg," she said, "that we need not worry about such impossible contingencies. Have a ginger-nut."

It was evident that the habitual tranquillity of Durham Square was now to be completely shattered by the dog question. Such disturbances occurred periodically: last year there had been a terrible to-do over a large flower-bed, which the Garden Committee had made at great expense. They had planted in it, in defiance of expert opinion, twenty rose trees which had all instantly died; the ructions that followed had taken their places in the annals of the Square as the Wars of the Roses. The course of these belligerences was that of an eruption; first there came mutterings and underground rumbles, then the volcano broke out, its lava and nether fires being represented by burning words and bitter retorts. It raged for a couple of days, then as its violence was spent it quieted down again. Flowers grew where the molten streams had flowed on their desolating way, wounds were healed, smiles blossomed on the faces that had been distorted with passion, and everybody was friends again.

The Garden Committee consisted of four persons: the Vicar (chairman), Mrs. Mantrip, Jimmie Mason and Elizabeth Conklin. Two were anti-dog, and two pro-dog, and some very stirring events began (as R. da V. would and did say) to transpire. Elizabeth started her house-to-house canvass, calling on all dog-owners and begging them, for the sake of their pets, to come to the meeting. This valuable device had not yet occurred to the anti-dog party, but next morning, Margaret Mantrip, meditating on Papa's parochial work at the window of her library, observed Elizabeth on the doorstep of No. 43 just opposite. There was nothing much in that, though the middle of the morning was an odd time to pay a call; but when she saw Elizabeth emerge again, stand on the pavement consulting a slip of paper, and then, passing by Nos. 44 and 45, ring the bell at No. 46, where there was a griffon which was a great nuisance in the garden by reason of its frequent bilious attacks, she began to

watch her with the closest attention, and forgot all
about Papa's farewell sermon at Screwby. Elizabeth
then visited Nos. 47 and 48, left out the next four
numbers and called at No. 53 where there was a
poodle. Margaret's synthetic mind grouped these
facts together, and she instantly guessed what Elizabeth was at. Full of indignation at so underhand a
trick, she hurried out herself, and began calling on
all the householders, who, since they owned no dogs,
might be expected to vote anti-dog, in order to urge
them to come to the meeting. She moved in the wake
of Elizabeth, and in the same direction, for it was more
seemly that they should not meet, and visited all the
houses Elizabeth had left out. But it so happened
that just as she came out of No. 44, Elizabeth found
she had left out No. 39 (Welsh collie) and was retrac-
ing her steps. An acid " Good morning, dear "
passed between them, and Elizabeth rang the bell at
No. 39 and Mrs. Mantrip at No. 45.

The vile devices of each were now manifest to
them both, and they threw all attempt at surreptitious-
ness to the winds and went steadily round the Square,
ringing, between them, at every door, like postmen in
quest of tips at Christmas time. Susan Leg, who was
very busy writing to the gay accompaniment of her
gramophone, happened to stroll to her window for a
brief rest, and saw them performing this species of
ladies-chain at the houses opposite. This was so
interesting that she turned off the gramophone and
watched them. Almost immediately she remembered
that Mrs. Conklin said she was going to call on all
dog-owners, and now Mrs. Mantrip was evidently
calling on all the rest. " Very stirring ! " she
thought.

She was engaged to go to lunch with Lady Eva
Lowndes, and as she approached the house she saw
that her hostess was out on her balcony, observing
the postmen through an opera-glass.

" They've *both* called on me," she announced
in a tone of triumph as she shook hands with
Susan.

" And have I guessed right? " asked Susan.
" Is it about dogs in the garden? "

" Naturally. You see Conklin called on me
because she knew I used to have a dog, and Mantrip
called because she knew a little more than that. She
knew that my dog died yesterday at a nursing-home,
and that therefore I hadn't got one. I call that up-
to-date. Conklin has called on you, I suppose? "

" I went to tea with her yesterday," said Susan.

" You had ginger-nuts made of granite then,"
said Eva, " and of course she wanted you to come
to the meeting and vote pro-dog. Let's go in to
lunch, Leg. You and I are alone because my
husband has gone to be X-rayed for cancer."

" Oh, dear me, I am sorry! " said Susan. " A
most distressing complaint, isn't it? "

" Oh, he hasn't got cancer," said Eva. " He only
goes to be X-rayed once a month to be sure about it.
He keeps the photographs of his inside in an album.
Quite a collection, but it's embarrassing if visitors
open it by mistake. By the way, he isn't Lord
Lowndes, if you don't mind my mentioning it, but
Captain Lowndes. And I'm not Lady Lowndes, but
Lady Eva, just like that. Dogs! I thought it was
coming. We have a sporadic outbreak of that kind
every now and then in the Square over something or
other. There hasn't been one for some months, and
a new one was due. Barrel-organ and street-singers
was the last. Mason put up three notices on the
garden railings that they weren't allowed in the Square,
entirely off his own bat, because he doesn't like them.
' No street-music is allowed in the Square. By
order,' in large white letters. Such impertinence!
So one night I erased ' No ' from his boards, and
painted in ' All ': ' All street-music is allowed in the

Square.' Brilliant success. We had five barrel-organs next morning and two baritones."

" How delightful! I should have liked that," said Susan enthusiastically. " And what happened next? "

" Mason had voting cards printed with ' For or against street-music,' stamped and addressed to himself, and went round the Square with them, popping them into letter-boxes. I lost. Nobody voted for music except me. But it was the principle of the thing I went for. You can't have one householder playing Mussolini like that."

" I should think not," said Susan. " Most public-spirited of you. And how are you going to vote about the dogs? "

" I've not made up my mind. It depends whether Conklin or Mantrip annoys me most at the meeting. I can't bear Conklin's dogs, but on the other hand I can't bear Mantrip's assumption that we must do as Papa would have wished. I'll tell you an odd thing about her. You know I see haloes. Well, Mantrip says she's writing her father's life——"

" Yes. Two volumes. She told me about it," said Susan proudly.

" Of course she did. She tells the bus-conductors and the lamp-lighters. Now it's a most extraordinary thing, but whenever she speaks to me about her writing her father's life, her halo changes completely. It becomes the colour of anchovy paste. Poisonous sort of dull red. Now I need hardly tell you what that means."

" I'm afraid you must," said Susan. " I know nothing about haloes."

" It means lies. Great, whacking lies, Leg. I can't be wrong, for the science of haloes is as exact as arithmetic. Besides, when I last had a séance with Corisande, my mother's voice came through, and she said, ' Little Doodleums, don't trust that lady who lives near you. She is not what she seems. She has a literary secret that falsifies her soul. There will be an exposure, and all will come out.' Corisande's very words, and she was in a deep trance, because I tried a pin on her arm. Now to whom else could that possibly apply except to Mantrip? Corisande is never wrong."

It flashed into Susan's mind that Corisande might be perfectly right, though her remarkable and oracular words did not bear the interpretation that Lady Eva put on them.

" Well, that is very curious," she said, " for it certainly looks as if Corisande was talking of her. And how curious about the anchovy paste. But do you think it means that she's not writing her father's life at all? Two volumes would take a long time for most people."

" Corisande couldn't have meant anybody else," said Eva. " Who else can there be in the Square who has a literary secret? Conklin isn't writin, a life of her dogs, I don't suppose."

" But you can hardly call Mrs. Mantrip's life of her father a literary secret," said Susan, " if she tells even the bus-conductors about it."

" No, but the literary secret that falsifies her soul is that she isn't writing it at all. Short of mentioning her name, my mother couldn't have given me a more direct warning. And then an anchovy halo is quite unmistakable. What enormous fun her exposure will be. I hope I shall be there."

Susan gently edged away from the subject of Mrs. Mantrip and literary secrets.

" Do you always see haloes round everybody? " she asked. " What a wonderful gift! "

" Always if I abstract my mind. I saw yours at Mantrip's party the other day."

" Oh, do tell me about it. Is it a nice one? " asked Susan.

" Gorgeous. A blaze of golden yellow. You're one mass of imagination, Leg. That's a tremendous responsibility, and it's your duty to use it. Think of the parable of the talents. Write a book, paint a picture, go on the films instead of listening to the gramophone all day. I can promise you that, if you took up some work which requires imagination, you would have a colossal success."

" Well, that would be pleasant, Lady Lowndes—I mean Lady Eva," said Susan. " But I fear you see my halo with too kindly an eye."

" Not a bit. It's stupendous. Rouse yourself and do something. Now's the time. It's the age for women. All the best work in every line is being done by us. Cigarette? Let's go upstairs and see how the dog-fiends are getting on."

The canvassing had already begun again, and the two ladies were moving methodically down the opposite side of the square, each of them with her list of doggy and dogless houses. The calls they paid were seldom of the same duration, for the owner of a dogless establishment might not be at home, and then Mantrip went on past the dog-house to which Conklin had been admitted, and shot ahead of her. Then Conklin drew blank, and passed Mantrip again. (Surnames are used because they were no longer on Christian name terms.) Sometimes they came out of adjacent houses simultaneously, but they appeared not even to see each other, and walked with averted heads.

" They're warming up beautifully," said Eva as she followed them with her opera-glass. " Dead cuts already. There'll be a wonderful meeting to-morrow; my God, what a bust up! Look, Leg! There are only about ten houses more. Which of them will you back to have finished first? There! Mantrip leads! No, Conklin has been told that No. 8 is out, though I see him at his drawing-room window. Conklin leads. There are a lot of dogs in that corner; on the other

hand, Nos. 1 and 2 don't keep them. A fine finish,
isn't it? Conklin's a long time in No. 4; Mantrip leads
by a house. Damned if I don't believe it will be a dead
heat!''

Mr. Heinrich Raphael Cartwright, who was dining
alone with Susan that night, was easily the most
adventurous and successful publisher of the day. He
had a matchless flair for distinction, both in the matter
of the books he published and in the manner of their
presentation. He brought out new editions of ancient
masterpieces at ruinous prices, printed on peerless
paper in exquisite type, with prefaces by the most
highly paid authors of the day, and somehow managed
to sell sufficient copies to repay him for his outlay.
Not long ago he had come across a Bible, and had
been immensely impressed by the admirable style of
it, and was thinking of bringing out an *edition de luxe*
of it on vellum, when he discovered, much to his
chagrin, that the copyright of this volume had not
yet expired. . . . He had now just returned from a
journey to Lake Garda in order to induce d'Annunzio
to let him produce an English translation of his
volume of stories, published ever so many years ago,
called *Le Novelle della Pescara*, but he had been
unable to secure an audience with the lately ennobled
Principe di Monte Nevoso. Monte Nevoso simply
would not see him. No matter. He spent a week
in Venice instead, and arranged for a series of photographs by flashlight to be taken of all Tintoretto's
masterpieces. Being an expert in distinction, he found
an exquisite, affectionate and expensive young lady at
the Lido to beguile his leisure, really superb modelling.
Then he discovered that *Le Novelle della Pescara*, by
reason of its antiquity, did not come under the regulations of the Berne Convention, and telegraphed to his
office in London to speed up the translation of it. That
was business: if the Principe had condescended to

see him, he was prepared to offer a most liberal royalty for his permission, but now as the Principe had proved himself so Nevoso, he would save himself the outlay that proved to be unnecessary.

Plans buzzed in his head like a swarming hive in May: some were concerned with the honey of distinction, others were equally intent on the flowers of business and the sweet harvests that could be reaped by shrewd husbandry. He did not confine himself to literature, for he bought pictures by modern artists, provided they were sufficiently weird, and sold them again. He bought large quantities of the produce of fine vintages, for they lay in his cellar and earned their dividends. He bought Queen Anne silver, which he kept at his bank, and disposed of it very profitably when silver was booming. Seldom did he make a bad purchase: the egg of a great auk, which subsequently proved to consist of plaster of Paris, cunningly coloured, was perhaps the worst of them. But even there the thirst for distinguished objects was the cause of that unfortunate error. There were so few eggs of the great auk. But this was not one of them.

To get rich was among the least of his conscious ambitions. Anyone as clever as he got rich without making that a definite goal, provided he kept his eye always alert for likely or even speculative opportunities. Such an opportunity had occurred when, six years ago, a perfect stranger, signing herself Susan Leg, had written to him from an address in an unknown street in Brighton, and had sent him the manuscript of a novel. The only distinguished thing about it, from a literary point of view, was its unique lack of distinction. It was preposterous to the last degree, but there was a sumptuousness about it, and, though nauseatingly moral in its conclusion, there was also fierceness, a sadism running like a scarlet thread through its portentous pages. Above all, it was written *con amore*; the gusto of Susan Leg blazed in it like some magni-

ficent conflagration, and Cartwright knew very well
that gusto in a writer begets gusto in a reader of similar
tastes. From the selling point of view, no book can
have a more valuable quality. In a word, it seemed
to him to have all the atrocious qualities of a possible
best-seller.

He went down to Brighton, a favourite resort of
his at any time, in order to see Miss Susan Leg. There
was a drop or two of satyr-blood in his veins; most
good-looking women, however inexperienced, could
make a guess as to what he was thinking about, and
at the back of his mind, as he waited for Miss Leg at
the Regency Palace Hotel, on that first occasion of her
entering that sumptuous caravanserai, he wondered
what she was like. . . . But when "A lady to see
you, sir," was conducted to where he expectantly sat
in the lounge, he felt not the smallest pang of disappointment, so gloriously rich to his dramatic mind
was the contrast between the physical plainness and
insignificance of this small woman, no longer young,
and her fiery and exotic mind. Often he made much
of the authors from whom he hoped great things: he
gave parties for them; he took them to fashionable
restaurants; he obtained their photographs and sent
them to chatty journals with little paragraphs; he got
them interviewed. But he saw at once that personal
publicity would be of no use in Miss Leg's case, and so
as they lunched he impressed on her the value of
mystery. Properly handled, mystery was quite as
good an advertisement as publicity.

"It's a very remarkable book you've sent me, Miss
Leg," he said, "and I will certainly publish it. We
will talk over terms presently: you will find me easy
to deal with. But I should certainly recommend you
to adopt a pseudonym; a good pseudonym often has
a selling value. People may ask, 'What's in a name?'
and my answer is, 'A very great deal if you think of
the right one.' I should like to make a mystery about

the author of this book. Mind you, I'm going to make
a feature of it. I think it has qualities that may give
it a very large sale. If it has the success I hope for,
thousands of readers will want to know all about you.
My office will be deluged with letters from unknown
correspondents wanting your photograph. It would
be a very charming picture, I needn't say, but don't
let them have it. Don't be Miss Susan Leg; the name
is really not suitable for the book. Think over one;
I am sure you will find something excellent. Then
there's the title: I notice you haven't given me a title
at all. I want a suitable title also; something in the
style of the contents. But I beg you not to let anyone
know that you are the author.''

Susan felt a momentary disappointment. Her
imaginative mind had been busy as he spoke, and
already she had seen herself taking her manuscript to
the office, and giving it to one of the typists. How she
would watch her as she worked, and perhaps observe
her eyes growing round with suspense or dim with tears
as she clicked the pages on to her sheets. Then, when
the typescript was complete, she herself would compute
its length, see that its pages were correctly numbered,
perforate the sheets for the ribbon to bind them together, and give it its jacket of thick red paper. And
then the typist would ask where it was to be sent,
and Susan would answer, '' It is mine. I wrote it.
I will take it home with me. To be published immediately by Mr. Cartwright! '' . . . Again her vivid
imagination had seen herself pictured in the illustrated
papers, as authoress of that wonderful book which
everybody was talking about. But now these bright
dreams must be given up, for Mr. Cartwright was very
insistent that she should not publish under her own
name, and no doubt he knew best.

Presently terms were discussed. He proposed a
most reasonable contract, for he was not so bad a man
of business, when he was engaged in the purchase of

what he hoped would prove an extensive and valuable estate, as to attempt to save a few pounds over acquiring the first acre or two of it. He could no doubt have secured this book for a cheque for £50, but what he was really after was the future output of Susan Leg's brain. If this first novel sold as he hoped it would, he would have little chance of getting the next, when, gorged with success, she found that he had made a fortune out of the first, and she only that squalid sum down. He therefore proposed a very fair royalty from the start, but stipulated that she should give him the first offer of her three subsequent books.

All the rest of that day Susan had racked her brain to think of a suitable title and pseudonym, but without success. But she woke up that night with a crow of triumph and said aloud, "*Apples of Sodom* by Rudolph da Vinci." She telegraphed the inspiration next morning to Cartwright, who was as delighted as herself.

Publisher and author linked together in this most successful partnership, which had continued ever since, had soon grown to be great friends. He was Nunky and she Susanna, and it was as such that they hailed each other when he came into her mahogany-panelled room to-night. He had not yet seen this new house of hers in Durham Square, which she had furnished according to her own taste, and he felt staggered by this fresh revelation of it.

"But a creation, my dear Susanna," he said as he entered. "What a chimney-piece! Mahogany panels! An Aladdin's cave, a palace of Haroun al-Raschid."

"Who was he?" asked Susan.

"*Arabian Nights*. I am bringing out a marvellous new edition of them in four volumes. I will send you a copy if you will promise not to read it. You would find some of them not quite nice. And orange legs to your piano! There is no one so original as you.

Tell me how you like your new neighbours.   Any
material?   Not that you want material: there is plenty
in that brilliant little brain of yours.   And how is the
new book getting on?   I am most impatient to see it.
Rosemary and Rue will make a new record: it is going
extremely well."

Bosanquet came in to announce dinner, and Susan
gave Nunky a warning look not to talk secrets before
him.   She believed that Bosanquet had no idea who
was the author of *Rosemary and Rue* and the rest of
the series, which was a most pathetic fallacy.   For
often when Susan was out, he went discreetly to the
drawing-room, where he took out from the drawer of
her writing-table the manuscript of the story which was
on the stocks, and read all that she had written that
day.   He was a devoted admirer of Rudolph da Vinci;
in his pantry, as in Mrs. Mantrip's library behind the
baize curtain, were all the master's published works,
and from internal evidence Bosanquet felt perfectly
certain in his own mind that no one but Rudolph da
Vinci could have written the wonderful tale on which
his mistress was now engaged.   He took the greatest
pride in serving such a genius, and was just as impatient for the completion of the new book as was
Nunky himself.

They went down to dinner, and as long as Bosanquet
was present talked about public topics.   The dining-
room, Nunky saw at once, was evidently decorated
according to the exquisite taste of the Duchess of
Plymouth who, in *The Dutiful Duchess*, had restored
the fortunes of that impoverished family by starting
a furnishing establishment.   She served behind the
counter : she trudged on foot to the houses of low-born
millionaires, where she went in by the area gate, and
was admitted through the back door under the name of
Miss Plymouth.   She decorated their houses for them,
often submitting to outrageous rudeness on the part of
the low-born, and gradually, gradually she paid off the

ruinous mortgage on the family castle, rescued her weak
but devoted husband from the clutch of money-lenders,
and had another baby on Christmas Day. Her furnish-
ings and embellishments, which were so justly popular,
were largely composed of Arabian chairs studded
with turquoises, velvet carpets and draped amorini
sprawling on the ceiling among pink clouds. The
taste of this admirable Duchess was evidently responsible for Susan's dining-room. At the end of dinner,
when Bosanquet had given them their coffee and
brought on a silver salver the *mouchoir* Susan had
left in the drawing-room, she began to talk more
confidentially.

"I've got lots to tell you, Nunky," she said.
"First of all, you were very wise to insist on my not
writing under my own name. I'm making new friends.
My neighbours are very highly cultured people, and I
think I shall get on very well with them. There's Mrs.
Mantrip who is writing the life of her father, the
Reverend Bondfield. There's Mr. Mason who has
Maharajahs to dinner and is most musical. There's
Lady Lowndes, Lady Eva, I should say, who sees
haloes: I've got a beauty. There's the Vicar who
knows all about reincarnation. But it's so lucky that
they don't know I'm Rudolph da Vinci, for some of
them shriek with laughter when he's mentioned, and it
would handicap me terribly if they knew he was me."

Nunky felt slightly disturbed at these signs of
mental aspiration. A mind that could pour out an
apparently inexhaustible stream of Rudolph da Vinci
stories ought not to be interfered with: any attempt to
improve or educate it might lead to disastrous results.

"Don't bother your head about culture and
reincarnation, my dear," he said. "It's full enough
already of far better stuff."

"But I should like to be able to talk as they do,"
said Susan. "Then again, when I was down at
Brighton last week-end, there was Mr. Arthur Arm-

strong at the Regency Palace, where first I met you,
and I felt envious of his high aims, his wonderful books,
his speeches and poems, and his review articles."

She broke off.

"And what do you think he was reading all the
time he was having dinner?" she asked.

"Some book of his own," said Nunky. "I'm told
he reads nothing else."

"Wrong, Nunky. He was reading *Rosemary and
Rue*. Wasn't that a thrill? And oh, how I wonder
whether possibly he may write about it next Sunday!"

"Why should you care whether he does or not?"
demanded Nunky.

"Because his approval would make me terribly
happy," said Susan. "I'm sure he's got a marvellous
mind, and I want one like it. There are scenes in my
new book which I do believe dig down into the very
heart of human nature, and if he felt that, too, it
would be such a joy to know I was in tune with him.
'Borne along on a wave of beauty.' What a line
to have written! It was in his last volume of poems."

"I've read those poems," said Nunky, "and
they're pretentious rubbish. 'Borne along on a wave
of balderdash' would describe it perfectly. Get all
that sort of stuff out of your head, Susanna. An artist
like you should never want the appreciation of a man
like him. Be content with your own mind, and don't
try to make it like his."

Susan was not yet satisfied.

"Nunky, why is it that the critics never take the
least notice of what I write?" she asked. "Never a
word about me, unless it's some scornful allusion. I
believe it's a conspiracy of silence. Years ago I subscribed, under Rudolph's name, to a press-agency,
and I haven't got to the end of my first hundred
cuttings yet."

Cartwright communed rapidly with himself. It
would never do if Susan began to long for the critical

appreciation of educated people, and in the effort to
attain it might seriously imperil the gusto with which
she wrote. He must try to restore her confidence; it
was safe to lay encouragement on with a spade.

"Of course it's a conspiracy, Susanna," he said.
"But did you ever hear of one that failed more utterly
all the time? Jealousy, my dear. They were furious
at the success of your first book, which none of them
had the brains to appreciate, and they boycotted you.
They set themselves to kill you by silence, and every
book of yours that comes out proves you're more alive
than ever. Besides, aren't you in good company?
Think of the great authors of the past, the Brontës,
Meredith, Hardy. Every one of them was violently
abused by the critics or utterly neglected. Go on doing
your work on your own lines, and don't heed what they
say or what they don't say. The only thing I could
wish for you is that one of them would single out one of
your books for a scathing attack. I should like that
immensely: it would make a wonderful advertisement,
and I would use it for all it's worth. If you feel sore
about their neglect of you, write a book about a critic.
Make him a loathsome reptile."

Susan brightened up at this.

"What a good idea!" she said. "I'll remember
that."

"Do. Now I've got news for you, though, in your
ungrateful frame of mind, perhaps you won't be
pleased with it. I ordered this afternoon a third big
printing of *Rosemary and Rue*."

"No, really?" said Susan. "That is quick, isn't
it?"

"Of course it's quick. And then I thought it was
time to have something in the papers about Rudolph
da Vinci, so I sent a paragraph to Ulrica for her social
column in the *Evening Chronicle* to-morrow. I've
said that he is in London for a short visit, and is on
the eve of completing his new book. Ulrica will have

seen him with his magnificent Alsatian in the Park
to-day, walking by the Serpentine. And his publisher,
Mr. Cartwright, dined with him to-night."

"Oh, how exciting!" said Susan, whom these
occasional paragraphs never failed to delight. "And
to think it's all about me really, and nobody knows.
Quite the hidden hand, isn't it? But, Nunky, was it
prudent to say you dined with him? If Bosanquet
sees it, he will know you dined here."

"That will give Bosanquet something to think
about, then," said Nunky. "He will come to the conclusion that you cannot trust what you see in the
papers. No more you can."

Susan had no return of high aspirations that evening, for Cartwright's spade had done its work well, and
they settled down for a little business talk. There was
the new novel, which was now nearly finished, and his
plan was to bring it out rather late in the autumn
season, when people would be beginning to think about
Christmas presents. Susan thought that would be very
suitable, because there was to be a fine Christmas scene
towards the end of it. And wouldn't it be nice to have
it illustrated? she asked. Frankly he was against the
idea. Readers did not want illustrations to books like
hers. They preferred to form mental pictures for
themselves of the great scenes. Besides, unless they
could find an artist whose conceptions were wholly
harmonious with the author's, the illustrations must be
unworthy of the book. Inwardly he writhed at the
thought of issuing such a volume from his house.
Illustrated da Vincis would be an artistic crime almost
beyond pardon.

"I can't think of an artist who could do it," he
said with the greatest tact. "Neither Orpen nor John
is your natural collaborator. And who else is there?"

"Still I do think a picture would be nice in a book
that is sure to be popular as a Christmas present," said
Susan. "You could have a charming frontispiece in

colour of snow-clad house-roofs and a church steeple. And you often have pictures in your books, Nunky."

"Well, give me time to think it over," said he. "Now I must go. A delicious evening, Susanna, and what a good talk we've had. And my final word is: go on doing your own work your own way, and don't try to emulate Mrs. Mantrap, if that's her name. It sounds as if she ought to be a good-looking woman."

"Naughty Nunky," said Susan. "She's got an interesting face, I should say, rather than a handsome one. A fine forehead."

"You damp my ardour. I find I have little in common with women who have fine foreheads. And don't mind what your friends with high foreheads think of Rudolph da Vinci."

"But how I shall seize the *Sunday Chronicle* next week to see if Mr. Armstrong has written about *Rosemary and Rue*," said Susan.

VI

IN spite of the zealous canvassing that had gone on, the meeting about dogs next day was so sparsely attended that Mrs. Conklin and Mrs. Mantrip could hardly believe their eyes. But the fervour of it was to compensate for the lack of numbers. A much larger attendance had been expected, and so it was held at the reading-room of the Parish Institute. This was an austere and educational apartment, pervaded by a faint smell of oilcloth and children, for the Band of Hope had only lately quitted it, and the oilcloth was still there. There were pictures on the walls of

the late Vicar and his wife, of the Bishop of the
Diocese, of the Mount of Olives and of the Sea of
Galilee. Also a chart showing the various stages in
the life of a mosquito, monstrously enlarged. Book-
cases which could not possibly have held all the books
of the Reverend Bondfield stood against the walls,
and on a platform at the end of the room was a table
round which sat the members of the Garden Committee. Rows and rows of chairs arranged for the
seating of the Band of Hope were ready to accom-
modate the householders of the Square and their
representatives, but of these there were only four.
There was Susan, there was Lady Eva Lowndes, and
there were the two Gandish twins, undergraduates at
Cambridge, who scented excitement and sat by themselves close to the door, where exit was easy if their
feelings overcame them. They were exactly alike,
except that one was very dark and the other an
albino: they were therefore known as Black and
White, though no innuendo as regards whisky was
implied. They were charming boys, cursed with a
streak of irreverence which those brought into contact
with them sometimes deplored.

The Garden Committee sitting on the platform also
numbered four persons, and consisted of the Vicar
(chairman), Mrs. Mantrip (secretary), Mrs. Conklin
and Mr. Jimmie Mason. Though there were actually
four of them present, they behaved as if there were
only three, for the two ladies, after their canvassing
adventures yesterday, did not appear to see each
other. There was sometimes one of them and sometimes the other. The Vicar opened the proceedings.

" If we are all assembled," he said, " I will put
the business of the meeting before you. Apart from
the accounts, which you all have seen, it is dogs.
The question profoundly affects every one of us.
There is, as you know, a regulation in force, or rather,
I should say it has not been repealed, which definitely

states that dogs are not allowed in the garden of our Square. ' No dogs allowed in the garden,' that is the notice on all the gates leading into the garden, and I am sure it is familiar to everybody present and admits of no misunderstanding. It has been in force, or I should say in existence, for thirty-four years——"

" Thirty-five," said Mrs. Mantrip, in the kindly, helpful tone of a prompter.

" For thirty-four years or thereabouts," said the Vicar, who did not like interruptions. " Now that regulation, as we all know, is not, at the present moment, being strictly obeyed. Some householders in our Square—I will mention no names, for I wish to keep the discussion quite impersonal, and I hope you will all do the same—some householders are in the habit of exercising their dogs there, and I myself "—he referred to his notes—" have seen with my own eyes, and at one and the same time, no less than seventeen dogs careering about the garden, as follows: eleven Pekinese——"

" Never! " said Elizabeth, not with the kindly note of the prompter, but with the harsh, disagreeable accent of the heckler. " Never more than ten."

" Eleven was the number," said the Vicar firmly. " There were ten of yours—I should say ten belonging to one owner, and one belonging to another owner. Ten plus one. You can do the sum, ladies and gentlemen, for yourselves. To resume: eleven Pekinese, one Alsatian, one fox-terrier, one poodle, a griffon, a collie, I think Welsh, and another animal, of which I could not specify the exact species. Let us say—ha—of mixed extraction——"

" Dachshund father, out of a Clumber," said Elizabeth, merely prompting this time.

" Golly! " said Black.

The Vicar raised his voice.

" Whatever its father and mother was—were," he said, " it was a dog. Now really, you know, ladies and gentlemen, there's not a particle of use in our regulations, which were wisely designed to give the greatest benefit to the greatest number, if nobody pays the slightest attention to them."

Jimmie rose.

" Pardon me, Vicar," he said, " but they do. I never take Atahualpa into the garden."

Elizabeth rose also.

" I beg to agree with your last observation, Mr. Chairman," she said. " Nobody pays the slightest attention to this regulation, because it is obsolete, and the sooner it is abolished the better."

Mrs. Mantrip rose.

" If I am not mistaken," she said, " I heard the word obsolete applied to this regulation. I object to it. The law against murder is not obsolete because it is broken. You are hanged just the same. These regulations about the garden were wisely framed, and they are binding on us all to-day just as much as they were thirty-five—*five*—years ago. More so in fact, because there are more dogs. Many more."

The Committee suddenly perceived that they were all standing up. They sat down again as if controlled by some common mechanism that affected them all simultaneously. Black was rapidly becoming hysterical, and now burst into a sudden hoot of laughter. The Vicar became officially aware of the presence of the twins and stood up again.

" We shall presently come to vote on the dog question," he said. " Every householder in the Square—I am sorry there are so few of them—is entitled to vote, or a duly-qualified representative may record it for him, but he is only entitled to one vote. One house, one vote."

The twins looked at each other, and now both broke into shrieks of laughter and hurried out. They nearly cannoned into a very smartly dressed lady who was just coming in. She took a modest seat close to the door. Mrs. Mantrip gave her one swift, scrutinizing glance which appeared to be enough for the present.

The Vicar remained standing during this unseemly interlude.

" What it comes to," he said, " is that we are here to vote whether dogs should be allowed in our garden."

" I wish to move an amendment to that," said Elizabeth, rising again. " My amendment is that only dogs of a certain size should be allowed in the garden: little dogs that can't hurt anything or anybody."

The Committee was becoming more domestic.

" Dear Liz-Liz," said Jimmie, " dogs are dogs. You can't get over that. And unless you have weighing machines at all the garden gates——"

" Order, please,' said the Chairman. " There is an amendment being proposed. Yes, Mrs. Conklin."

Elizabeth suddenly realized that the introduction of *avoirdupois* might alienate both Jimmie and Susan, who owned monstrous dogs.

" No, I withdraw that amendment," she said.

" Very well, we go back to the original motion," said the Vicar. " Are dogs to be allowed——"

Jimmie interrupted again: he was getting as talkative as usual.

" I should like to say a word first about the griffon," he said, " to which Mr. Chairman has briefly referred. I was sitting in the garden the other morning, and he stole up under my deck-chair and was sick. Quite disgusting. I'm all for having dogs in the garden, but a little dog that is sick is far more objectionable than a big one that isn't."

" A very wise suggestion, Jimmie," said Elizabeth, currying favour with him again. " I feel very uneasy when that horrible little creature is there, if I'm exercising my Pekinese. I should not wonder

if it had jaundice, which they believe now to be
infectious among dogs, though of course it isn't among
human beings. I'm very glad you thought of that.
I propose then that no dogs should be allowed in the
garden unless their owner can guarantee that they
are not suffering from any infectious ailment."

Mrs. Mantrip rose, turning her back on Elizabeth.

" May I ask if this is an amendment to an amendment, Mr. Chairman? " she asked in a refrigerating
voice. " I only want to know where we are, or if
that is impossible whereabouts we are."

She sat down and Lady Eva got up.

" I beg to second that," she said. " Are we
about to vote on the original proposal or on Conklin's
amendment or on her amendment to her amendment? "

Elizabeth rose.

" I distinctly said that I withdrew my first amendment, Eva dear," she said. " But all about the
griffon stands. Jimmie proposed it—oh, no, I did,
but I've no doubt he'll second it."

She remained standing and Mrs. Mantrip got up
again.

" Before the question of voting comes on, Mr.
Chairman," she said, " I wish to call your attention to the presence of a lady who is sitting at the
back of the hall. You so rightly said, ' One house,
one vote,' and we take that as your ruling. But I
assert, without fear of contradiction, that the house
to which she belongs is already represented."

Elizabeth cast a hasty glance behind her: she
guessed what this meant. Expecting a full meeting,
she had directed her cook to come quietly in when
business had begun, so that when a show of hands
took place on the vote, she might, from a modest
position near the door, support the pro-dogs. But
before she could look round the smartly dressed
lady was no longer there. Unable to face this public

identification, she had slipped out again in a state of high fury against that lynx-eyed woman. Mrs. Mantrip was not likely to get a very good dinner next time she came to spend the evening at No. 26. That day, however, in the present state of tempers, was probably far distant.

Mrs. Mantrip remained standing.

" As all of us present are now properly constituted voters," she said, " I should like to offer a few remarks before we proceed to business. It is most unfortunate that so few householders have had the public spirit to attend this meeting, but I think the Committee ought to know what their real feeling about the matter is. I devoted some valuable hours yesterday to calling on many of them personally, and I can say, again without fear of contradiction, that all whom I saw were unanimous in their support of the existing rule being retained. They all expressed a hope that the Committee would rigidly enforce it."

Elizabeth got up.

" Mrs. Conklin, *please*," said the Chairman in an imploring voice.

" Do be quiet, Liz-Liz, just a minute," put in Jimmie. " If you don't, I shall vote against you."

Elizabeth sat down.

" Yes, Mrs. Mantrip? " said the Chairman.

" That's all," said Mrs. Mantrip. But it was a score to have made Elizabeth sit down. She did the same and Elizabeth rose.

" Any of us, Mr. Chairman," she said, " is liable to be contradicted whether we fear it or not, and I feel it my duty to tell the Committee that the opinion of the Square about dogs in the garden is precisely the opposite to that which we have just heard stated. I devoted the greater part of yesterday to ascertaining it, and the result does not admit of argument. The rule was universally regarded as being quite obsolete. A remnant of outworn Victorianism, was a phrase I heard. As to its being strictly enforced, all I can say is that I hope the word ' Pooh ' will not be regarded as an unparliamentary expression.''

There was dead silence as she sat down. There was an ominous stillness as before (not after) a tropical storm.

'' If no one has anything more to say,'' said the Chairman in a quiet voice, '' I will propose that the existing rule about dogs in the garden be retained and that necessary measures be taken to enforce it.''

'' I beg to second that,'' said Mrs. Mantrip.

'' Will those in favour kindly hold up their hands? '' said the Chairman.

Lady Eva hesitated. On the whole, the dastardly trick of telling your cook to slip in and vote was more objectionable than anything Mrs. Mantrip had said or done. She held up her hand.

'' Against,'' said the Chairman, and Elizabeth, Susan and Jimmie voted against.

The Chairman engaged in the necessary mental arithmetic.

'' Three for the motion and three against,'' he said. '' What on earth are we to do now? ''

'' Surely the Chairman has a casting vote,'' said Mrs. Mantrip.

'' Certainly not,'' said Elizabeth. '' Preposterous. His ruling was ' one house, one vote.' If it applies to my cook, it applies to him.''

'' I think that is the case,'' said the Chairman. '' I put it to the meeting as to what we are to do next. We are equally divided, and to judge by the reports given us by the two ladies who have so generously devoted their time to making extensive inquiries, the rest of the Square appears to be equally divided too. Is there no compromise we can arrive at? ''

'' In my humble opinion,'' said Mrs. Mantrip, with so arrogant an air that Lady Eva regretted not

having voted against her, " in my humble opinion,
none. Where does compromise come in? The rule
has not been repealed, Mr. Chairman, and I therefore conclude that it remains in force."

" And in my humble opinion, Mr. Chairman,"
said Elizabeth, " the rule remains in force to exactly
the extent that it has done for the last five or six
years, and that is not in force at all. Such is my
interpretation of the vote you have just taken."

" The Committee, no doubt, Mr. Chairman," said
Mrs. Mantrip, " will devise a method of making the
rule obeyed. I should suggest that any householder
who infringes it should be deprived of her—I should
say his or her—key of the garden."

" I do not think that the last suggestion, Mr.
Chairman, is of the smallest practical value," said
Elizabeth. " It would necessitate a burglarious
entry into his or her house followed by theft, or a
personal assault, if he or she was in the garden and
had the key on his or her person."

The unfortunate Chairman was sitting between the
two ladies, and as they addressed their remarks
directly to him, he had to turn his head rapidly from
left to right and back again, like a spectator watching
a lawn-tennis match. Each time he looked at the
speaker, he encountered a face before which he
quailed, Mrs. Conklin's very red, Mrs. Mantrip's very
white, but both Gorgon-like. He almost wished they
could both be reincarnated instantly.

" Well, ladies, there are two sides to every
question," he began.

" Not to this," said Mrs. Mantrip.

" Hear, hear," said Elizabeth.

Their eyes softened with a momentary reconciliation, so fervent was their abhorrence of the notion
that there could be two views about this. But the
softening was inconceivably transient, and their eyes
again looked like hard-boiled eggs split in half.

" Order, please, for the Chair," said Jimmie. " I want to hear what Mr. Chairman has to say."

" Thank you, Mr. Mason. I was not conscious of putting forward a proposition that would be likely to arouse such strong dissent. Let me say, then, that there are two sides to most questions, in fact to every question but this. When dealing with other questions I have invariably found that a compromise between extreme views may be arrived at, and seventeen dogs careering uncontrolled about the garden means ruin for the flowers——"

" Seven geraniums in a rustic vase," said Elizabeth. " Also quite out of reach of any moderately sized dog."

" Silence for the Chair," said Mrs. Mantrip in a nasty voice, but looking quite away from Elizabeth at the picture of the Sea of Galilee.

" Ruin for the flowers," repeated the Chairman, " and a complete sacrifice of tranquillity for everybody else. If dogs are to be allowed in the garden——"

" Never," said Mrs. Mantrip.

" Silence for the Chair! " said Elizabeth, looking at the Mount of Olives.

" If dogs are to be allowed in the garden, they must be under their owners' control. Dogs must be on leads. How about that? "

" Now we're getting at something," said Jimmie encouragingly. " I had almost given up hope."

" Not very practical," said Elizabeth. " Nobody can walk about with any sort of freedom with ten Pekinese on leads. Impossible. It's as much as I can do to get them across the road. But I quite agree that dogs should be under control. Mine always are. May I propose that dogs should be allowed in the garden, but their owners must keep them under proper control. Not leads."

" But then there's the dogs' own control to think

about," said Jimmie. " If dogs are to be allowed in
the garden they must be under their owners' control
and their own control. I told you about the griffon."

The Vicar looked at his watch.

" I am afraid I have not time to discuss the health
of every dog in the Square," he observed with great
suavity, " and I must remind you, ladies and gentlemen, that two suggestions have arisen out of our
impasse on the main question. These are: (1) that
dogs should be allowed in the garden on leads, and (2)
that they should be allowed in the garden under their
owners' control. These alternatives are, of course, at
present mere suggestions which have arisen at our
meeting, and the opinion of the householders in the
Square must be obtained. It seems that the vast
majority of them are not sufficiently interested in the
whole matter to attend a meeting, in spite of the
laudable and self-sacrificing efforts "—he bowed to the
two protagonists who took no notice whatever of this
pretty courtesy—" that have been made to induce them
to do so, and I therefore propose that our Honorary
Secretary, Mrs. Mantrip, be asked to draw up a
memorandum and send typewritten copies to every
householder containing these suggestions, and ask for
an immediate reply. Will those in favour? Thank
you. Carried. . . ."

Mrs. Mantrip had a momentary impulse to resign
from the Committee at once, in order to mark her
entire disapproval of the whole proceedings. But
she thought better of it, for her powerful imagination
could not picture herself not being on the Committee:
it was one of the unthinkable things. Besides,
if she resigned, she would leave Elizabeth triumphant
on the battlefield. She therefore consented to follow
these instructions, and the meeting was adjourned,
pending the result of the plebiscite. The Honorary
Secretary then swept from the room without a word
to anybody.

" Well, we have had a nice talk," said Jimmie, with the amiable but futile design of making everything as pleasant as possible. " I've quite enjoyed it. But I shouldn't wonder if we're all much worse before we're better. Good-bye, everybody."

This hopeful prophecy seemed highly likely to be fulfilled. Those who knew the usual course of the disturbances that periodically turned Durham Square into a volcano felt that the eruption had not yet attained its maximum. The Vicar went off in a great hurry to hold a confirmation class, Jimmie to have a rest before going to a concert, Elizabeth to take her Pekinese for an extra walk in the garden by way of keeping the flag flying, and Lady Eva to keep vigil by a tombstone in the disused graveyard above which she had seen a very dreadful emanation which showed that he who lay below was earth-bound in death and had been a parricide in life. The sound of a gramophone mingling with the voice of a lecturer on the wireless discussing the tendencies of modern fiction, which presently poured out of the window of Susan's drawing-room, indicated that she had lost no time in getting back to her work.

Mrs. Mantrip addressed herself without delay to the task that had been forced upon her. Bitter indeed it was, for the prohibition on dogs being taken into the garden was a definite, indeed a notable contribution to Papa's life-work in the Square. He had rid the garden of dogs, just as he had rid the houses of other undesirables. Naturally she felt bitter at the opposition of her fellow-members on the Garden Committee, but she resented even more Susan Leg's vote. She had behaved to her in the most friendly and encouraging manner: she had been the first to call on her, she had told her about Papa's life, she had asked her to lunch and shown her Papa's library, and now Susan Leg had bitten the hand that fed her, and, though feigning an intelligent interest in the Life, had voted with those whose object it was to render void a valuable achievement in Papa's work in the Square. Everyone had seen at her luncheon-party that Susan Leg was a silly, affected little woman with all those artificial tricks of speech and manner which the ill-bred think ladylike, but though deficient in brains and breeding, she had seemed a well-meaning creature. Now she had proved that she was nothing of the sort, and Mrs. Mantrip's sentiments of mere neutrality towards her were superseded by a definite hostility. The dog-volcano would die down again, and she would be friends once more with Elizabeth and Jimmie, but her resentment against her tenant, in spite of the fact that she had put into her house a service-lift and another bathroom, was of sterner quality.

She drew towards her the writing-pad hitherto dedicated for notes on the Life, and composed herself for the distasteful task that had been committed to her. There had been a lot of twaddling talk about dogs on leads and dogs in the owners' control, and dogs in their own control (a shocking piece of bad taste on the part of Jimmie, but in spite of his Maharajahs he never was *quite*). It was impossible to give an accurate account of all that had taken place, for everybody had talked at once: the point was to give an opportunity to all those who disapproved of dogs being allowed in the garden at all of expressing their feelings about it. Her communication, therefore, ran as follows:

" To the Householders of Durham Square.

" Sir (or Madam),—It was resolved at a General Meeting summoned by the Garden Committee to-day, that the following question should be put to the householders in the Square, viz., ' Do you approve of dogs being allowed in the garden on leads and under proper control ? '

" Please write ' yes ' or ' no ' at the foot, with any

other remarks you may care to make, and return to me as soon as possible."

She took this round to a typewriting agency in Durham Road, asking for fifty-eight copies to be made. She saw, to her disgust, that the garden was full of Elizabeth's Pekinese, and heard, with more disgust, a babel of jazz music and lecturing pouring out of her tenant's windows. She felt too angry and ruffled to hope to recapture the tranquillity necessary for continuing her notes on " Personal Characteristics," but there was a medicine on a curtained shelf below the window of her library which never failed to be efficacious. Thank God, she thought, there was a sure refuge from the malicious pettinesses of which life was so inconveniently full, in the pages of one who transported you into an ampler ether. . . . Half an hour's reading restored her, and taking up the evening paper, she saw on the page that recorded the movements of the mighty, that Rudolph da Vinci was in London. Ulrica had seen him walking with his beautiful Alsatian by the Serpentine, and his publisher, Mr. Cartwright, had dined with him last night. The mention of an Alsatian aroused disagreeable associations, but it was an uplift to know that Mr. da Vinci was not far away. Some day she felt she would have to write to him, and tell him all he had done for her. Some day, she hoped, she might meet him. A dream, perhaps? But no one is too old to dream.

Elizabeth, issuing out next morning with her full tale of Pekinese, each on a lead, till she had conveyed them across the road into the garden, saw there a sight that instantly appealed to her sense of humour: it was very funny indeed. There was the black Gandish twin walking very demurely along the gravel path, towing behind him a large toy bulldog on wheels. Very naughty, of course, to make fun of Jimmie and his

Atahualpa like that, but who could help laughing? Jimmie came out of his house exactly as she passed it.

"Look!" she said. "Really that boy is most amusing. Atahualpa to the life."

Jimmie made a stony face.

"I see nothing to laugh at," he said.

"Oh, but really, Jimmie," said she. "How can you fail——?" She broke off, for from the opposite direction there appeared White. He towed behind him ten toy Pekinese dogs, all on wheels. The brothers passed without apparently seeing each other.

"Oh, look," said Jimmie. "There's White. One, two, three, four, ten Pekinese dogs. Just like yours, aren't they, Liz-Liz? What fun those boys are! And now you're going into the garden with nine, and altogether that will make twenty. Beats what the Vicar saw."

Off he went, walking like a starling.

Elizabeth crossed the road, getting into dreadful entanglement with her leads, for some dogs were moving straight on towards the garden gate like castles at chess, and others were hopping about like knights in oblique directions, and there were all sorts of unedifying delays owing to their excellent health. Never had it taken longer to get to the gate, but eventually she arrived, and banging it behind her she unloosed her flock. Their rage at seeing ten woolly counterfeits of themselves was indescribable, and they bounded on these unnatural mockeries. White pulled them in with cries of dismay.

"Call off your dogs, please, Mrs. Conklin," he shouted. "They're not in proper control, and they're not on leads. You haven't read the new voting-paper."

This was the case. The Gandish house had got theirs, being lower down in the Square, and Mrs. Mantrip was now engaged in delivering them at the top end of the Square, and had not yet reached Elizabeth's house. Mrs. Mantrip thought that both the toy bulldog and the toy Pekinese were very amusing, thereby proving that she had exactly as much sense of humour as Jimmie and Liz-Liz put together. She went on popping her notices into the few remaining letter-boxes, which made up the complete circuit, and hurried up a little towards the end, for she saw that Elizabeth was cutting short the exercise of her pets and beginning to attach the canine swarms to herself. A meeting in this crisis between two old friends, she felt, might lack cordiality, and she glided into her house just in time to avoid it.

Delirium followed. Elizabeth, on her return, found the notice in her letter-box, and thereupon suffered a complete loss of self-control. She dashed round with it to the Vicarage and ascertained that the Vicar was doing deep breathing in the back garden, and must not be disturbed. So in order not to disturb him she went out there herself, and issued from the door like a round red cork out of a pop-gun.

" Good morning, Vicar, perfectly infamous," she said. " Margaret Mantrip was directed to put two alternatives before the householders. Look at that, please ! She asks householders to vote as to whether they approve of dogs on leads and in proper control being allowed in the garden. Where are the alternatives, I ask ? Show me them ! We compromised, subject to the approval of the Square, that dogs should be allowed in the garden either on leads or in proper control. Alternatives ! Instead she asks whether dogs should be allowed in the garden under both. I could not have believed it even of her."

The Vicar was alone with this female. Deep breathing ought to have produced in him the requisite calmness to deal with tempestuous situations, but he was not aware that it had done so. He wished he was at Benares. He murmured " *Om mani padmi hum* " to himself, but he felt that instead of being in a holy calm he was under the wheels of Jagenath's car.

" Dear me, yes," he said, after studying this misleading document. " It does seem at first sight as if Mrs. Mantrip had not followed out the directions given her."

" Look at it again then," said Elizabeth, " and see if second sight will help matters."

Matters remained much as they were.

" What do you propose to do ? " asked the Vicar. (*Om mani padmi hum.*)

" Show her up. Issue another report of our meeting to all the householders——"

" Fifty-eight copies ? A great additional expense."

" I'll bear it. Another report stating that the question on which the Committee asked their vote was whether they desired that dogs should be allowed in the garden on leads or (or, mark you) under proper control."

" Hadn't we better first offer Mrs. Mantrip an opportunity——" began the Vicar.

" Certainly not. We've seen enough of the use she makes of her opportunities. Another leaflet is the way of dealing with her, and I shall ask you and Jimmie to sign it with me. Be fair, Vicar. You put those alternatives to the Committee yourself, and all I ask is that you should say so."

There was no denying that justice demanded some peremptory measure of this sort, and three hours afterwards Elizabeth was hurrying round the Square, no longer calling only at pro-dog houses, but at all, with the amended information succinctly conveyed on fifty-eight typewritten leaflets signed by herself, the Vicar and Jimmie. It ran :

" SIR (or MADAM),—By an unfortunate misunderstanding the notice left on you this morning by the Honorary Secretary for the Garden Committee was wholly erroneous. The Honorary Secretary was directed to ask you whether you desired that:

   (*a*) Dogs should be allowed in the garden on leads, or

   (*b*) Dogs should be allowed in the garden under proper control.

The Committee therefore request you to disregard the previous notice altogether, and earnestly ask you to answer the above queries without delay, returning them to Mrs. Conklin, No. 26 Durham Square.''

With the delivery of those amended notices, the volcano stoked up to what may be considered full horse-power, and the householders of the Square who had been so culpably apathetic yesterday in failing to attend the meeting, made up for it now. Mr. Salt, that notable hater of all quadrupeds and many bipeds, returned answers at once to both notices, merely scribbling across them '' Poison the lot,'' but by mistake he put the one that should have been returned to Mrs. Mantrip into Elizabeth's letter-box, and the other into Mrs. Mantrip's. He gave a thunderous knock on each door as he delivered these ill-localized missives, and both ladies hurried down because it sounded like telegrams. Elizabeth at once destroyed what Mrs. Mantrip should have received, owing to the odious brutality of what Mr. Salt had written there; but Mrs. Mantrip kept what Elizabeth should have received, because it evidently counted as an anti-dog declaration, for if Mr. Salt wanted all dogs to be poisoned, *a fortiori* he did not want them in the garden. . . . Round about a quarter to three that afternoon, the full fury of the eruption was reached. Householders had read both notices, and as they went out on their usual afternoon errands and pleasures, did their duty with regard to the politics of the Square. There was almost a queue on the pavement between Mrs. Mantrip's door and Elizabeth's, for most of them took no heed of the instructions conveyed in the second notice that the first should be disregarded, and showed their awakened zeal by answering both. When the rush had subsided Mrs. Mantrip gathered up the papers which had been pushed through the letter-box, and analysed their contents. Most of them, apparently assuming that the Committee had repealed the rule that no dogs should be allowed in the garden at all, approved of leads and proper controls; only a comparatively few who preserved their clearness of head under the strain of assimilating both notices, were logical enough to say that they objected to dogs altogether. Since then the spirit of the voting went against her and Papa, and since treacherous Elizabeth had stated definitely that the first notice should be disregarded, Mrs. Mantrip destroyed the lot. If the spirit of the voting had been the other way, she would have summoned a meeting of the Garden Committee.

Pending the result of the voting (though there was considerable divergence of opinion as to what they were voting about), all spirited dog-owners that afternoon, at great personal inconvenience and the cancelling of other engagements, took their dogs into the garden, with or without leads, for a demonstration in force in favour of dogs. This was not a concerted demonstration: it seemed to every pro-dog householder, quite independently, that it was the proper thing to do. The result was that no such gathering of dogs had ever been seen there before. Jimmie and Susan were among these demonstrators, and just as shrieks of dismay and frenzied whistlings to small dogs not on leads hailed the entrance of Jimmie and Atahualpa at one gate, Susan and Sigurd entered at another. The two noble animals instantly perceived that they had met the friends of their hearts, and gambolled round each other with the liveliest expressions of delight. They ran races up and down the length of the garden, Sigurd occasionally leaping over the lady if she got in his way. They rolled and wrestled on the grass, biting each other with the soft tooth of love, and in three minutes every other dog in the garden had been buckled up to its terrified owner and dragged out of the perilous precinct, amid a babel of yells and yappings. Sigurd and Atahualpa had it all to themselves.

Mrs. Mantrip had observed this frightful scene from her balcony and a holy glee warmed her heart. She felt like Miriam: she could have sung a pæan of victory at the panic and confusion that had fallen on her foes. Valiant fox-terriers, now in safety outside, were madly barking through the railings at the amorous giants within; the Welsh collie was being severely slapped by Mrs. Gandish for not coming sooner; the bilious griffon was being sick; the poodle was fighting with the dog of mixed parentage; and best of all, there was Elizabeth so tightly wound about in the leads of her Pekinese, who were dancing frenziedly round her, that she could not move at all, and had to shout to her parlourmaid, who had run out on to the balcony to see what the din was about, to come down quickly and unwind her. Papa, true Christian that he was, and of no revengeful spirit, would have rejoiced to see what discomfiture had overtaken those who transgressed his wise regulations. So far did Mrs. Mantrip's feelings carry her that she heard herself murmuring, "Good Sigurd, pretty Atahualpa."

Susan had been rather nervous at these evidences of romantic affection between the great dogs, but Jimmie had told her that Atahualpa was not like that now. Presently she saw that her motor was waiting at her door, and she went off to give Sigurd his run in the Park while she took her walk; for whatever crisis was threatening in her story, or in whatever

maelstrom of whips and scorpions her characters were
involved, she made a rule to spend an hour in the
open air during the day, and tried to think of something else, in order to rest her brain and relax the
prodigious tension. To-day, as she walked beside the
glittering Serpentine where Rudolph da Vinci had been
seen by Ulrica with his magnificent Alsatian (and
where he might be seen now if people only knew), she
had dogs and Garden Committee to think about.
That meeting in the parish room yesterday had been
a painful affair. It had lacked dignity; it had lacked
restraint; it had not been conducted with the
scrupulous attention to the sensibilities of others which
should accompany discussion between well-bred ladies
and gentlemen, however acute their differences of
opinion were. The members of the Committee,
especially the female part of it (which made it worse),
had snapped and snarled at each other—" really it
made me quite hot and uncomfortable," thought
Susan—instead of talking quietly and calmly and
remembering " who they were." Mrs. Mantrip had
been the worst of the lot.

Susan was accustomed to spend many hours of
the day and many months of the year in the deft
dissection and delineation of the characters of the
bright children of her imagination, and in forming
sentences in her head about them, which were fit to
be printed straight away. Her trains of thought, too,
even when she had no idea of publishing them, were
much more consecutive than the disconnected and
broken fragments of reflections with which most of
us flutter round the subject we have in mind, and
now without any effort at all she was ready to sum
up in clear and characteristic language the conclusions
she had arrived at.

" Mrs. M.," she thought, " is far from being what
I had hoped and imagined of her. She showed a
commonness of nature and an irritability of temper

that anyone should be ashamed of. A nasty,
sarcastic manner: she cannot be as truly refined and
such a perfect lady as I believed. Then again, no
lady would have left the meeting without a smile or
a word to anyone; that was a piece of ill-breeding
indeed! I cannot help remembering, too, that very
unique circumstance that Lady Eva told me about her
halo: how it turns the colour of anchovy paste whenever she talks about the progress she is making with
her father's life, and shows she is not telling the truth.
Then again, there was that message from Lady Eva's
mother telling her to beware of the lady with the
literary secret that falsifies her soul. With the other
painful lights which are thrown on Mrs. M.'s
character, and her nasty temper at the meeting, and
taking one thing with another, I can well believe that
she has a falsified soul. Straws show the set of the
tide, and blood will out. It would be wiser for me
not to see too much of her. I shall be quite affable
if we happen to meet, but the next time she asks
me to her house I shall be engaged. What a gulf of
deception opens before me if she is not writing the
life of her father at all, just to make us believe she is
literary. . . . Bless me, if that isn't she coming
towards me now. I shall just bow to her, but no
more than that. Come to heel, Sigurd.''

This small sacrifice on the altar of politeness was
not, however, demanded of Susan. As the two
approached, Mrs. Mantrip became violently interested
in a pair of tufted ducks that were paddling near the
margin of the water, and observed their pretty ways
with fixed attention till Susan had passed. Disappointment for the moment had soured her: it was not only
her resolve to have no more to do with Susan that
caused her to turn so uncompromising a back. For
remembering that Rudolph da Vinci had been seen
two days ago by Ulrica walking with his Alsatian in
the Park, she had taken this walk in the hope that he

might be taking it again. She had seen the great Alsatian coming, and with eager, expectant eyes she had scrutinized the figures of approaching pedestrians. And then, after all, it was only that tiresome little woman with her dog!

Though Susan usually abstracted her mind from her work when she was taking her outing, to-day her story forced itself upon her, and she lingered by the rails of Rotten Row drinking in local colour, for as soon as she got home she would plunge, to the accompaniment of all kinds of music, into the romantic scene which was to take place in these very surroundings. The main features of the place would do very well, and it should be just here that Julian Beltravers with his pure Hellenic face, his Herculean frame and those powerful arms which had won so many boat-races for Cambridge on the Isis, should be standing beneath the plane trees in front of the flaunting bed of glocksinias (or was it gloxinias? She must look it up). He had already seen among the riders who were galloping up the Row the sinister but terribly handsome face of Prince Igor Ekaterinburg, and knew that since he was in London the day of reckoning between them was near. Then a buzz of excitement arose among the loungers by the rails: all looked, all pointed in one direction, as there approached the Lady Cynthia Balestine. She was mounted on a thorough-bred Arabian stallion whose tail swept the ground. She wore a hat with blue feathers that drooped over her cheek; she wore a riding-habit of cut white velvet, and her Alsatian trotted by her side. Julian had seen her last at a *soirée* given by the King of Roumania in his summer palace, and by a timely intervention had saved her from the odious persecution of Prince Igor. She saw him now; she reined up her Arab steed on its haunches; she advanced to the rail to greet him, with a mantling blush below the blue feathers. She had just extended her exquisite hand to him, he was just kissing it, when the sinister Prince came galloping back down the Row. With one hand he seized the silk bridle of her Arab steed, with his whip he cut savagely at Julian's face. . . . Yes, the general surroundings would all do beautifully: the plane trees, the flower-bed, the idle loungers by the rails, the coo of pigeons. All these made a correct and realistic setting. Susan could not see any ladies in white cut velvet riding-habits or any wearing blue feathers, but it was possible to be too servile a practitioner of realism.

She turned homewards full of garnered impressions. With all her aspirations after culture and her reverence for the mind of Mr. Arthur Armstrong, sinister Russian princes and velvet riding-habits and Arab stallions were by no means dispossessed from her heart. She felt at home with them; she knew how to handle them; her gusto was undiminished. One prolonged spasm of work, two days perhaps, in which she would be blind to the world in the intoxication of her romance, would see the book done. She would be justifying her right to a halo of golden radiance. So different from poor Mrs. M's.

VII

AFTER the demonstration in force the volcanic eruption about dogs began swiftly to subside, according to the usual behaviour of volcanoes in Durham Square. The energy of the nether fires was exhausted and lava ceased to flow. The majority of the householders had signed two documents, one set of which had been destroyed by Mrs. Mantrip, while Elizabeth, after vainly trying to determine whether the votes of her set were in favour of leads or proper control, had given it up as a bad job, and destroyed the other. It was impossible for a woman with so many dogs to devote the time fully to unravel all the conundrums that these answers asked. Some people before committing themselves to " leads " required to know what the length of these leads would be. (A hundred yards clearly was no lead at all.) Others, before committing themselves to " control," asked to be told precisely what control meant. Did it imply that when you exercised your dog in the garden, the pet must go to heel all the time? Elizabeth very wisely decided that the best thing to do was to take her Pekinese out exactly as before, and make a strong personal appeal to Jimmie and Susan if their monstrous creatures appeared there again. She felt sure that everybody after this explosion was sick and tired of the whole affair, and did not want to hear the word " dog " again for a month or two at least. Temporary estrangements, as usual, must be cancelled as well. So when on Friday morning she set forth, like the old balloon so familiar to everybody, to take her dogs

into the garden, and when Mrs. Mantrip (appeased by
the hurly-burly of the afternoon before) simultaneously
stepped out of her front door on morning errands,
the eyes of the two protagonists met, and they smiled
at each other. Instead of saying " Ill met by sunlight, proud Titania," or saying nothing, but cutting
each other, they both said, " Another hot day, dear."
The volcano was extinct.

Mrs. Mantrip (" Margaret " once more) was on the
way to the lending library to change two books. But
she was quite disposed for a stroll in the garden first,
and as they crossed the road together she lent a kindly
hand to the unwinding of some of the leads. She
patted the murderous Bully Boy on the head, and
in the warmth of reconciliation she said:

" And I suppose that before long, Liz-Liz, you'll
be taking some of Sabrina's puppies out for their first
walk with the others."

A handsomer olive-branch could scarcely be conceived: it was indeed handsomer than Margaret had
intended, for no sooner had she emitted these ultra-
generous words than she saw that they implied not
only that bygones were bygones, but that she had
abandoned all opposition, on behalf of *père et fille*, to
the presence of dogs in the garden. But in these early
stages of reconciliation, when everybody must be
quixotically generous, she made no attempt to withdraw or qualify them.

Elizabeth took her words at their face value, and
now she had to make her contribution.

" Oh, not for a long time yet, dear," she said,
" and Sabrina will be absent too, for she's such a good
mother. As you see, I have only nine. And how do
things go with you, Margaret? That life of your
father—how is it getting on? "

" I haven't had much time to devote to it these
last few days, dear," said Margaret

There was again a slight awkwardness. It

occurred vividly again to both of them why there had
been so little time lately to devote to anything except
that bitter business of dogs, to which neither of them
intended to refer. But in these repatriations, after the
volcanic disturbances were over, there was always the
need of careful walking: the ground was still hot
and a careless heel might break through the cooling
crust. Just a little tact, a little ignoring of the obvious
was required.

"I'm sure I don't wonder that you've been so
busy," said Elizabeth hastily. "June in London is
always such a rush. How you manage to work at the
Life at all just now is a perpetual mystery to me. . . .
Why, what on earth——"

There was evidently about to be an urgent S.O.S.
for tact, for just as the two friends sat down on an
adamantine garden seat below one of the ancestral
sumacs, there entered from a gate lower down in the
garden the Black and White twins. One again towed
his toy bulldog, the other his string of ten Pekinese.
Whoever else was tired of dogs they were not; whoever else did not appreciate their clumsy satire they
did. Both ladies saw them about simultaneously, and
both became stone-blind.

"I am taking back to the library a volume of
Tchekov's plays," said Margaret, in her most detached
literary voice. "Something terribly poignant about
them. Heartrending in a way. Have you read *The
Cherry Orchard*, dear?"

Elizabeth cast one fleeting glance at the twins.
They had separated, and, as before, appeared to have
nothing to do with each other. Black, with his bulldog, was approaching by the left-hand path; White,
with his string of Pekinese, was coming up on the right.
Elizabeth opened the volume of Tchekov's plays of
which she had never heard before, and intently studied
it. Margaret continued to look straight in front of
her.

" No; I've not read *The Cherry Orchard*," said
Elizabeth. " Not read it: not done more than glance
at it. I was wanting something to read. Do you
recommend it? "

" I find it difficult to answer that, dear," said
Margaret very earnestly. " Personally it absorbed
me. There is a sad, a bitter sweetness about it which
haunted me for days. But I can easily understand
that to many it would be meaningless if not distasteful. A matter of temperament."

Elizabeth, without raising her eyes, shut up
Tchekov and opened the second of the books that
Margaret was returning to the library.

" The other," said Margaret, " is Walter
Pater's——"

" No, dear," said Elizabeth. " It's Rudolph da
Vinci's *Rosemary and Rue*."

Sight was instantly restored to Margaret, and she
almost snatched the book out of Elizabeth's hand.

" Good gracious me, what can have happened? "
she said. " A book by that comical Rudolph da
Vinci? It must belong to my parlourmaid, and she
must have left it in my library, where I picked it up.
What a queer thing! "

The twins were now quite close to them, one to the
right, one to the left, but still completely invisible.
Their childish conduct was too sharp a reminder of
the late crisis to make it advisable to be aware of them
at all. Sometimes one of the toy Pekinese upset on
the uneven gravel path, and then White stopped and
put it on its wheels again. Then suddenly the pack
of real Pekinese became aware that they were being
mocked, and in violent excitement rushed upon their
images. The ladies rose, as if by a preconcerted
signal, and though they were still stone-blind, something had to be done.

" Well, dear, I must be getting on," said
Margaret. " I shall have to go home first and get

Walter Pater's *Appreciations*. Fancy if I had taken *Rosemary and Rue* (is it?) to the library! What would they have thought of me? And you will be wanting to exercise your pets."

The pets were already exercising themselves; a combined assault was going on. Elizabeth drove them off without apparent knowledge of what they were attacking, and with so grim a face that White, having cried out "Oh, Mrs. Conklin!" did not venture to say anything more. Cowed and snubbed.

Elizabeth put all the real dogs on their leads. It would be too great a strain to remain here unconscious of the twins.

"I shall be getting home too," she said. "And on Sunday night if you are disengaged, Margaret, won't you come and have a little meal with me and one of our battles at piquet?"

"Charmed," said Margaret. "Good-bye, dear, for the present."

All this had been beautifully managed: the two left the garden without having seen the twins at all. But Elizabeth had seen on the title page of *Rosemary and Rue* Margaret Mantrip's name, written large and clear with the date. She would have liked to point that out when Margaret had said that the book must belong to her parlourmaid, but it was wiser in the first glow of reconciliation to say nothing about it. It was most mysterious, but it was not the time to ask awkward questions. How nimbly Margaret had snatched the book from her: how voluble and fallacious had been her explanations! As Elizabeth drifted up the Square like a balloon in a very light air, for the dogs were far from unanimous about going home so soon, she heard floods of melody proceeding from the open windows of Susan's drawing-room, and had a glimpse of Susan herself busily writing at her table, with her head in the very mouth of the loud-speaker.

That day anyone who looked for Mr. da Vinci and his Alsatian in the Park would have looked in vain. Susan was in the rapids and could not stop, and she abandoned her usual outing altogether. Throughout the afternoon melodies poured forth, to the accompaniment of lectures and children's hours and other pieces on the wireless, and with only the briefest pauses for the readjustment of the gramophone needle.

Jimmie was out in the afternoon attending a concert at the Queen's Hall, where a Scandinavian protégée of his was playing the 'cello, but when, on getting back, having just heard the overture to the *Meistersingers* at the conclusion of his concert, that noble contrapuntal piece began over again next door, he felt that such goings on could be tolerated no longer. He went to see Elizabeth, who was Susan's neighbour on the other side, to see if she had anything to suggest.

Elizabeth was reading *The Dog-Lovers' Quarterly* when he came in. She had stopped her ears with wads of pink cotton-wool.

" I know what you've come about," she said, uncorking herself. " It has been going on without a break since breakfast. Something must be done. The only question is ' What? ' That's so often the case."

" It's simply driving me mad," said he. " I've been thumping on the wall with my poker, but it makes no difference. The woman's got no imagination; she doesn't realize what an agony it is for me. One damned tune after another, and that awful overture on the top. I'm worn out. And this evening I've got a little dinner-party, and I'm going on to a boy-and-girl dance, and there'll be a band there."

" I've been thumping on the wall, too," said Elizabeth. " But she won't take hints. She doesn't care."

Jimmie gave a despairing squeal.

"There's that overture begun again," he cried. "Liz, I've got an idea. Pay her in her own coin. Reprisals. We've got as much right to turn on gramophones for ever and ever as she."

"But that doesn't make any difference to her," said Elizabeth. "She can't hear our gramophones when her own is going on. It only makes it twice as bad for us."

"No, but listen. I see it all. The time for our gramophones is when hers stops. Now will you sit up, say, till two o'clock to-night?"

"Till two hundred if it's to do any good," said she.

"Well, my plan is worth trying anyhow. As soon as her foul machine stops to-night, you put your gramophone close to her wall and begin. Go on firmly without any pause till two o'clock. I shall be back by then, and I'll put my gramophone close to her other wall, and give her a couple more hours of it. She won't get a wink of sleep, for her machine sounds quite loud in my bedroom, so mine will sound loud in hers."

"Not very neighbourly, Jimmie," said Elizabeth. "Shan't we first ask her to stop because we can't bear it? She may think we like it."

"How can she when we've been thumping at her wall with pokers? Besides, I'm out for vengeance now. Give her a dose of her own medicine. Let her see if she likes our music. I don't care whether it's rude or not. She's been rude without ceasing all day. She wants a good sharp lesson, and then to-morrow, perhaps, we shall have a bit of peace."

"Very well," said Elizabeth.

That night Susan had a tray brought her, for she could not spare time for dinner. Never in all these six years of passionate authorship had she known so high a level of lyrical inspiration. The great tide of imagination flowed stronger than ever, and that very

night, with any luck, it would waft her story into its
haven.   Close by her left elbow stood her wireless, and
the gramophone on her table poured its music into her
right ear.   Hour after hour went rapturously by, she
rising now and then to put a fresh needle into her
gramophone, or to readjust it (this she could do without rising) to the beginning of the piece.   She did not
bother herself to-night to change the record: the same
one, over and over again, was perfectly efficacious,
and the famous overture to the *Meistersingers* continued to inspire her.   Such a fine loud tune !   At
half-past eleven the wireless finished its programme
for the evening, but the other was quite sufficient,
and Bosanquet, as he went up to bed, promised himself an immense treat when, as he hoped, she would
go out for her walk in the park next day.   There
would be lots to read, for never could he remember
so unremitting an orgy of music, and this implied an
orgy of work.   How many pages would there be?

   At a quarter to twelve tragedy descended on Susan's
loud, creative Eden.   The gramophone emitted a
short, sharp croak, and became dumb.   It was in
vain that she dug in its vitals with nibs and hair-
pins: she had no mechanical knowledge, and for all
her proddings it remained mute.   She sat down again
and tried to continue in spite of this deadly silence.
Her brain, she knew, was full of ideas, red-hot and
noble, all waiting for her pen, but some co-ordination
between the two had snapped with the cessation of
noise, and the door of her mental treasure-house was
slammed.   She wrote and she erased the feeble, un-
inspired stuff; she took fresh sheets of foolscap on
which to make a new start; she drew pictures on her
blotting-paper; she stared out into the silent, unsympathetic night; she said over the last of the inspired
sentences; she invoked the names of Julian Beltravers
and the Lady Cynthia, but all was fruitless.   It was
too cruel that within sight of the end this wretched

machine should fail her. Fool that she was not to
have had two gramophones !

But now with the relaxation of the bent bow, which
had been shooting these silver arrows of romance so
incessantly into the very bull's-eye of the target, she
was conscious of an immense, an overpowering fatigue.
Too tired and too nerveless for the moment to make
the effort to go upstairs to bed, she turned out her
electric light and dropped on to the sofa to get a recuperative snooze. She instantly fell into a dreamless
sleep.

Elizabeth next door was waiting for the cessation
of Susan's gramophone, for that was the signal that
it was time for her to begin. She listened a minute or
two for its renewal: Susan might be putting a fresh
needle in, or even changing the record, but there was
unbroken silence. She wheeled a comfortable chair
up to where her gramophone stood close to the wall;
she stopped up her ears again with cotton-wool, and
put on a record. A loud, cheerful piece of jazz music
would be nice to begin with.

Immediately Susan awoke. Her brain was heavy
with the dreamless sleep from which she had been
recalled, the room was dark, and at first she did not
know where she was. Then through her drowsiness
there pierced like a beam of celestial light the sound
from next door. Instantly she remembered everything: the collapse of her own machine, her struggles
and her writhings to get on without it, her despair, her
throwing herself down on the sofa. How loud and
lovely this noise was; it might almost be in her own
room. It had sprung up out of the horrid silent night
like the singing of angels on Christmas morning.
Surely it was loud enough. . . .

She clicked on her light, she took up her pen, she
read the last sentence or two which she had written
before her own music failed, and with a sob of relief
she found that the co-ordination was established again:

the words she had sought for were streaming on to the
paper. On and on went the heavenly music, on and
on poured out the torrent of her thoughts now un-
congealed again, but the authoress was unconscious of
the passage of time. She could have wished that the
music was louder, but it did very well.

Jimmie Mason returned from his dance rather
earlier than he had intended. He had had a good
substantial supper, for there was a long vigil before
him, and it was about half-past one when he came
upstairs to the place of execution. He had seen that
Elizabeth's drawing-room was lit; he had heard as he
let himself into his house that her gramophone was at
it, but there was no reason why he should not begin
at once. All the better, in fact, if he did, for then
there would be two gramophones going on simultaneously, one on each side of the beleaguered Susan. He
provided himself with his copy of *Rosemary and Rue*,
which would be sure to afford him the highest entertainment, and drawing a comfortable chair close to
the gramophone, which stood against Susan's wall, he
turned it on. " Now she'll begin to see what it's
like," he said to himself.

Susan, reinspired by Elizabeth's gramophone but
not quite satisfied with the volume of it, had arrived,
a quarter of an hour before, at the climax in the last
chapter of her romance, and she had been unconsciously muttering to herself, " Louder, louder ! " as
Prince Igor's servants carried into the sumptuous
dining-room of their master's magnificent mansion in
Belgrave Square the gagged and bound figure of Julian
Beltravers. It was the night of Christmas Eve; a
glowing fire of cedar logs burned on the hearth between
the lapis lazuli Caryatides of naked nymphs that supported the elaborate chimney-piece, and into the heart
of the fire was thrust a poker which was now quite
red-hot. . . . After that powerful scene in Hyde Park,
Julian and the Lady Cynthia had become engaged, and

the wily Russian had apologized to them both for all
past violence on his part, and had convinced them that
he was now their true friend. He had therefore asked
the poor lambs to a little supper-party to-night, and
there was the table adorned with priceless gold plate
and groaning beneath every kind of unseasonable
delicacy, such as strawberries and asparagus. The
Lady Cynthia was due now; as soon as ever she
entered the marble hall she would be gagged and
bound also, and brought into the room where lay her
trussed lover. Prince Igor would then have his own
supper in a leisurely manner and, after his coffee and
cigarette, he proposed to blind the gentleman with the
red-hot poker in front of her eyes, and ravish the lady.
He had already procured his passport under an
assumed name, and would leave Victoria by the boat-
train next morning.

Such a situation, it will easily be understood,
required the most powerful handling. The suspense
must be terrific, the reader's anxiety perfectly sicken-
ing, and Susan knew that in order to secure that, her
own imagination must be screwed up to the highest
possible point. She felt it all tremendously, her brain
was all on fire with it, but she wanted more noise,
much more noise, to enable her to concentrate, to
sharpen her power of expression, to develop the full
horse-power of her pen, and now in an agonized
whisper she again muttered, " Louder, please, much
louder." Providential as had been the starting of
Elizabeth's gramophone, which shattered the barren
silence, that bounty lacked the volume of noise for
which she thirsted. Already Julian was lying ready
on the floor, bound like Isaac for sacrifice; a faint
scream, instantly stifled, showed that the Lady Cynthia
had been gagged and would now be brought in, but
the tension must grow till the final moment when her
intelligent Alsatian, whose instinct told it that his
beloved mistress was in imminent peril, jumped

through the window of the dining-room from the
pavement in Belgrave Square, and regardless of the
red-hot poker, flew at Prince Igor's throat. . . . " Oh,
my God, can't you give me anything louder than
that? " exclaimed Susan in an imploring and yet
irritated voice. " I *must* have it louder."

At that moment of her greatest need, Jimmie turned
on his gramophone. A heavenly smile spread over
Susan's face, making her plain, insignificant features
look almost beautiful, and dashing away the tears of
thankfulness that sprang to her eyes, she heaved a sigh
of deep content, and her pen streaked across the paper.
She was blind to the world in this bloody intoxication
of her brain. Just once or twice, as she took a fresh
sheet, she murmured " Thank God! " to herself.

Two o'clock struck: that was the hour at which
Elizabeth's ministrations were over, and she was free
to go to bed, leaving the rest of Susan's punishment
to Jimmie. But she did not feel tired, and this number
of *The Dog-Lovers' Quarterly* had a very interesting
article about canine jaundice, which the writer regarded
as certainly infectious. " And as we're at it," she
thought to herself, " we may as well do it thoroughly.
Miss Leg might possibly go to sleep with only one
gramophone at work, but I don't think she can with
two. We'll give her such a dose as she won't forget."

The hours passed on; occasionally Elizabeth dozed
a little, but roused herself to attend to the gramophone
when the record was finished. Soon the short summer
night was drawing to its close, and so also, ever more
swiftly under this riot of inspiring noise, there drew
to its close the final scene of Susan's romance. Outside the sky was growing dove-coloured at the approach
of day, and the sooty sparrows of London were vocal
with their earliest chirrupings when the Alsatian
jumped in through the window and Prince Igor soon
lay dead on the floor with his throat incredibly
mangled, while the red-hot poker burned a hole in the

carpet. There was to be no epilogue or chapter beginning " About a year later . . .": the book was to end
on this top note. Just the sound of Christmas bells,
and that was all. Susan set them ringing at 3.50 a.m.
(summer time), and fresh as a daisy and infinitely
happy, she wrote " Finis " across the last sheet of her
manuscript. She kissed her hand, right and left, to
the houses that had showered on her so generous a
supply of sorely needed music, and went upstairs to
bed with a singing heart.

" Was anything ever so fortunate," she thought to
herself, " as that dear Mr. Mason and sweet Mrs. Conklin should both have such a go at their gramophones
just when I wanted them so badly? It's strange
that they should be playing so late: never before has
anything of the sort happened. What a lovely coincidence ! " She was not yet in bed when the sound
of both gramophones, which were quite loud, even up
here, abruptly ceased. " Almost more than a coincidence, was it? " she wondered. " Really it looks
as if it had been specially arranged on purpose for
me," and for the second time that night she fell, just
as dawn grew rosy, into a dreamless sleep.

Though much fatigued by so long and loud a vigil,
the two conspirators, who had both put notices on their
bedroom doors that they were not to be called till nine,
congratulated themselves next morning that their plot
had succeeded, for not a sound came from the inter-
vening house of noise. For the last few days gramophone and wireless had both been going at full blast
by this hour, and Elizabeth, wearily dragging herself
from bed, was pleased to think that Susan had taken
the hint so loudly given, or at any rate was still sleeping
the sleep of a thoroughly exhausted woman. But,
when she looked out from her bedroom window on to
the garden, she perceived that the latter supposition
was not tenable, for there was Susan herself tripping
gaily about the grass with that monstrous hound

cavorting beside her. She picked up sticks and threw
them for his retrieving. She playfully dodged behind
the rustic chalice that held the seven geraniums provided by the Garden Committee, and like a child
bounced out on him this way and that, saying " Bo ! "
and pretended to run away. Elizabeth thought that
she had never seen anything more degrading and disappointing: not only was the victim out and about,
but she seemed possessed of an elfin sprightliness, as
if she had passed a night of recuperative rapture or
refreshment. It was most unsuitable conduct in any
plain, middle-aged woman, and positively indecent in
one who should have been kept awake till four in the
morning by the dissonances of two gramophones.
Monstrous that Susan, who ought to have been tired
out, should caper about in that artless, rejuvenated
manner ! Did music have the same effect on her as
monkey gland? What else could account for that
magical briskness?

The first duty of Elizabeth's day was to drink a
glass of hot water, the second to refrain from breakfast
while engaged on a cross-word puzzle, which was sufficient by itself to take away the healthiest appetite, and
the third to take her dogs into the garden. Sigurd and
his mistress had come home before she had finished
having no breakfast, and she listened to hear if the
gramophone would now begin. There was not a
sound, and this seemed to indicate penitence, or at least
an appreciation of the punishment she had undergone.
Full of hope, Elizabeth proceeded to the third duty of
the day, and went out with her dogs. Susan's motor
was standing at the door, and Bosanquet emerged
carrying a gramophone, which he deposited on the box-
seat. That was capable of a disappointing interpretation to the analytical mind: it might be argued that
Susan's gramophone was dumb this morning merely
because it was out of order, and that it was being sent
to the specialist so that it might make its old godless

noise again. But it could equally well be argued that, however indisposed Susan's gramophone was, she would by this time (10.47 a.m.) have had recourse to her wireless, and at present the wireless had been dumb also. There had been no daily service (Elizabeth felt sure) at 10.15, nor any announcement of the correct time and the state of the weather at 10.30. If there was no organ recital or other music during the morning, Elizabeth felt that there would be good grounds for hoping for the best. She let loose all her dogs and sat down to finish her cross-word.

Immediately afterwards Susan came out of her house. She carried a substantial packet done up in brown paper just about the size of foolscap folio. She caught sight of Elizabeth, and, giving her packet to Bosanquet, tripped across the road to the garden railings and called to her.

"Good morning, Mrs. Conklin," she said. "Thank you ever so much for your sweet music last night. How I enjoyed it! I felt I must tell you!"

She got into her car, and told her chauffeur to take her to Mr. Cartwright's office. Off she went, in her hat loaded with bunches of polychromatic grapes, as gay as the flowers that bloom in the spring. Tra-la.

Bosanquet turned back into the house as soon as she had gone. His fine features, which usually were composed into a mask of imperturbable complacency, were soured with the pain of his disappointment. He had already overheard (or rather heard, so ringing was his mistress's voice that morning) Susan telephoning to Nunky, saying that "it" was finished, and that she would bring it round to him during the morning. After that she intended to go down to Brighton for the Sunday. Bosanquet could easily conjecture what this meant, and all his hopes of enjoying a unique literary banquet were dashed to the ground. The most exciting story he had ever read was snatched from him before he knew how it ended, and now he would have to

wait till the typewritten copy came back. He had
only got as far as the great scene in the Row, which
Susan had finished two nights ago, and since then he
had had no opportunity of reading more, for all yesterday she had sat immovable at her table, only quitting it
for the briefest periods during the course of the day.
She had had a tray in the evening, and after that the
gramophone had gone on till he went to bed. He had
not been able to sleep (no more had M. Rouen, who
was in a very bad temper this morning), because music
of some sort had been continuous till four o'clock. He
could not quite localize it: sometimes it had seemed
to come from neighbours' houses, but without doubt
his mistress had sat up writing till dawn, for he had
heard her come upstairs. He had not minded (though
M. Rouen had) being kept awake like that, for Susan
was awake, too, and working, and he would have a
more than ample recompense for his vigil when he read
what she had written. It was monstrous that she should
have taken the finished manuscript away to Nunky's
office to be typewritten in such a desperate hurry. The
day was Saturday: the typist would not get to work on
it till Monday, and with Susan at Brighton, what a
wonderful Sunday he might have enjoyed, reading it
quietly and carefully in the manner of Mrs. Mantrip's
second perusals.

To make sure that his depressing conclusions were
correct, Bosanquet looked into the manuscript drawer
of Susan's writing-table, which during this past week
had been so rapidly filling up with foolscap; but, as he
feared, it was empty, and the only shred of evidence
as to what had happened in the concluding chapter or
chapters was a few crumpled sheets of paper which the
housemaid had omitted to empty from the waste-paper
basket. He smoothed these out and tried to decipher
them; there were one or two highly stimulating
sentences, showing that Julian lay on the floor somewhere, gagged and bound, but these were all the clue

he could find, and the rest of the paper was so full of incomplete sentences, of erasures, of interpolations, of scribbled pictures on the margin, that he could make nothing of it. It was clear that Susan had had a difficult time during the night, when her work would not go well, but the inspiration must have returned again. Bosanquet gave the housemaid a sharp word or two for the slovenly way in which she had tidied the drawing-room, and then betook himself to the telephone, where he rang up the *Evening Chronicle*, and had a short conversation with a male who called him Uncle Bob. After that he retired, baffled and ill-content, to the pantry and finished cleaning "his" silver.

Despite the joyous exhilaration which always followed on the completion of a romance, and made her feel infinitely young and infinitely kindly towards all the world, Susan was conscious as well of an undercurrent of flatness. The princes and prelates, the high-bred and the dastardly folk, who for the past weeks had drawn their shining furrows, meteor-like, across her brain, had fulfilled their destinies and gone out like candles. They had been lovely or atrocious realities to her, and now they were extinguished; thus the triumph of achievement was mingled with this sense of loneliness and of reaction. As she drove to Nunky's office this morning, both these emotions were vividly at work, and, while she looked forward to a week-end at Brighton, which she always found bracing and agreeable, she considered what she should do to occupy herself on her return. She must set to work at something, she must have some employment for her hours; but there was no reason to begin another book for the present, for Nunky was intending to bring out the romance she had just finished in the late autumn, so that it should catch the book-buyers of Christmas presents, and there were weeks and weeks yet before she need think about a publication for the spring.

She determined to devote herself in this interlude to some course of intensive culture, such as she had contemplated since she had come among these highly educated ladies and gentlemen in Durham Square. Nunky had not thought much of her aspirations when she had talked to him about them the other night, nor had he entered into her adoration of the mind of Arthur Armstrong, and it was no use asking his advice as to what species of enrichment to dig into her mind. There was a wide choice: English history, philosophy, astronomy, politics, Italian painters, the study of a foreign language, all these liberal subjects, and no doubt many, many more would conduce to that sort of ripeness of the mind which it would be so pleasant to acquire. Then there was reincarnation, the Indian question, and spiritualism, which had made such glib and stimulating conversation at Mrs. Mantrip's luncheon-party. What a lot there was to be learned: she wondered whether a steady course of reading the Encyclopædia would be a sound step.

She wanted advice, and the thought of consulting Mrs. Mantrip occurred to her. True, she had made up her mind to keep her distance from the lady, and not cultivate her acquaintance, for she certainly had shown an absence of true breeding at that meeting over the question of dogs in the garden, and Lady Eva had made dark speeches about the gloomy character of her halo. On the other hand, it was perhaps the force of Mrs. Mantrip's filial piety that had led her into unseemly behaviour at the meeting, and though Lady Eva had been so discerning over her perception of Susan's own halo, it did not follow that her eye was unerring. Susan felt that she might be wronging Mrs. Mantrip and coming to a too hasty conclusion about her. The picture of her, surrounded by grave books, engaged in the high-minded and far from remunerative task of erecting a literary monument to her father's memory, had elements of nobility. That was the sort of person whose advice would be valuable, so after leaving her manuscript at Nunky's office and depositing the gramophone at its maker's, Susan returned home and wrote her a note that could hardly fail to please. She began by asking her to a little dinner she planned to give next week, and supplemented this by a very humble request that Mrs. Mantrip would kindly recommend her two or three serious and improving books.

The answer came back just before she left for Brighton.

" DEAR MISS LEG,—I fear it would be useless for me to recommend you such books as I am personally interested in, as our tastes, I am sure, lie in such different directions. It is most kind of you to ask me to dinner next Thursday, and I much regret that I am unable to accept.

" Yours truly,
" MARGARET MANTRIP."

Susan stepped into her car.
" Hove," she said. Not a word more.

Bosanquet was still so morose from his disappointment that he had not intended to see Susan off, but remembering who she was, and what hours of happiness she had given him, his better nature reasserted itself, and he came up from below in a great hurry, with the 6.30 edition of the *Evening Chronicle*. (It was really much earlier in the afternoon, but the *Evening Chronicle* was famed for looking ahead into the future.) There was a paragraph in it which he was sure she would like to read, though Susan did not know that Bosanquet knew that.

For quite a long while Susan sat without looking

at the paper at all, outwardly composed but seething within, and it was not till her powerful imagination devised several awful catastrophes for the misguided writer of the note which she had torn to fragments, that she was sufficiently mistress of herself to conclude that the woman was not worth thinking about, and to see what the 6.30 said. Nunky had been busy, and Nunky had been very quick, for though she had only told him shortly before ten this morning that her book was finished and that she was off to Brighton for the week-end, he must have sent this item to the *Evening Chronicle*; for in Ulrica's column she read that Rudolph da Vinci had penned the last words of his new romance, which would be published by Messrs. Cartwright early in November, and was spending the week-end, as he so often did, at the Regency Palace Hotel, Brighton, or Brightelmstone, as Ulrica reminded her readers, was the older appellation of the place. Ulrica had spread this information over a couple of handsome paragraphs, bringing in the Alsatian again, and the customary thrill of pride and excitement visited Susan at the thought that it was all about her. It was great fun being the hidden hand and going down to Brightelmstone incognita, but then again there were drawbacks. She felt sometimes that she would enjoy life more, if everyone knew. Rudolph was having all the glory, and by the very nature of the situation he could not enjoy it since he had no existence. " It's rather a waste," thought Susan, " but then there's culture to be thought about."

There was nothing else of interest in the paper, and after planning a few more tribulations for Mrs. Mantrip, she threw it out of the window just as her car emerged on to the glittering esplanade, and she passed Ascham's Typewriting Agency and soon identified the shelter in which Arthur Armstrong had sat disapproving of the moonlight with a copy of *Rosemary and Rue* by his side. She could hardly

believe that it was only a week since she had made
that stroll along the sea-front, so much had " trans-
pired " in the interval. There had been that battle
of the dogs, there had been the disclosure of her own
magnificent halo, there had been the completion of her
new story with that night of melody so kindly arranged
by Providence and her neighbours to counter the
machinations of the devil in causing her own gramophone to collapse, and finally there had been that note
which Mrs. Mantrip had been rash enough to write
and for which she would fully deserve whatever she
happened to get. All in a week !

The hotel, as she noticed when she came down to
dinner, was very empty : all told, there were not more
than a dozen tables occupied. Of those who had been
there the week before, there was only the Semitic
family who held their mouths open and played bridge.
But in spite of this slackness, there was an air of
inscrutable alertness about the staff. All the waiters
stood at attention; the controller of the wines held his
missal of choice beverages in his hand, with his
finger inserted in the pages of champagnes; the cocktail-
mixer peeled his thinnest rinds of lemon and speared
his preserved cherries with unusual care. A highly
finished and polished young man who vaguely
reminded Susan of Bosanquet came in and sat himself
at a table not far from her, and at his entrance Susan's
waiter, who was handing her grated cheese, turned
swiftly round, jerking the spoon out of her hand, and
then, seeing who it was, gave a small sigh of disappointment and picked up the spoon. The entry of
a second young man with a pale, puffy face, as if
he sat indoors a good deal, produced a similar
alacrity, followed by a similar depression. He carried
a small writing-pad of the sort used by stenographers
and he was known to the first, for they exchanged
nods, but did not seem to like each other.

Then at last came he who doubtless was the

lodestar of all these expectant eyes, and whose entry,
a week ago, Susan had observed with reverential
awe. But to-night Mr. Armstrong, evidently to his
own astonishment, produced no effect of any sort.
He paused half-way to his table as if to give everybody a second chance, but, metaphorically speaking,
he had fallen flat. The head waiter just beckoned to
him to indicate his reserved table, the merchant of
wines sauntered across to him, and he had to call
the cocktail-mixer himself. The two young men near
the door passed a smile to and fro between them, in
which derision had a share, and Mr. Armstrong sat
down looking offended, and, as before, propped a
book against his standard-light.

Susan felt sore and indignant at the shabby reception accorded to the great man; she would have liked
to stand up and curtsy to him. What a moment
was now drawing near for her, when, to-morrow
morning, she would open the *Sunday Chronicle*,
which she had already ordered! Perhaps he would
say nothing in his article about *Rosemary and Rue*,
which he had been reading a week ago: that would
certainly be a sad disappointment, but she must be
prepared for that. Perhaps he would criticize it; he
might even from the heights of his own superb technical
knowledge be severe on her handling, or from the
heights of his knowledge of the human heart find
fault with her psychology. How she would pore over
every word, striving to benefit from his blame, and
learn wisdom from his chastisement! And then there
was the third chance, which her pride in her work
forbade her altogether to rule out, namely that he
would hail *Rosemary and Rue* as a masterpiece, and
award it his unqualified praise. Her imagination was
working brilliantly now, and she determined in that
case to write to him, and, over the signature of Rudolph
da Vinci, express in fervent terms how eagerly Rudolph
clasped to his bosom (no, breast—she had forgotten his

sex) the appreciation of such a master. Mr. Armstrong, no doubt, would answer that in suitable terms,
similarly expressing his delight at being called a master
by one who was so supreme a master himself. Quite
a romantic sequel, though only sketchily outlined,
formed itself in Susan's brain as she ate her strawberries. She would get to know him in the incarnation
of Miss Leg, and the day might come when, under
promise of secrecy, she disclosed Who Else she was.
The rest, she realized, must depend on him.

As she went out, she got a fleeting glance at the
book he was reading. The title was *The Brothers
Karamazov*. She had never heard of it, and
wondered if, as naughty Nunky had suggested, it
was one of his own novels. The two young men who
did not seem to like each other had already gone to
the lounge, and the puffy one was speaking in a
querulous voice.

" But they tell me at the bureau that they've
received no news of his coming," he said. " He
hasn't engaged a room, and as for his often coming
here, as you said he did, they say he's never been
here at all."

" Can't understand it," said the other, whose
features again recalled those of Bosanquet. " The
information came straight to me from Jerusalem
Cartwright, his publisher, and so naturally I took it
as O.K., and made a par about it. Sorry you've
had a disappointment. *Très ennuyant*, but so have
I."

" Damned sell I call it, unless he comes to-morrow.
What about a stroll on the pier? "

" I think I won't. I shall try to get a few words
with Abstemious Armstrong. Better than nothing."

" *Un peu*," said the other, in a less admirable
French accent, and walked off.

Suddenly the truth flashed upon Susan, and she
was astonished at herself for not having thought of it

before. There she inconspicuously sat drinking her coffee, as if she was nobody in particular, and it had been for the sight of her that the eyes of all the staff had been fixed on the door at every entry: it was for her that the controller of wines had kept his finger in the champagne page; for her the mixer of cocktails had peeled his lemon so exquisitely thin, for they all had seen in the *Evening Chronicle* that Rudolph was spending the week-end here. Never yet had she witnessed a public though a disappointed demonstration of her sovereignty over the hearts of her readers, and used though she was to the thousands of letters from unknown correspondents who told her with the most touching confidence what her books meant to them, and how they had helped them in times of trouble, the ocular witnessing of the suspense of the hotel staff was a revelation to her. Even Mr. Armstrong attracted no attention; nobody paid the least heed to him, when there was a chance of seeing her. The sense of her secret power was positively intoxicating: but at the same time she longed to disclose herself to somebody and satisfy his yearning. That polished young man, for instance, with the exquisite French accent: she knew now by his own admission that he must be Ulrica of the *Evening Chronicle*, and he, poor fellow, on the strength of Nunky's information, had come from London at the expense of a railway ticket and an hotel bill, on the chance of getting an interview with her. Really it was a great shame to disappoint people like this, and yet even if she had gone up to him and said, " Excuse me, Miss Ulrica, but I thought you would like to know that I am Mr. Rudolph da Vinci," it was exceedingly unlikely that he would believe her. There was nothing to be done, though her heart bled for him, and she picked up a copy of the *Evening Chronicle* and read about herself over again.

Before long she began to observe that he was casting

piercing glances every now and then in her direction.
He was young, twenty-four, she guessed, or thereabouts, and she thought she might almost, though not
quite, have been his mother if she had been married,
or indeed, even if she hadn't. Soon he got up, evidently still puzzling over some mental problem, and she
saw him go to the bureau, where he inspected the
visitors' book. Then he came back with a brisker step
and seated himself considerably nearer to her than he
had been before. Was he screwing up his courage to
speak to her? It seemed highly likely, and Susan was
bursting with curiosity to know what he wanted to say.
She was safe, whatever he said, with so many people
about. Mr. Armstrong, having finished his dinner,
came out into the lounge, but the sight of him and the
chance of getting some copy out of him appeared to
appeal to the young man no longer, for he took no
notice of him. Susan felt it was only kind to help him,
and she dexterously let a sheet of her paper fall to the
floor. It was very well done and looked quite acci-
dental. Instantly Mr. Ulrica sprang from his chair
and picked it up for her.

"Miss Susan Leg, surely, *n'est ce pas?*" he said
in a most respectful voice. "I have had a glimpse of
you more than once from the window of your servants'
sitting-room in your house in Durham Square as you
got out of your motor."

This was surely a remarkable way to introduce
himself. Susan could think of nothing better to say
than "Indeed." This she did.

"Perhaps I had better explain," he said. "I am
Ulrica of the *Evening Chronicle*, but the real key to
the situation is that unprofessionally I am Augustus
Bosanquet, nephew of your butler, than whom, as I
know from his own lips, you have no warmer admirer."

It seemed a little unusual that a butler should
(with his own lips) express his sentiments towards
his mistress in such terms, but Susan was pleased to

know that Bosanquet found her so satisfactory. She hastened to respond with equal cordiality.

" And I, too, have found your uncle the most excellent servant," she said. " Always willing and obliging. Really, I look upon him as a friend as much as a butler."

" Uncle Bob will be overjoyed when he hears that," said Augustus fervently.

There was a pause. Having given this handsome testimony to the qualities of Uncle Bob, Susan could not think of anything more to say about him.

" And do you often come down here, Mr. Bosanquet? " she asked. It was odd to be calling the uncle Bosanquet, and the nephew Mr. Bosanquet.

" Too busy, alas, usually," he said, " though perhaps I shouldn't say ' alas,' for I love my work and am very proud of it. But we social specialists of the press have our hands pretty full. In the season we can hardly keep pace with fashionable news, and out of the season we have to be veritable sleuth-hounds in order to find it. I see, Miss Leg, that you have been looking at my jottings *du jour*," and he pointed to the open page.

Susan glanced at the paper as if she had not seen the jottings *du jour* before.

" Ah, yes, I see," she said. " All about Rudolph da Vinci and his book and his spending the week-end at Brighton."

" Quite. I was afraid that I had had my journey for nothing," said he, " and my poor colleague, Esmeralda, who has just gone out, still thinks that he has. But when you came in here after dinner I began to wonder if I had, after all, wasted my time and my money. I thought I recognized you, Miss Leg, but the glimpses I had got of you from the servants' sitting-room were only of the briefest. So I went to the bureau to find out. I was right; it was you."

As Mr. Augustus Bosanquet spoke these cryptic

words, a slight buzzing arose in Susan's ears and a slight mist before her eyes. She recognized these symptoms as those of cerebral excitement, such as she had often experienced before when a crisis was approaching in the writing of romance, and some weighty disclosure was imminent. They (the buzzing and the mist) were louder and thicker than usual: she attributed this to the conjecture that a disclosure personal to herself and not merely to her puppets was at hand. It was the wildest of conjectures, but sufficiently substantial, apparently, to cause these symptoms. She could, however, still assume an outward calm, though involuntarily she trifled with her pearls and fanned herself with the *Evening Chronicle*.

" Pray explain what you mean, Mr. Bosanquet," she said. (She heard her own voice saying these words, which was another symptom of suspense, as she had often described it to be.)

Augustus Ulrica Bosanquet also exhibited the correct signs of masculine discomposure. He cleared his throat; he tugged at his collar; he quenched the dottle of his cigarette in his ash-tray, exactly as Susan had often divined that an agitated male would do. Then he spoke with a flippant lightness.

" I'll make a clean breast of it, Miss Leg," he said, " though I assure you I had a bath before dinner. Ha ! "

" Ha ! " said Susan in a faint echo. Then she thought she had not shown sufficient appreciation of his humorous observation and said " Ha " again more warmly.

" *À nos moutons*," said Augustus in his very pure French accent. " We must revert to Uncle Bob. I told you, Miss Leg, that he was one of your warmest admirers. As a mistress—if you'll excuse the word— he does regard you with the most respectful feelings. But it is for another aspect of you that he feels the admiration of which I spoke."

The loudness and the thickness of the buzzing and the mist grew in intensity as Augustus made a dramatic pause. The crisis was come.

"Pray continue," said Susan, unable to bear it.

"Uncle Bob," said Augustus, "is a very observant man, and he has long had his suspicions, and, I may say, more than suspicions. He noticed, for instance, that when I, in the performance of my social duties, once stated, on information derived from Mr. Cartwright, that Mr. C. had been dining with Rudolph da Vinci, he had been dining with you. I naturally thought that he had mixed his dates up. I wronged him. Then again, Uncle Bob, in the performance of his domestic duties, and even exceeding perhaps what was strictly required of him, has often looked in the drawer of the writing-table in your *salon*, and found there, when you were working, an ever-increasing pile of manuscript. He dropped into the habit of reading it when you were out, and he felt certain that it could be by no other hand than that of the author for whom he has the warmest admiration. The name of that author, Miss Leg, is Rudolph da Vinci."

"You are telling this excellently," interrupted Susan, quite carried away by her admiration of his technique. "Yes, Mr. Bosanquet?"

"I treasure that praise," said Mr. Bosanquet. "Well, when Uncle Bob assured me that he had been reading thus clandestinely, instalment by instalment, a new romance, written by you, which he was certain was by Rudolph da Vinci, I was much impressed, for no one knows the work of our *premier romancier* better than he. Still I was not wholly convinced until this evening. Follow me closely here, Miss Leg, for chronology is important."

"I am all attention," said Susan.

"Well, about ten o'clock this morning, you rang up Mr. Cartwright to say that your book was finished

and that you would bring the manuscript to him at
once.   Uncle Bob heard that: he was cleaning silver.
It was a terrible disappointment to him, for he had
so eagerly looked forward to reading the end of your
story, and now you had taken the manuscript away
and deprived him of his chance.   He rang me up,
very much cast down by this, for, as he told me,
gramophones had been going all the night before,
which implied that you were at work, and he had
consoled his own sleepless hours with the thought of
the substantial treat that awaited him, and had now
been snatched from him.   I condoled with him as best
I could, and immediately afterwards there came down
to the office of the *Evening Chronicle* a special
messenger from Mr. Cartwright with the information
that Rudolph da Vinci had finished his book and was
going to spend the week-end at the Regency Palace
Hotel.   Uncle Bob had not told me that you were
going there for the week-end, and though it was undoubtedly very curious that you (who, Uncle Bob
always insisted, were Rudolph da Vinci) had finished
your book on the same day as R. da V., I still did
not believe that his theory was proved.   But on this
information from Mr. Cartwright, I came here too, on
the chance of getting an interview with R. da V., whom
I still thought would turn out to belong to the sex to
which—to which I myself belong.   He did not seem
to be here: Esmeralda (poor Esmeralda) learned at
the bureau that he was not expected, and so far from
his often paying visits here, he had never been to the
hotel at all.   Then, I must confess, I felt very indignant with Mr. Cartwright for having given me false
information which had caused me to mislead Ulrica's
innumerable (if I may say so) readers, my poor
colleague among them.   I did not observe you in the
dining-room, but when you came into the lounge just
now, the glimpses I had had of you, when, in your
servants' sitting-room, I was having a cup of tea with

Uncle Bob, flashed into my mind. I made an inquiry at the bureau, which I trust you will not think was a dishonourable thing for a social specialist to do, and found in the visitors' book the corroborative testimony of your autograph. Then all was clear. Rudolph da Vinci had fin shed his book this morning and was spending the week-end at the Regency Palace Hotel. Miss Susan Leg had finished her book this morning and was doing the same. R. da V. was apparently not here, but Miss Susan Leg was. So Mr. Cartwright's information was correct, and Uncle Bob had been right all along. Oh, Miss Rudolph Susan da Vinci Leg, *quel moment* ! "

Susan drank in from the reverential face and the fervent accents of Augustus, as he made this eloquent and lengthy speech, the intoxicating draught of personal recognition, and this single direct tribute to Susan was worth all the homage of countless correspondents to R. da V. *Quel moment* indeed (for she knew the meaning of many French words) for her also ! Then swift on the heels of that heady rapture came the sobering thought of the pseudonymity to which she was pledged. But to deny the truth was beyond her; besides, to tell such a whopping lie to so devoted an admirer as Augustus evidently was, would be nothing short of wicked. All she could do was to beg that it should go no further.

" Mr. Bosanquet," she said, " I cannot deny the justice of your conclusions. But I entreat you to respect the secret which you have discovered."

He looked at her in blank surprise.

" Why, whatever else do you suppose I should do ? " he asked. " What's the use of a secret to a social specialist if he gives it away ? He only makes one paragraph of it, and then it's public property. Not to mention, of course," he added hastily, " that an appeal made by a lady—*Ça va sans dire*. But it was a pretty little bit of detective work, wasn't it, Miss Leg ? If I wasn't Ulrica I should seriously think of becoming Edgar Wallace."

" But what about Bosanquet, about your Uncle Bob? " asked Susan. " Will he keep my secret too? "

" Uncle Bob is the soul of honour," said Augustus, with a burst of family pride. " Never hitherto has he communicated his conviction to anyone but me, and now that the truth of it is proved, he will be even more mum than ever, if that was possible, for he will know what tremendous value secrecy is to me."

" In what way? " asked Susan.

" A hundred ways, and not to me only, but, if I dare say so, to R. da V. also, and to Miss Leg. Hitherto all information about the mysterious R. da V. has come to me from Cartwright, and I think you will agree that it is often very crude, obvious stuff about your dog. All that can be made far more telling, far more subtle and seductive if you will let me handle such information about R. da V., his ways of work, his theories about romance-writing, as you may graciously give me. Wonderful material for me, and, I assure you, very useful to him. Then again, there is Miss Susan Leg to consider, and I flatter myself I can be of use to her. You have an original house; you have your own personality; you have only lately settled in London. No charming lady is without social ambition, and you would not be averse to seeing paragraphs in my organ constantly, about your wonderful parties, your fork-luncheons——"

" Oh, what are fork-luncheons? " asked Susan eagerly. Never had the hotel been so bright a fairyland.

" My own invention, though not out yet, and, indeed, not quite complete. Designed for those who in the maelstrom of social engagements have no time for a long and elaborate luncheon. Miss Leg's Thursday fork-luncheons can be the rage of the season if properly handled and given a dainty publicity. And

how pleased your marvellous chef will be, for I may
tell you that in Uncle Bob's opinion he does not find
enough to do, and was thinking——"

"Oh, dear, he mustn't go," said Susan.   "Shall
I raise his wages, Mr. Bosanquet?"

"Certainly not.   Give him more work.   That is
what all we artists want.   But that's a *bagatelle*.
What I want to tell you is that Ulrica's knowledge of
the world and Ulrica's pen are henceforth laid at Miss
Leg's feet.   You will amply repay me by letting me
come and dine quietly with you now and then, and
giving me real intimate stuff about R. da V. for my
column."

"But won't that be rather awkward, as your——"
began Susan.

Augustus instantly divined what she was about to
say.

"Not in the least, I assure you," he said.   "Uncle
Bob will not feel either himself or me to be in a false
position when he gives me my soup, or whatever it is.
He is quite accustomed to it.   Before he came to you
he was one of the most respected waiters at the Savoy
Hotel, and he has often waited on me when I was dining
there with social aspirants.   I assure you there will be
no *gêne* at all, Miss Leg.   After all, butling is an art,
and he is justly proud of it.   Well may he, for in a
wide experience I have never met with any butler who
has a finer natural pomposity than dear Uncle Bob.
How he appreciates the privilege of being of your
household, Miss Leg!   And if I may venture to say so,
he might be of great use to you occasionally in other
ways, if you will officially recognize that he is in the
great secret.   Molière's housemaid, in fact, if I may
so express myself."

"Yes, I suppose she was a wonderful housemaid,"
said Susan, a little vaguely.   "But Bosanquet's a
butler——"

"That is not exactly what I meant, dear Miss

Leg," he said. "Molière, the renowned French play-
wright, used always to read his dramas to his housemaid. He made her the test, the touchstone of the
great public to which he so powerfully appealed.
Uncle Bob's criticisms might similarly be of use sometimes to R. da V., for he has a considerable knowledge
of high life, and think what a treat to him ! "

Vistas, only narrow before, were enlarging themselves before Susan's desirous eyes. This young man
seemed singularly intelligent; indeed, his status as
Ulrica was sufficient evidence for that. He had divined
her hidden identity with hints from his uncle; he had
divined, with no hints at all, her craving for a brilliant
social life independent of R. da V., and the prospect
of getting Ulrica to fan the flame of them both was
dazzling indeed. The notion of Miss Susan Leg's fork-
luncheons, duly recorded by that decorative pen, was
enough to make the mouth of anyone who had social
ambitions water. But if they were to be associated
in this grand design, she must open her heart to him,
she must let him know more about herself, she must
make a clean breast of it. But after all he had already
done that, and why should she be shy?

"Mr. Bosanquet, it all sounds quite delicious," she
said, "and how well you've guessed all about me—
Susan, I mean, not only Rudolph. I, Susan, do want
a brilliant social life, full of culture, of course, but also
smart—such a horrid word, but I can't think of any
other. I should love to have fashionable people
dropping in with a fork. The worst of it is, that I've
only just come to London, and I don't know anybody
yet. Some of my neighbours have been very civil.
Mr. Jimmie Mason, for instance, has called on me——"

"Jimmie Mason? Jimmie Mason?" said Augustus. "I know I've heard the name. Yes, of course,
I've often written about him. Maharajahs and music.
He's all right: a useful friend. Lots of my clients go
there. Who else? "

"Lady Lowndes," said Susan. "I mean Lady Eva Lowndes."

"Oh, yes: the witch of West Endor. Quite good. Haloes are very fashionable now, everybody wants to be tested. In fact they are the *dernier cri*. Who else?"

"Mrs. Conklin," said Susan.

"Pass on," said Augustus. "The name is enough: I can do nothing with it."

"The Vicar who is most interesting about reincarnation."

"I know. He preaches about Yoga and draws similes from golf. A straight drive in life, though short, is worth all the crooked screamers. He and the witch of West Endor would be a good nucleus for a psychical symposium after a fork-lunch. Who else?"

"Then there's Mrs. Mantrip. I was much drawn to her at first, but the way she's behaved, well, really! I thought her so cultured."

"Uncle Bob thought her repellent when she came to have tea with you," said Augustus. "He's a very good judge of character, and if you agree with him, I should say ' Don't touch her.' "

"I won't," said Susan with decision. "Then there's Captain Lowndes. I've met him, but there's nothing particular about him, except that he doesn't have cancer. Positively those are all the people I know in London as yet. So hard to begin."

"Not a bit," said Augustus cheerily. "You take my hand, so to speak, Miss Leg, and trust me. Besides, there's your chef. You wouldn't believe me if I told you how many fashionable folk in Mayfair will go blindfold to a house if they know they will get a really good dinner, and more especially if they think that Ulrica will write something about it next day. My word! The power of the pen! But who am I to say that when you know it so much better than me? I await your orders."

Susan, who had a practical side to her imaginative mind, thought it would be an excellent plan to take him at his word, and begin at once. She indicated with a graceful turn of her short neck and a swift sideways glance of her eyes the figure of the second most important person present in the lounge. He sat a little aloof with his coffee and his second brandy and his *Brothers Karamazov*. The dinner had not been quite up to the mark, he had not been greeted with the obsequious attention to which he was accustomed in this hostelry, and he was seriously considering whether he should not put Dostoevski in his place when he wrote about him next week, or whether even he would not write about him at all, poor man.

"There's one of the people I should most adore to have visiting me," said Susan in a low voice. "What a red-letter day it would be if I could get Mr. Armstrong's legs under my table, as they say. Do you know him, Mr. Bosanquet?"

"Him?" said Augustus. "Why, of course. I arranged that luncheon-party he gave for Brazilian men of letters last week. He hadn't an idea how to run it. He would have asked a lot of measly, highbrow authors and critics to meet them, but I told him that a few pretty women would be far more to the point. Glad he was that he called me in: *grand succès* in consequence. Do you want to know him? Nothing easier."

"Oh, if I could!" said Susan. "One of my dreams."

Augustus got up and crossed over to the discontented poet, novelist, critic and M.P. There was an inaudible word or two and they returned together.

"My friend, Mr. Armstrong, is most anxious to be introduced to you, Miss Leg," said Augustus. "Mr. Armstrong: Miss Leg."

"Very pleased, I'm sure," said Miss Leg, hardly able to articulate the words of welcome.

They all sat down.

VIII

SUSAN awoke next morning in just such a state of vague rapture as that in which the old-fashioned breed of children (now unhappily much depleted by education and other hurtful influences) used to awake on Christmas morning. Christmas Eve had been exciting and unusual, carols had been sung by voices in the night; there was an atmosphere of presents about, for mysterious parcels had been hidden on their approach, and perhaps there was a sleepy memory that, during the night, some juggling had been in progress with the stockings they had attached to the foot of their beds. Then there was the sure anticipation of a festal day to follow with crackers and an unlimited licence with regard to rich and agreeable foods. In just such a state of happiness derived from pleasant and exciting incidents that had already occurred, and from the expectation of their being renewed to an intensified degree, did Susan awake on this Sunday morning.

What an evening it had been! What a time both she and R. da V. had had! There had been the dramatic epiphany of Augustus Bosanquet with his hands laden, so to speak, with presents for them both. Augustus was pledged to give a far more subtle and suggestive publicity to Rudolph than Nunky's little wooden paragraphs had ever done, and to make Susan's beautiful house in Durham Square a lodestar for esurient and fashionable folk, and to write her up in his influential column with the same zest as he was to devote to Rudolph. Then there was that

touching disclosure about Uncle Bosanquet: she freely
forgave him for his pryings in her manuscript drawer
for the sake of the fervent devotion to the eminent
author which had inspired them. Indeed she did
much more than forgive him: she was full of the
warmest feelings towards him, and realized what a
treasure he was. She would let him read the last
chapters of *Julian Beltravers* the moment they came
back from the typist, and would give him an autographed copy on publication.

Then (here she had to thank Mr. Bosanquet) there
was the introduction she had achieved to that great
and (she was sure) good man, whom only a week
ago she had been worshipping from afar. " *O noctes
cœnæque deorum!* " she would have exclaimed, had
she only known Latin as well as she knew French,
when she thought of that hour she had spent in con-
verse with him, as he sipped his brandy and puffed at
his cigar. He might almost have been dictating a
Sunday article to one of his typists, so wise, so
peremptory, so cultured, so literary was the talk that
flowed from his lips. He spoke of the Russian trinity
of immortal novelists, and Susan trembled at the
thought that by some unfortunate turn in the conversation she might be forced to acknowledge that she had
not the slightest idea who these high personages might
be. Perhaps henceforth, he said, only two would be
immortal, for he had read *The Brothers Karamazov*
again and had revised his opinion of Dostoevski.
But Tolstoi and Turgenev remained, and Susan could
cease trembling, for now she knew the names of them
all. He mentioned a whole string of contemporary
authors of whom Susan had never heard, and she
could hardly breathe, such was her suspense as to
whether he would say something about Rudolph da
Vinci. She would almost have taken the plunge and
asked him what he thought of *Rosemary and Rue* if
there had been an opportunity to get a word in edge-

ways. Then he mentioned a name which she had
heard before: Milton, he said, was terribly over-rated
as a poet, though his prose had a certain stiff-jointed
dignity. But as a poet he was obsolete: who could
read any longer those stilted dialogues between God
and Satan in *Paradise Lost*? He was thinking of
putting Milton in his place some Sunday soon, and
Susan was pleased to think that in her programme of
intensive culture she could omit Milton's name, for the
list threatened to be a long one.

Presently, in consequence of a question or two she
managed to put to him, he saw that what would interest
her most would be to hear him talking of himself, and
lighting another cigar he magnificently indulged her.
He told her how much he paid for his evening shoes,
how many printings of his last novel had been sold,
and how few of his poems. He was not bitter about
that: he was quite content to await the verdict of
posterity. But it was with real bitterness that he spoke
of the abominable and expensive lunch that had been
served him at a wayside inn that day on his journey
from London. A wait of half an hour. No fish.
Cold meat, not bad as far as it went. No salad.
Apple-tart. Dough instead of pastry. Cheese. Stale
biscuits. No fresh fruit. Bottle of mediocre hock.
Price, nine shillings. Then Augustus—and oh, what
a brilliant creature he was—had said, "Bad food is an
insult, but Miss Leg is always polite. The best chef in
London." For a little longer Mr. Armstrong swept on
his course again, like a critical comet blazing in a
gastronomic sky, but when, at the end of a fine description of a *soufflé* of persimmons, Susan got up to go to
bed, he shook hands very warmly and said that he
hoped she would give him an opportunity before long
of testing her invariable courtesy. In a flash she saw
what he meant by this beautiful phrase: he was
positively asking to be bidden to dinner. A date was
settled there and then, and on Thursday next she

would indeed be a happy woman, for Mr. Armstrong's legs would be under her table. Oh, that dear Mr. Bosanquet!

All this mingled in her happy dreams that night, and now, opening her window, Susan saw the pretty sunlight sparkling on the sea, and heard the noises of little ripples breaking on the shore. It was evident that Nature, as R. da V. had often acutely observed, was showing in her sunny way her sympathy with Susan's joyousness. And what a nasty one for Mrs. Mantrip who had so curtly declined to dine with her that night! It would be a long time, thought Susan, before she got another opportunity to refuse. She would be certain to see in the *Evening Chronicle* on the day following—Ulrica could be trusted for that— that Miss Leg had entertained Mr. Armstrong, M.P., etc., and a few friends to dinner that night. A fine example of Natural Retribution for being stuck-up! That was what had happened, without any machinations on Susan's part, to that ill-starred, anchovy-paste-haloed woman. Then there was Mrs. Mantrip's refusal to recommend her a book or two to read on the ground that their tastes were so different. More Natural Retribution had speedily overtaken that snorting piece of vainglory; for now Mr. Armstrong had recommended her what to read (a volume of short stories of his own was the first on the list), and with him as guide and counsellor Susan felt that she could manage to get along without any supplementary aid from Mrs. Mantrip. This pleasant thought was a source of extreme satisfaction to her. Sympathetic Nature positively beamed as she dwelt upon it, and the prattle of the breaking ripples was like gay, winsome laughter at the expense of Mrs. M., poor thing.

Finally there was a great excitement in the immediate future. The *Sunday Chronicle* would come up with her breakfast which her maid would

bring to her at nine o'clock. After that, more
pleasure; a stroll on the sea-front, already arranged,
with Mr. Bosanquet, and a consultation with him as
to the other guests on Thursday.

Nature became almost a nuisance when Susan's
maid came in with her breakfast, for the window was
open and so brisk a draught came dancing in that
some papers on her table fluttered into the air and fell
all over the carpet. But that was Nature's way of
showing a delicious, sympathetic excitement. Then
Susan teased herself. She went out on to her balcony
for breakfast, and there ate a crisp roll and butter and
drank some tea before she opened the paper at all, and
even then she did not look at *the* page. She tried the
cross-word; she glanced at the centre-sheet where the
news of nations was recorded. But nothing of the
smallest significance seemed to have happened anywhere, and no atom of the cross-word was soluble.
Then Nature joined in the teasing. When Susan
wanted to turn over, she made the paper struggle in
her grasp, she blew it against her face, she caused
sharp angles to form themselves in the sheet, which
were most difficult to negotiate. But eventually Susan
succeeded in folding the naughty thing back, and the
fateful page was open to her perusal.

She gave a sigh and a squeal of rapture, for what
first caught her eye seemed almost too good to be true.
Mr. Armstrong's column and a half was headed
" Rudolph da Vinci," and it began as follows:

" I have repeatedly stated in these articles of mine
that it is the first business of a critic to find beauty in
the literary work which he is examining. I state it
again. Again and again. To find and point out fresh
ugliness and stupidities in a world that already teems
with them is idiotic. That is my rule. I affirm a
hundred times that I am right. A thousand times.
A book that does not arouse my admiration is not

worth criticizing. Incidentally I may find faults in it. I usually do. But my mission is to find beauty. I can soon see if a book has beauty. A score of pages suffices. Or less. If it has none, it is not worth reading, far less writing about. I toss it aside. My time is too precious. I can use it better."

" The dear creature," whispered Susan to herself. " And, oh, what lovely writing! So noble in style, so brisk and brilliant, so authoritative, so——"
The opening words of the next paragraph came under her eye:

" There are exceptions to every rule. To-day I am forced to break the rule that generally guides me. It is not my fault. Quite the contrary. Books occasionally appear which call for my severest condemnation. Especially if they have a considerable sale. They must be annihilated. Such a one I took down into the country last week. It was called *Rosemary and Rue* (Rudolph da Vinci, Cartwright, 7s. 6d.) The publisher states that it is in its third large reprinting. He ought to state the actual number of copies sold. Large is a relative term. I find it difficult to believe that three substantial bona fide printings of such rubbish have already been sold. However, I will assume that this is correct. Though I should like to see his figures. Now I know nothing about Rudolph da Vinci. Possibly it is a writing-name. (I refuse to say *nom de plume*, because such a phrase does not exist in French.) Or possibly it is the writer's real name. He may be English, or he may be Italian. Withal more probably English. An Italian who writes in English has probably been taught grammar. Rudolph da Vinci has not. (p. 221: 'Who are you looking for?'; p. 236: 'to intensely enjoy,' etc.) I therefore assume that Rudolph da Vinci has been at Eton and Oxford."

The words began to dance before Susan's eyes, and
she found it impossible to read the lines consecutively.
She dipped here, she pounced there, she skimmed about
like a swallow hunting poisonous flies, and caught
a quantity of them. " Nauseating sentimentality . . .
mawkish trash . . . childish sadism . . . a valet's
view . . . lispings of a lady's maid . . . titterings of a
typist . . ." Such were a few of the alliterative tit-
bits so lavishly spread for her. Then steadying herself
down again, she read Mr. Armstrong's peroration :

" Such is the rubbish which has been reprinted three
times in ten days. I do not blame Mr. da Vinci.
On the contrary. I applaud his acuteness. I always
applaud the acuteness of a charlatan who makes money
out of the folly of others. ' Lord, what fools these
mortals be,' said Puck, and Mr. da Vinci has demonstrated the truth of that. He has already a considerable
list of books to his credit. And discredit. They have
all sold largely, and as each one appears Mr. da Vinci's
readers increase. *Apples of Sodom*, six printings;
Noblesse Oblige, eight printings; *Heart's Queen*, ten
printings, etc. But it is time to put a stop to this sort
of thing, and I fancy, after what I have said, that
Rosemary and Rue will not make a new record. But
I blame any publisher who will issue such piffle. Publishers are supposed to issue books, and such a firm as
Mr. Cartwright's ought to be ashamed of itself. Enough
of Mr. Rudolph da Vinci. R.I.P. Next Sunday I
shall speak of *The Brothers Karamazov*. There are
many beautiful things in it. I shall point them out.
But it is a book with which it is worth while finding
serious fault. Most people regard it as a classic. My
answer is monosyllabic. Rats."

The mind of any authoress less well-balanced than
Susan might well have been knocked out by the perusal
of such an article by one whom she so revered. Her

temper saved her, and instead of being plunged into a
gulf of stricken bewilderment, she felt perfectly herself,
except that she was trembling with passion. Her first
thought was that she would cut that pretentious monster
the next time she met him, and send him a note
written in the third person in which she regretted having
to cancel her dinner-party next Thursday, without
assigning reasons. But that, it soon appeared to her,
would be a very feeble reprisal. Greedy as he
evidently was, it would not hurt him enough to be
deprived of M. Rouen's masterpieces: that was not the
da Vinci touch. To let him go free without branding
some mark of Cain on his ignoble brow would be a
grievous failure to meet this situation. But what
should that stigma be? Fruitlessly she questioned the
sunshine and the sea. How bald and unsympathetic
Nature was!

The telephone bell interrupted these dark and passionate musings. It was Nunky, ringing up from
London, and Nunky was evidently in high good
humour.

"Good morning, my dear Susanna," he said. "I
rang you up in London quite forgetting that you were
gadding about at Brighton. Any nice young men?
But, my dear, was there ever such a piece of good
fortune? Have you seen the *Sunday Chronicle*?"

"Yes," said Susan.

"Good gracious me, what a voice! It sounds as
if you had kept it in cold storage. Or is there white-
hot anger in it? It's the greatest stroke of luck, I tell
you. Armstrong's done the trick for us. I'm drawing
up a blurb now, and I shall have a new jacket made
for *Rosemary* at once, with a quantity of the phrases
out of his article printed on it."

Susan interrupted.

"Oh, Nunky, I'm so upset," she said; "that—
that viper was introduced to me only last night, and I
thought him, oh, so wonderful. I was thinking of

putting him into my next book, as a perfectly splendid
person, chivalrous and cultured and altogether noble.
And then he goes and does this wicked, wicked thing ! ''

" All the more reason for putting him into your
next book," said Nunky cheerfully. " A slightly
different view of him. There'll be plenty of gusto in
it."

" That's an idea ! " said Susan. " Nunky, you are
clever ! But then he's coming to dine with me next
Thursday. I call it biting the hand that promised to
feed him."

" Better and better. You can study him. I'll send
word to Ulrica that he's dining with you."

" No need, Nunky. Ulrica is here. We're such
friends. Quite a romance. One of the most wonderful things that ever happened. You couldn't guess."

" Dear Susanna, is it a schwärm ? " asked Nunky.
" Are you a burning Sappho ? "

" What ? " asked Susan. " I don't understand.
Am I a what ? "

" No, never mind. But keep friends with Armstrong. Quite worth studying, and also a most
amusing situation. He'll adore your food. He
deserves it, too, for he'll have given Rudolph the most
priceless advertisement. You'll leave that to me.
But who is Ulrica ? Is she pretty ? "

" I can't talk about it down a telephone, Nunky.
But thanks for your idea. I think I——"

Then they were cut off.

Nature was still smiling, but now Susan read into
that brightness a very sinister intention. There might
be lightning in yon cloud. Instantly her mind took
hold of clever Nunky's idea and found it brilliant
beyond compare. Mr. Armstrong should indeed come
to dine with her; he should give lustre to the parties of
Susan Leg; he should launch her on the sea of culture
(with Mrs. Mantrip looking enviously on from the
shore) and all the time Rudolph da Vinci would be

studying him for purposes of ruthless satire. What measly adventures Rudolph da Vinci would invent for him! What revolting falsities he would probe into!

Swiftly to and fro flew the shuttle of thought through Susan's weaving brain. Armstrong should be an eminent critic, dominating the literary taste of the people, but inwardly he should be a ruffianly black-mailer. His procedure was to write to a rising author, saying that he would shortly receive an advance copy of his forthcoming book, and would so much like to have a personal talk about it. Twenty pounds in cash, he would then hint, might make him take a more favourable view of the forthcoming work than he otherwise would. He had an immense reputation, and a really favourable notice from him would easily be worth that. Most young authors would agree to this base proposal, and then he had them in a cleft stick. They could not make this infamous transaction public, for then they would stand convicted of having bribed the press to give them enthusiastic reviews. But one day he caught a veritable Tartar. . . .

Susan was off now. Inspiration was in full spate, and with a happy smile on her lips she was borne along by the torrent of it. So strong was it that she wanted no gramophone.

" A veritable Tartar. . . . There was a young woman, scarcely more than a girl, called Serena Lomond (Susan Leg) who lived in a country cottage covered with roses, with her old nurse and her noble Alsatian. (No: the Alsatian was overworked. A Great Dane.) Though quite untaught, she improvised on the piano in a marvellous fashion, and when asked where she got her tunes from, said that she heard angels' harps in the air, and just played what they did. Serena had already written one book, which had made a profound sensation: it dealt with visions and glimpses of the unseen world which was so real to her. Though the critics had scarcely noticed it at all, and

that only with scornful mockery, many very exalted
persons, princes and poets and prime ministers, considered her a heaven-born genius, and thought it an
honour to come and have tea with her in her cottage;
but, however eminent the visitors, Nursie always had
tea with them, sitting in the best arm-chair. . . . Now,
on the approaching publication of her second book,
Amor Vincit, Armstrong called on her and made his
infamous business proposal. At first Serena hardly
understood: her grey eyes with sapphire lights in
them '' (Susan glanced at her looking-glass) '' wore a
puzzled look. But by degrees it dawned on her what
he meant, and then her eyes flashed with electric
fire. . . .''

Susan began walking up and down her bedroom;
her excitement was prodigious.

'' Serena rose,'' she said to herself in a low voice,
vibrant with emotion. '' ' Do you mean that for this
paltry bribe you promise to write a favourable review
of a book you have not yet read? ' she cried. ' You
dare to suggest to me, Serena Lomond, that I should
pay you to puff me in the press? Is a leading critic,
such as you represent yourself to be, so venial [*sic*] a
cur? Out of my presence: never again presume to
tempt me with your monstrous propositions! Go!
Do your worst! Dip your foul pen in poison! I
laugh your threats and promises to scorn.' ''

Susan liked that. The speech of the impassioned
Serena had fallen into blank verse without any effort
on her part. She regarded this as the most signal
evidence of high inspiration. Her prowling steps
quickened, her face flushed, her plump little hands
gesticulated, her voice sank to a whisper.

'' He snarled at Serena in a very sinister manner,
but she had cowed him, and he crept from her
presence like a beaten hound. On his way down
the rose-wreathed pergola to her rustic wicket-gate,
he encountered her Great Dane, who always welcomed

my (I mean Serena's) visitors, be they princes or paupers, and gave him his paw. The thwarted critic struck at the dog with his stick, and out I flew with my riding-whip in my hand. . . ."

Susan wiped the dew of excitement from her intellectual forehead and went on in calmer tones.

" So *Amor Vincit* was published, and Mr. Armstrong wrote the most ungrammatical and scathing attacks on it in all the numerous papers in which he was the literary mentor." (" I shall give several quotations," thought Susan, " taken straight out of his article this morning.") " The cringing crowd of critics followed suit, and *Amor Vincit* was hailed with a chorus of bitterest contempt. Serena subscribed to a press-agency, and she and Nursie sat over the fire (for it was winter now) and read these revilings with peals of merry laughter, and then gave them to the great Dane to worry and tear to bits. The faithful animal seemed to know that they were attacks on his beloved mistress, for he pounced on them, not playfully, but with angry growls, showing all his beautiful white teeth. But this flood of contemptible contempt made not the slightest difference to the sales of *Amor Vincit*; printing after printing was called for, and the cheery old postman who brought Serena's letters staggered under the load of letters she received from total strangers, telling her how her book had strengthened and comforted them. Almost simultaneously a novel appeared by Mr. Armstrong, and though the entire press saluted it as a work of the most transcendent genius, it never got beyond its first printing, which consisted only of one thousand copies, whereas Serena's printings were each of thirty thousand. Serena was full of commiseration for him, for, in spite of his dastardly conduct to her, she believed that in him, as in all other of God's creatures, there was something good, if she could only find it. She made it her business to find beauty everywhere. (A nasty one !)

"One day," continued Susan, now completely
identifying herself with Serena, "I was coming home
after visiting some poor people, when I saw a man
lying in the snow just outside my garden gate. It was
Mr. Armstrong, and when I asked him what was the
matter, he ground his few remaining teeth and spat
at me, and then became unconscious. I quieted my
Great Dane, who would have torn him limb from limb,
and then Nursie and I carried him into my cottage, and
sent for the doctor. He at once pronounced that he
was suffering from a malignant and infectious form of
brain-fever. He warned me of the risk I ran in taking
him in, but I paid no attention to that, and when the
doctor had put him to bed in my room, which was the
best in the house except Nursie's, I tended him myself.
I fed him with cooling fruits, I improvised to him on
my piano, and after many days of shocking delirium
and a very high temperature, he fell into a long, deep
sleep from which he woke perfectly well."

Accustomed as she was to her own swift swallow-
flights of imagination, Susan was amazed at the richness and vividness of this series of visions which flashed
into her mind. Never in her previous romances had
she fashioned herself into her own heroine, nor stoked
up the fires of personal vengeance for the roasting of
a personal enemy, and the gusto these actualities gave
her was astonishing. "How clearly I can see myself
running out from my cottage to slash at that cur with
my riding-whip," she said to herself, "and throwing
his dirty review of *Rosemary* for Sigurd to worry!"
With hardly less vividness she could see herself nursing
Mr. Armstrong through his infectious brain-fever, for
she felt that such a capacity for nobility and forgiveness certainly existed somewhere in her soul, though at
present it was slightly obscured by the violence of her
loathing for him. . . . How the story would proceed
when she had tended him into convalescence again she
did not at present investigate. She had the main motifs,

namely, the reptilian quality of the great man, and her
own exquisite charity, burning like a beacon in her
brain, and (so at least she had always found it happen
before) the rest would unravel itself when she got started
on her story with a powerful gramophone.   The acces-
sories pleased her also: she liked the visits of royal
and eminent folk to Serena's rose-wreathed cottage.
These noble personages, who cared nothing for the
contempt of the press nor for the venomous outbursts
of Mr. Armstrong, of whom they had never heard,
found it the greatest intellectual treat to be allowed to
have a cup of tea with Nursie and Serena, and bask
in the sunshine of that lovely mind.   (Moreover, with
Ulrica to help her, might not Susan presently be enter-
taining in Durham Square just that class of visitor
which flocked to Serena?)   Then perhaps she might
work in Mrs. Mantrip: she could be Mr. Armstrong's
discarded mistress, or if that was not quite nice, his
mother, which would be just as stinging.   Yes, that
was a good thought.   She should have awful tea-
parties for pompous frumps and highbrows; she should
hold forth about literature, and pretend to be writing
a life of Julius Cæsar; she should talk in a learned
manner about all the books of which she had only read
her son's reviews; she should hate dogs.   That would
all work itself out in time, but what was quite certain
at this moment was that, though Susan had only yesterday completed her new romance, *Julian Beltravers*,
she would instantly set to work on *Amor Vincit*, while
the fires of vengeance were roaring up the chimney.
Nunky must bring it out this autumn as a Christmas
book, postponing *Julian Beltravers*, and she must buy
a second gramophone in case of accidents.

She tripped downstairs after this fruitful hour of
meditation and went out on to the gay and sparkling
sea-front.   Sitting in one of the shelters, and actually
reading his own vile work in the *Sunday Chronicle*,
was her victim.   He rose to greet her, and Susan, after

overcoming a qualm of nausea, sat down by him. It was worth while making that effort, and she began studying him at once.

"You seemed interested last night in my work, Miss Leg," he said, " and I suppose I need hardly ask you whether you have read my article in the *Sunday Chronicle* this morning. I am not displeased with it now that I read it in cold blood. I was afraid that my feelings about that trash had led me to express myself with too great warmth. Quite the contrary. I have been no more than just."

"Oh, I read it with such admiration," said Susan. "Very severe, but so convincing. Do you suppose that he—what is his name? Rudolph da Vinci—do you suppose he will ever publish another book after what you have said? He must indeed be brazen if he does."

"He would be wiser not to," said Mr. Armstrong. "There will not be much sale, I should think, for his next. I am sorry for him as an individual, but I have to consider my duty to his deluded public."

"A masterpiece of criticism!" cried Susan. "And what a tremendous responsibility is yours. There is no one who counts like you. And can it be really true, do you think, that hitherto Mr. da Vinci has sold hundreds of thousands of copies? All those printings! Just fancy!"

"I referred to that in my article. Surely you cannot have missed that. Nobody knows, I said, what a printing means. It may consist of one copy. Why not state the actual number of copies sold as I always do? I have challenged Cartwright to produce his figures. No doubt he will do so, when he sees my article."

Susan began to feel again the secret rapture of being the hidden hand. Rudolph da Vinci was not having all the fun after all. She was having the fun now, and would hand it on to him. Carefully she studied her victim: she saw now that the massive intellectual

forehead she had once so much admired was but the
beetle-brow of a badly swollen head.   The sensitive,
full-lipped mouth was the snout of a sensual animal;
the lean, ascetic cheeks and chin were the jaws of a
pike.   She would feed them; she would stuff them, as
they stuffed a Strasbourg goose, with M. Rouen's most
artistic concoctions; Mr. Bosanquet would describe
Susan Leg's dinner-party at which Mr. Armstrong was
present, and then R. da V. would make a bubble and
squeak of him in *Amor Vincit*.   Even now Nunky was
devising a new blurb for the jacket of *Rosemary and
Rue* which would make him supremely ridiculous.
What a marvellous thing this double life was!   How
truly exhilarating the air on these twin peaks of
existence!

Mr. Bosanquet drove up to London with her on
Monday morning and came to lunch.   The meeting
between the uncle and the nephew on the threshold
was very pretty.   Even as he had said, there was no
awkwardness about it at all.   Instead of going down
the steps by the area gate, which was his wonted mode
of access to Miss Leg's house, Mr. Bosanquet stepped
after her through the front door, carrying Susan's
cloak, and Susan said, " Mr. Bosanquet is coming to
lunch with me, Bosanquet."

Augustus said, " Good morning, Uncle Bob."

Bosanquet completely grasped the situation, and
doubling the character of perfect uncle and perfect
butler, said, " Good morning, Gus.   Shall I take your
coat, sir?"

" Thank you, Bosanquet," said Augustus, for he
was now speaking to his friend's butler.

So there they all were.   Perfect.

They went upstairs for the interview which R. da
V. had been induced to give Ulrica, and though there
were only two persons apparently present, there were

really four. There was the eminent novelist, there was
Ulrica, there was Augustus Bosanquet, and there was
Susan Leg. The peccant gramophone had come back
that morning, and before the two main personages
settled down for their talk, Susan turned it on. It
was louder, she thought, than ever: most satisfactory.
Augustus already knew from his uncle that Susan
always wrote under the stimulus of this melodious
uproar, but it was truly astonishing to think that anyone could do anything except go mad while it was at
work. She turned it off.

" I should like to bring that into my interview if
I may, Miss Leg," said he. " I could make something
very picturesque about Rudolph da Vinci drawing inspiration from music. I shouldn't, of course, say that
the music was that of a gramophone, for that might
give undesirable hints to your neighbours, but something of this sort——"

Augustus pressed his hand over his eyes for a
moment.

" I was ushered, I should tell my readers," he said,
" into the sanctum of the great novelist, an immense
salon furnished in the most exquisite taste. (Something about your fireplace.) Mr. da Vinci was seated
at his *escritoire*, absorbed in his work, and did not at
once perceive my entrance. At the far end of the
room was a magnificent three-manualled organ, on
which one of his secretaries, evidently a skilled
musician, was playing one of Bach's most elaborate
organ fugues. . . . Something of that sort."

" That would be lovely," said Susan enthusiastically; " but would it all come in the Ulrica column in
the *Evening Chronicle*? "

" Oh, no. This would be a bigger thing than
those mere jottings. One of my ' Chats with Cele-
brities ' which you may have seen in the *Weekly
Telegraph*. I write for them under the name of
Leonora. Ulrica will be busy this week with Miss

Susan Leg and her parties. We will discuss those
presently. Let us do Mr. da Vinci first. And do you
mind, Miss Leg, if I call you Mr. da Vinci as we chat?
It makes it more vivid to me."

" By no means," said Susan.

" Well, Mr. da Vinci," said Leonora, " may I
first ask you what you felt about that article by Mr.
Armstrong on your book, *Rosemary and Rue*, which
appeared last Sunday? "

Susan felt a billow of rage rising within her, but
she instantly suppressed it.

" Poor man, I was simply sorry for him," she
said. " As far as he was concerned, I felt unadulterated pity for a nature so sadly soured by
jealousy. But for myself, unadulterated amusement.
Roars of laughter, I assure you."

Leonora nodded.

" I'll say that you broke into ringing peals of
merriment at my question," she said. " That will be
the way to put it. And afterwards you said, ' Poor
fellow. Soured with jealousy.' A very good point:
he can't help hating it. Now what is the truth about
these four printings which Mr. Armstrong suggests
are not bona fide? "

" Better leave that to Nunky Cartwright," said
Rudolph. " He's sure to answer that in his new
blurb."

" Very well. I'll just say, Mr. da Vinci, that you
felt it beneath you to take any notice of such contemptible insinuations."

" Quite right," said R. da V. " Just what I felt.
Far beneath me."

" Now to save time," said Leonora, " I just jotted
down yesterday a few thoughts that came into my
mind about the manner in which you plan and execute
your romances. Shall I read them, and see if you
sanction them? "

" Please," said R. da V.

Augustus referred to his note-book.

"Leonora says, ' A dreamy look came into Mr.
da Vinci's eyes as I put this question to him about
his methods, and he sat silent, stroking the silky curve
of his black moustache——' "

"No, I'd rather be clean-shaven," said R. da V.

"It shall be done. . . . 'A dreamy look came
into his eyes. "It is difficult," he said, "to tell you
how the first idea comes to me. Perhaps some spirit
of the air, one of those celestial intelligences which
hover round us, whispers something in my ear.
Perhaps it comes to me in a dream, when, as you may
remember I said in *Absinthe and Aloes*, our souls
escape from our sleeping bodies, and wander far and
wide through the starry sky, and even behold the
golden gates of Heaven itself." ' "

"Oh, I'm so glad you put that in," said R. da V.
"Azaliel says that, and it's one of the most poetical
passages I ever wrote."

"Thank you. . . . Rudolph speaking: ' Then,
as I figure it, the idea takes root in my brain, and
puts forth leaves and flowers and luscious fruit. It
gains complete possession of me, and as soon as I
begin to write, I live in my book. It is more real to
me than my material existence, and when it is done
I feel lost and uncharted. Then perhaps for a little I
plunge into the gay world of Paris or Rome or London
again, but oh, how hollow I soon find it. I go back
to my country cottage——' "

"Why, that's just like the book I'm planning
now," said R. da V.

" ' I go back to my country cottage and my
solitude,' " resumed Leonora, " ' though how can I
call it solitude when the glories of nature are spread
around me, and I can commune with the immortal
minds of Shakespeare and Dante and Milton.' How
does that strike you as a framework, something to
work on? "

"Oh, it's beautiful," said Susan. "So noble and lofty. And I mean to read some Milton, just because Mr. Armstrong says he is overrated. I know who's overrated," she added with extraordinary venom. "And those who live in glass houses ought to know what they shouldn't do."

"I'll work that up then," said Leonora, "and send you a rough proof to-morrow, Mr. da Vinci. And now for Miss Susan Leg's dinner-party on Thursday."

Augustus was seized with the enthusiasm of the true social specialist.

"I've had many bits of interesting work in my time," he said, "but never such a dramatic job as this. Straight from R. da V.'s withering scorn of Mr. Armstrong we pass to Miss Leg's dinner-party at which he will be so honoured a guest. There's a situation for you! Now I should keep it small and cosy, Miss Leg, if I were you. There's Lady Eva Lowndes whom you thought of asking, and Mr. Jimmie Mason, and Mr. Armstrong and yourself——"

"And you, please, Mr. Bosanquet," said Susan.

"Very proud, I'm sure, and I wonder if I might suggest a great friend of mine. Lady Mackleton. She and I constantly meet at houses, which, if I may say so, we are fostering. There's not a woman whose name you see more often as being at luncheons and dinner-parties, and she's the best listener in London. I'll get her, if you approve."

"She sounds just the thing," said Susan. "Mr. Armstrong wants some strong listeners as I know very well. But do you think she would come?"

"Certainly. It's her profession. I ought to explain perhaps that she has a regular tariff, two guineas for dinner, or dinner and theatre, and one guinea for lunch with her taxi-fares. Or if you engage her for a series of six, she pays her own taxi. She is well worth it, I assure you."

" Oh, but is that quite safe? " asked Susan. " Suppose she told people that I paid her to come and dine? "

" And suppose you told people that she was paid to go out to dinner? " retorted Augustus.

" Yes, there is that," said Susan. " Please engage her. Then how about Mr. Cartwright? "

" Wiser not, I *think*," said Augustus. " If his new blurb for *Rosemary and Rue* is out, there might be a little stiffness between him and Mr. Armstrong. Six is an excellent number to begin on, Miss Leg. It will be one of those *intime* little parties, which are much more chic than any large party. And Ulrica will do it justice, I assure you. Now if you'll ask Uncle Bob to telephone round to your guests at once, we shall be fixed up."

Susan had never spent a more interesting week, or one more packed with excitements, since *Apples of Sodom* first started her career. She seemed to be living in one of her own books: life was opening out before her, right and left, like some great panorama of sunny and fruitful stretch of undiscovered country. *Rosemary and Rue*, terrible as an army with banners, was achieving such triumphs as never yet fell to the lot of the best of best-sellers, and her social career, to the sound of the honey-sweet flutings of Ulrica, kept step with it.

" To the delight of her numerous friends," said Ulrica, in the *Evening Chronicle* of next day, " Miss Susan Leg is now settled in her veritable *petit palais* in Durham Square, and will at once be commencing a series of those entertainments to which those who are fortunate enough to be invited so keenly look forward. A few of her *intimes* are dining with her on Thursday, among them being Mr. Arthur

Armstrong, M.P., the world-wide critic and novelist, Lady Mackleton, Mr. ' Jackie ' Mason, as his friends call him '' (an error on the part of Ulrica), '' Lady Eva Lowndes and others, and we hear talk of several fork-luncheons to follow.

'' This charming form of entertainment, devised by Miss Leg, bids fair to revolutionize social habits in the smart world. Busy men and women have not at this time of the year leisure for a long, elaborate lunch-party, so Miss Leg provides for them an exquisite cold buffet where guests help themselves, and sit where they please at one of the colour-scheme little tables for four persons, where they chat with their friends, taking their next course, if they choose, at some other table. I shall give my readers more detailed information about these dainty *al fresco* gatherings when I have been to Miss Leg's first party, which takes place on Friday in next week. With her well-known thoughtfulness she will provide *déjeuner maigre*, for her Roman Catholic friends. . . .''

Susan was delighted with these sumptuous para-graphs, and how generous it was of dear Mr. Bosanquet to credit her with the invention of fork-parties! Her delight was doubled when the next morning she got a note from Mrs. Mantrip, couched in the most polite terms, saying that she was sending with it an extremely interesting book that had just come out, called (oddly enough) *The Snake in the Grass*. Mrs. Mantrip felt sure that Miss Leg, like herself, would vastly enjoy it. Then followed (in this engaging note) a passage that was clearly the result of Ulrica's announcements. Mrs. Mantrip found that, after all, she was free on Thursday evening, since the lecture she meant to attend on the less-known novelists of the reign of William IV was cancelled, and she would be delighted to dine if Miss Leg had still a place for her. . . . Susan positively smacked her lips as she wrote an equally

urbane reply to Mrs. Mantrip, saying that she was
returning, with many thanks, the book she had so
kindly lent her, as, in the rush of social engagements
just now, she would never have time to read it, and
that she much regretted that her little party on Thursday was now complete. So that was that.

On the same morning there arrived for her, by
special messenger from Nunky, a copy of *Rosemary
and Rue* in its new jacket. The front cover had the
title at the top, and on the rest of the page, running
over on to the back, in startlingly vivid green letters
on a red ground, appeared a stunning manifesto:

" Mr. Arthur Armstrong, M.P., devotes one of his
famous articles in the *Sunday Chronicle* to *Rosemary
and Rue*. He says:

" ' Books occasionally appear which call for my
severest condemnation. They must be annihilated.
Such a one is *Rosemary and Rue*. . . . Nauseating
sentimentality . . . mawkish trash . . . a lady's
maid's lispings . . . twitterings of a typist. . . .
Enough of Mr. R. da Vinci.'

" The verdict of the public does not coincide with
that of Mr. Arthur Armstrong, M.P., for the fourth
printing of *Rosemary and Rue* is now being rapidly
exhausted. The public will, no doubt, correctly
estimate the value of his literary judgment. Moreover, he has the elephantine effrontery to call in
question the bona fides of these printings, and asks
for the number of copies actually sold. We readily
comply with this insulting request, and inform him
that up to date the sale has been 109,624 copies. We
await his apology for his insolent suggestion, and shall
probably continue to do so.

" H. R. CARTWRIGHT (*Publisher*)."

" That's a nasty one," said Susan with glee, as she

pored over this withering statement. " That's what
they call pulling the hair of the dog that bit you!
Clever Nunky!" And was there ever a neater
situation? For here was Rudolph da Vinci vicari-
ously smacking the face of Mr. Armstrong, M.P., and
Susan was welcoming him at her house, where he would
be helping her social career, while she studied him for
the fell purpose of *Amor Vincit*. " I seem to score all
round," said happy Susan.

Then came Thursday, and what a triumphant evening! Susan was free from care about the dinner itself,
for she could trust M. Rouen to give her guests all that
most flattered the palate, and Bosanquet saw to the
wine. He, too, was to be trusted, said Mr. Bosanquet,
for he had once been wine-waiter at a club for gour-
mets. As for any anxiety about the social side, the
moment Susan set eyes on Lady Mackleton all her fears
were at rest. Such a good-looking woman, such ease,
such agreeable manners! She sailed into the room, she
advanced to Susan with both hands stretched out, as
if meeting an old friend. " My dear, too delicious to
see you again," she said, " after all this long time!"
She was introduced to Lady Eva, and said something
very pleasant about Brosely Castle, implying that she
had once stayed there with her brother. She said to
Mr. Armstrong, " I know you don't remember me, but
I haven't forgotten. And, oh, your last book, Mr.
Armstrong. Perfect!" Her geniality, her mastery
at once set Susan at her ease, and she felt that all
she need do was to enjoy herself. Mr. Bosanquet had
supplied her with a rare bargain at the price of two
guineas and taxi-fare.

They went down to dinner, and Mr. Armstrong had
hardly tasted his soup before he asked Susan to come
to tea with him next Friday on the terrace of the
House of Commons. Then Lady Mackleton told her
she mustn't forget the Charity Concert at Norfolk
House. Would Susan pick her up, and they would

go together? Then Lady Eva asked her to come to
the meeting of the Psychical Research on Tuesday,
where she was reading a paper on haloes. Bosanquet
glided round the table in orbits as regular and noiseless
as the planets. Once only did anything occur to upset
his composure, and his hand trembled when, as he
was refilling Mr. Armstrong's glass with Chateau
Yquem 1864, Jimmie Mason said in that silly voice
of his :

" I saw your article on Rudolph da Vinci, Mr. Armstrong. Superb ! I read *Rosemary and Rue* till four
o'clock in the morning the other night. Laughed till
I cried."

" I have said my say," replied Mr. Armstrong, and
a marked acidity in his voice made Susan feel certain
that he had seen the new jacket.

But Bosanquet controlled himself, and the anxious
moment passed. With all these gratifying invitations
showered on her, Susan felt she was penetrating like
a steel drill into these high circles of culture and social
distinction which were her goal, while Rudolph was
battening on Mr. Armstrong. From now onwards, he
took possession of the whole table, and Lady Mackleton
settled down to listen.

Next evening Ulrica wrote such things about the
brilliance of the party as must have made Mrs. Mantrip writhe, and on Sunday came the crowning glory.
Susan had ordered the *Sunday Chronicle* on purpose
to read Mr. Armstrong's article on *The Brothers
Karamazov*, wanting to soak herself (for purposes of
reproduction) in his authoritative and pontifical style,
and her eyes grew wide with joy, as, breakfasting in
bed, she read the opening remarks.

" A rare experience has been mine this week. So
rare as to be almost unique. At least in England. I
dined at a house where I had never been before.
Though I expected a pleasant evening (or else I should

have refused), I found infinitely more. I had a perfect,
not a pleasant evening. The dinner was perfect. Five
courses. Not too many, and each a masterpiece. The
wine was perfect. The conversation was perfect. Six
people, all adepts in the art not only of talking but
of listening. After dinner a quarter of an hour in the
dining-room with a perfect cigar. Which is nearly as
rare as a perfect dinner.

" It is this instinct for perfection in life that I am
always seeking for. I seek for the same in literature.
I long to give undiluted praise. I seldom have the
opportunity. Last week I dispensed undiluted damna-
tion to Mr. Rudolph da Vinci. A painful duty. I
hated it. But I got my reward in that perfect dinner
on Thursday. This week I shall speak about Dostoevski's famous novel. It is not perfect. I wish it was.
Withal, passages of rare beauty."

Susan, like the saints, was joyful with glory, and
rejoiced in her bed. Those who had read Ulrica either
on Tuesday or Friday would know where Mr. Armstrong dined on Thursday, and those who read Mr.
Armstrong on Sunday would know what sort of an
evening he had had. Mrs. Mantrip took in both these
interesting journals, and the thought of that ill-judged
little note, which merely caused Susan to say " Hove,"
must be choking her. But Susan scarcely gloated over
that, for all her gloating powers were occupied with her
own progress and her great revenge, and there was
nothing to spare for that pitiful little ninepin, which
she had knocked down with but a cursory flip of her
fingers. Besides, Mrs. Mantrip was to cut a sordid
figure in *Amor Vincit*: it would be time to think of her
then. . . .

Though there was nothing more about her dinner,
Susan read the rest of Mr. Armstrong's article on *The
Brothers Karamazov* with great care, for the purpose
of caricaturing his style. She snipped out the first

paragraph for pasting into a scrap-book, which already
contained Leonora's chat with Rudolph da Vinci and
Ulrica's news about her forthcoming fork-luncheons.
The first was to take place on Friday, and she would
have tea on the terrace of the House of Commons
afterwards. Monday and Tuesday would see her at
the Charity Concert with Lady Mackleton and at the
meeting of the Psychical Research Society with Lady
Eva. '' The pace is getting terrific,'' thought Susan
as she went to her onyx bath with nickel fittings, '' but,
thank God, I'm strong.''

Then, in addition to these social triumphs, Susan
was already tremendously busy over the new book.
Never yet having drawn from life, she found it added
a scarifying vividness to her pen, if, before settling
down to the delineation of the critic, she read over
a paragraph or two of Mr. Armstrong's review of
Rosemary and Rue. The sense that she was writing
about the author of that outrage—he was to be called
Francis Grout—gave a new power to her elbow, and
she was astonished at the heat of the furnace that blazed
in her brain. Pre-war vitriol of the strongest grade
was her ink: the paper on which she wrote should have
hissed and bubbled and grown black (as indeed it
rapidly did) with such acidity. Then at the opposite
pole of her creation was Serena Lomond, this young
woman hardly more than a girl, on whom Nature had
lavished beauty and genius and the pure, untainted
soul of a child. Here the living model was herself,
even as the initials were hers: she saw herself
endowed with these admirable qualities, and lent them
to Serena. She had told Leonora in her interview
with Rudolph that the ignoble Armstrong's review had
only roused in her unadulterated pity for a nature
soured by jealousy, and for herself unadulterated
amusement. That was how, artistically, she regarded
herself, and she worked off in her picture of Armstrong
the chattering rage which really filled her when she

stoked herself up with the outrageous stuff. Bosanquet, going up to bed, sometimes heard, mingling with the strains of the renovated gramophone, little peals of silvery merriment: it was easy to guess that Serena-Susan was laughing with Nursie over the press-notices before giving them to the Great Dane to tear to pieces. Or there might come from the room a tentative tinkling from the piano with orange legs: that was Susan-Serena improvising. She had always written from the heart, but never yet with so superb a gusto.

It was no longer necessary now for Bosanquet to make surreptitious visits to the manuscript-drawer when Susan was out, in order to keep abreast of the romance on which she was engaged. He read it day by day, like a serial, for when she left the house for her airing or some brilliant social engagement, she always gave him the numerous sheets she had written since the previous day; and, when he returned them, sometimes his eyes were soft with emotion, sometimes glittering with indignation, and as often as not his wide experience of the world was useful, his taste, his quality as Molière's housemaid.

" If you'll excuse my saying so," he burst out one evening when Susan was having a tray in the drawing-room, " I think that Francis Grout is quite one of your most powerful creations. I almost seem to know him, if not quite. Wasn't I glad when Miss Serena went for him with her riding-whip! Fancy a man who called himself a man striking that beautiful Great Dane of yours—I should say of Miss Serena's—when it gave him its paw! "

Susan was charmed with the way in which Bosanquet instinctively identified Serena with herself.

" I'm glad you liked that piece, Bosanquet," said she. " I thought it was pretty powerful myself. Any criticisms? "

" Nothing to mention, miss," said Bosanquet.
" But when you—I mean Miss Serena—has the Earl
of Kent—what a nice nobleman, miss !—to tea he
shouldn't be the son of a viscount. That wouldn't
be quite regular. An earl, I should say, might be
the father of a viscount, but I've never observed one
who was a viscount's son. And when the Earl sends
Miss Serena that case of Chateau Margaux, which she
gives to the consumptive railway-porter, it mustn't
be described as a rich champagne. More of a claret,
miss."

" Thank you, Bosanquet," said Susan; " if you're
quite sure about those, I'll correct them."

The resumption of work only a couple of days after
the completion of *Julian Beltravers* implied a resumption of the gramophone which, so boundless was the
flow of inspiration, was practically incessant, except
when Susan was engaged on social success. Maddened
by music, Elizabeth went in to consult Jimmie as to
what further steps could be taken, and also to talk
over Susan generally. There was a growing feeling
in the Square that there was something mysterious
about her, which it would be nice to fathom. Elizabeth often dropped in to see a friend a few minutes
before lunch-time, and that was the hour she chose
now.

" It's getting intolerable again, Jimmie," she
said. " From ten till half-past one yesterday, and
from two till half-past four, and from six till eight,
and from nine till eleven. I think we had better give
her another dose. It answered excellently last time:
there was no gramophone next morning. Just to
remind."

Jimmie hesitated. He still remembered the
marvellous dinner, and he had been asked to a fork-
luncheon. He did not want to risk his footing, for
never was there such food.

" I dined with her the other night," he said. " So I don't want to do anything she might take as unfriendly."

" Good? " asked Elizabeth, diverted for the moment.

" My dear, a dream. In fact I did dream about it. And you must have seen what Mr. Armstrong said about a perfect dinner last Sunday. That was the one."

" Well, I haven't been so favoured," said Elizabeth, " and I must get on without any dreams. All I know is that she's making the day a nightmare to me. I vote we give her an all-day concert. I've got rather a cold and I don't mind stopping in to-morrow. Morning till night I vote for."

" All right. I shall be out all day. Dentist in the morning, concert in the afternoon, and dining out. I'll tell Figgis to keep my gramophone at it."

Elizabeth waggled her hand to Mrs. Mantrip who passed the window with a book in her hand. Elizabeth stealthily leant out and saw that she was standing on Susan's threshold. So much for Margaret's determination to have nothing more to do with her !

" I can't make out who Miss Leg is," she said, " and I've a feeling she's somebody. It's little more than a month since she settled in, and nobody took much notice of her, and here she is now, with her parties in the papers, not taking much notice of us. Did she shine at her own house more than she shone at that dreadful lunch of Margaret's, when the fish was putrid ? "

" Not much opportunity for anyone to shine," said he. " Mr. Armstrong held forth the whole time. Golly, what a lot of books that chap must have written ! He talked about them and his speeches in the House the whole time, whether his mouth was full or empty. It was generally full."

" But she can't be anything literary," said Elizabeth. " Totally uneducated, I should say."

Lunch was announced. Jimmie had no opportunity to tell Figgis not to say it was ready till Elizabeth had gone, as he had meant to do.

" Come along in to lunch, then," he said, without any warmth in his voice.

" Dear me ! Half-past one. So it is," said Elizabeth. " So kind of you, Jimmie."

" Not at all," said he. " I hope there will be enough."

Next day accordingly, as an encore to the device that had been successful before, the grinding of the gramophones at Nos. 24 and 26 Durham Square (Jimmie's house and Elizabeth's) was incessant, and Susan revelled in the punishment that was being inflicted on her. Occasionally she turned off her own instrument, for there was something wonderfully satisfactory in the muddle produced by those of her neighbours playing different tunes. She had not known how far-reaching in its effects was the power of music. At one period, Beethoven's famous symphony in C Minor was going on, loud and strong, on the left, and Melba and Caruso were singing their equally popular duet on the right. She did not know what either of these classical pieces happened to be, but the effect was tumultuous and most stimulating. But admirably as these loud dissonances suited her, Nos. 23 and 27 were not so appreciative. As the day went on Mr. Salt, the Serpentine swimmer in No. 23, and Elizabeth's outside neighbour (from the point of focus) in No. 27, grew frenzied with the unceasing melodies. Without any consultation at all, they both of them determined that next day they would administer to Jimmie and Elizabeth the treatment that the latter were administering to Susan.

In consequence, next day the beleaguerers became the beleaguered, and hour after hour these two unfortunate householders in the Square that was usually so peaceful, were subjected to incessant music from both sides of them, for Susan's book was progressing so well that again she did not take her usual airing, and Nos. 23 and 27 were giving them the drastic hints that they had been administering to her. Elizabeth was driven to sit in the garden most of the afternoon, and, in the intervals of playing Patience in a high wind, to give her Pekinese, now augmented by Sabrina's three surviving puppies, more exercise than they had ever enjoyed before. Jimmie's case was even more ghastly, for he had caught Elizabeth's cold, and had had a really horrid visit to his dentist. (" Come again in two days if the pain continues.") So he was house-bound, and at uncertain intervals, as he tried to recapture his amusement in *Rosemary and Rue*, he kept exclaiming, " Oh, my God, won't it ever stop? " (referring not only to toothache but to music). Right in the centre of this disturbed area sat industrious Susan, scribbling away like mad under the inspiration of her own wireless and gramophone.

Though so short a period had passed since the crisis of pro- and anti-dog, it looked as if more trouble, and that of the acutest and most unusual kind, was brewing. What if Nos. 22 and 28, exterior neighbours of Nos. 23 and 27, began to take the same reprisals against them as Nos. 23 and 27 had taken against Nos. 24 and 26? There seemed no logical end to it. From No. 25, as if a stone had been dropped into the tranquil pool of the Square, there spread these concentric circles of incessant melodies, this ever-widening epidemic of mechanical music. At this rate it might spread over the whole of the district in a few weeks. Musical as English people were, they might well be driven mad with so much melody.

About six o'clock that evening Jimmie could stand
it no longer. Susan's music from No. 25, " Land of
Hope and Glory" from No. 23 and his tooth had,
between them, driven him nearly crazy. Regardless
of his cold, he went out without a hat, and rang the
bell of No. 25. Bosanquet, beaming with pleasurable
anticipation of a great literary treat after this musical
day, opened to him.

" I want to see Miss Leg," he said. " Most
important."

" I'm afraid, sir, it's impossible to disturb Mademoiselle," said Bosanquet. " I know she's busy."

" But, good God, how can she be busy with that
infernal din going on ? " cried Jimmie.

" I couldn't say, sir," said Bosanquet, " but the
facts are as I represent them."

" But I must see her," said Jimmie. " My
mental equilibrium is tottering."

" Very sorry to hear it, sir," said Bosanquet,
still holding on to the door.

Jimmie tried to remember that he was a gentleman and not a burglar, and miserably failed. He
dived under Bosanquet's arm, and with the agility
of despair scudded up the staircase. He knocked at
the door of Susan's drawing-room, and without waiting for the lady's answer plunged in, for Bosanquet
was close on his heels. There at her table Susan was
sitting. The trumpet of the loud-speaker was bellowing into her ear, and she was swiftly writing on a
sheet of blue foolscap paper. Other sheets covered
with script paved the table. On the wireless the
"Foundations of music " were being well and truly
laid by an accomplished pianist playing Chopin's
Études. Against the brazen hubbub of the gramophone they sounded like the singing of a tea-kettle
soon about to boil.

Some echo of Jimmie's knock must have subconsciously penetrated into Susan's brain, for, while she

went on writing as busily as ever without looking
up, she gave a little silvery laugh as if distantly aware
that somebody had entered. She began to speak in
an artless treble voice like a young girl.

" I know you've come to scold me, Bosanquet,"
she said. " I'm very naughty. But I will be good.
I'll go out at once, so ring up for my car. Such a
lot for you to read."

The agitated Bosanquet had now entered.

" Very sorry, miss," he said, " but I did my
best. Mr. Mason, he ducked under my arm——"

Susan looked up for the first time, and gave a
slight scream. There was a strange gentleman there.
Even so had Francis Grout forced his way into
Serena's presence. Nature copying Art.

" I'm sure I apologize, Miss Leg, for intruding
like this," said Jimmie, " but really I'm on the
verge of madness between your gramophone and my
toothache and No. 23's gramophone. I know you
wouldn't like to see me taken away in a strait-waist-
coat."

Susan came to the surface, gasping for breath
like a diver after a prolonged immersion. With a
sweep of her hand she thrust those numerous sheets,
those pearls she had gathered, into the manuscript-
drawer.

" I am astonished at this unwarrantable intrusion,"
she said, quoting verbatim what Serena had said to
Francis Grout in the same circumstances.

" I know," wailed Jimmie. " I admit it.
Quite inexcusable of me. I forgot that I was a
gentleman. I forgot that an Englishwoman's house
is her castle. But I appeal to you, Miss Leg, in
the sacred name of humanity. I throw myself upon
your mercy. Anything you like."

They both had to shout to make themselves
heard, but it occurred to neither of them to turn off
the bellowing gramophone.

"But what is it all about?" yelled Susan. "Sit down, dear Mr. Mason. Oh, of course, I accept your apology completely. But tell me what's wrong. You look so worried. Bosanquet, a chair for Mr. Mason."

Bosanquet drew up a throne sumptuously inlaid with tortoiseshell and mother-of-pearl and patines of bright gold.

"Well, it was yesterday that Elizabeth Conklin and I felt we couldn't bear it," he shouted, "and so as a protest against your gramophone, which really, dear Miss Leg, went on the entire damned day, we started ours. We thought that would give you a hint, as it had done once before when we played all night."

(Outside in the Square a wild excitement was brewing. The Vicar, Elizabeth and Mrs. Mantrip all happened to meet on the pavement just outside, and through the open window came the frightful sounds of Jimmie and Susan yelling at each other. Some awful quarrel, such as had never been known in the tranquil precinct since the purging of it by Papa, was clearly in progress. Would it culminate in the report of firearms and the ultimate shriek of the victim? They stared at each other with a wild surmise, and did nothing at all.)

Bosanquet intervened. His good sense seldom failed him.

"Shall I turn off the instrument, miss?" he bawled. "I think you and Mr. Mason would save your throats if I did."

"Yes, please do, Bosanquet," screamed Susan. "What a good idea. There! Now go on, Mr. Mason."

("All has ended well," said the Vicar, as the storm was stilled. "Bosanquet has joined them. I heard his voice. Thank God!")

"You see on that night," said Jimmie, feeling as if he had come out of a roaring tunnel, "we thought we would show you what it felt like to have that row eternally going on, and we thought we had succeeded, for you didn't give us any music next morning. So we reminded you again. Ghastly failure. You didn't stop, and now the houses outside Mrs. Conklin's and mine have been giving us a hint. We're between two fires, each of us, and I'm nearly crazy. That's why I forgot myself, and why I throw myself on your mercy."

The fierce fire of R. da V.'s genius faded out of Susan's eyes, and left those insignificant orbs mildly glowing with womanly compassion.

" Dear me, what a trying situation for you, Mr. Mason," she said. " I am so sorry. You must have had a dreadful day, toothache and all, in spite of your love of music. I remember that night you spoke of so well. My instrument had bust up, or, I should say, was incapacitated, and I was so glad of your delicious music and Mrs. Conklin's, too, of course, for I'm devoted to the gramophone, and can't have too much of it. But certainly it mustn't spread like that: I quite realize. And all my fault."

" Not at all," said Jimmie eagerly. " Don't reproach yourself for the past, Miss Leg. But it would be so nice if, for the future, an hour's music a day, or perhaps two, would be sufficient for you."

Rudolph da Vinci, banked down for the moment by Susan's womanly compassion, shot forth a fierce finger of flame in protest. Two hours a day, when his furnace was in full blast and his metal molten, was a ludicrous and pitiful allowance. Though Susan felt kind, he was blazing with indignation.

" I quite see your point of view," she said, torn in two between these conflicting claims, " but there's mine as well. So difficult to explain. Isn't it called something congenital, when you must have certain conditions for—— Bosanquet, help me."

"It's quite true what Mademoiselle says, sir," said Bosanquet. "At certain periods it's most necessary for her to be steeped, you may call it, in loud noises. Her nature demands it, sir, and two hours a day would be quite insufficient. It's congenital, sir, just that, as Mademoiselle puts it."

"But who could work or eat or sleep or anything else with that going on?" cried Jimmie.

A gloomy silence descended on the three. No further explanation could possibly be given, and that which had been given was such as would be expected only from the very worst wards of Bedlam. But again Bosanquet proved his quality.

"Excuse me, miss," he said, "but, if I might make a suggestion, what about my pantry? It's in the basement, it's got a baize door, and it has outside walls, not contiguous, if I may use the expression, to your neighbours. I'm sure I could make you comfortable there, miss, with the chair and table to which you're accustomed, and I could easily do my work in the servants' hall and the scullery. I don't think any noise to speak of would penetrate outside."

Susan hailed this hopeful idea with enthusiasm, and the necessary experiments were at once made. Bosanquet carried the gramophone down to his pantry and closed the baize door, while Jimmie went back to his house to listen. He returned with the glad tidings that only the faintest tinkle of sound, rather agreeable than otherwise, could be heard. So without delay the table with the manuscript-drawer was brought down from the drawing-room, and Susan's accustomed chair, and a stock of the regulation blue foolscap, and the malachite inkstand. A Persian rug was spread over the oilcloth on the floor, an Oriental embroidery was cast over the sink, and on the wall hung Bosanquet's book-shelf containing a Wesleyan hymn-book and the published works of Rudolph da Vinci: the pantry became the most beautiful little boudoir. As soon as all was ready, Susan came down the kitchen stairs, while the gramophone bellowed louder and louder as she approached this improvised shrine. She shut the baize door and fairly clapped her hands for joy, for the noise was magnificent: in the more confined area of the pantry the air was thick with trumpeting melody. As soon as she took up her pen she knew how harmonious were her surroundings, and telling Bosanquet that she would not go out at all to-day, she plunged into her work at the point where Jimmie's incursion had interrupted it.

M. Rouen, an ardent votary of Terpsichore, as Rudolph da Vinci would have described him, was equally pleased with this new arrangement, and had several brisk turns with the first kitchenmaid, in the intervals of his professional art. She danced beautifully.

IX

THE weather broke, and in accordance with established ritual, a taxi came up the Square at five minutes to eight the next evening through the pouring rain, and stopped opposite No. 22, loudly hooting. Mrs. Mantrip, as soon as the driver condescended to open the door of the vehicle, made a rush across the pavement and got in, calling out in her shrill voice: " No. 24, please, next." There she had to wait, for Jimmie, deeply mistrusting Lady Eva's cook, the fruits of whose kitchen he was shortly to eat, was having a cupful of very strong soup and a sandwich; and, distrusting Captain Lowndes's wine, was enjoying a nice glass of old brown sherry. Thus fortified, he could last through the evening, even if he was obliged to drink water and to conceal the greater part of the viands he was given below his knife and fork. He was sorry to keep the taxi waiting, but the soup was very hot.

He came out with galoshes over his evening shoes, and an umbrella over his head. The rain was exceedingly heavy and drummed on it. Having arrived at the door of the taxi, he had a polite word with the driver about this horrid night, said " No. 26, please, next," and got in, furling his umbrella. He had sat down by Mrs. Mantrip's side, but then, recollecting that there was to be another lady, put down an extra seat. He bumped his head in this polite transference of himself, and left his umbrella leaning against the back seat.

After a further journey of the same length as the

last, the taxi stopped again, the driver trumpeted and
clicked the record of a third passenger on to his dial.
When the door of No. 26 was opened a quantity of
dogs poured out. Elizabeth shepherded them back
again and got in. In the agitation of the moment, for
Sabrina had a cold, she gave No. 64 as the final stop-
page: this was a mistake, for No. 46 was the correct
destination. There was a board up at No. 64 to say
it was to be let furnished, and her error was discovered.
In the meantime a large van had backed across the
road just behind, and as no amount of hootings would
induce its driver to move it, the taxi had to drive on
into Durham Road. It was delayed some little while
owing to the stress of traffic, and then, entering the
Square again where it had done some minutes before,
made the circuit till it came to No. 46. In consequence
of Elizabeth's stupid mistake, the two others had been
rather cold to her, but now it was discovered that
Jimmie's dripping umbrella, leaning against the seat
between the two ladies, had wet their stockings. Instantly there was a re-shuffling of sentiments, and the
two sisters in misfortune hurried into the house leaving
Jimmie to pay the entire costs of this protracted
expedition. They were ten minutes late.

Captain Lowndes was not dining at home that
night: he was so pleased with the result of his X-ray
examination that day that he was having a " jolly "
all by himself at a restaurant where dancing was to be
had, and so there were just the four of them. The
soup was a judicious mixture of pepper, sherry and hot
water in the old English style. Lady Eva apologized
for its being only tepid, and everyone knew that a
reproach for their lateness was intended. Then, oddly
enough, considering that they were all such tried and
trusted old friends, there was a long silence. The
hostess was psychical, Mrs. Mantrip was literary,
Elizabeth was canine, and Jimmie was musical. Perhaps this very diversity of tastes caused the silence:

there was so much to choose from. Or it may have been the depressing influence of the soup. Eventually Lady Eva broke it.

"I went to the Psychical Research meeting a few afternoons ago," she said, "and read a paper——"

"You took Miss Leg with you, didn't you?" asked Elizabeth.

"Yes, we went together," said Lady Eva.

This seemed to come to much the same thing: Elizabeth had guessed right.. Then fish.

"I was going out shopping this morning," said Elizabeth—"really the price of the ox-liver I always give my dogs is monstrous—when I met that French chef who has lately come to the Square. An Alsatian was carrying his market-basket for him."

"Miss Leg's chef and dog, I suppose," said Jimmie, making a careful cache of his fish. It was soft, grey, dead fish, which in life, he imagined, must have fed on duckweed.

"I came across the most interesting book the other day," said Mrs. Mantrip. "*Stories from the boyhood of Charles Kingsley*. A book that I should have thought everybody would have been interested in."

"That was the second book that you lent to Miss Leg, wasn't it?" said Elizabeth. "You took it yourself, just before lunch, two days ago."

Mrs. Mantrip said that that was the one.

"I had a horrid day of toothache yesterday," said Jimmie. "I disliked every hour of it till the evening. Altogether a day of worries——"

"When Miss Leg's gramophone went on without ever stopping," interrupted Elizabeth. "Oh, yes, and we heard your voice and hers bawling at each other. What *was* happening?"

Here, then, were these four old friends full of various interests. One had started the subject of Psychical Research, another the price of ox-liver, a third the boyhood of Charles Kingsley, the fourth toothache.

These covered a vast range of topics; it should have
been easy to have a lively and pleasant discussion on
any of them, but no sooner had each been introduced
than, in the manner of a transformation scene, it faded
away and the figure of Miss Leg superimposed itself.
They had all tried to talk about something else, but
such efforts were vain, and they gave it up.

" Tell us all about it," cried the three ladies. If
they had been singing in a glee, with their eyes fixed
on the conductor, they could not have made a more
pat and punctual entrance.

" There she was," said Jimmie, " with her head,
I assure you, *in* the gramophone trumpet, writing away
for all she was worth on blue foolscap."

" That's what I told you all ever so long ago," said
Elizabeth. " I saw her one night sitting in the window
hard at it. When she writes, she always turns on the
gramophone, and when the gramophone's on you may
be sure she's writing."

" Not proved by any means," said Mrs. Mantrip.
" A very hasty conclusion, Liz."

Elizabeth hated that argumentative manner and
she wanted to hear more about Susan. So she snubbed
her friend.

" I know you don't turn on the gramophone when
you're writing your father's life, Margaret," she said,
" but then, you see, other people are different. Go
on, Jimmie."

" I believe you're right, Liz," he said. " At any
rate there's a great deal in what you say. Bosanquet
had already told me that she was busy and that I
couldn't see her, but when we had—had settled that
and I went upstairs, there she was, so busy that she
never saw me come in."

" Then she's stopped being busy," said Mrs. Mantrip. " There hasn't been a sound to-day."

" Wrong again, dear Margaret," said he. " The
gramophone hasn't ceased from morning till night,

though you haven't heard it. But I have: very faint
and rather pleasant. But where do you think she's
been busy? That's a teaser. You shall guess."

Mrs. Mantrip gave a shrill laugh to show that these
snubs made no difference to her natural gaiety.

"Really, I don't know why we're all talking about
poor Miss Leg," she said. "There are surely more
interesting subjects."

"I don't know of any," said Elizabeth. "I guess
she's been in the wine-cellar, Jimmie."

"No, but you're hot. Nobody else guessing?
Well, she's been in the pantry. Bosanquet took the
gramophone down there to see if it could be heard
from my house, and, as I tell you, only so faintly that
it was rather agreeable. That's where she's been, for
I looked in this afternoon to tell her how satisfactory
it was, and she came up the kitchen stairs with a great
ink-mark on her finger, and said the pantry was ever
so comfortable."

"It's a very good pantry," said Mrs. Mantrip.
"My last tenant built it out. And a very suitable
place for Miss Leg. I should think she would be much
happier among her servants. Bosanquet sits with her,
I suppose, and cleans the silver. I wonder if he's
married to her."

"My dear, don't be so poisonous," said Lady Eva.
"So bad for your halo. And you know you would go
to dine there if she asked you."

"Unfortunately for the truth of that supposition,"
said Mrs. Mantrip, "she did ask me on the night on
which you went, and I refused. I merely want to have
nothing to do with her. That's all."

"Oh, skittles, dear Margaret," said Jimmie in his
cosiest manner. "How can you say such things?
Why, you asked her if you mightn't come after all,
when you sent her the first book which she sent back.
She told me so herself. And Bosanquet doesn't sit with
her; he cleans the silver in the servants' room and the

scullery. . . . Well, while I was there chatting to her this afternoon, Mr. Cartwright called, and she said, ' Go down into the pantry, Nunky, and see my new study——' "

" The publisher? " asked Lady Eva.

" Yes. So he must have known about her work. The whole thing begins to hang together, and if you ask me, I believe she's writing a book for him to publish."

" Life in a butler's pantry," said Mrs. Mantrip meditatively.

" No, dear Margaret, because she was working at it before she went to the pantry. That was only yesterday. And then there's her friendship with Mr. Armstrong. I believe there's a literary side to her, though she won't read your books. And now I come to something that only happened to-day, and I'm not sure that it's not the most interesting of all."

" We are still speaking of poor Miss Leg? " asked Mrs. Mantrip.

" I am, but you needn't listen."

Mrs. Mantrip assumed an expression of infinite patience, and with an absent smile balanced her coffee-spoon on the edge of her saucer.

" It concerns her past, and it's most curious," said Jimmie. (It was no use: Mrs. Mantrip let her coffee-spoon fall on to the tablecloth, and attended violently.) " As far as we've known hitherto, she's had no past. She just happened. But to-day I sent for my accountant to do my July bills, and her name's Miss Mimps. Middle-aged. She adds them all up for me, and goes into them, and draws a cheque which I sign and she pays them. Never a mistake——"

" Dear Mason, we don't want Mimps's present, but Leg's past," cried Lady Eva.

" A little patience," said Jimmie. " I'm coming to it. Well, this morning I was standing on my balcony expecting Miss Mimps, when she appeared coming up the Square, and at the same moment Miss Leg came out of her house. As soon as Minnie Mimps saw her she called out quite loud: ' Why, if it isn't Susan ! How are you, Susan ? ' ''

'' And what did Susan say? '' asked Mrs. Mantrip breathlessly, quite forgetting that she deplored their interest in so trivial a topic.

'' She said ' How-de-do.' Like that. Quite coldly, and walked quickly on. Then up came Minnie Mimps looking vexed, and though I make it a rule not to talk to that sort of person about my friends, there come times when you can't help it. This was one of them. I had to know.''

'' I should think so, indeed,'' said Elizabeth. '' Well? ''

Jimmie made a dramatic pause and tapped the table. It was like the knocking in *Macbeth*.

'' Six years ago,'' he said, '' Minnie Mimps and Susan Leg were employed in a typewriting agency at Brighton. Susan didn't type: she sat at a larger table, and punched holes and counted words and looked for misprints. Then one day she went out to lunch at the Regency Palace Hotel with a gentleman friend of hers. Susan told Minnie Mimps so herself. Very shortly afterwards, Minnie Mimps thinks at the end of that week, she left the agency. She still lived in Brighton, for Minnie saw her about occasionally, and she said that an uncle had left her some money. She had lodgings, facing the sea, rather expensive, and Minnie Mimps went there to tea once, and remembers she had a gramophone. Then she drifted away from all her old friends, and Minnie hadn't seen her for several years till this morning.''

'' I don't believe in that uncle,'' said Mrs. Mantrip, who could no longer make a feint of not being interested.

'' Nor do I particularly,'' said Jimmie. '' But one can't help believing in the money.''

Lady Eva rapped the table.

" I've thought of something," she said. " She calls Mr. Cartwright Nunky. I heard her at the fork-luncheon."

" My dear, you *are* brilliant," said Jimmie. " But there are objections. He can't have left her all that money, because he isn't dead. Who can have left it to her? Was it the gentleman friend at the Regency Palace? And if so, who was he? You won't persuade me he was what they call her protector."

A glance at the faces of the three ladies showed him that they had no thought of persuading him of anything of the kind.

" No, poor thing, not *that*," said Mrs. Mantrip. " But——"

" I've another idea," cried Lady Eva. " How about the gentleman friend being Mr. Cartwright? I suggest he became Nunky to her afterwards when she got to know him."

" But then there's the money," said Elizabeth.

Jimmie became thoroughly excited.

" I believe we may be on the right track," he said. " I suggest that all the money does come from Mr. Cartwright, *qua* publisher, not *qua* Nunky. She's always writing. What happens to it all? I believe he publishes her books."

Mrs. Mantrip gave a loud, acid laugh. She had been almost too kind about Susan's moral integrity.

" How sarcastic you are, Jimmie," she said. " Making fun of poor Miss Leg like that! "

" Anything is possible with a woman who sits and scribbles with her head in a loud-speaker," said he.

" Then let us go to the library to-morrow," she said, " and ask for Miss Susan Leg's latest book. Such a run on them I expect that they'll have no copies in."

Lady Eva rose.

" Well, how about bridge ? " she said. " But I stick to it, that Leg's got a stupendous imagination. I told her she ought to cultivate it, and perhaps she is writing a book. How's Papa's life getting on, Mantrip ? "

" Wonderfully well. Such a busy week I've had over it."

Lady Eva looked fixedly at her hair as she passed her in the doorway.

" Anchovy-paste," she murmured to herself.

Jimmie went up with the ladies though he felt himself quite safe alone against the seductions of a pale, tawny port. He knew it. Sweet to the mouth but of an incomparable bitterness later on. The card-table was ready, and also a copy of the rules of auction-bridge. Durham Square treated contract with contempt, and said very severe things about it. Elizabeth had lately made a brilliant *mot*. " If you want your partner to go five spades," she said, " all you've got to do is to ask for the matches." That quite killed contract in Durham Square. But a copy of the rules of auction was still useful if there was a divergence of opinion about penalties or dealings out of turn. This latter irregularity was of very common occurrence when Mrs. Mantrip was of the party, for she had an absent-minded habit of picking up the pack, when, at the conclusion of each hand, she criticized the play of her partner and of her opponents, and presented it to be cut to herself. She then dealt and continued to talk with great rapidity, so as to complete the deal before her right was challenged. These manœuvres, however, were widely known now, and whenever she began to deal, even if it was quite proper that she should do so, calculations had to be made. Again, she often made underbids, and a copy of the rules was required. . . .

The game to-night went on to an unusually late hour, and Captain Lowndes had been heard to go stealthily upstairs while the gamblers were still at it. There were passionate interludes when the fresh light thrown on Susan by her discarded friend Mimps was warmly discussed, and it was after midnight when the joint taxi was rung for, as the rain still fell heavily, to convey Lady Eva's guests to the opposite side of the Square. Jimmie had ordered a little cold supper to be left ready for him, and this was a prudent measure, for he had eaten next to nothing. As he partook of it in his silent house, he could hear through the drip of the rain outside the faint noise of the gramophone from his neighbour's pantry. From a back window he could see the pantry itself, and, sure enough, there was still a light from it shining out on to Susan's back yard. " I feel convinced that it's a book she is writing," he said to himself, " and it must be a long one, for, barring a couple of days, the gramophone has been going on ever since she came here."

August was now at hand, and the householders in the Square were completing their holiday plans. Elizabeth laid hers with considerable foresight, and generally managed to quarrel with her cook early in July. Her cook thereupon gave her a month's notice, and thus there would only be two servants to support in idleness during her own holiday. Their mistress betook herself to a farm-house high up on Dartmoor, taking the entire kennel of dogs with her, and walked about incessantly all day trying to reduce her figure. This healthful and economical existence, however, gave her a prodigious appetite, and though her friends, when she returned, were unanimous in telling her that she looked very well, nobody but a sycophant could say that she looked thinner. Jimmie Mason went down to his house at Cookham for a couple of months, and rejuvenated himself with parties of bright young people, much romping and bathes in

Cookham Weir if the weather was very warm. He wore a bathing-dress of the Bath Club colours, a coquettish straw hat to protect him from the sun, and paddled about at the tail of the pool when there was no undertow. He had a gondola, too, in which he rowed old ladies of title up and down Cookham reach, dressed in spotless white flannels, with a scarlet sash round his waist and a scarlet cap with a tassel on his head, and called out "Stali" or "Sinistra" to approaching traffic until everybody felt they were back in Venice.

The Vicar went to play golf at Westward Ho! and subsequently to study Yoga with a saintly Hindu, who could swallow his tongue, at Bournemouth. Lady Eva and her husband went to Harrogate for a cancer-cure, and Mrs. Mantrip stayed on in the Square throughout the month with the avowed intention of finishing, or rather beginning, if the truth was known, the Life of her father. Her annual announcement was that she intended to stop in London during August and to have a couple of months on the Riviera in the winter, or to go to Cairo to see the treasures of Tut-ankh-amen. On the approach of winter she usually altered her plans and decided to go to Madeira in the spring. When spring came, she made more plans for going to the Land of the Midnight Sun in August. By these judicious postponements, she gave the impression of travelling a great deal, and accomplished her object of never leaving London at all.

So, morning after morning now, as the Square grew emptier, she sat in her library surrounded by all the influences which should conduce to the successful handling of her literary aim : there were her father's diaries, his letters, his voluminous sermons; there were stacks of the lives of notable ecclesiastics by the study of which she could learn how this sort of thing was done; there was her schedule of the contents of

her book; there was plenty of ink in her ink-bottle.
Nothing, in fact, was lacking except the elementary
accomplishment of writing down what she wanted to
say. It was indeed time to begin, for had she seen
(or only fancied she had seen) faint smiles on the faces
of her friends, when she had told them how well the
great work was progressing?

But, morning after morning, the same inexplicable
barrenness persisted, and though the schedule grew
more and more detailed, and a whole fresh page of
notes on " personal characteristics " was added to the
firm framework, she could not get started on this or
any other chapter. How was it done? . . . She took
Rosemary and Rue from behind the baize curtain:
there was a notable paragraph describing the Earl of
Truro, the fine oval of his face, his high-bridged,
aquiline nose, his mouth, sensitive as a woman's, his
curly golden hair, his great stature, his fine long-
fingered hands. To read that through was to realize
the magic of the man at once, and if, *mutatis mutandis,*
she followed the lines of that, she could hardly help
producing an equally vivid portrait of her father. He,
too, had a magic of his own; few came in contact
with him without feeling spiritually and intellectually
braced. With *Rosemary and Rue* propped up in front
of her, she began to write.

" My father's face was square rather than oval, and
conveyed an impression of power. His nose was
somewhat short. Not much of his mouth could be seen
as he grew a beard and moustache from the time he
took Holy Orders, but an earlier photograph of him
when a boy shows that this feature had a remarkable
firmness for one of his tender years. In later years his
hair, never very abundant, became streaked, though
no more, with grey. He was about five foot eight
in height, and his hands were of normal size and
shape. . . ."

Mrs. Mantrip paused and read this over. She glanced at the portrait of her father that hung above the mantelpiece, and wondered whether anyone who read what she had written would derive as vivid an idea of Papa's appearance as she did when she read those few lines about the Earl of Truro. It did not seem probable, but perhaps more detail would give her portrait the vividness that it at present lacked. She wrote again:

" His forehead was of no very marked type, his eyes were hazel in colour, and in later life he wore tortoise-shell spectacles for reading, though his sight was very good otherwise. His eyebrows were slightly arched, and in cold weather he wore mittens. His chin, like his mouth, was concealed by his beard, which was slightly reddish in hue, and he wore a signet ring on the third finger of his left hand. . . ."

" That is more like him," she thought. " There are a great many true touches in that. Anyone who reads that carefully ought to get a very fair idea of him."

She began a fresh paragraph.

" Such was his general appearance when he gave up parochial work and came to live in Durham Square, where he died of asthma, and suffered from hay-fever. This distressing complaint, which he bore with Christian fortitude, did not, except when it was very bad, really incapacitate him, though often in the summer months he had sharp attacks. This he attributed to the pollen of flowers and grasses, which even in the middle of London was probably present in the air. The Square, in those days, though outwardly much the same as it is now, was internally of a very different character, and he laboured in his vineyard till from its being, as he so aptly called it, an Augean stable, he had made it what it is. He also improved the garden very much, planting there at his own expense several sumac trees which have now grown to be of fine proportions. This was rather of the nature of a horticultural experiment, for it was not then known whether sumacs would flourish in the fogs and winter-darkness of London, but when friends tried to dissuade him from making it, his invariable reply was, 'We can but see.' Before his death his faith in the hardy character of these trees was amply justified.

" But it was the moral character of the Square in which he made the most sweeping changes. It was by no means a respectable place, and there were many difficulties to contend with. Without going into detail over such painful matters, it may be stated that by the judicious purchase of a number of freeholds, and by close inquiries into the characters of those to whom he let them, the leaven brought forth good fruit, and in course of time, in Biblical phrase, the whole was leavened. Not content with such activities, he wrote many sermons, the most of which, alas, he could not personally deliver owing to his asthma, and he kept a very full diary till a week before his death, writing it in the front room on the ground floor where he kept his books. These gradually increased in number, and fresh shelves were added as required. Though in no sense a trained musician, he delighted in it, and more than once attended the Handel festival, which he described in his diary as being ' glorious.' Though fond of cats, and also of dogs in their proper place, he was altogether against their being allowed in the garden of the Square, where he walked every morning before his lunch from a quarter to half an hour, sometimes resting on the seats he had placed there, having been in his youth a very active pedestrian."

Mrs. Mantrip felt much happier. She had had secret qualms as to whether, when it came to actual writing, she was capable of the feat. But it was going swimmingly now; she had embodied a quantity of those personal characteristics, which she had entered on her schedule, and this particular chapter was not likely to present any new difficulties. Refreshed and encouraged by her success, she clipped these pages together, and she resolved, now she had caught the trick of it, to begin at the very beginning of her book, and write steadily on. Birth and parentage then:

" My father, George Frederick Bondfield, was born on the 25th of August, 1860, and thus, had he lived to the present year, he would now have been seventy. His mother was Edith Springfield, an old family in Salisbury. The marriage was a very happy one, and the birth of this their only child was a great joy to his parents. He was christened in Salisbury Cathedral, where his father was a most respected solicitor and senior partner in a well-established firm, and which my father always regarded as the finest, or nearly so, of the great English fanes. By a curious coincidence the christening ceremony took place in one thunderstorm, and his death in another. As a child he was rather delicate, and among his earliest recollections, as subsequently recorded in his diary as having made a deep impression on him, was being taken to church there, when he cannot have been more than four years old. Throughout his life his memory was always extremely retentive, and remained so up till the end."

Again Mrs. Mantrip paused, and read over this opening paragraph. She seemed to have said that her grandfather was a solicitor in Salisbury Cathedral, and that must be corrected. Otherwise these topics of her father's infancy seemed to lead on, one to the other, very naturally, but there was a sort of speckled, streaky effect about the whole which vaguely dissatisfied her. Rudolph da Vinci was never speckled, he carried you on with a more even progress, and though the adventures he recorded were so enthralling, what could be more intensely interesting to a serious mind than the spiritual adventure, that was coming, of a retired clergyman who purged Durham Square of cocottes? The early years and childish recollections therefore of such a man, his development into the spiritual athlete that he became, must surely be interesting too. But she saw clearly that when she came to the Augean stable again, she must enlarge on it, however painful the subject was, for its cleansing was really the climax of the book. At least she could not think of any other.

Mrs. Mantrip, rather tired with her morning's work, and not yet quite confident about her biographical powers, spent a couple of hours that afternoon in the garden. With the departure of Elizabeth and other dog-owners on their holiday, the tranquil place, which had lately been no less than an Augean kennel, was for the present purged of these odious creatures; and, with one of the earlier works of Rudolph da Vinci, she promised herself a congenial and unharassed time in a deck-chair. Authorship, the passion to give a message to the world, was a strange instinct. It affected the most noble minds, like Rudolph da Vinci's, but it swayed the common and the ignoble also, and as she mused on this interesting theme, it was natural enough that her thoughts should stray to her tenant in No. 25, who was one of the few householders who still remained in the Square in this second week of August: everywhere else blinds were down and shutters up. Mrs. Mantrip had been loath to accept Jimmie's theory that the raw, pert, uneducated woman was engaged with literary labours in the butler's pantry, but the evidence was indeed very strong; and as Mrs. Mantrip got drowsy with the heat of the afternoon, she half pictured, half dreamed that she saw Susan scribbling away below stairs, with the gramophone close beside her, and covering sheet after sheet of blue foolscap with fluent and unhesitating script. Then she was aware that she must actually

have dropped into a doze, for she had the sensation of
awaking abruptly, and was conscious that a noise had
roused her.

She looked up at the windows of No. 25, and saw
that the main features of her dreamy imaginings were
fulfilled, for there was Susan sitting with her head in
the loud-speaker, as Jimmie had described, writing on
sheets of blue foolscap. From the open window there
poured out the strident tones of her instrument: this
no doubt was the noise that had awakened Mrs. Mantrip. It was easy to conjecture what had happened:
with Jimmie away at his house at Cookham, and
Elizabeth with her dogs on Dartmoor, the houses to
right and left of No. 25 were empty, and Susan, knowing that she would not disturb her neighbours, had
come back from the pantry to her sitting-room. Ocular
evidence, which could not be distrusted, confirmed the
substantial truth of Jimmie's statement.

Mrs. Mantrip watched her with eager attention.
Some unwilling kinship with another authoress stirred
in her breast; she wondered whether Susan found
grammar and the logical sequence of sentences as
difficult as she herself did. Apparently not: her pen
scudded over the paper with the most enviable facility;
it was as if the woman was a skilled practitioner. Then
her motor drew up opposite her house, the gramophone
ceased, and Susan vanished. In a minute or two she
appeared again at her front door with her hat on, and
stood there talking to Bosanquet for a few seconds.
Whether in consequence of his wit or her own she broke
out into a peal of girlish laughter, which was quite
unlike the titter which Mrs. Mantrip remembered had
enraged her so much at her luncheon-party. Apparently she had been acquiring a new laugh, but Mrs.
Mantrip did not like it any better than the old one.
That horrible great Alsatian hound sprang after her into
her car, and off she drove.

Mrs. Mantrip opened her well-worn copy of *Heart's*

Queen, where she would find, in an ampler ether, escape from these dreadful artificialities of her tenant. Heart's Queen was a wealthy landowner in her own right, who set herself to raise the moral tone of those squares and streets in Westminster which formed the bulk of her enormous property. These chapters were great favourites with Mrs. Mantrip, for the noble work of that pure young woman reminded her very much of Papa's work here in the Square, and she often wondered whether Rudolph da Vinci had based this part of his romance on something he had heard about what Papa had done. But to-day for the first time, it struck her with an unpleasant shock how very different were Heart's Queen's methods from Papa's. True to the fine maxim on which so much of Rudolph's work was based, that (with the exception of principal villains) you could find good in everybody, if you set about it in a truly loving and indulgent spirit, Heart's Queen used to visit the gay, disreputable ladies on her property and persuade them to mend their ways. She brought them flowers, she talked to them of their younger years when they were innocent girls, and by the very charm and sweetness of her often caused them to burst into tears and lead a new life. Papa never tried that sort of thing at all; he did not attempt to exercise his charm, but only refused to let them live in his houses. He never tried to influence them for good: he only said " Get out of my Square," and having done that, did not bother his head about them any more. They could make another Augean stable somewhere else for all he cared.

Viewed in this light, his activities seemed to lose their bright sheen, and the operations which Mrs. Mantrip had always regarded as being so important and edifying a piece of his life-work, presented a different aspect. They had been highly remunerative, for with the purging, the Square had become a far more desirable residential quarter, but there was no reason to suppose that he had raised the moral tone of London in the beautiful manner of Heart's Queen. She began to wonder whether the section of his life's work which dealt with the Augean stable would prove as edifying as she had hoped. Much, of course, would depend on the manner in which she handled it. Could she indicate that he had their spiritual welfare, as well as that of the Square, very much at heart? It would need to be very subtly conveyed, a delicate piece of work, quite unbased on actual facts, and remembering the struggles she had gone through before she could get down on paper at all the barest incidents about her father's christening and Salisbury Cathedral, her misgivings about her own capacities returned again. Perhaps she had better leave out the part about the Augean stable altogether, and yet that would be a lamentable omission, for only this morning she had felt most strongly that the rest of her book would lead up to that: that it was indeed the crown of his life's work, which would make all that went before so interesting. Now quite suddenly and most inconveniently it represented itself to her candid mind as merely a piece of shrewd business. Rudolph da Vinci, she felt, could have made a marvellous chapter of it: he would have painted the evicted ladies in such repulsive colours that the reader would have followed the process of the purging with enthralled interest, drawing a long breath of edified thankfulness when the last of them took her eyebrows and rouge-pots away. He would have forced you to feel that Papa was one of those who left not only the Square but the world better than he found it. Oh, for the pen of that transcendent artist just for the writing of that one section!

She got up from her deck-chair, leaving *Heart's Queen* on it, for the garden was quite empty and her name was written large inside the book, and strolled down the shady side of the Square and out into Durham Road for the purchase of an evening paper. The Park

was only a few minutes away, and she walked up there
to sit and read it. The world seemed to have fallen
asleep: not a murder, not a railway accident, not a new
disturbance in the Balkan States broke the monotonous
calm of the columns. Turning quickly over leaf after
leaf, she soon came to " The Way of the World," by
that delightful writer, Ulrica. The season, Ulrica told
her readers, was quite over, but a few London-lovers
still lingered here, and Ulrica had met Miss Susan Leg
walking in the Park a few afternoons ago with her
Alsatian. She was soon off now on a round of visits,
but though London was so empty, she was still able
to collect a few people for her *intime* dinners. Ulrica
had dined with her last night, and had a great talk
with Mr. Rudolph da Vinci. . . .

The letters danced before Mrs. Mantrip's eyes, but
when they had finished dancing they sat down again
and she read on.

The great novelist had talked to them about the
new book which he had lately finished. Much that he
had said must not be divulged, but it was violating no
confidences to say that its title was *Julian Beltravers*,
and that the *dénouement*, the scene of which was laid
in Belgrave Square, was perhaps the most powerful
thing that Mr. da Vinci had ever penned: the suspense
was intolerable. As usual, he had composed it while
his musical secretary played the organ to him. He
had meant to bring it out during the autumn, but
perhaps its publication would be postponed, for Mr.
da Vinci was already deep in another romance, which
would probably come out before *Julian Beltravers*. . . .

The sense of what she had missed made Mrs. Mantrip feel positively unwell, and the cool seat where she
had been reading became intolerable. Regardless of
the duty of tidiness in public places, she left her paper
there to scud about and disfigure the grass, and took
a swift and agitated walk beside the rails of the Row.
Who could have foreseen the hideous consequences that

would follow on her refusal to dine with Susan and to
recommend her a book to read? Was there ever so
ill-judged a snub? Had it not been for that, she might
now have met Mr. Armstrong, M.P., and Mr. Cartwright (and how useful that would have been when
Papa's Life was finished!), and Lady Mackleton, have
gone to fork-luncheons and, though she despised
publicity most heartily, have been mentioned by
Ulrica as an *intime* at No. 25. But this last stroke
was far more staggering than all the rest put together:
it was a cruel blow above and below the belt: it was
almost a knock-out. If only she had taken the trouble
to be polite to Susan she might have been present last
night, have seen and spoken to R. da V., and heard
from his own lips about the new book. Of all people
in the world to whom one would have thought that a
snub might be administered without fear of missing
something agreeable in consequence, Susan Leg was
she, and retribution of the most dire kind had resulted.
Bitterly Mrs. Mantrip regretted it; despairingly she
wondered if the damage she had done herself was
irreparable. Could she at the cost of any humiliation
make friends again with her tenant, or by any exercise
of penitence and patience re-establish relations with
her, and thus have the chance some day of meeting
the great romanticist?

While Mrs. Mantrip was writhing in the talons of
remorse by the Row, Susan had returned from her
drive, and had let herself and Sigurd into the Square
garden for a further stroll before she returned to her
gramophone. The book was getting on at a tremendous pace, and the end of August ought to see it
completed, but till that was done she had no intention
of leaving London. But she found she did not write
with such headlong facility in the drawing-room as in
the pantry: the reverberation of the instrument in the
confined area was wonderfully conducive to inspiration,
and though, knowing that there were no neighbours

now who would be disturbed, she had to-day moved into the drawing-room, she determined to go back to the pantry again, for she missed that atmosphere of closeness and concentration. . . .

She paused, as she paced up and down the grass, beside the chair in which Mrs. Mantrip had been sitting, and noticed that there was a book lying on it. With a rapid glance round to make sure that the owner was not within eyeshot, she picked it up in order to see, as she ironically reminded herself, what were those literary tastes of Mrs. Mantrip which differed so much from her own. To her amazement she found that she was holding a copy of *Heart's Queen*, a well-thumbed volume, bearing authentic signs of long and loving study, and on the title-page was written large and clear the name and address of its owner.

Susan felt that her firm and well-justified dislike of that rude highbrow widow with the anchovy-paste halo was thawing just a little round the edges. It was not a real thaw, but there was a perceptible softening. The book was so evidently a favourite with its possessor, so evidently had it been read and re-read, and no author, however well-used to flattering tributes from hundreds of readers, could fail to be touched at this mute but eloquent witness of devotion. Susan's grim hostility melted: she perceived that in spite of many (God knew how many) disgusting characteristics, Mrs. Mantrip had just one saving grace. In the book, on which Susan was so busily engaged, Mrs. M. was coming in for some pretty severe treatment as the false highbrow mother of the venial critic, but the end, the general winding-up of the characters, with dismal fates in store for the damned, was not absolutely fixed yet, and Susan felt like relenting towards her, now that she had discovered that there was some good in the creature after all. She determined to go through her work and insert some redeeming features in that despicable character, and mitigate her fate in the last chapters. "I must be just to her," thought Susan, "now that I know this about her."

Before getting to work again on the delirious ravings of Francis Grout in the attack of brain-fever through which Serena nursed him, Susan glanced at the evening paper and saw, just as Mrs. Mantrip had seen, that she was still able to collect a few *intimes*, and that Ulrica and Rudolph da Vinci had dined with her last night. This was a new phase: Ulrica had often chatted or dined with Susan Leg, or seen her in the Park, and Ulrica, during this past month, had become quite intimate with R. da V., but never before had direct personal contact been established between R. da V. and Susan. It was a different way of putting things, and Susan was not quite sure that she liked it. There was nothing absolutely false in the account, for Ulrica had dined with her, and she had told him about the great scene in Prince Igor's house in Belgrave Square, and so it was quite truthful that he had dined with and heard this from R. da V. But to advertise all three of them as dining together (though still true) was to introduce a new note. It made for complications, and though Susan revelled in complications when she was writing, she did not want to have more of them than was necessary in her private life. She could not undertake to be two people simultaneously: Ulrica might come to see Susan as often as he cared to do so, or he might come to see R. da V. But not simultaneously.

She pondered a little over this and over other subjects which it suggested. There had been that short encounter with Minnie Mimps in the Square, and she had not liked that. She wanted her past life to be simple to the point of non-existence, and Minnie had turned on her a fox-like look, when, in answer to her greeting, Susan had just said "How-de-do?" and passed on, and that fox-like look still dwelt in her mind and made her slightly uneasy. She did not know what the woman could do to hurt her, but conceivably

the woman might think of something, for assuredly
she had not been pleased at being treated so curtly.
. . . Then there had been a coolness also with Lady
Mackleton, who had sent her in so outrageous an
account for taxis in addition to her ordinary charges
for lunching and dining, that, though Susan had paid
it, she had intimated that for the future she would send
her own car to convey her friend forth and back.
Slight recriminations had passed. Lady Mackleton
had said she was sorry Susan did not trust her. All
rather unpleasant. She had referred the matter to
Ulrica, and Ulrica, though with great tact, had rather
taken Lady Mackleton's side. Lady Mackleton was
part of his social firm, so to speak, and he told Susan
that he could not believe she would be guilty of
charging for taxis that she had not taken. He urged
her to pay the account, and, if she could manage it,
to regret that she had ever called in question the
correctness of it, for it was as well to keep on good
terms with Lady Mackleton, who went about so much
and was a good talker as well as a good listener. Susan
had managed it, but the incident had left her with the
feeling that she had been done and also that her position
was not secure yet.

That evening the work did not go very well, and
next day, though she moved back to the reverberating
pantry, she again failed to attain the fine free rapture
in which alone her most supreme flights were accomplished. These little annoyances came between her
and her page; they distracted her; they were like a
mosquito trumpeting close to her in the dark, and she
had an ominous feeling that a poisonous bite might be
the result. She was doing slack work; she was not
concentrating on it to the exclusion of all else, and after
erasing several sentences, which was very rare with her,
she put down her pen, went upstairs, and rang for
Bosanquet to come and cheer her up and restore her
confidence in herself and Providence. A chat with him

always had a stabilizing effect: his outlook on life was so calm, his common sense so rich, and his devotion to her so unquestionable. In all things concerning the gaieties, the splendours, the ambitions of her life, she sought the advice of Augustus, whose imagination was so fiery, but when homely words of peace and consolation were required " Give me Bosanquet," thought Susan.

He brought up with him the evening postal delivery. This consisted of a large packet from Messrs. Cartwright containing the letters of all the adoring readers who had written to R. da V., c/o his publisher, soliciting alms, proposing marriage, or merely stating how much he had changed their outlook on life, and Susan put these aside for future perusal. Besides them there was only one letter, but that was addressed to Rudolph da Vinci, c/o Miss Susan Leg, 25 Durham Square.

She stared at this, stonily distrusting it.

" Good gracious me ! " she said. " What can this mean ? Look, Bosanquet ! "

Bosanquet shook his head.

" Yes, miss, I have looked," he said. " Never before has that happened in my knowledge."

" Care of me. I don't like it," said Susan. " I wonder whom it's from."

" A glance at the inside, miss, would tell you that," said Bosanquet, with that unfailing grasp of the obvious which Susan found so comforting.

Susan tore it open and found the most disconcerting contents. It was from Minnie Mimps herself, and after a lyrical passage declaring her boundless devotion to R. da V., she requested the favour of an autographed photo. So far there was nothing unusual in this letter, but then there followed the disconcerting matter :

" I saw, dear sir," wrote Miss Mimps, " in the

paper last night that you had been dining with Miss Susan Leg, and I feel I ought to warn you that she is a mere upstart and quite unworthy of your friendship, having sprung from what I may call the dregs of the population, and having been for years in a type-writing office of low class in Brighton. I know this for certain, because I worked there myself, and now she hasn't a civil word for me, but a ' how-de-do ' and passes on. Oh, shame on those who throw over their old friends, and flaunt about in pearls and what-not, just because their uncle, so she said, left her some money as if we weren't all equal in the sight of God. So I felt impelled to warn you against her, for she's beneath you, dear sir.

" Enclosing a large stamped envelope for the photograph, and thanking you again and again in anticipation, I am,

" Yours, etc.,
" MINNIE MIMPS."

Susan read this forceful but devastating composi-tion with a furrowed brow. She had intended already to seek from Bosanquet comfort and consola-tion in the worries of her social life (of which Mimps was one), but she hesitated before revealing to him this secret part of her past which she would so much have preferred should have remained buried at Brighton. Could she seek Bosanquet's counsel in such a matter? Though she had sent for him to consult him about her general apprehensions concern-ing Mimps and Mackleton (as Lady Eva would have said), it was a different thing altogether to expose to him this exhumation of her vanished years: she did not know how he would take the revelation of her plebeian past. But she decided to chance it, for she wanted comfort and counsel, and having begged him to take a seat, she read him, in all its horrid complete-ness, this warning to her to beware of herself.

Bosanquet had preferred to stand, and when Susan
had finished he was silent. She looked at his trusted
face: he was staring out of the window, but the
twitching of the muscles of his throat showed that he
was in the grip of some strong emotion. Seeing that,
Susan's heart misgave her: was he of that aristocratic
type of butler familiar to readers of R. da V. who will
only take service, so they proudly put it, with gentle-
folk?

" Well, Bosanquet? " she said.

He turned his devoted eyes on her.

" Oh, miss, is it all true? " he asked. " Did you
have your origin in the dregs, and make your living
in a typewriting agency? "

(Was there disillusionment or reproach in his
voice? Susan decided that there was not.)

" Yes, Bosanquet," she answered confidently.
" I am sprung from the dregs, if you consider a
draper's assistant to be dregs. And I did make my
living as Mimps alleges."

Before she had finished speaking, she knew how
right she had been to trust him.

" Oh, miss, what a joy to me! " said Bosanquet,
in a voice that trembled with emotion. " I always
felt sure that you were like that in your origins,
though there have been two opinions about it in the
house: M. Rouen, for instance, but I told him he
knew nothing about our upper classes in England.
And now I know from your own lips that you are
one of us, who has raised herself by her own abilities,
very much as Augustus has done, though to a far
lesser degree than you. I *am* pleased."

It was a relief to Susan to find that Bosanquet was
so fervent a modernist in his views about classes, but
for some reason, which she did not care to go into, it
was a slight jar to her that he had never been under
any misapprehension about her origins. What a
keen eye he had!

" Now this letter, Bosanquet," she said. " What do you recommend me to do? I don't like it."

Bosanquet recalled himself from the happy contemplation induced by the knowledge that he was serving a mistress who had raised herself from the dregs by the exercise of her pure genius.

" Well, miss," he said, " it doesn't do you any harm as far as I can see. This Miss Mimps, nasty though her intention was, is only telling you under another name what you knew yourself under your own——"

" Say that again, Bosanquet," interrupted Susan.

" Put it like this then, miss," said Bosanquet lucidly. " She's only telling Mr. da Vinci about Miss Susan Leg."

Bosanquet paused.

" But I'm beginning to see a bit further into it, miss," he said. " There's others as well. She might tell somebody else about it, and with all the false notions that people have about classes, you wouldn't like that so much! "

" It would be dreadful," said Susan. " You see, I met her just outside only ten days ago—she was going into Mr. Mason's house. I shouldn't like it at all if she told him! "

" Quite natural, too, miss," said Bosanquet, who, like Susan, was blissfully ignorant that the disclosure had already been made. " What we must think of is how to stop her tongue. Evidently a low woman, if you'll excuse my speaking so of one who was once your friend."

" You may speak of her exactly as you like," said Susan. " And I was pretty short with her. She may have told Mr. Mason about me. Oh, Bosanquet, if she has! He may have told others as well. Lor! "

Bosanquet glanced at the incriminating letter again.

" There's a nasty tone about it, and I don't like

it, miss," he said. " But isn't she gone on Mr. da Vinci? "

" Yes, but I can't stop her tongue by telling her that he is me," said Susan.

" I wasn't going to suggest such a thing, miss," said Bosanquet. " I only meant that you had her weakness for him to play upon. I think I should, if I were you, write to her as from Mr. da Vinci."

" But she knows my handwriting," said Susan. " She saw it every day for years. Of course I could type it."

" No," said Bosanquet decidedly. " What you want is to send her a letter from Mr. da Vinci himself, to show how important he thinks the matter. It would be a privilege to me to be allowed to write it for you. But before we get to that, we must think what would be the best nasty thing to say to her."

Susan had a brain-wave.

" Oh, Bosanquet, I believe I've got it," she cried. " You must write a letter to her from Mr. da Vinci, saying that he is astonished and shocked (I'll make it up for you) at being told such scandalous things about Miss Susan Leg, whom he has known all his life, and that she must instantly withdraw them, because there's no word of truth in them. She must also tell anybody to whom she has mentioned them—that's in case she's told Mr. Mason—that they are all wicked lies."

" Well, you are a one, miss," said Bosanquet, unable to contain his admiration. " Why, it might all have happened in one of your books——"

" ——and that if she promises to do that, no further proceedings will be taken," continued Susan, acknowledging Bosanquet's handsome tribute by a gracious inclination of her head.

" Quite so, miss," said Bosanquet rather doubtfully. " But if she refused to promise anything of the sort, might I ask what your proceedings would be? "

" I'm sure I don't know," said Susan, " and I

don't suppose it matters. But we've got to say that proceedings will be taken. That always frightens blackmailers and people like Minnie Mimps. It sets their imagination working, and they lie awake at night."

This was quite in the R. da V. style, but in practical life it did not seem to Bosanquet to promise much success. He stared out of the window again, dissatisfied and lost in thought. Quite unconsciously, to aid meditation, he took a gold-tipped cigarette from Susan's enamelled box on the table and lit it. A sparkle returned to his eye; his face grew animated again.

" Excuse me, miss, but I've got a new idea, and a real beauty," he said excitedly. " Let Mr. da Vinci write to Mimps as per how we've settled already, and say that he has reasons to believe that she has told other people besides yourself about your past life, and that she must own up and say it's all lies. And if that's done to Mr. da Vinci's satisfaction he will send her the signed photograph of himself that she asks for. From the tone of her letter, miss, I should say that she would close with that at once, and think herself very fortunate."

" But how can I send her a photograph of Mr. da Vinci? " asked Susan. " There isn't such a thing in the world. I can't send her one of my own, for that would give the whole secret of my life away."

Bosanquet pondered over this little difficulty.

" Well, it must be somebody else's photograph, then, miss," he said, rather lamely.

" And he must be in the conspiracy, too," said Susan.

Bosanquet chucked his cigarette-end into the fireplace.

" I've got it, miss," he cried. " It's Augustus's duty to do the needful here. It's his privilege, too. He must give you a nice photograph of himself to be autographed by Mr. da Vinci and sent to Miss Mimps, if she withdraws all she's said."

"Bosanquet, you're wonderful!" cried Susan. "You shall write the letter, which I'll make up for you, and you shall sign the photograph."

"Thank you, miss, a thousand times for the honour," said he. "I shall be proud to do it. I think we shall put a stop to her now. And Mr. Bosanquet is a good-looking young fellow, though perhaps I shouldn't say that, knowing how strong you think the family likeness to be, and you won't feel let down by his featuring Mr. da Vinci. He'll do it very naturally, if I may say so, for having been Ulrica and Leonora so long, he's well used to impersonation."

"Ring up Mr. Bosanquet, then," said Susan, "and ask him to dine with me to-night, and bring a recent photograph of himself."

"Yes, miss, and I'll see that he does it," said Bosanquet.

Bosanquet instantly became the perfect butler again.

"You rang your bell, miss," he said, "before we got talking about this."

Susan recalled her mind from the conspiracy.

"I know I did," she said. "Really it was to talk to you, Bosanquet. I felt bothered. I couldn't concentrate. I was thinking about Mimps, and my meeting with her in the Square."

"Well, that's off your mind now, I hope," said he. "You won't bother about that any more."

"I hope not. I think she is sure to accept the terms on which she can get Mr. da Vinci's photograph. Then again I was a little bothered about Ulrica saying that she had dined here with Mr. da Vinci and me. I like her dining with me, and I like her having talks with Mr. da Vinci. But I don't think it's wise for Mr. da Vinci to dine with me."

Bosanquet nodded.

" I felt the same myself, miss," he said. " I thought, ' Where there's smoke, there's fire.' You see, you've already got an Alsatian that's seen with you in the Park, and so has he, and your neighbours in the Square know that you write with a gramophone close by you, while Mr. da Vinci has his organ played when he's at work. People will begin to put two and two together if we're not careful. I hope you'll point that out to Augustus. Nothing more to bother you? "

" Lady Mackleton, just a little bit," said Susan. " We had a few words about the charges she made for her taxis, as I think I told you, and there has been a coolness. Could she turn nasty too, do you think? "

" Don't get worrying about her ladyship," said Bosanquet decidedly. " After your season and all its successes, mark my words, miss, you'll soon be of more use to her than she is to you. You wait till your friends come back to London in October and November and you'll have her ladyship wanting to come to your house without any honorarium at all, not to mention taxis."

" Do you really think that? " asked Susan.

" I'm sure of it. So I'll ring up Mr. Bosanquet, shall I, and ask him to dine with you to-night, and bring a nice photograph of himself. Better say that dinner's at half-past eight, so that, now these little worries are off your mind, you'll get a couple of hours good work. I'll put a fresh record on the gramophone for you."

Augustus, as his uncle had anticipated, was more than willing to oblige, and that very evening Susan dictated to Bosanquet a pretty stiff letter from Mr. da Vinci to Miss Mimps, demanding a plenary withdrawal of all the libellous facts she had promulgated about Miss Susan Leg's past, and promising, if this was done to Mr. da Vinci's satisfaction, that she would receive a signed photograph of himself. They passed a most pleasant evening, and drawn closer together by the conspiracy, Susan and Augustus arrived at Christian-name terms, calling each other by them with quite unnecessary frequency, in order to get used to them as soon as possible. On his departure, Susan, invigorated by intrigue, and now quite unharassed in mind, betook herself to the pantry, and worked at *Amor Vincit* for a couple of hours more with redoubled gusto.

X

THOUGH Jimmie Mason was, as Mrs. Mantrip often lamented, sadly lacking in intellectual fibre, he was the soul of honour (so much more important), and when Miss Mimps wrote to him, as she did without a struggle, to tell him that she was under a complete misapprehension as to Miss Susan Leg's past, and that all she had said was lies from beginning to end, he was very much concerned to think that he had repeated them. He was shocked also to think that so admirable an accountant could be so prodigious a liar. So in order to minimize the harm he might have done in repeating these wicked falsehoods, he not only wrote to Susan to tell her that a ridiculous story had reached his ears about her having been employed in a typist's agency, which he now knew was completely untrue, but wrote also to Lady Eva, Mrs. Mantrip and Elizabeth, among whom he had disseminated it, to the same effect. He also invited Mrs. Mantrip to come and spend a few days at Cookham with him, where they were having great fun.

Then he decided to forgive Miss Mimps for the lies she had told, for she had confessed to them, and was probably penitent: besides, she was an excellent accountant, and he did not know whom else he could get. So, since it was time for his August accounts to be made up, he wrote to ask her to come down for a night, and prepare his budget for him. This was perfectly usual: she always came down for a night when he was at Cookham, and of course, he paid her journey both ways. The day before the arranged

date, she had received a beautiful photograph of Mr.
Augustus Bosanquet, signed by Bosanquet under the
pseudonym of Rudolph da Vinci: a very pleasant little
letter also from R. da V. accompanied it. Naturally
she took these treasures with her, and put the photograph on a small table near her bed, so that it would
be the last object she saw before, and the first object
she saw after her night's rest.

There were two or three brisk young people in the
house, to all of whom their host was Uncle Jimmie,
and they set forth after breakfast next morning in
punts and bathing-dresses to romp in Cookham Weir.
Miss Mimps could not go with them, for she had her
work to do, and Mrs. Mantrip flatly refused to romp,
for she found the society of the young ageing and
exasperating to the last degree. But she had brought
down with her an early work of her favourite author's,
and, for the sake of her reputation, a volume of her
father's diaries, and was delighted to see these nephews
and nieces safely off the premises till lunch-time. She
established herself in a shady corner of the lawn with
her literature, and, since she was intending presently
to complete a section of her father's life as Vicar of
Screwby, she first read some pages of Rudolph da
Vinci, in order to tune up her sense of vivid and
picturesque English. Miss Mimps, with packets of
bills around her, settled down to her work in the
room which was known as Jimmie's study.

There was a big writing-table with its back to the
door, a sofa where the owner was accustomed to rest
after lunch or after romps, but not much else to
remind one of a study. As she was now alone in the
house and secure from interruption, she propped up
on the table in front of her Augustus's photograph,
and in the intervals between adding up figures and
making entries in the ledger, gazed long and fondly
at it, and returned refreshed to her bills. She herself
just now was very hard up, for she had been out of

regular work for some weeks, and it seemed to her monstrous that Jimmie should spend so much money at fishmongers' and fruiterers' and florists'. Quite a small fraction of that would procure for her no end of things, including a new hat, of which she stood really in need. But when she looked at her photograph, she felt that a pearl of great price was hers. His photograph never appeared in any paper, and precious though it was to her, she began to wonder what it was worth.

Outside on the lawn, Mrs. Mantrip read a stimulating chapter, and then closed the book with a sigh. It was time to get to work on the diary, in which were several very important entries about a ruridecanal meeting: she must read these through and take some notes before embarking on her account of it. She found she had brought out no paper with her; but Jimmie's study was close at hand, and she would find materials there, and thus save her going upstairs.

She entered: Miss Mimps was sitting with her back towards the door gazing at a cabinet photograph propped up in front of her. It was that of a good-looking young man, with a very interesting expression of face. Her entry seemed to be unperceived, and taking a step nearer she saw that in a dashing hand across the white mount was scrawled the name of Rudolph da Vinci. Miss Mimps, recalled from her reverie, turned quickly round, and with a slight scream and a trembling hand slid the picture back into its envelope.

" I came to get a few sheets of paper, if you can spare me them," began Mrs. Mantrip in a calm and distant voice. . . . Then her emotion, secret and stifled for years, welled forth, sweeping her self-control completely away.

" Miss Mimps," she said, " please, please allow

me to see that photograph. I saw by the signature
whom it represented, and it would mean so much to
me to have a good look at it. I admire that man's
work more than I can possibly tell you, and I have
never seen him. Oh, Miss Mimps! "

Mrs. Mantrip had been rather condescending to
the accomplished accountant, and it was very pleasant
to have her suing like this. Miss Mimps could con-
descend too.

" Certainly," she said with great amiability.
" Was it not nice of Mr. da Vinci to send it me, the
sweet thing? It doesn't quite do him justice though.
Fancy you not knowing him! Such a delightful little
note he wrote me. Now what can I have done with
it? Don't tell me I've thrown it away before answering it."

" Thrown it away? " said Mrs. Mantrip in a
curdled whisper.

" No, I don't think I have. Ah, there it is in the
envelope. Read it if you like."

Mrs. Mantrip transferred her reverential gaze to
the letter. It was dated from Susan's house.

" DEAR MISS MIMPS,—I've just got your note.
All quite right now, so don't think anything more
about it. So I send you a recent photograph of my-
self to show we're friends again, though why anyone
should want my dull old phiz is more than I know.
Just off to Norway on a yachting cruise.
" Cordially,
" RUDOLPH DA VINCI."

Mrs. Mantrip clasped her hands together.
" But how delightful for you to possess such
treasures," she said. " And such modesty in him to
say that he can't imagine why anyone should want a
photograph of him. Signed, too, by himself! How
you must value it! "

The astute Mimps guessed that there might be something doing. It was worth while anyhow to ascertain that. She adored her photograph, but she wanted cash.

" I should think so," she said. " I shouldn't wonder if a signed photograph of Mr. da Vinci and a letter from him weren't worth anything from five to ten pounds."

Mrs. Mantrip was in no mood to bargain. Besides, she was rich.

" I'll give you ten pounds for them on the spot! " she said.

Miss Mimps recognized the accent of desire, and wished to God she had mentioned a far higher figure in her extempore valuation. But perhaps it was not too late.

" Well, really, I hardly know what to say," she answered. " One doesn't like parting with such treasures. They may be worth much more than that for all I know."

Mrs. Mantrip gave her a penetrating glance. She had observed the astonishment of Miss Mimps when she made her princely offer, and had likewise observed the look of greed that sharpened her features immediately afterwards.

" That is the utmost I am prepared to give," she said. " It is ' yes ' or ' no.' "

Miss Mimps surrendered. She clapped her hands with charming gaiety.

" Going, going, gone! " she cried, " and I shall much prefer Treasury notes, as I haven't got a banking-account just at present. And mum's the word for both of us, isn't it? You don't want to be known as having such a crush on Rudy as to buy a photograph and a letter of his sent to somebody else, and I don't want him to know I've parted with them. So grasping it would appear to be. You'll be discreet then, won't you, and me likewise."

Mrs. Mantrip firmly grasped these auctioned objects.

" Treasury notes it shall be," she affirmed, " and mum it shall be. But one thing more, Miss Mimps. Could you, of course in the strictest confidence, tell me the nature of your little disagreement with Mr. da Vinci which was so happily righted? It would add such interest to my property."

" Ah, that's a little matter between him and me," she said. " Can't betray a friend's confidence."

Mrs. Mantrip bore these treasures back in triumph to Durham Square next day. The secret shrine in which she worshipped the genius of Rudolph da Vinci was now enriched with two relics of undoubted authenticity. Though that lovely little letter, which she felt sure was characteristic of his simple and manly nature, was not addressed to her at all, and though the photograph had been signed for somebody else, they were tokens of his presence, for he had sat for the one and he had written the other. They had cost her a considerable sum of money, and though she was far from regretting the outlay, it was bitter to reflect that a little politeness on her part to Susan, or even a little abstention from rudeness, might easily by now have brought her into personal contact with him, which would have been so much more satisfying than a purchase of mementoes not designed for her, and also much cheaper. Ignorant as she was that Susan's congealed heart had thawed its edges towards her owing to that discovery of *Heart's Queen* in her deck-chair, she did not at present feel equal to the risk of incurring another snub by making fresh overtures to her tenant: besides, as the acquired letter to Miss Mimps stated, Mr. da Vinci was just going off on a yachting cruise to Norway. But when he returned (Ulrica would be pretty certain to make that announcement) she resolved to open negotiations with Susan, and, chanc-

ing the most staggering initial rebuffs, to persevere in
establishing friendly relations again.

Susan was still in London when she returned from
Cookham, as she ascertained by a few simple recon-
naissances: her windows were unblinded, Sigurd bayed
at the top of the area steps, and returning one night
from a cinema down the footpath that led by the back
of her tenant's house, Mrs. Mantrip heard rich melodies
pouring out of the pantry window. That odd habit of
Susan's, confirmed by Jimmie, of writing to the strains
of a gramophone, was paralleled in a more sumptuous
manner by that of Mr. da Vinci, who, so Leonora testi-
fied, wrote his immortal work to the accompaniment of
fugues played by his musical secretary on the organ.
There might be something in this idea, she thought, and
so in the hope that noise might be more conducive to
literary inspiration than was generally known, Mrs.
Mantrip tried the effect of the Queen's Hall promenade
concert on the wireless when, after an early dinner, she
sat down to the reluctant account of her father's life
at Screwby. But instead of producing the required
abstraction, she found that the Pier Gynt music had a
most distracting effect, and she could not frame a single
sentence. Perhaps it was an acquired habit, like the
taste for oysters or caviare, but a second and a third
experiment only led to the conclusion that the acquisition of it would take a long time. And she was in a
hurry to get on with that chapter about Screwby.

In the intervals of literary composition, there were,
for diversion and sweet refreshment, the treasures she
had brought from Cookham, which must be set up
worthily. Secret though they were, and mum though
she was pledged to be, she could not bear merely to
keep them in a drawer, and take them out of the
envelope addressed to Miss Mimps, for surreptitious
glances at them. Dust would accumulate on them, and
their edges get worn with handling. Something more
permanent must be devised. The photograph, she

determined, must be handsomely framed, and glazed both at back and front, so that the letter could be displayed at the back.   But the invocation of the letter " Dear Miss Mimps," was acutely distressing.

One morning as she looked at it, there arose out of the unexplored regions of her secret life, an insidious temptation.   Before she realized what was happening, it had got a strangle-hold on her.   The letter in itself was thrilling: it intimately alluded to a tiff of some sort and a reconciliation, sealed by the gift of this signed photograph.   But there was one blot on its beauty, one blemish on its perfection, for it was not addressed to her.   Inward voices clamoured that it should begin " Dear Mrs. Mantrip." . . . She knew perfectly well, thanks to her Christian upbringing, that forgery was seldom practised in really moral circles, and was even considered definitely wrong, but there was an easy answer to that objection.   For this kind of forgery was not an enrichment of herself at the expense of others; it was pure gain to the voluptuousness of her own secret life, and injured nobody.   It would add such richness to her private perusal of that letter, if it appeared to be addressed to herself.   She might almost be able in time to imagine that it had been.   It might be self-deception, but it would be such fun.   And the changes required to make the document perfect were so small. . . .

Caution was necessary.   A clumsy or a hasty erasure of the " iss " of " Miss," and the " imps " of " Mimps " would show that she had committed an illegal operation.   So, before getting to work on the falsification of the manuscript, she made some careful experiments on a page of her father's diary with an ink-eraser which she had already found most useful in removing stains from her own forefinger.   She moistened the paper a very little according to the directions, and then applied the eraser.   In quite a few seconds the gingerly application of this brave expunger had completely removed the words on which she was experimenting, and when the paper had dried again, the most minute scrutiny showed no sign that it had been tampered with. Then with the delicacy of a skilled surgeon making some incision close to a vital organ, she repeated the process on the " iss " and the " imps " of the letter, for the two capital M's would form part of the forgery. Success crowned her care, and now the letter began, " Dear M . . . M . . ."

The way was now clear for the forgery itself. She studied how Mr. da Vinci (Bosanquet) shaped his " r " and his " p " and the other letters which composed her own name : she observed the stress of his thick strokes, and the lightness of his thin, and presently on her practice-sheet she produced an " rs." and an " antrip " which would surely deceive an expert in the detection of forgery. She went on practising these till she could write them with cursive ease, and then, screwing her courage up and holding her breath in, she wrote in the required syllables after the initial M's. She watched the ink dry without blotting it, and then taking her work to the window, she examined it again. Nothing could have been more neatly done, and with the difficulties attending literary composition in her mind, she almost felt that she had missed her vocation. She went out at once to a trustworthy framer of pictures, and gave the most minute instructions as to how she wanted the letter set up at the back of the photograph. Probably the courteous carpenter was himself a student of Rudolph da Vinci, for having seen what she brought, his manner became almost fulsomely respectful. He assured her that the greatest care should be exercised over the job.

Elizabeth came back to the Square from her holiday on Dartmoor at the end of August. She returned with more dogs than she had taken there (for Eusapia had followed Sabrina's fruitful example); she was much bronzed by wind and sun and stouter than ever, owing

to the ungovernable appetite which an outdoor life had
given her. Indeed that was why she had left the
country nearly a week sooner than she had intended.
She dined one night with her friend, with the usual
piquet to follow, but, as once before, the cards lay long
untouched, so much news was there, obstetric on the
one side and literary on the other, to be exchanged.
The mother was doing well and the puppies were doing
well, and Papa's Life, so Mrs. Mantrip bravely maintained, was doing well, though privately her doubts
about it had become very painful. But she could not
bring herself to give utterance to these: the Life had
been her stunt for so long that it was impossible to
confess that when this morning she had read over the
now finished chapters on " Early Life " and " Personal
Characteristics," she had been very much cast down
about the results of her industrious August. Somehow
they did not resemble a book, or even parts of a book.
. . . But why climb down before the ladder of her
spurious reputation began to totter beneath her ? Not
being omniscient she could not tell that Elizabeth had
long ago ceased to believe that she was writing the Life
at all, and that Eva, whenever she alluded to it, saw
her halo turning to such an unpromising hue. So,
once more she nailed her false colours to her worm-
eaten mast, and held forth for a long time about literary
composition. She must soon be getting in touch with
a publisher.

Elizabeth changed the subject as soon as she could
with her usual abruptness.

" Most interesting," she said. " Now I must tell
you about Eusapia. Three beautiful puppies, but
rather a difficult confinement. I'm going to call
them Dartmoor and Devonshire King and Devonshire
Queen."

" Devonshire Cream ? " asked Margaret.

" No : Queen," said Elizabeth. " King and
Queen."

" Beautiful names," said Margaret. " Shall we have our piquet? "

When the game was over Mrs. Mantrip went out with her friend to see her to her door. The night air was warm, the moon shone brightly in a clear sky, and she continued her stroll a little before she retraced her steps, for any lady of any age could, since the purging of the Square, loiter here at any hour without sinister encounters. She admired the graceful foliage of Papa's sumacs, and looked up at the windows of the houses she passed to see if other neighbours had returned from their holidays. Susan Leg's drawing-room was lit, so, too, was the Vicar's (so he was back): Eva's house and Jimmie's were still shuttered, and Mr. Salt's and Mr. Gandish's. . . . She must certainly devise some avenue of approach to Susan again, for Susan was her tenant, and Papa used to make a point of keeping up friendly relations with his tenants after he had got rid of the Augeans: the pleasant tradition must be kept alive. There were other reasons as well.

She turned and was approaching Susan's house again, when the door was thrown open and three things came out. The first was a flood of light from within; the second was that girlish peal of laughter which Susan had invented for Serena Lomond, and now used quite naturally herself. The third was a young man, bareheaded, with his hat in his hand, who stood talking on the doorstep. The light from within and the moonlight from without shone strongly on his face. Recognition followed in a flash, and instantaneously, from Mrs. Mantrip's secret life, there leapt out a plan that was worthy of the lofty emotion which gave it birth. She hurried on: if, while the two were still talking, she could get within sight of Susan, she was resolved, whatever snubs had been given and taken, to step forward with an affectionate word of greeting. Short of slamming the door in her face, Susan could thus hardly fail to introduce Mr. da Vinci to her.

Alas! she was just too late. "Good night then, my
little Rudolph," Susan called out (for after the affair
of the photograph she often playfully called Augustus
Rudolph). "See you again on Tuesday, one-thirty,
and Nunky's coming too." So before Mrs. Mantrip's
heart-born ingenuity could be rewarded the door was
shut, and little Rudolph was stepping briskly down the
Square in front of her.

The disappointment was severe, but though this
admirable *coup* had not come off, it was something,
indeed it was much, to have seen Rudolph, to know
for certain, apart from Ulrica's chat, that he did in
very person visit her tenant, and that he was coming
again on Tuesday. She had one glance at her photograph before she went to bed. Quite a good one.

During the days that intervened before Rudolph
was expected again, Mrs. Mantrip did all that a forgiv-
ing Christian woman could, to establish friendly
relations with Susan. She asked her to tea one day
and to lunch the next. Both of these invitations Susan
refused, but in a kindly fashion that kept hope alive,
for she had not forgotten her discovery of *Heart's
Queen* on Mrs. Mantrip's deck-chair, and she meant to
be nice to her again when she had leisure for that sort
of thing. But just now she had absolutely no time
to spare, for such had been her industry throughout
August that the next morning after this nocturnal
encounter, she got into the rapids which always ran
swift and powerful towards the end of a book, and
for these days she hardly left the pantry during her
working hours, except for hurried meals, or when
Bosanquet insisted that she must take a little air and
exercise in the Park. Very soon now she would have
done, but no external distraction must interrupt her.
Day by day Bosanquet feasted on great chunks of
marvellous manuscript, and on Tuesday morning,
shortly before Augustus and Nunky were due, the
last words of *Amor Vincit* were inscribed. In spite

of Susan's multitudinous social engagements in July, the time it had been written in established a new record for Rudolph.

That day Mrs. Mantrip found herself unable to take the slightest interest in ruridecanal meetings; it was no use trying. About one o'clock she entered the garden, and established her deck-chair directly opposite Susan's house, where, half-screened herself by the luxuriant foliage of Papa's best sumac, she could get an uninterrupted view of the front door. Presently Susan came out on to the balcony of her drawing-room with that great hound of hers. She called it baby-names, she toyed with it, but she seemed to be keeping watch also, for often she leaned over the railing and gazed down the Square. Then she began violently waving her fat little hand to some-one she had espied, and as quick steps came nearer up the pavement she called to him.

" So it's finished, finished, finished," she cried. " Speak to Uncle Rudolph, Sigurd. Say ' Good morning, Uncle Rudolph ! ' "

But Mrs. Mantrip scarcely heeded her, for there was Rudolph, and her eyes were riveted to that revered face. By the strong midday light she could see him more distinctly than before, and the photograph that lay in the table-drawer of her library did not do justice to his animated expression. He bounded up the steps, and Bosanquet admitted him. There was a distinct facial resemblance between him and Bosanquet; Mrs. Mantrip noticed it instantly, now that she saw them together.

Susan had gone in, but she reappeared again on the balcony with Rudolph; she took a sip of his cock-tail, and he did not seem to resent that ill-bred familiarity, which was so painful to the watcher. Both of them now were watching for somebody else, and presently there drew up at the door an open taxi, containing a brisk little man of middle age. Susan

SECRET LIVES

nice news for you." Mrs. Mantrip remembered
whom Susan called Nunky, and drew the sound conclusion that this was Mr. Cartwright.

Mrs. Mantrip went back to her house when the
door was shut behind Mr. Cartwright, and ate a quick
lunch: after that she returned to her deck-chair in
the garden, bringing with her the well-thumbed
volume of *Heart's Queen*. But the anticipation of
what might possibly happen so occupied her, that for
once she found it impossible to concentrate on that
favourite masterpiece. What had happened already
indeed was sufficient to distract her, for it was clear
that Rudolph had finished the new book of which
Ulrica had spoken. Doubtless, he had telephoned to
Susan to tell her so, and Mr. Cartwright had come to
talk over the date of publication. But the anticipa-
tions of what might happen were even more enthralling. Susan might bring her distinguished guests out
into the garden after lunch, and, if that excellent idea
occurred to her, who could tell what delicious develop-
ments might follow? Mrs. Mantrip would certainly
address a friendly greeting to her, as she had planned
three nights ago, and that was bound to lead to something. Or that great hound might come gambolling
up, and Susan would call him off. Then Mrs.
Mantrip, abandoning all her feelings about dogs in the
garden, would (in Susan's own playful language) say,
" Beautiful doggie: come and talk to Auntie Mantrip." Again the volume of *Heart's Queen* might
come in useful: she would drop it when they came
nearer, and then either Rudolph or Nunky Cartwright
could hardly fail to pick it up for her, and to see what
it was. Having seen that, they could scarcely fail, as
one wrote it and the other published it, to make some
kindly comment. There was, in fact, no wile, however low, to which she was not prepared to descend,
if only Susan would bring her guests into the garden.

Meanwhile, inside her tenant's *petit palais*, as Ulrica had so justly and so often called it, a sort of Cabinet meeting was discussing da Vinci politics and, simultaneously, the luscious fruits of M. Rouen's kitchen. All the three ministers were there, the author, the press-agent and the publisher: indeed Bosanquet himself, after his brilliant management of the Mimps-imbroglio might almost be considered of Cabinet rank. He wore an apt and complacent smile, as Susan told Nunky of the admirable device, so largely contrived by him, through which, at the comparatively trifling cost of a photograph of Augustus, Mimps's highly libellous truths about Susan's past had been formally recanted by their disseminator. Discreetly behind his hand, as he offered a *purée* of mushrooms to his nephew, Bosanquet joined in the laugh that followed Susan's narration.

" Very ingenious, Bosanquet," said Nunky, nodding at him. " I think that as far as you are concerned, Susanna, you may consider that Minnie Mimps won't tell any more truths about the typewriting office. What is she like? She sounds as if she might be a bright, tricky little thing."

"Nunky, what a naughty Satire you are!" cried Susan. " At least I mean those goaty people in Greek forests who weren't quite proper. Besides, she's hideous. Go on: you were going to say something else: I saw it in your eye before you got naughty."

" Well, Susanna, if I've got to give up Minnie," said Cartwright, " I'm not quite sure that I like the idea of there being in existence a signed photograph of Rudolph."

" But it isn't Rudolph, silly Nunky, it's Augustus," said Susan lucidly.

" I know that. But it purports to be Rudolph and is signed by Rudolph, and there is also that ingenious letter of Bosanquet's confirming that it is.

Supposing that this hideous Mimps—I take your word for that—chooses to sell it to some illustrated paper which reproduces it with the letter?"

"Oh, but the copyright of the photograph is mine," said Augustus. "Nobody could publish it without my consent. And the publication of letters without the consent of the writer is illegal. Bosanquet would put his foot down there as he wrote it. We could prosecute."

"Yes, but *who* could prosecute?" asked Nunky. "Who could stop it? Susanna, in point of fact, is Rudolph, but she couldn't stop a photograph of you being published, unless she came forward and said that the whole thing is a fake, and that she is Rudolph. In which case there would be an end of the mystery about him, and that I should deeply regret. As for you, Augustus, I'm afraid you've been privy to a fraud. That photograph of you, purporting to be Rudolph, but really of you, was a bribe to Mimps to stop her telling the truth about Susanna. It's as much a fraud as if you had sent her Treasury notes which you had forged yourself. Then again, supposing Mimps happens to show the photograph of you to someone who knows you. Her friend will say at once that it is you impersonating Rudolph."

Augustus's jaw fell. But he took some more mushrooms and bucked up again.

"I don't mind about that," he said. "I'm used to impersonation, after being Ulrica so long."

"Yes, but you *are* Ulrica," said Nunky; "that's where the difference comes in. It isn't fraudulent to say you're Ulrica, or to sign your photograph as Ulrica. But if you consent to a photograph of yours being signed by Rudolph, in payment for the silence of Mimps, it is."

A slight gloom fell on the Cabinet.

"Dear me, I wonder if we acted precipitously," said Susan. "Or do I mean precipitately? Either will do. But it was such fun, Nunky, making Mimps recant the truth.''

'' I'm sure it was, but I'm not sure that I like it. What I personally find fault with, for I've got nothing to do with the fraud, is the breaking down of the mystery about Rudolph. There now exists a signed photograph of him, though it happens to be Augustus, which there never has been before. We shall be in a mess presently. You never know where these little things will end.''

They had all long ago finished their mushroom *purée*, but Bosanquet was attending so closely to their rather disconcerting conversation that he forgot to change their plates. Suddenly he remembered that he was butler as well as being Rudolph, and, whisking them away, he hurried to the service-lift just outside the door, in order to bring in the next course as quickly as possible, and thus miss the minimum of this rather ominous talk.

'' Well, Susanna was in a hole,'' said Augustus, '' and both Bosanquet and I thought we ought to help her out of it. And surely your notion of Mimps selling my photograph to an illustrated paper is rather far-fetched.''

'' It's the far-fetched that often comes closest to us,'' said Nunky, so epigrammatically that Susan made him repeat it for future use. '' Or supposing she sells it to anybody who has a passion for Susanna's work? Awkward things might arise from it. I don't deny that you've been doing excellent propaganda work both for Susanna and Rudolph all this summer, but I cannot like a false photograph of him having gone abroad like this. And as we're on the subject, I don't like the way you've brought them together and given them such similar tastes and dogs and eccentricities. He is becoming too like Susanna. He oughtn't to have dined here——''

'' I'm getting confused, Nunky,'' said Susan.

" Do you mean me by Rudolph, or do you mean
Augustus's photograph? Or do you mean Ulrica
dining with both of us? "

" Whichever you like. Any of you," said Nunky.
" And then what I called their tastes and dogs.
They've both got Alsatians and they both write to
the strains of loud music."

Bosanquet could not help interrupting.

" Just what I said to miss the other day," he said.
" Where there's smoke there's fire."

Nunky did not quite recognize Bosanquet as a
member of the Cabinet and ignored this.

" You see, Susanna," he said, " it's certainly
known to your neighbours that when you're writing
busily, the gramophone is at it, and Ulrica has told
everybody that when Rudolph is at work, he gets his
musical secretary to play fugues on the organ."

" Oh, but how different the instruments are," said
Susan.

" There's a dangerous analogy. And then when
Ulrica's been dining with you, she writes that she and
Rudolph have been dining with you. On the top of
that there's a photograph of her signed by Rudolph."

" But you're not logical, Nunky, you're not fair ! "
said Augustus, with some warmth. " If Rudolph is
me, as per signed photograph, he quite certainly isn't
Susanna. The photograph makes for secrecy as far as
Susanna is concerned ; it puts people off the right scent
magnificently. If you blame me for putting people on
the scent with their Alsatians and their need for music
when composing, you ought to thank me for putting
them off the scent by the photograph. Unfair, I
say ! "

" Yes, that's right enough," said Susan.

" I disagree," said Nunky. " Augustus has given
them two clues, one of which is the right one. I don't
want any clues at all, even wrong ones."

" But it's the essence of a mystery that there should

be wrong clues, *mon cher*," said Augustus in tones of considerable annoyance.

The Cabinet meeting was getting stormy. Susan poured oil.

" Never mind, Augustus," she said. " You showed yourself a true friend to me, and I'm grateful to you. Besides, talking is always puzzling work, and I'm getting mixed with everybody being so many people. But I do agree with Nunky in one thing. I think we acted precipitously about the photograph, and I should like to get it back."

" I'm sure it would be wise," said Nunky, " and get the letter back as well. Offer Miss Mimps five pounds for it. I'll pay. I wish my photograph would fetch as much. And I'm sure I never intended to hurt Augustus's feelings. But whether the clues are right or wrong it takes the cream off the mystery of Rudolph, to my mind, that there should be any clues."

" It shall be done," said Susan. " Bosanquet and I will write another letter, sending five pounds and asking for it back. We'll manage it all right, so make your mind easy, Nunky. And now I want to talk about the new book I finished this morning. I'm terribly keen that it should come out before the other one, the one, I mean, about the Russian Prince and the Lady Cynthia. Dear me, I've forgotten the name of it."

" *Julian Beltravers*, miss," said Bosanquet quietly to her, and he handed her some grouse covered with *pâté de fois gras*.

" Yes, of course, thank you, Bosanquet," said she. " *Julian Beltravers*. I want *Amor Vincit* to come out as soon as ever you can manage it, Nunky. It's a corker. It's my best. Also *Julian Beltravers* is just a bit like *Rosemary and Rue* in parts. Much better to separate them."

" Yes, it could be done if you're really keen about it, Susanna," said Nunky. " *Julian* hasn't gone to the printers yet, as I didn't mean to bring it out till the middle of November.''

'' Then will you get going with *Amor Vincit*, as soon as it comes back from the typist's? '' said Susan. '' Let's see: it's barely September yet. You can have it out by the middle of October. It's really a personal document, Nunky, and it's brimming with gusto. It's about me, living in a cottage and scorned by the critics. Arthur Armstrong, you know: you remember his disgraceful article in that Sunday rag. I give it him hot: he's a venial critic, and he blackguards me in the press, and then I nurse him through brain fever. You gave me the idea yourself, the morning his article came out, down the telephone. It is good, isn't it, Bosanquet? ''

'' Yes, miss: quite your top note,'' said Bosanquet.

'' Very well,'' said Nunky. '' I'll take the manuscript away and send it to be typed.''

Augustus drew out a pocket writing-pad.

'' That's settled then, is it? '' he said. '' *Amor Vincit* to appear in October, instead of *Julian Beltravers* in November. What may I say about it, Susanna? I must have one interview with Rudolph about it.''

'' Just say that it's about a wonderful young authoress whom the press always snubs, and whom all thinking people with any sense of beauty adore, and who gives the press-notices to her Great Dane to tear to bits without even opening them——''

'' Why does she subscribe to a press-agency then? '' asked the carping Nunky.

'' Don't be silly, dear. Oh, I forgot: she does read them with shrieks of laughter first, so that makes it all right. Then another thing, Nunky, I want to write a short preface saying that no copies of *Amor Vincit* will be sent out for review. That will be a slap for the critics, won't it, and I don't believe it will make any difference to my sales.''

'' I think I must send one to Arthur Armstrong,''

said Nunky, " in the hope that he'll abuse you again. My putting extracts from his article on the new jacket of *Rosemary and Rue* certainly stimulated the sales."

" Very well, if you wish it," said Susan, " but not to the others. Just think of their buying it themselves and then finding out what I think of them! And how I shall look forward to Mr. Armstrong dining with me again, when the book is out. That'll be a bit of irony all right! "

Mrs. Mantrip, even with so great a prize in prospect, had almost got tired of waiting, when at the conclusion of this long and weighty Cabinet meeting, the distinguished company actually came out of Susan's house and entered the garden, with Bosanquet carrying deck-chairs for them. Sigurd did not accompany them, as he preferred to dally with Atahualpa through the railings of the area gate next door, and so Mrs. Mantrip's ingenious dodge of calling herself Auntie could not be executed. But there was no need for that, since Susan, now at leisure and feeling kindly disposed to her, owing to her discovery of the well-thumbed *Heart's Queen* in her chair, tripped towards her with a far more cordial expression on her face than it had previously been wont to wear on chance meetings. Her two companions followed a step or two behind.

Mrs. Mantrip struggled to her feet: the difficulty of getting out of a low deck-chair with ease and dignity was very great, but she surged upwards somehow. Had Susan been alone, she would probably have remained sitting and not tried to be an acrobat, but she could not bear not to rise up in reverence at the presence of the " original " of her newly acquired photograph. What a speaking likeness the photograph was, and now it looked very much as if the original would speak too. Her right hand was advanced to take Susan's: in her left she held the book so that its title was clearly displayed. Susan saw it and her cordiality rose (as R. da V. would have said) correspondingly.

" Good afternoon, dear Mrs. Mantrip," she said. " How charming and shady the garden is. Your father's trees, I remember you told me. May I introduce to you my friends, Mr. Cartwright, the famous publisher, and Mr. Augustus Bosanquet? "

For a moment, when she heard this totally unexpected name, the whole garden, deck-chairs and publishers and Papa's sumacs and all, seemed to whirl giddily round. But then almost instantly she understood, for she knew well how the great author always shunned personal publicity when meeting strangers. (He had once gone up the Nile as Mr. John Smith, so Ulrica had told the world.) Had he seen perhaps how like he was to Susan's butler, and had humorously said he would be Mr. Bosanquet for the time being? Charming playfulness! It was only good manners to respect his incognito.

Bosanquet had placed the deck-chairs he brought out so as to form an intimate group.

" But aren't we interrupting your reading? " asked Susan.

" No, not at all, not at all," cried Mrs. Mantrip. " I was only just glancing at my book: I open it anywhere, for I know it so well. Have you read it, Mr. Cartwright? Dear me, how silly I am, considering you published it! *Heart's Queen*. Quite one of his best, I think."

This was all perfectly correct conduct. She quite respected Mr. da Vinci's incognito (just as if she had not the faintest idea of his identity) and merely expressed a reader's enthusiasm. As for keeping up the highbrow critical attitude with regard to his work, here and now in his presence, such a notion was that of a lunatic.

" I've got good news for you then, Mrs. Mantrip," said Cartwright, " if you are an admirer of Mr. da

Vinci's work. I've just arranged to bring out another book of his in October."

"Oh, that will be a treat," said Mrs. Mantrip, still not even glancing at Augustus. "I had seen somewhere in the paper—Ulrica, I think, of the *Evening Chronicle*—that we might look for another in November, but the earlier the better. That will be *Julian Beltravers*, I suppose?"

"No, another one which he has just finished. *Amor Vincit* is the title of it."

"How I shall look forward to it! *Amor Vincit*. What a beautiful title! I must remember to order it at once."

Mr. Bosanquet glanced across at Susan, and Mrs. Mantrip caught that look. There was sly, playful mischief in it, which immediately made itself audible as well.

"I can't share your enthusiasm, Mrs. Mantrip," he said. "How that man can go on turning out and the public go on devouring all that rubbish is beyond me altogether. I consider Mr. Cartwright is a criminal for aiding and abetting him."

"Dear Augustus! How severe you are on him!" said Susan.

"But surely you agree," said he, "that it's all the most wretched stuff. And the pace he produces it at! One would think that he wrote two books together, one with each hand."

This was too utterly delightful. Mrs. Mantrip felt she was witnessing, even taking part in, some delicious comedy full of witty double meanings. Only Rudolph could have spoken thus.

"Oh, Mr. Bosanquet?" she cried. "How can you say such shocking things? I regard him as quite the most brilliant and beautiful author of the age."

"I can't agree," said Augustus. "I was never more pleased than when Mr. Armstrong put him

properly in his place in the *Sunday Chronicle*. That
man has got a prodigious brain."

" I was pleased too," said Cartwright. " It sent
up the sales instantly."

Susan gave her silvery laugh.

" Poor Mr. Armstrong ! " she said. " His malice
sadly miscarried then. He's rather a friend of mine.
If I was Mr. da Vinci I should write something scathing about him. I should make him a venial critic.
I should scarify him."

Mrs. Mantrip duly noted " venial critic." So like
the poor uneducated thing ! But she forgave her
(though she would probably tell Elizabeth), for she
had brought about this wonderful meeting.

" Precisely what Rudolph has done, I believe, in
Amor Vincit," said Cartwright. " He gave me a
little sketch of it not very long ago."

" But how interesting ! " said Mrs. Mantrip.
" What a privilege to have heard about it ! "

Susan felt that she must return some of these extra-
ordinarily handsome compliments that Mrs. Mantrip
was showering on her. Only fair. She was, after
all, a most agreeable woman and parts of *Amor Vincit*
would need a drastic revision.

" I must tell you that you're talking to another
author, Nunky," she said. " Mrs. Mantrip is engaged
in writing a life of her wonderful father. Such a
good man. How is it getting on, Mrs. Mantrip ? "

Mrs. Mantrip was covered with pleasing confusion :
never had confusion given so much pleasure.

" Dear Miss Leg, how can you allude to my little
scribblings ! " she cried. " I'm shocked. But just
for your ear I may say that I've been very busy lately
and not wholly displeased at what I've done. But
it's a long way from complete yet. A good deal of
research necessary."

" But such interesting research," said Susan, paying back compliments in ringing coins. " And how

he raised the tone of the Square! What a delightful chapter that will be, though I believe naughty Nunky would have liked it best before.''

A slight blush rose to Mrs. Mantrip's face at these indelicate observations: she hastened to sponge it off.

'' Almost reminds me a little of what Heart's Queen did on her estate,'' she said. '' Such a beautiful description.''

Before long Bosanquet came out to say that Susan's car was round, and the two ladies strolled away together towards the garden gate. It would not be indiscreet, when he was no longer within hearing, for Mrs. Mantrip to indicate, ever so delicately, that she knew that Mr. Bosanquet was really somebody else, though she would keep the delightful mystery up and not suffer the great name to pass her lips.

'' So interesting and such a privilege to have met Mr. Cartwright and Mr. Bosanquet,'' she said in a low voice, for the others were following. '' And would it be very wrong of me, dear Miss Leg, just to hint that I think I've heard of Mr. Bosanquet under another name? ''

Susan could not imagine how Mrs. Mantrip knew that Augustus was Ulrica, but she nodded.

'' Yes, you're quite right,'' she whispered. '' But not a word, please. The sanctity of private life. How did you know? ''

Considering all the circumstances, purchase and forgery and the rest, it was better not to be explicit.

'' I think I must have seen a photograph of him,'' said Mrs. Mantrip cautiously. '' Certainly I recognized him at once. But his secret is quite safe with me.''

The two men joined them and Mrs. Mantrip saw Susan and Rudolph da Vinci set off for a drive in the Park. Sigurd sat, large and panting, on the front seat. It would have been nice, she thought, if Mr. da Vinci had brought his Alsatian as well. But perhaps it did not get on with that great awkward dog of Susan's.

She returned to her house in a highly braced condition; she trailed clouds of glory. Susan had been most cordial. She had said that she was going off to-morrow or the next day for a little sea air at Brighton, but when she returned and began to get her friends round her again, she hoped that she would see her landlady much more frequently than had been the case lately. The landlady heartily concurred, and other meetings with Rudolph da Vinci might confidently be anticipated. But far transcending this, as a tonic, was the thrilling meeting which had already taken place. It inspired her to tackle her literary labours with a wholly new ardency to be aware that a fellow craftsman (and such a fellow craftsman !) saw little merit in his work. She had had her doubts about the value of her own, but it was an easy matter now to dismiss so false a modesty when she found that the very greatest authors shared such misgivings and spoke of their own work as rubbish. His photograph, standing on the table in front of her, became an inspiration; it filled her with courage to tackle the difficulties that bestrewed her path. She must wield a more romantic pen, produce something with the da Vinci touch, and she plunged into the account of the Augean stable. All the next day she worked, and it was not till her parlourmaid came in to tell her that it was seven o'clock and to bring in the evening paper, that she finally left the table on which now lay so many sheets of finely-wrought manuscript.

With a sigh of well-earned relaxation, she opened the *Evening Chronicle*. There was little of interest in the more solid news of the day; the pictures of an abortive attempt of a lady swimmer, who looked like

a sausage with goggles, to negotiate the English
Channel did not rouse her admiration. " Better go
by the Calais-Dover boat next time," she thought
ironically, and turned to brighter pages. Ulrica had
a column and a half of chatty paragraphs, and
instantly her own name caught her eye. That had
not happened since she married. When she had
overcome a natural dizziness she read:

" Miss Susan Leg, who is leaving London very
shortly, has been seeing a few friends. I found her
in the pleasant garden of Durham Square yesterday
afternoon, with a *partie carrée* of literary folk. There
was Mrs. Mantrip, her neighbour, who is busy with a
life of her father; Mr. Cartwright, the famous
publisher, and Mr. Rudolph da Vinci. Only yesterday morning the latter finished the book which has
kept him so closely employed throughout August, and
which will be published by Mr. Cartwright during
October, under the title of *Amor Vincit*. He now
hopes to get away to Brighton for a brief rest, the air
of which he finds so invigorating after long hours in
his study. He had with him, as usual, his magnificent
Alsatian."

Mrs. Mantrip's first emotion on reading this was,
of course, one of undiluted exaltation. Her work
had been mentioned in the papers (or paper) long
before its appearance and in the most highly distinguished company. The potent wine of publicity
mounted to her totally-abstaining head, and snipping
this paragraph out, heedless of what might be at the
back of it, she sent her parlourmaid out to purchase
three more copies to send to friends. Jimmie should
have one, Eva another and Elizabeth the third, and
she would put a red pencil direction on the first page
to " see p. 13." She had long been aware that there
was an impression among them that the wheels of

her literary chariot were tarrying, but this would give
them the welcome assurance that it was bowling
along.

The pleasant fever subsided, and reading the
paragraph through once or twice more she began to
see that in some respects it was most inaccurate: it
was full of mistakes. Certainly there had been a
partie carrée in the garden yesterday afternoon, but
they had not all been literary, for there was Susan
among them, and Ulrica had not been there at all.
Again, it was not Rudolph who was just off to
Brighton, but Susan, and the magnificent Alsatian
spoken of was not his, but hers. Yet Ulrica must
have been present, for she had heard a quantity of
things they had said. Could she have been sitting up
in Papa's sumac, concealed by the abundant foliage,
and taking down in shorthand the conversation of
these literary folk? It did not seem likely: in fact,
without hesitation, Mrs. Mantrip ruled out the
possibility.

Then suddenly like a crash of thunder immediately
overhead the solution came to her. There were four
of them: that was right. There was herself, there
was Mr. Augustus Bosanquet, whom she knew to be
Rudolph da Vinci, there was Mr. Cartwright, and
there was Susan, who was evidently Ulrica. No
longer need the Square puzzle itself about her and
her secret, for it was here revealed, and here, in the
snipped-out paragraph was a sample of the literary
work on pieces of foolscap that her gramophone
inspired. All this summer, every week and even
oftener, she had been boosting herself and her parties
and her friendship with Rudolph da Vinci and Lady
Mackleton and Mr. Armstrong, M.P., using her position on the press as a ladder for social climbing.
Mrs. Mantrip had constantly wondered why Ulrica
was for ever harping on Susan's Alsatian and her
fork-lunches and her little hole-in-the-corner parties,

and now the reason was absolutely plain. Artful
Susan was Ulrica.

There was no other conclusion possible. The
proposition was Q.E.D., as Papa used to say when he
taught her the elements of Euclid, and that meant, when
translated from the Latin, " which was to be demonstrated." Poor dear Jimmie had got very much
excited one night at the notion that Susan's income was
derived from the books which she wrote to the braying
of the gramophone, and which Mr. Cartwright published. Ingenious, though, as she herself had maintained at the time, quite ludicrous, but Jimmie had
a knack of getting hold of the wrong end of a stick,
and here was a conclusive instance of his erroneous
imaginings. Susan got her money from being Ulrica,
and though it was surprising to find that this type of
journalism was so extremely well paid, there was no
getting away from facts.

It was distressing to find that Susan was a spy for
the press and retailed her own activities and the doings
of her friends to the advantage of her purse, and Mrs.
Mantrip felt that she would be bound to tell her circle
of the discovery. It was only right that they should
know that what they said to Susan in the closet might
be bawled out to the world by Fleet Street, and they
would all have to be careful. Yet there was another
side to it. Only a few moments ago, she herself had
been justly intoxicated with the thought that all
students of the press would learn that she was writing
the life of her father, and had been chatting with
Rudolph da Vinci, and, to do Susan justice, it was she,
and she alone, who had brewed for her that heady joy.
She owed Susan something for that: besides, she hoped
to owe Susan many more similar debts of gratitude of
the same type. She decided to overlook all such
duplicities in the past as concerned herself, and any
similar ones she might be guilty of in the future.

XI

MISS MIMPS received a most friendly letter from Rudolph da Vinci next morning, enclosing five pounds and requesting the return of the signed photograph and of the last letter she had received from him. R. da V. was sorry to trouble her, but a complicated question of international copyright was concerned, and he hoped the apparent ungraciousness of this request would be atoned for by the enclosed Treasury notes. This letter, though superficially simple, was of mixed parentage: Susan had dictated it to Bosanquet, Bosanquet wrote, as before, over the signature of Rudolph da Vinci, and Nunky had supplied the Treasury notes.

Had Miss Mimps known its history, she would certainly have sat down and thought what further bonus could be made out of it: as it was, the problem presented to her fine judgment as to what a perfect lady should do in these rather exceptional circumstances was very simple; indeed every course but one was ruled out. She could not possibly answer that she had sold the letter and photograph to Mrs. Mantrip (22 Durham Square) for ten pounds, for such a statement in black and white would make her look a very mercenary person. Besides, it had been agreed between the high contracting parties that all lips were to be sealed, and a perfect lady, after having given her promise, would scorn to go back on it. She could not point-blank refuse to do as requested, because that would be unfriendly to kind Mr. da Vinci. She there-

fore wrote back to say that she much regretted that she
had lost the letter and the photograph: otherwise she
would have been very glad to accede to Mr. da Vinci's
proposal.   With regard to the Treasury notes, the
simplest plan was to keep them pending future events.
She might be obliged eventually to return them, but
it seemed very unlikely that a gentleman like him would
take summary steps to recover them.   In fact, Miss
Mimps's acute business-sense detected something odd
about the whole affair.   She guessed there was a
sleeping dog somewhere (though of what species she
could not exactly say), which Mr. da Vinci might
easily prefer should be let lie, even at the cost of five
pounds.   That allusion to international copyright was
pure rubbish: she felt sure there was some other reason
behind that, why he wanted the things back.   Five
pounds, too, was rather a paltry sum to have sent her,
when Mrs. Mantrip had been so prompt with an offer
twice as handsome, but, given that all went well, she
would have got fifteen pounds out of the transaction,
which, as far as she was concerned, was impeccable,
for all she had done was to tell Mr. da Vinci the truth
about that Susan Leg's past.   That was the penny she
had put in the slot, and the agreeable machine had
vomited fifteen pounds at her.

Miss Mimps's letter of regret announcing, though
not explaining, the sad loss of the photograph, arrived
at Susan's house just as she was preparing to start for
Brighton.   It was rather disquieting, for, knowing
Mimps, she naturally did not believe that the photograph had been lost at all, and Nunky's dark speeches
about forgery recalled themselves to her mind.   She
rang him up to tell him what had happened, and he was
not consoling.   He was sorry about it: he agreed that
the photograph was not lost, but was probably being
withheld for some sinister purpose.   Also he was very
much vexed with Ulrica for the paragraph about the

partie carrée. It gave Mrs. Mantrip a broad hint as to who R. da V. was. He scolded Susan as if it was her fault, and she had answered him with some clever tears in her voice, and said he was very unkind and ungrateful.

"You mustn't bully me like this," she huskily whispered. "You expect me to produce beautiful work for you and give me no freedom. Perhaps you're tired of publishing what I write. Please say so if you are, and I'll find somebody else."

She winked at Bosanquet who was listening with an anxious face to this colloquy, and Nunky climbed down at once. Finally he told her not to bother herself any more about the photograph: no doubt he was making a mountain out of a molehill. He would try to get down to Brighton on Sunday on purpose to be forgiven. He would have read *Amor Vincit*, he hoped, by that time. These agitating topics caused them both to forget that Mimps had retained the five Treasury notes which had been sent her in payment for the return of the photograph and letter, thus her caution in not acting hastily about that was amply justified.

Though Ulrica had briefly announced that Rudolph da Vinci was going to Brighton, she did not follow that up with the news that he had arrived at the Regency Palace Hotel, because the editor of the *Evening Chronicle* had sent her a peremptory note saying that he had had more than enough of R. da V. and of Miss Susan Leg for the present, and preferred that they should be left yachting in Norway or rotting in Durham Square for a while. Augustus had not, of course, communicated this editorial surfeit to Susan, but, in consequence of it, the arrival of neither of her incarnations in Brighton was heralded by the press. But she had been working very hard—she had finished two full-length romances in a little over three months—and she was not sorry to have a complete relaxation out of the public eye, and to feel that the crowd which thronged the hotel had no idea that the small lady with pearls, who sat alone in the restaurant or quietly dozed over cross-word puzzles in the lounge, was the much sought-after Susan Leg whose fork-luncheons had been so brilliant a feature of the London season. Nor was anybody looking out for the appearance of Rudolph da Vinci; no eager eyes were raised to the door, only to be dropped again in disappointment when they saw it was nobody at all. No one was on the look-out for either of her.

Incognita⁰ ⎱ she strolled or sat on the sea-front, she toyed with penny-in-the-slot machines on the pier, she thought a man was following her one evening in the dusk, but found to her great relief that she was mistaken, and returned to the hotel feeling rather flat; she went on a marine excursion down the coast in the *Eastbourne Belle*. This was not a great success, for though there was a band on board, she was not in need of loud noises just now, and before the pleasure-trip was over, the sea got up, and the *Eastbourne Belle* proved to be a very frolicsome lady, fond of dancing. Susan made some mental notes which might come in useful for future scenes, about bulwarks with surges dashing over them, but she had made plenty of these and was tired of the pranks of the surges before they were.

After that she lived her recuperative holiday life ashore. There was a luxurious sense of internal splendour veiled from every eye in being thus unknown, and she passed a fortnight in peaceful and expensive solitude in a small, convenient suite on the first floor of the hotel. Nunky came down for a couple of nights and told her that the proofs of *Amor Vincit* (of which he highly approved) would require her attention when she got back to London, but she saw little of him as he

had with him a companion who greatly engrossed his
attention. He introduced her to Susan as his cousin,
but Susan, though steadily refraining from thinking
evil things, concluded that the relationship was a
distant one. Mr. Armstrong, M.P., was also down for
this Sunday, but he seemed to look coldly on the
publisher, possibly remembering the use that Cartwright had made of his scarification of *Rosemary and
Rue*. Susan had some pleasant lectures from him on
the subjects of himself and food, but, after what he had
said about R. da V., she had entirely ceased to revere
his literary gifts. He asked if he might dine with her
again when she got back to London, and he remembered with astonishing vividness and detail the perfect
dinner he had eaten at her house in the summer. She
was delighted that he should come again, for he might
say something further in his weekly column about her
cuisine. She must also remember when she came to
correcting the proofs of *Amor Vincit* to insert a paragraph about the loathsome greed of the venial critic
when he partook of Serena Lomond's hospitality.

While Susan was enjoying this Arcadian existence
without any of the limelight which the publicity of
either of her incarnations would have shed on her, the
houses in Durham Square were swiftly filling up with
those who had returned from their holidays, and were
settling in to do nothing at all at home. Mrs. Mantrip,
as in duty bound, had wasted no opportunity of
acquainting her friends with her discovery that Susan
was Ulrica, and that all those fulsome paragraphs in
the press about her parties and her fork-luncheons were
written by herself. These communications were made
in strict confidence and under the stern bidding of duty,
for Susan might resent the disclosure of her secret life.
That would never do: nothing must imperil the friendly
relations which had begun, and which Mrs. Mantrip
hoped would speedily ripen into intimacy. She wanted

lots more talks with R. da V.: his modesty about his own work had already given her a stimulus which was being immensely fruitful with regard to her own. Swiftly and confidently now she scribbled away at the Life.

"I felt you ought to know, about Miss Leg," she said to Eva, "for we must all be a little careful what we say in front of her. One doesn't want confidential conversation repeated; one must be on one's guard. I should never, for instance, have told her about my father's life, if I had known she would make use of it."

"How is that getting on?" asked Eva suddenly, unfocussing her eyes in that disconcerting manner of hers, and gazing dreamily at Mrs. Mantrip's hair.

"Very well indeed, dear Eva," she answered. "I've been working very hard and, I think, successfully. I've never got on so fast and well before."

Eva waited to see the glow of anchovy-paste tinge, like a dyspeptic sunset, Mrs. Mantrip's grey locks, but it did nothing of the kind. Her halo remained of that crude topaz hue (denoting an unsympathetic but truthful nature) which was usual with her. She must be writing the Life after all.

"Glad to hear it," said Eva. "Also most interesting about Leg. But I'm disappointed if that was all that her corn-coloured halo meant, though to be sure Ulrica is imaginative enough. Are you sure you're right?"

"Positive. There were just the four of us that afternoon in the garden. Rudolph da Vinci, Mr. Cartwright, she and I. And there it all was, with all we said, in the paper next day. I sent you a copy."

"I must get hold of her when she comes back," said Eva. "I'm the President of the Halo Society this year, and the papers will never publish the accounts we send them of our meetings. Splendid to get Ulrica."

" But don't tell her I told you," said Mrs. Mantrip.
" Evidently she does not want it to be known, and I'm
sure I don't wonder, considering the way she has used
her position."

" Naturally I shan't tell her. I shall just chat to
her about the Halo Society as if to a sympathetic friend.
I shall ask her to a meeting. Glorious discovery of
yours, Mantrip."

Mrs. Mantrip sighed; she could seldom resist a
sprinkle of Papa.

" Poor Miss Leg ! " she said. " But perhaps I'm
a little old-fashioned. Papa always brought me up to
think that our private lives were our own."

" But you've got over that," said Eva encouragingly, " as you're going to publish all you can
remember of his. I shall make much of Leg."

Elizabeth was the next confidante. She took exactly
the same line as Eva.

" My word, what a piece of luck," she said. " It
was clever of you, Margaret, to find that out. I shall
ask her to be an honorary member of the Dog-Lovers'
Association. Social paragraphs are just what we want.
They make no end of people join."

Mrs. Mantrip had not intended that her revelations
should have the effect of causing Susan to become such
a popular person, but wherever she made them the
result was the same. Jimmie Mason, who had come
up to London for a couple of days (the same tooth)
but was going back to spend the rest of September at
Cookham, instantly wrote to Susan, asking her down
for a particularly smart week-end party that he was
giving, and the Vicar sent her the prospectus of the
Christian Reincarnation Club which met every fortnight at his house. Mr. Gandish, the President of the
West London Badminton Association, the membership
of which had been falling off sadly, hoped for a revival
of interest in that health-giving game (which could be

played by artificial light, and was independent of weather) if Ulrica would only give it publicity in the press. Mr. Salt, the dog-hater, who bathed in the fresh waters of the Serpentine every morning, especially when it was frozen over, foresaw that if only Ulrica would become a bather, which she might easily do, now that mixed bathing was sanctioned by an enlightened Government, her popular pen could be of no end of use to the Hyde Park Swimming Club.

So when Susan, braced by the Brighton air to an unexampled pitch of energy and having no novel on hand, returned to London, she found that the Square, now fully believing that she was Ulrica, was panting for her presence and her power. On the very afternoon that she arrived, she went to tea with Lady Eva, at whose house the Halo Society was to meet. Before the business proper began, Lady Eva established her on a throne-like chair, and a string of members were brought up to her for audiences. They had the distraught and hungry aspect of those who concern themselves much in occult matters, and told her the most remarkable stories. A presidential address followed, in which Lady Eva said that everybody had haloes, and that the power of seeing them was a gift that could be cultivated and certainly should be. When once you could see haloes, you had an infallible guide as to the character of those with whom daily life brought you in contact, but this was not generally known. People were slow to take in new ideas, and the press was afraid of them. What the Halo Society chiefly needed was publicity; they wanted some very well-known and gifted journalist who would constantly, in social paragraphs, write about the Society and its work, and keep it continually before the public. Haloism would then soon be admitted to be an exact and most useful science, and they might all, especially the youngest, live to see it taught in elementary schools. Children of six would then be able to discern good and evil from this opening of the inward eye, and a race of supermen and women could be confidently expected. Hitherto the crass ignorance and timidity of the press had kept progress back, but if only one of the great journalists would give the lead, the rest would follow.

During this eloquent address Susan had become aware that the hungry eyes of many Haloists had been fixed ever more and more firmly on her. She could not imagine why, unless it was that they all saw round her head the very gratifying emanation that Lady Eva had noticed there. That was very pleasant; she liked to let them feast their eyes on her golden halo, and at the conclusion of the meeting she applied for membership. She was instantly enrolled amid long and loud applause, and the President, warmly shaking her by her hand, felt sure that she would do her best for the welfare of the Society. And would she not look in on Saturday next at 3 p.m., to see a demonstration of halo-reading? Lady Eva had procured from a trustworthy board-school teacher in a sealed envelope the written characters of six of her pupils. These six children would be present, and Lady Eva would vivisect their characters by their haloes and her pronouncements would be taken down. The sealed envelope would then be opened, and its contents would certainly be found to verify her vivisection. That sounded interesting, and Susan promised to come.

She went back to her house and found a note from Elizabeth asking if she might look in for a few minutes. She looked in and brought with her the last three numbers of *The Dog-Lovers' Quarterly*.

"The subject nearest my heart," said Elizabeth. "And I knew that you, with your interest in dogs, which you showed so strikingly when you supported the admission of our angels to the garden, would be a sympathetic listener. How is your beautiful Sigurd?"

"Very well, thank you," said Susan. "How is—I should say how are—yours?"

" All flourishing, including Eusapia's latest," said Elizabeth. " This *Dog-Lovers' Quarterly* now. It only requires to be known to be appreciated. The diet and general management of our pets, distemper, their nuptials, everything. Many thousands of dog-owners want to know much that they will find lucidly described here with copious illustrations. What they don't know is where to look for it. Thousands of canine lives have been lost because owners do not take it in. Publicity, dear Miss Leg, is badly needed. An occasional paragraph in the press, though, of course, the less occasional the better, would be most useful to all dog-owners, and would also send up the circulation by leaps and bounds. You ought to belong to the Association, and I'm sure the Committee would make you an honorary member. Your name and influence would help it enormously."

Bosanquet entered.

" Could you see the Vicar, miss? " he asked. " A matter of some importance, his Reverence says."

" Yes, show him up, Bosanquet," said Susan. " I should indeed be honoured, Mrs. Conklin, by being made an honorary member of the Dog-Lovers' Association, and I will certainly take in the *Quarterly*."

" So kind of you," said Elizabeth. " And you'll work for us, won't you? I'll leave these numbers of the *Quarterly* with you, and then I'm sure you will. Good evening, Vicar."

" A hasty call, Miss Leg," said he. " Charmed to see you back and looking so well. We had a most interesting talk once on the subject of reincarnation. You may not remember it, but I do."

" But dogs have souls, Vicar," said Elizabeth. " Don't try to make Miss Leg think they haven't. I've seen a look in Sabrina's eyes that spoke direct to me, heart to heart. Good-bye, dear Miss Leg; so good of you to have seen me. Do come to the general meeting of the Dog-Lovers' Association on Saturday at noon at my house."

She shook a playful finger at the Vicar and said
" Bow-wow " by way of salutation. Bosanquet took
her away, and the Vicar leant in a thoughtful attitude
against the alabaster chimney-piece.

" So well do I remember it," he resumed. " You
told us at a luncheon-party given by our excellent
friend Mrs. Mantrip, that you felt sure you had once
been Marie Antoinette. That made a deep impression
on me, for these instincts are to be trusted, and, from
that moment, I knew that you were one of us. Reincarnation to me, and I am sure to you, is a part, and
no meagre one, of religion. It is a facet of the great
diamond of truth that flashes the rays of its illuminating
spectrum in every direction. Others may approach
truth from other quarters, but you and I, I know,
approach it from the same. Our doctrines have only
to be more widely known to be accepted by all earnest
Christian people. Several bishops, to my knowledge,
believe in them, but they are afraid of confessing it.
The Church is sadly hide-bound in many ways. What
all reincarnationists long for, aye, and indeed pray for,
is that their beliefs should be made more familiar to the
people. Church papers are shy of alluding to them:
it is to the secular press that we must look."

" All most interesting," said Susan, " and I am so
pleased to know that you think I may really have been
Marie Antoinette. Why don't you write a letter to *The
Times* about it all ? "

A look of pain crossed the Vicar's face.

" I have done so on many occasions," he said.
" So often, indeed, that I feel we must approach the
public in lighter fashion. More chattiness. I should
like when I picked up, say, an evening paper, to see
that at some little, or indeed big gathering of distinguished people, the subject of reincarnation was
much discussed over the tea-urn or the walnuts and the
wine. I should like to see some such paragraph as
that again and again, until the ordinary man in the

street—never mind the bishops at present—began to feel an interest in our beloved doctrines. Many of them will have experienced those sacred convictions, of which they are too shy to speak, that they have lived and loved on this earth before. But when they feel that others have felt them also, they will lose their diffidence.''

The eternal verities did not interest Susan nearly as much as the fact that this highly spiritual man thought that she might have been Marie Antoinette. If she was widely known as the reincarnation of that distinguished lady, that would surely be a valuable social asset.

'' I'm so glad you think that I was the Queen,'' she said. '' And you've got a Society about it? ''

'' That, dear Miss Leg, is what I came to you to speak about. The Christian Reincarnation Club is at present the only organized body which works for the propagation of our precious knowledge. It meets every fortnight at the Vicarage; in fact, now I come to think of it, there is a meeting in three days' time. We would all welcome you most warmly if you could, among your many engagements, honour us by attending it, and, I hope, by becoming a regular member. We need all the help we can get, not so much in the way of money as of truly influential support.''

Susan felt very much flattered, and to be sure the support of the reincarnation of Marie Antoinette would be much appreciated by the Club, and would be indeed influential. She made a note of the day and hour, and promised to be at the meeting. It had been fixed for Saturday at four o'clock in the afternoon, but there would be plenty of time after that to drive down to Jimmie Mason's house at Cookham for the week-end party. How right Bosanquet had been when he had assured her that her wonderful social successes of the summer would render her independent of Lady Mackleton !

Next day Susan received an afternoon call from
Mr. Gandish, a lean, elderly gentleman with a fringe
of hair encircling a bald scalp. One half of this was
pure white, the other half coal black, which accounted
for the colouring of the twins. He was as lively as a
grig and extremely brisk in his movements for one of
his years. A ring of the curtains stuck as Bosanquet
was drawing them, and in a moment he had hopped
on to a chair to release it.

" Yes, indeed, I'm pretty nimble yet," he said, as
Susan congratulated him on his agility, " and I put
it down to regular Badminton. During the winter
months in our foggy, rainy climate, it is impossible to
walk with any enjoyment, and it is in the winter, if
you follow me, that our joints therefore get stiff with
disuse, and our muscles flabby for want of full, brisk
movements."

Susan had come across the word Badminton in her
study of the *Peerage*.

" A wonderful house, is it not? " she asked. " Or
is it a game of some sort as well? "

Mr. Gandish looked shocked.

" You astonish me, Miss Leg," he said, taking a
large slice of rich chocolate cake. " Badminton is the
king of indoor games, and it is regular Badminton, I
repeat, which keeps me in such perfect condition.
What man of my age, do you think, could eat so
large a portion of your delicious rich cake at a late
tea and yet be as hungry as a hunter for his dinner?
But I can, for from half-past six to half-past seven this
evening I shall play Badminton single-handed against
my two boys, in the garage at the back of my house,
which I have fitted out as a court for our club. I used
to suffer at one time from indigestion, loss of appetite,
liver and kidney trouble, constipation, corns, depression, and cramp. Never a trace of any of them now,
since I have taken to Badminton. Vanished, Miss
Leg ! "

Even Susan's powerful imagination could not picture the idea of waking up in the morning suffering from all these distressing ailments at one time. She hastened to applaud any treatment that would get rid of them.

" But surely we ought all to play Badminton every day then," she said. " I never heard of anything so wonderful."

" Exactly so, Miss Leg. You take the words out of my mouth, and I perceive that you are an enthusiast already. You must experience the benefits of Badminton for yourself. You must come down to my house, my humble little temple of health, and have a game. Now on Friday afternoon I have a few other enthusiasts dropping in. Rain or fine, light or dark make no difference to our pursuit, for I have an admirable electric arc-lamp. May I not persuade you to honour me? "

Susan had to look at her engagement book. There were meetings of the Dog-Lovers' Association, of the Halo Society, and of the Reincarnation Club at which she had already promised to be present, but Friday afternoon was luckily free.

" Dear me, what a whirl London is," she said delightedly. " I am always worked to death between this and that. But I'm glad to say I can manage Friday."

" Capital! Capital! " ejaculated Mr. Gandish, taking some more chocolate cake. " I regard you already, Miss Leg, not as a convert merely, but a fanatic. It only needs that Badminton and its benefits —a most amusing game too—should become known, for it to be among the foremost of our national sports. At present it is practically boycotted by the press. Occasionally you may see some notice of a county match in an obscure corner of a sporting paper, but what we want are constant little allusions to it in the daily paragraphs we all read so greedily. Think what

an impetus it would give to the game, if we saw now
and again in the paper that Miss Susan Leg, shall we
say, and Mr. Rudolph da Vinci had been having some
great tussles lately. He, I know, is a great friend of
yours. What a genius! I read little else."

It was only natural that Susan should feel strongly
predisposed towards Badminton after these handsome
remarks, and though a series of tussles (or even a single
one) between her and Rudolph da Vinci would be
harder to stage than Mr. Gandish could have any idea,
she willingly promised to do her best for Badminton.
He finished his cake and leapt to his feet.

" I must be off," he said. " All lovers of Badminton will be overjoyed to hear that I have enlisted
your sympathy. Friday afternoon then, at half-past
two."

Bosanquet entered. He was not accustomed to go
up and down stairs so frequently and looked tired.

" Mr. Salt is below, miss," he said wearily. " Can
he see you for a few minutes? "

" By all means. Show him up," said Susan.
" Friday afternoon then, Mr. Gandish. Such a
pleasure."

Mr. Gandish skipped from the room after picking
up a teaspoon from the floor without bending his knees,
and Susan heard him leaping downstairs. The house,
in fact, seemed full of athletes, for hardly had the sound
of his downward activity ceased than somebody else
came bounding upstairs, and apparently waited outside
the door till Bosanquet caught him up and announced
him. In came Mr. Salt with the bloom of youth on
his face and a mop of thick white hair standing straight
on end by reason of its native vigour. Sigurd gambolled round him, thinking he wanted to play.

" A beautiful dog of yours, Miss Leg," he said.
" Usually, as you know, I detest dogs, but upon my
word I must make an exception here. Is he fond of
the water? "

" I can't keep him away from it," said Susan. " Whenever I walk in the Park by the Serpentine, he plunges in. Lie down, Sigurd."

Mr. Salt slapped the tea-table and made the tea-cups tinkle in their saucers.

" That's the bond between him and me then," he said triumphantly. " I can't be kept out of the Serpentine either, and woe be to anyone who tried ! Every day, Miss Leg, I have my morning swim there. Hot or cold, rain or fine makes no difference to me. Swimming's food and drink to me, and washing as well, if it comes to that."

In spite of swimming being food to Mr. Salt, he was easily persuaded to supplement it in the more ordinary way. In fact, he ate as heartily as Mr. Gandish: swimming seemed as good for the appetite as Badminton.

" I have an astounding fact to put before you, Miss Leg," he said, " and one which will fill you with horror. Out of the entire population of our island, which I need hardly remind you is completely surrounded by water, only seven per cent. can swim. Ninety-three per cent. would infallibly drown if they got out of their depth. How could seven swimmers save ninety-three non-swimmers, I ask you ? A holocaust."

" Dear me, that does seem a lot," said Susan.

" In London, the percentage of non-swimmers is even higher," said Mr. Salt. " I dare say it's ninety-five, though I haven't worked it out accurately. And, mark you, there is no excuse for them. I consider that any man or woman who is drowned has committed suicide."

" I see your point of view," said Susan sympathetically. " You mean that they might have learned to swim and didn't."

" Precisely. You take the words out of my mouth. But anyone who joins the Hyde Park Swimming Club at the purely nominal subscription of five shillings a

year, with a big reduction for families, can be taught
swimming for nothing, and thus be enabled not to save
his own life alone, but that of others. Then there is
no such health-giving and enjoyable exercise in the
world. And then the excitement of our swimming-
races! Prodigious! On Saturday morning next we
hold the Serpentine Derby. Three furlongs finishing
close to the bridge. You ought to see it, Miss Leg:
indeed you ought."

" I should so much like to," said Susan. " I am
sure I should be thrilled. But I'm afraid Saturday is
rather a full day for me already."

" I promise you that it will not interfere with your
other engagements," said Mr. Salt. " It takes place
at a quarter to eight in the morning. From the bridge
you will see it admirably. Quite like the grandstand.
And, I'll be bound, if you see it once you'll never miss
it again."

She got her engagement book and found there was
nothing to interfere with her seeing the Serpentine
Derby except sleep.

"Thank you so much for telling me about it," she
said. " I will certainly come. Shall I have to arrive
very early to get a good place? "

Mr. Salt smote the table again. The sugar-basin
upset.

" It's a national disgrace that you won't, Miss Leg,"
he said with some heat. " The public apathy with
regard to swimming altogether is truly nauseating.
Again and again I have written to the papers giving
many more statistics than those which I have put before
you, and never once have any of my letters, though
very reasonable in length, been accorded the most
humble position in the columns of the press. But the
public, I am determined, must not be allowed to remain
in ignorance. The danger is a national one."

" It's difficult to know what to do," said Susan, " if
they won't publish your interesting statistics."

Mr. Salt gazed abstractedly at the ceiling.

" There are other ways of bringing the facts of the case before the public," he said. " People are like sheep. Let one take the lead and the rest will follow. Much can be done to prepare the nation for statistics. For instance, if readers of some paper which gave fashionable news saw that Miss Leg was an enthusiastic spectator of the Serpentine Derby, they would say to themselves, ' What is this Serpentine Derby that brings Miss Leg out into the Park at a quarter to eight in the morning, after some brilliant gathering at her house late into the night before ? She must know that she will be amply repaid for her early rising.' They will go themselves to see what it is all about. They will see there young men and women, and old men like myself, ever so many of them, and some older, revelling in the pure water, foaming along, side-stroke, breast-stroke, truncheon, diving, taking headers, floating, treading water——"

Mr. Salt had sprung to his feet and illustrated these movements with great vigour. Susan had to quiet Sigurd's barking, and Mr. Salt sat down again and made his peroration.

" This will all be new to them," he said, " and they will begin to say to themselves, ' Why were we not told ? We must learn to swim too ! ' They will peel off their coats and trousers; bathing costumes are supplied at the sheds. But the way to begin to rouse interest is by letting people know that the fashionable world goes to see the swimming, and by rubbing that in. The time for my staggering statistics will come later. I see that now. You must help me, Miss Leg."

Bosanquet showed Mr. Salt out, and had to come upstairs once more with a note from Mrs. Mantrip which had just arrived.

" DEAR MISS LEG,—Just a line to welcome you home to our beloved Square, where you have been sadly missed. When we last met (what a delicious talk: how I enjoyed it), you took such a vivid interest in my little literary project, that I feel sure you will be pleased to hear that the first half or thereabouts of my father's life is now finished. Such a source of thankfulness to me, and you are the first person I have told about it!

"It has now gone to be typewritten, but I should be so pleased if, when it comes back, you would give me the privilege of reading to you any portion of it that you might care to hear. I want to get the public interested in it before it comes out, as I am told that a little curiosity about a forthcoming book is worth all the reviews in the world. But I hope we may meet before I get my MSS. back and then we can make an appointment.

" Sincerely yours,
" MARGARET MANTRIP."

Susan felt that it was only fair that she should take an interest in Mrs. Mantrip's work, since the latter (though she did not know it) was so ardent an admirer of her own, but she was glad that this literary treat was not to take place just yet, for really the end of this week was a mosaic of unexpected engagements. She looked at her engagement book. She was to play Badminton on Friday at 2.30 p.m., with tea to follow, and Nunky was dining with her. As for Saturday:

" Serpentine Derby (Bridge in Park)—7.45 a.m.
Dog-Lovers' Association, General Meeting (Mrs. Conklin)—12.
Halo-reading (Lady Eva)—3 p.m.
Reincarnation Society (Vicarage)—4 p.m."

And after this day of varied interests she had to drive down to Cookham for Jimmie Mason's Saturday-till-Monday party. She felt that she had really

arrived: she had become a social power, and now
instead of having to hire Lady Mackleton to confer
lustre on her parties, all these champions of world-wide
interests, this spectrum of enlightened pursuits, were
clamouring for her to confer lustre on their meetings
by her presence. Without exception they had implied,
or even definitely stated, that if she would support these
different objects which were so dear to their hearts progress would be assured. The papers would record her
presence at their meetings, she would be a bell-wether
for others who moved in cultured and fashionable
circles.

She was delighted to do her best for them all. She
would get Augustus to come and see her when she got
back to London on Monday and give him the news of
all she had been doing. Ulrica had already written
several paragraphs saying that London was filling up
again, but, very oddly, he had omitted to say that she
had returned from her holiday. Perhaps he did not
know, and he would be pleased to hear what a budget
she had ready for his column. She wondered how she
could ever have thought that Rudolph da Vinci had
all the fun, for in her own private capacity as Susan
she was fast climbing to a height of culture and social
fame that bid fair to rival his literary peaks. The
votaries of Badminton, swimming, haloes, dogs, reincarnation and week-end parties all sought and sued
for the favour of her influential patronage. Indeed, it
seemed as if it was she who was having all the fun, and
R. da V. was being left out in the cold, for since June
he had not published a single book, though he had
written two.

Then once more the fatigued Bosanquet entered,
and Susan wondered who else wanted to enlist her
support. But this time R. da V. had his turn, for
Bosanquet brought a large square registered packet
which must be the proofs of *Amor Vincit*. This was
the case, and Susan directed that the pantry should be

put into commission again on Monday. She always did her proof-correcting to the gramophone, for the noise helped her to a vivid realization of her own work, and enabled her to insert fresh sensational adverbs and adjectives which gave an added sparkle or sombreness as required. It was not worth while starting on these proofs before Monday, but next week Rudolph would come into his own again, and Susan's social splendours be eclipsed for the time. No more Badminton or reincarnation for her till Rudolph had finished his work. Not even any swimming in the Serpentine on these brisk autumnal mornings.

It was a satiated Susan who sank into her car on Saturday afternoon to drive down to Cookham. She had got up before seven o'clock in order to be in time for the aquatic Derby, barely able to drag herself out of bed, so stiff was she from the health-giving Badminton she had played the day before. It was a cold, raw day with a boisterous wind and squalls of rain that churned the pure waters of the Serpentine into foam, so that from the grand-stand of the bridge it was most difficult, in the general flurry of the surface, to distinguish the particular patch of foam which indicated that some athlete was working away, with side-stroke and truncheon, among the waves. Mr. Salt had begged her to give to the winner (who turned out to be himself) the prize which he had himself presented, and which was held by the winner for the ensuing year. They all stood shivering in the inclement air, while he made a tooth-chattering but polished oration about the honour she had conferred on the Club by attending the fixture at great personal inconvenience, and expressed the ardent hope that next year the bridge where Miss Leg had been the solitary spectator (shame !) would be as crowded as was Hammersmith Bridge on the day of the comparatively unimportant University Boat-race. Susan had replied in modest terms, saying how proud

she was, and had given Mr. Salt a striking Staffordshire
pottery group of Leander, after swimming the Helles-
pont, locked in a passionate embrace with Hero. Susan
did not get her allusion to this handsome piece quite
right: she thought that Leander (Leanda) was the lady,
and Hero the gentleman who had done the swimming,
but it made little difference for there they were. . . .
Mr. Salt took the prize home with him and put it back
in the china cupboard till next year, as Mrs. Salt did not
consider it the sort of ornament that she liked to have
in her drawing-room.

After breakfast and a much needed rest Susan
attended the meeting of the Dog-Lovers' Association,
at which her presence was equally appreciated, and
after lunch she had gone to the exhibition of halo-
reading. Lady Eva fixed her dreamy yet menacing
gaze on the heads of six small children in turn, and
passed very gloomy verdicts on the character of all of
them. Her reading was amply confirmed by the
contents of the sealed envelope. Both then and at the
meeting of the Reincarnation Club that followed Susan
was treated with the most gratifying deference: it
almost surprised her (though not quite) to find to how
high and influential a pinnacle her social successes of
the summer had raised her.

As she drove off through the darkling day (for
this last meeting had been unusually protracted) she
wondered whether some hint of her secret life had
leaked out, for her reception at these meetings recalled
to her the suspense at the Regency Palace Hotel when
Rudolph da Vinci had been expected. But that
seemed disproved when, on her arrival at Cookham,
she found her host reading aloud some of the most
powerful passages out of *Rosemary and Rue* to a couple
of his guests, who rocked with ribald laughter. Surely
he could not have been doing that if he knew that the
author might arrive any minute. . . . Then, after
finishing the chapter, Jimmie put the volume aside, and

devoted himself in the most deferential way to her. It was quite his grandest party this year, numerous and highly distinguished, and he had drawn up for Susan a list of his guests stating exactly who they were. There was the Dowager Duchess of Middlesex and an Italian count, a Czecho-Slovakian diplomat and a very old man who would be an earl if five much younger people died first without leaving any children, an R.A., and an eminent authoress whose romances sold by the ten thousand (Susan smiled at that, and said, '' How lovely for her ! ''), the poet-critic-novelist, Mr. Arthur Armstrong, M.P., two English countesses, an actor, a female member of Parliament, and a baroness in her own right. There they all were, neatly written down for Susan's special information. In spite of all her fork-luncheons, she had never met any of them before except the monstrous Armstrong (though she fully intended to meet them all again), and she thought it most friendly of Jimmie to have asked her to this galaxy, and to have provided her with so careful a map of the stars. A most pleasant evening with romps.

Further raptures awaited Susan next day. She found the Duchess all alone, surreptitiously reading *Rosemary and Rue*. There was a distinct moisture visible in her fine eyes, and though last night she had joined in the ribald laughter, and even now, on Susan's entrance, tried to conceal the book behind a sofa-cushion, it had fallen to the floor, and Susan picked it up for her. Then in a burst of confidence Her Grace confessed that she was a secret devotee. She was thrilled to know that Susan was quite intimate with R. da V., and plainly hinted that she would like to be asked to meet him. An agonizing moment for Susan: the temptation to tell the Duchess that she was even now talking to the famous novelist was almost irresistible. Susan said that R. da V. was not at present in London (which in a literal sense was quite true), but held out hopes for the future, for when it came to such

a pass as this, it was surely time to consider whether the
great secret could be kept any longer. She must really
speak to Nunky about it, for if there was added to her
own social effulgence as Susan Leg the literary effulgence of R. da V., her social career, now that she knew
that duchesses longed to meet him, would be one of
almost intolerable glory. But at present her promise
to Nunky forbade her to speak.

Susan and her comfortable car were very popular
on Monday morning. Lady Rye (baroness in her own
right) asked if she could give her a lift back to London,
as railway trains always made her feel faint. Mr.
Armstrong, M.P., took the box-seat and the two ladies
with the Baroness's maid came inside. This necessitated that Susan should send her own maid back by
train in charge of the surplus luggage of the rest, which
she would deliver at their addresses by taxi. But it
was easily worth such inconvenience, though it was a
slight shock to Susan that the Baroness was staying
at a boarding-house in Cromwell Road: Susan had
hoped to drop her at some mansion in Grosvenor
Square. Mr. Armstrong, however, wanted to be
dropped at the House of Commons, which was something. Before the journey was over they were both
engaged to dine with her early next week, and the
female M.P. had been already bidden. Susan felt that
she was beginning to add a political circle to her other
spheres of influence.

A quantity of communications concerning Badminton, swimming, haloes and the rest were waiting for
her at home, and she would have a mass of rich
material for Ulrica, when Augustus came to dine with
her to-night. But, with the arrival of the proofs of
Amor Vincit, she would be entirely occupied this week
with R. da V.'s interests, for time was short, and
Nunky had told her she must be industrious. She at
once shut herself up in the pantry, and turned on the
gramophone.

That afternoon, while Susan was lost to all but
Serena, a wave of horrid disappointment swept over
the Square. The Vicar, Mr. Salt, Mr. Gandish, Mrs.
Conklin, Lady Eva and Mrs. Mantrip all opened their
6.30 *Evening Chronicles* with high expectation and
turned at once to page 13, on which Ulrica recounted
the pleasures and pastimes of fashionable folk. Not
only was there no mention of Miss Leg in any of these
succulent paragraphs (they could have borne that),
but not a word about reincarnation, Serpentine Derby,
Badminton, haloes, dogs or ecclesiastical biography.
In vain their champions and practitioners scrutinized
Ulrica's columns. She had not seen Susan anywhere.
Susan might have been dead instead of having spent
such a busy Saturday. There was nothing to be done
except to wait for Tuesday evening's issue. Very
disappointing.

But though Susan had been so remarkably alive
all Saturday she might truly have been considered
dead to-day, so absorbed had she been, ever since
she went down to the pantry on her arrival home, in
the affairs of her secret personality. She gloated as
she read her proofs: vengeance had indeed made a
dagger of her pen when she wrote of the venal critic
(the press corrector had seen to this), and she felt,
when in short interludes of Susanhood she remembered
that Mr. Armstrong was dining with her on the following Monday, much as some Borgia might have felt,
when he had invited his special enemy to dinner.
She would be feeding her foe with the most delicate
and unseasonable dainties, and all the time her
poisoned stiletto would be ready for plunging in his
heart on the day of publication. Eagerly she inserted
a whole new series of contemptuous and stinging
epithets, not forgetting to add a special paragraph
about his greediness and his lean, pike-like jaws:
tenderly she adorned Serena with fresh garlands of
graces and genius: mercifully she cut out libellous

touches about Mrs. Mantrip, for R. da V. was never insensible to appreciation. It was not till Bosanquet had knocked on the pantry door for the third time, and, shouting at the top of his voice to make himself heard above the jubilation of the gramophone, had told her that it had " gone eight " that she came forth and hurried upstairs to dress. Augustus was her only guest, but there were many topics.

" Well, I have got a budget of news for you, Augustus," she said as they sat down. " Susie has been working hard for Gus," and she proceeded to recount all the activities which had made Saturday so busy a day.

This was uncomfortable for Gus : the editorial boycott on Susan's name had not yet been lifted, and even if it had, Badminton, reincarnation, haloes and the rest were most unattractive topics for social columns. Miss Leg would lose caste if she was known to support such dreary cranks.

" And then after the reincarnation meeting," continued Susan, " I hopped into my motor and whirled down to Mr. Mason's house at Cookham. Dear thing ! So thoughtful and welcoming, and really a quantity of bright people in the house. He had written out a list of them for me, in case there were some of them I did not know. The dear Duchess : sweet Lady Rye, etcetera. Lots of counts and things. I kept the list for you : Bosanquet, did I give you the list ? Thank you. Just look, Augustus ! Why, with all my Saturday's doings and a party like that to follow, your column for to-morrow is as good as written. Aren't I a fairy godmother to you ? "

Augustus's gloomy eye brightened as Susan handed him the list. He was very short of material to make up into personal experience, dinners, lunches, chattings in the Park and so forth, and this was indeed a trove.

" My word! That's more the stuff," he said.

" I should think so. And all of them so affable.
I feel quite friends with the Duchess already: she's
a tremendous admirer of mine—R. da V.'s—and
wants to meet him ever so much. I couldn't break
my word to Nunky, but fancy my being obliged to
put off a duchess, and tell her that R. da V. wasn't
in London at present, which was quite true as I was
at Cookham. Such a cosy talk we had. And this
morning I gave a lift to Lady Rye—that's the
Baroness in her own right—and Francis Grout sat on
the box-seat. There's irony again."

" My dear, you're a treasure," said Augustus
warmly. " There's the making of a column and a
half in that list of names. I shall say I came down
for lunch and stayed on for dinner and played backgammon: I want to bring in backgammon. But
about all those things you did on Saturday. I'm not
so keen about them. That *fête aquatique*, the
Serpentine Derby I think you said——"

" Oh, just a line," said good-natured Susan.
" Such enthusiasm in spite of the rain. Mr. Salt
was so anxious that it should be known that I
had been there. I should like to do them a good
turn."

There was no use in trifling.

" Dear Susanna, I can't," said Augustus firmly.
" My *clientèle* likes to read about the people it *savoirs*
about, and it doesn't *savoir* about Mr. Salt. *Pas de*
Derby."

" Well then, the Badminton on Friday," said
Susan. " I have promised to play Badminton again:
they say the stiffness goes off. And the Dog-Lovers'
Association. And the reincarnation thing. They
were all terribly honoured by my presence. Quite
touching."

A light began to break on Augustus: not the true
light but something akin to it. It had puzzled him

to know why the whole Square had suddenly found
Susan, on her return from Brighton, so essential to
the success of their absurd stunts.

" It's all rather odd," he said. " *Très curieux.*
Not, of course, that it's odd that everybody wants
you to join their societies: don't think I mean that
for a minute. But they all said that a little chatty
publicity would help them so much."

" Yes; that's why I told you," said Susan. " I
want you to give it them."

Augustus gazed earnestly at her.

" Susanna," he said, " mark my words. I
believe that is just what all those cranks wanted you
to do. I believe that somehow or other they've got
to know who I am. That old desiccated widow—
Mrs. Mantrip, wasn't it?—who came and sat with
us in the garden on the day you finished *Amor Vincit,*
and I crabbed R. da V.——"

" Well? " said Susan.

" I felt at the time that she had got some idea in
her head about me. She kept stealing reverential
glances at me. Not the glad eye, God help me, but
the adoring, the reverent eye. I believe she knew
or guessed that I was Ulrica."

Susan stared at him with open mouth.

" Let me recollect," she said. " What was it that
she asked me as we walked off together? Good
Lord, yes. She asked me if she had not heard of
you under another name, and I said you didn't like
it mentioned. The sanctities of private life. And I
never thought of it again from that day to this ! One
doesn't attend to what Mrs. Mantrip says. I believe
you're right: no doubt she knew somehow that you
were Ulrica."

" But how? " asked he.

"Whom else could she have meant," retorted
Susan, " when she said she had heard of you under
another name? Oh, I see it all! She must have

told everybody in the Square that you are Ulrica:
and that's why they all came swarming round me
when I got back from Brighton. The mean, false
creatures! They wanted me to tell you about their
measly stunts, so that you might give them publicity.
What do you think, Bosanquet?"

Bosanquet had been listening to this most intently,
and was looking very indignant.

" Indeed, miss, it does seem like it," he said.
" Not but what they must have been only too pleased
as Aug—as Mr. Bosanquet said, to get you to their
meetings, but it looks sadly as if they had the other
in mind."

" I won't go to a single one more of their meetings," said Susan. " I've been made a cat's-paw,
pulling the chestnuts of publicity out of Augustus for
them, and what not. The low things!"

Augustus felt as if Providence had specially
intervened to obviate his having to tell Susan that
his editor had boycotted for the present from his
social columns any mention of her and her fashionable
activities. Had she pressed him to give publicity to
those meetings of cranks where she had been so
honoured a guest, this prohibition, so difficult to
speak of tactfully, must have come out. She
wouldn't have liked that at all: she might even have
planned a new book to show up the vile ways of news-
paper editors. Her scornful refusal therefore to have
anything more to do with the cranks was indeed a
Godsend to him.

" Don't you put a single word about any of them
in your column, Augustus," she cried, reverting a
little to type in the bitterness of her personal feelings.
" If you mention a single one of them I'll never speak
to you again. They're beneath your notice and mine
too, making me stand on the Serpentine Bridge with
the wind blowing a gale and the rain soaking me to
the skin just that I might tip the wink to you and

get a par for them. That Mr. Salt with his sea-green
eye! I never trusted him, though I kept that to myself, and I'm not one that acts on suspicion, and that
indecent piece of crockery! They're all in one
boat, and there's not a pin to choose between them.
Dogs, haloes and Badminton and reincarnation,
they're all frauds and swindlers. And what about
Mr. Mason?"

Her voice dropped: she almost whispered the last
sentence, for hideous possibilities as regards the depths
to which seekers after publicity might sink, suggested
themselves to her inflamed imagination. Had that
nice Jimmie asked her to his week-end party at Cookham merely in order to get a par about his party from
Ulrica? The list of guests so carefully made out for
her added a lurid tint of likelihood to that supposition.
But she put it from her; she refused to admit into her
mind so ugly a thought about a neighbour. Besides,
even if it were true, she had collected out of that party
a baroness in her own right, and a female member of
Parliament, both of whom were coming to dine next
Monday, not to mention the discovery of a Dowager
Duchess's passion for the works of R. da V. Even if
Jimmie had been guilty of the same self-seeking as
the others in inviting her, she herself had scored
heavily.

" No, I don't, and I won't believe it of Mr. Mason,"
said Susan firmly, " and because he hasn't stooped to
those mean tricks of making a cat's-paw of me, just you
give him a jolly good par, Augustus. Merely mention
me; say that when you came on Sunday you found
me and the Duchess of Middlesex chatting on a sofa
about R. da V. I make you a present of all the rest,
and handsome stuff it is!"

" It is indeed, dear Susanna," said Augustus
warmly. " *Merci beaucoup*, you are indeed a fairy
godmother."

" Then there's Mrs. Mantrip," said Susan, still

continuing her judicial summing-up. "It's true that she wrote me a letter about her book, asking for publicity, but I can't forget how she stuck up for R. da V. when we were sitting in the garden and you ran him down. I feel sure now, after all that has been said and done, that she thought you were Ulrica, but those sweet things that she said about R. da V. show that her heart's in the right place. True blue she was. I shall ask her to my grand dinner next Monday with the Baroness, and if I let slip a sarcastic thing or two, about the deceitful ways of Vicars and Conklins and the rest of them, it will be them that's provoked me to it, for having got into their heads that I could do them a good turn with Ulrica. The impertinence of them, for as I happen to be R. da V., I'm sure you won't take it amiss, Augustus, when I say that such an idea is an insult."

Bosanquet, like the ranks of Tusculum in Lord Macaulay's beautiful poem, " could scarce forbear to cheer." Proud as he was of his nephew's journalistic eminence, he was infinitely prouder of his mistress's genius, and as she sat there violently gesticulating and betraying her origin in every word and inflexion of her voice, his heart swelled with loyal devotion. Besides, there were moments when he found it humiliating to wait on Mr. Bosanquet and call him " sir," and Susan had put him in his place, bumped him into his place, and Mr. Bosanquet knew it. Who, prithee, was Ulrica, when R. da V. was present?

Augustus winced, but he was wise enough not to take this amiss. He hastened to talk about Susan's coming party, which might exercise a soothing influence.

"Yes, dear lady," he said. " Ask Mrs. Mantrip by all means. You'll have a wonderful evening, quite one of your best. And who else? Are you thinking of asking Lady Mackleton? "

" Delighted to see her if she comes as an ordinary

guest," said Susan, remembering what Bosanquet had
said about that. " But no more two guineas a go and
taxis. Don't think I'm ungrateful to you, dear: your
pars about Susan Leg and her fork-luncheons helped
me very much, and there'll always be a knife as well
as a fork for you. But you must remember who I am,
and when it comes to chatting with a duchess about
R. da V. and telling you about it, you must allow that
I can stand on my own pins now, even before they all
know who I am. Now let's go upstairs."

All that week Susan remained sequestered in the
pantry, and every evening the seekers after publicity
vainly searched the 6.30 edition of the *Evening Chronicle* for Ulrica's advocacy. As the days went on
without a sign in the press that she had been swimming
or playing Badminton or being interested in the new
cure for distemper, the feeling in the Square about
Miss Leg took a very pessimistic turn. Mrs. Mantrip's
account of the literary *partie carrée* in the garden had
convinced everybody that Susan was Ulrica (for there
was no one else left for her to be), and it was thought
to be exceedingly shabby conduct on her part, with all
that space at her disposal, not to mention in her column
a single one of those clubs and societies which had given
her so warm a welcome. " Did the woman imagine,"
thought Elizabeth, " that I got her made an honorary
member of the Dog Lovers because she was just Susan
Leg? " Indeed, had there been a joint general meeting of the respective societies which had entreated her
to patronize them, a vote of censure followed by one of
expulsion would have been carried *nem. con.* and probably with acclamation. The only possible dissentient
would have been Lady Eva, who, though she thought
Susan had behaved very shabbily to the Halo Club,
could not be blind to the fact that her halo remained
of purest ray serene. Lady Eva saw her one evening
after dark, fresh from the proofs of *Amor Vincit*, taking

a few minutes' air and exercise in the garden, and her
halo positively illuminated the lower boughs of the
sumac with its richness and its golden radiance. She
could not think evil of one who emitted so royal an
emanation, and clung to her belief that there must be
a misunderstanding somewhere.

But about all these stormy politics, Susan knew and
cared nothing. She was like Serena Lomond in *Amor
Vincit* whom, with regard to the machinations of
the venal critic, she had compared to Galileo "who
cared for none of these things." (The proof-corrector
had queried in the margin "Gallio?" but Susan
crossed it out. She meant Galileo, the man who so
rightly said that the earth went round the sun, and
did not care what anybody else thought about it.) She
cared as little as Gallio and Galileo combined what
taunts and unkind sneers about Ulrica were popping
in the Square like squibs on the fifth of November.
Secure in her pantry with a gramophone to inspire her
vituperative insertions, and a dictionary to verify the
suggested corrections made by the proof-reader in the
margin about her spelling, she was as sundered from
the world as any diver among the pearls of the deep
seas.

A week of Herculean labour saw her task accomplished. As soon as the last page was done she turned
off the gramophone, to the great chagrin of M. Rouen,
who was dancing a very enjoyable fox-trot next door
with the kitchen-maid, and called for Bosanquet.

"Finished, Bosanquet!" she cried, "and much
my best. I had no real idea how good it was till I
worked over it. Send it down at once by special
messenger to Mr. Cartwright. I feel quite dazed.
I've been living only in my book. What time is it,
Bosanquet? What day is it?"

Bosanquet consulted his watch.

"Just gone three, miss," he said. "Monday
afternoon. October the second."

" Have I had lunch? " asked Susan.

" No, miss. You only said ' Take it away, Francis Grout ' when I brought you a tray."

" Oh, did I, Bosanquet? How rude of me ! "

" Not a bit, miss. I was pleased to see how your work was gripping you. Have a little something now."

" No, I don't want any," said Susan. " But did you say it was October the second? Then it's my political party this evening."

" Yes, miss. And glad I am that your work's finished. It's time Miss Leg had a bit of fun."

" She will, Bosanquet. Let me see: there's the Baroness and Mrs. Mantrip and Mrs. Bramham, M.P., and Mr. Armstrong, M.P., and Mr. Mason, Mr. Cartwright and Mr. Bosanquet. That's right, isn't it? Send round for the car, please, at once. I want a little air."

Dancing being no longer possible, M. Rouen looked in to see if Mademoiselle would not have a drop of soup.

" *Merci non*," said Susan, whose French was becoming extremely fluent. " *Mais j'ai fini mon livre. N'est-ce pas bon?* "

" *Mille felicitations, mademoiselle*," said M. Rouen, and Susan tripped up the kitchen stairs out of the basement into the light of day. As if to welcome her back from the deep seas of thought into the milder preoccupations of ordinary life, the post-box at the front door suddenly belched letters at her. In spite of the ungenerous silence of Ulrica, the propagandists had not yet quite given up hope, and there were lists of fixtures for the forthcoming season and notices of meetings from them all. Rightly incensed, as Susan still felt she had been, at their miserable overtures to her, not for the honour of having her as a member of these societies, but simply in order that she might procure for them the powerful support of Ulrica, the happy conclusion of her work and the conviction that it was far the most striking book that had ever come from her pen, made her feel compassionate towards all the world, and before taking the air she sent cheques for a guinea to aid the causes of Badminton, swimming, haloes, dogs, and reincarnation respectively.

XII

M RS. MANTRIP enjoyed every moment of Susan's party that evening. Like the rest of the propagandists who had not yet given up hope that Ulrica would advertise their stunts for them (and thus showered literature on Susan) she took it to be a very favourable sign that Susan asked most affectionately how the Life was getting on (just as if it was a friend recovering from illness) and put her to sit next Mr. Cartwright at dinner. There was most interesting political talk bawled across the table between the M.P.s, Mrs. Bramham and Mr. Armstrong. Both were of the Labour Party and both were exceedingly wealthy, he from his literary earnings, she from the chemical works founded and raised to a pitch of staggering prosperity by her late husband, who, like Mr. Armstrong, had once been an errand-boy. Mrs. Bramham therefore, as representing the deceased, was a worker too, and they agreed that workers were entitled to every penny that their industry earned, however rich they were. They ought, at any rate, to be assessed on the lowest scale of income tax, and the imposition of sur-tax on such as them was monstrous. Mr. Armstrong informed the table what difference surtax made to his income, and a dead silence then ensued, for everybody was engaged in mental arithmetic in order to calculate from this what his income was. Susan, from her experience in the typewriting office, was quick at doing sums in her head, and she was pleased to find that Mr. Armstrong was not nearly so rich as she. What a bombshell she could have lobbed

into the middle of her own dinner-table if she had stated
that her income, derived also from literary earnings,
suffered far more than his. Then both the Labour
members bitterly complained that the £400 a year
which they were paid for being M.P.s was a most
niggardly remuneration for the time and the brains
they devoted to the service of their country. " Mere
sweating," Mr. Armstrong called it. Mrs. Mantrip
enjoyed this discussion; it really looked as if Labour
and Capital were beginning to understand each
other.

But to her the real red-letterness of the evening was
the presence of Rudolph Augustus da Vinci Bosanquet.
She and he and Susan had a long talk afterwards in
which occasionally Nunky joined. Susan spoke of
the forthcoming appearance of *Amor Vincit* quite
detachedly, thought Mrs. Mantrip, as if she was not
conversing with the author of it, while he, with that
admired playfulness which he had already shown in
the garden, continued to run R. da V. down. He
called on Mr. Armstrong to support him, reminding
him of the frightful drubbing he had given him in the
Sunday Chronicle, and Mr. Armstrong, with a modest
shrug of his shoulders, said that he didn't suppose that
anybody would hear much more of R. da V., for he
had made his pronouncement. Mr. Cartwright did
not agree. A good many people in a few weeks' time
would be hearing more of R. da V., seeing that eighty
thousand copies of his new book, *Amor Vincit*, had
already been subscribed for. His reputation did not
seem to be quite annihilated yet, thought Mr.
Cartwright.

A look of anguish passed across the M.P.'s face
when this colossal figure was mentioned. But he
pulled himself together.

" Well, I've finished with the fellow," he said.

Mrs. Mantrip found that moment almost painfully
dramatic. Next him, and sharing the same onyx and

mother-of-pearl ash-tray sat Rudolph Augustus da
Vinci Bosanquet, and, with that perfect breeding of
his, he did not betray by as much as the movement
of an eyelash, far less by spitting in the M.P.'s face,
that he resented being called " the fellow." But his
friend Susan Leg flushed angrily: naturally she was
indignant at his being so contemptuously alluded
to.

" He must console himself for your scorn with his
circulation," she said sharply.

There was a suppressed fury in her voice that was
startling: Mrs. Mantrip wondered if, in the account
of this party, which was sure to appear next day in
the *Evening Chronicle*, Ulrica would say that Mr.
Armstrong, M.P., was looking very unwell or had
got drunk, or would omit his name altogether. To
her surprise she found there no mention of the party
at all, which was odd, considering how many
distinguished people had been there. But later in the
week she found by chance in the *Weekly Telegraph*
that Leonora had a very substantial account of it.
All the guests were mentioned by name, herself
included; there was much about Rudolph da Vinci's
forthcoming book and the number of the enormous
subscription was correctly given. Leonora had a
racy style, she put things in the same bright way as
Ulrica, and the conviction suddenly flashed into Mrs.
Mantrip's mind that Susan must be Leonora as well
as Ulrica, for the account was clearly that of an eye-
witness. What a wonderful secret life the woman
had in addition to her rising social value! It was
well worth while being friends with her, and though
the propagandists poured scorn on her for her petty
guineas, when she might have befriended them so
much more efficiently, Mrs. Mantrip now began to
take her part in such discourses. Besides, Susan had
promised to drop in some afternoon and be treated
to a short reading from that most sensational chapter

of the Life, which dealt with Papa's work in the
Augean Square. Mrs. Mantrip had thrown restraint
to the winds, and it was now a very daring piece. The
mercantile side of the transaction was lightly passed
over, and the reader would only feel that Papa had
done a most noble and Christian work in turning out
these frail and abominable ladies. She longed to read
it to Ulrica-Leonora, and told her parlourmaid to
admit Miss Leg whenever she happened to call. But
she had gone off to Brighton again soon after the
party so ably described by Leonora, and Mrs. Mantrip had to wait for her return. She was still away
when the great event of the autumn publishing season
took place and *Amor Vincit* was piled in stacks in the
windows of all the booksellers.

Susan came back to London a few days after. It
was a wet and cheerless afternoon, and Mrs. Mantrip,
after a fruitless attempt to concentrate on her description of Papa's asthma, left her library and went upstairs
to the seclusion of her bedroom in order to give herself
up to the unparalleled rapture which *Amor Vincit*
wrought in her. Never before had Rudolph da Vinci
been so sublime (and when occasion demanded so
withering), but in addition to the high emotional spell
of his work, there were elements of personal human
interest which were new. Almost as soon as the venal
critic had made his appearance Mrs. Mantrip felt sure
that he was drawn from life, and that the life from
which he was drawn was Mr. Armstrong, M.P. The
description merely of his personal appearance, of his
pike-like jaws and his waved hair, was enough, and the
conviction was endorsed when, on Serena Lomond's
rejecting with scorn his proposal that she should purchase his favourable notice of her forthcoming book, he
wrote a scathing review instead. Some of the sentences
from it were quoted, and they were familiar to Mrs.
Mantrip; she had read them with an indignation which
still burned in her when she remembered that despic-

able article by Mr. Armstrong in the *Sunday Chronicle*. " A valet's view " : ' lispings of a lady's maid " : who could forget his outrageous expressions ?

Then there was Serena Lomond herself. Serena laughed just as Susan Leg laughed : the description of her personal appearance (though Serena was young and lovely, and God knew that Susan was not that) somehow recalled Susan. And then there were her initials, the same as Susan's. It became absolutely clear that Rudolph da Vinci had taken Susan for his model, had beautified and adorned her with every grace and charm and gift of genius, and yet preserved a likeness. In the same way he had taken Mr. Armstrong for his villain, branded him with every deformity and disease of soul, and yet made him unmistakable. That was the stuff to give him !

Mrs. Mantrip suddenly remembered that she had left the photograph of the author on the table in her library, instead of shutting it up in the drawer, as she usually did, when she left the room. But it was of no consequence ; she did not expect anybody to call, and even if some neighbour like Elizabeth dropped in for a game of piquet on this dreary afternoon, she would be shown into the drawing-room. She lit the gas-fire in her bedroom, for it was chilly, and settled herself down for an hour of intellectual Paradise. From outside there came the sound of a few sonorous barks of a bass-voiced dog : they had no external significance, and only reminded her of Serena's Great Dane. She had got to the point where Mr. Armstrong had just been pronounced to be suffering from infectious brain-fever, and she left the dull earth below, rising on the wings of high romance.

The bass-voiced dog was in point of fact Susan's Sigurd ; so Mrs. Mantrip's association of ideas was correct. He was baying a welcome to Durham Square on his return with his mistress from Brighton. Susan found a telephone message or two to attend to,

but, having seen to them, she had nothing to do till tea-
time, when she expected Nunky to arrive with a batch
of letters from the office for R. da V. and some gratifying news about sales. It was a good opportunity to
call on Mrs. Mantrip and fulfil her kind promise of
listening to extracts from Papa's Life. She had a
feeling for struggling authors, having never struggled
herself, and if (as was highly unlikely) Mrs. Mantrip's
work possessed the smallest trace of skill or interest she
would get Nunky to look at it. On such a dismal
afternoon the authoress would probably be in, and off
she went on her errand of kindness and possibly
encouragement.

She was instantly admitted according to orders.
Mrs. Mantrip was up in her bedroom.

" No hurry at all," said Susan to the maid. " I'll
wait in that nice little library of hers where she does her
work. Just tell her Miss Susan Leg is here."

She went into the nice little library, and the maid
ran upstairs to tell her mistress. " Miss Leg has called
to see you, ma'am," was all she said, and Mrs. Mantrip,
speaking as if in a dream, for the tension was terrific,
answered :

" Tell her I'll be down in a minute."

There were three pages more to the end of the
chapter and it was no use attempting to leave them
unread. That was one of those things that merely
could not be done. Gratifying as Miss Leg's visit
was, Miss Leg must wait.

Susan meantime, alone in the library, hovered
about the book-lined walls, and the more titles she
read, knowing, as she now did, how staunch a da
Vincian Mrs. Mantrip was, the more she felt that there
must be a sort of arid nobility about a woman who thus
lived in the midst of missionaries and divines for the
sake of honouring her father's memory. From the
walls her eyes wandered to the table. There were
writing materials on it; there was a packet of type-

written manuscript which no doubt was the Life. There was a big framed photograph standing with its back to the light. Probably Papa, she thought; it was suitable that he should thus mutely preside over his daughter's pious industry. With only the mildest curiosity in her mind to see what Papa was like, she looked at it, and with a gasp of astonishment she saw that it was a photograph of Augustus. That was truly amazing: she had no idea that Augustus was on photograph-terms with Mrs. Mantrip; indeed, as far as she knew he had only seen her twice, and agreed with his uncle that she was a repellent woman. What could it mean?

The room was rather dark. She carried the picture to the window and observed that it was signed across the mount with the name of Rudolph da Vinci. A sudden illumination flooded her brain. The signature was in Bosanquet's handwriting; surely this must be the missing photograph which had been sent in a too light-hearted moment to Minnie Mimps. She turned the photograph round, and there on the back, below glass, was a letter signed by the same name. She read it, and it was certainly the letter, written at her dictation on her own note-paper by Bosanquet, which had accompanied the photograph. But instead of invoking (as it had once undoubtedly done) Miss Mimps, it invoked Mrs. Mantrip. "Dear Mrs. Mantrip": nothing could be plainer.

About one minute before Susan made this bewildering discovery, Mrs. Mantrip upstairs in her bedroom came to the end of the sublime chapter. She wiped the moisture from her eyes, and turned her tremulous smile into one of welcome, for it was very kind of Ulrica Leg to come and hear a reading from the Life. It was a pity that she had not chosen to-morrow instead of to-day for her visit, for then Mrs. Mantrip could have finished the second perusal of *Amor Vincit*. But she banished that regret and went downstairs to the draw-

ing-room. She entered, and found there was no one
there.

Till then, absorbed in the wonderful story, she had
again forgotten that she had left the photograph of
Rudolph on the table in her library. Now, with a
pang of alarm, she remembered, and bounded down
the flight of stairs to the ground floor as nimbly as
if, like Mr. Gandish, she habitually kept her muscles
in athletic condition by playing Badminton, or by
swimming with Mr. Salt in the Serpentine. But she
was too late. Susan was standing in the window with
the photograph in her hand, reading the back of it.

No word of salutation passed.

"Where did you get this photograph, Mrs.
Mantrip?" asked Susan in a low but penetrating voice.

There was no question in this world, nor any that
might subsequently be put to her by the Recording
Angel, that Mrs. Mantrip was more unwilling to answer
directly or, if she came to think of it, indirectly. She
had a horrid feeling that her knees were made of
blotting-paper or of quivering calf's-foot jelly. Susan
evidently knew something, but she had not the slightest
notion of what that might happen to be. She mastered
the jelly feeling and became extremely stately.

"I observe," she said, "that there is a photograph
missing from my table, and that you, Miss Leg, are
holding one of similar shape and size in your hand. If
that is the one, I must ask you to be so kind as to
replace my property where you found it."

Susan did not quail before this lofty austerity. She
saw with the eye of the practised psychologist that, in
spite of this iron front, Mrs. Mantrip was quaking with
some hidden apprehension. She gave one more glance
at the letter and, replacing the photograph where she
had found it, waited in silence till Mrs. Mantrip had put
on her glasses and surveyed it.

"Thank you, Miss Leg," she said. "That is my
missing photograph."

" I should call it *the* missing photograph," said Susan.

Mrs. Mantrip was feeling stronger. After all, no one could force her to say how it had come into her possession. Since her tongue still felt like a nutmeg grater (such had been the desiccating effect of that moment when she had come into the room and found Susan reading the back of the photograph), she thought it would be as well to give her the roughest side of it.

" Miss Leg," she said, " I have not the slightest notion what you are talking about, but may I just ask what business it is of yours? "

Susan pointed to the photograph.

" As you won't answer my question," she said, " I'll answer it for you. That photograph was given to an unscrupulous female called Miss Mimps, who subsequently said she had lost it. Does that convey anything to you? "

That was an unpleasant blow. Evidently Susan knew something about it. Mrs. Mantrip answered it by another punch.

" Certainly it conveys something to me," she said brightly. " It arouses associations, for it was Miss Mimps, whether unscrupulous or not, who said you had been employed at a typewriting agency in Brighton."

" She withdrew that," said Susan. " She said it wasn't true."

" I have no idea which of her two statements is correct," said Mrs. Mantrip, " though no doubt you have."

The jelly symptoms invaded Susan. She felt a strong desire to sit down, and gratified it. That made her firmer and she attacked at a fresh angle.

" Since last I saw the letter which is framed at the back of that photograph," she said, " it has been tampered with. When in its original state it began ' Dear Miss Mimps.' As it stands, it is a forgery."

" Most interesting," said Mrs. Mantrip, looking down her nose. " Have you anything more to tell me about it ? "

" Lots," said Susan. " The letter was not written by Rudolph da Vinci at all, nor was the photograph signed by him. They were both written by Bosanquet."

" By 'Bosanquet,' I suppose you mean the so-called Mr. Augustus Bosanquet? " said Mrs. Mantrip.

" No, I don't," said Susan. " I mean my butler. I happen to know because I was present."

Whatever revelations might be in store, Mrs. Mantrip could not repress a little crow of triumph.

" Now we're getting to something more like forgery," she said. " Your butler, you tell me, wrote the letter and signed the photograph. You appear to have been privy to it."

There flashed into Susan's mind some disagreeable remarks Nunky had made about forgery. She did not like them at the time, and she liked them much less now. Mrs. Mantrip saw a definite look of alarm come into her eyes, and followed up her advantage, though it necessitated an admission which she had determined never to make. But since Susan knew, it did not now matter, and such an opportunity could not be missed. Again she pointed to the photograph. They were both pointing at it with quivering forefingers.

" Mr. da Vinci sent that photograph to Miss Mimps," she said, " and I bought it from her for ten pounds. But as you now tell me that to your knowledge both the letter and the signature are forged, I shall insist on my money being returned, taking legal steps if necessary. You will be called as a witness."

" I'll give you ten pounds for it at once," said Susan, blanching visibly.

Mrs. Mantrip did not hesitate. A mystery had to be probed first.

" Certainly not," she said. " There has been some swindling going on, and I feel it my duty to expose it."

" And you in turn will have to explain how ' Dear Miss Mimps ' got changed into ' Dear Mrs. Mantrip,' " retorted Susan.

Mrs. Mantrip could not think for the moment of a satisfactory answer to that. Indeed, she doubted if there was one. To gain time, she took refuge in irony.

" I seem to have acquired what auctioneers call a doubtful piece," she said. " Perhaps you'll tell me next that the photograph isn't genuine either."

" Of course it isn't," said Susan. " That is no more a photograph of Rudolph da Vinci than you are."

" I am not aware of being a photograph at all," said Mrs. Mantrip. (What shocking grammar this woman spoke !)

" You see what I mean," said Susan, " so why be sarcastic ? It isn't a photograph of R. da V. at all. It's just Augustus Bosanquet. But my offer of ten pounds still holds good, though it's a monstrous price to pay for a photograph of Augustus."

Mrs. Mantrip's brain began to go round. Perhaps it would be more accurate to say that the thoughts which poured into it began to go round. They would not stop still for her to regard any of them firmly; they slipped out of her grip, and went off on orbits of their own. It was as if a kaleidoscope was being twirled round in front of her. Facts, or what she had taken to be facts, shifted and changed colour, the pattern altered and became something else. With a violent effort she arrested this twirling movement, so that she could regard a certain group of facts with steady vision.

"Miss Leg," she said, "either something is happening to my head or things are not what they seem. I want to recall to you a scene in the garden at which you and I were present. There were also there Mr. Cartwright, whom I have hitherto supposed to be a publisher——"

"O.K.," said Susan.

"And Mr. Augustus Bosanquet. That photograph"—and she looked at it as if she was afraid it would turn into something else—"was already in my possession. Naturally I recognized in Mr. Bosanquet the original of it. As we walked away, I asked you whether he was not known under another name. You said that he was."

Susan's brain was beginning to whirl too.

"Quite correct," she said. "But the other name by which he is known is not Rudolph da Vinci."

"Then what is it?" shrieked Mrs. Mantrip. "I think I'm going mad."

"He's Ulrica," said Susan. "But don't tell anybody."

Mrs. Mantrip's bewilderment, instead of clearing off, increased in density.

"But you're Ulrica, aren't you?" she cried. "You're Ulrica and Leonora surely? What's happening to everybody?"

This infamous suggestion stung Susan to the quick. She recoiled from Mrs. Mantrip with a gesture of infinite scorn.

"Me Ulrica?" she said. "Me Leonora? I have never been so insulted before. How dare you?"

Mrs. Mantrip recoiled from her. Not even now did she conjecture the colossal truth.

"Then are you only just Miss Susan Leg?" she said. "Is it all lies when Ulrica says that he—or she—dines with you and Rudolph da Vinci? I don't believe you know him at all. You've been using your supposed intimacy with him for purposes of social success. You get Ulrica to say Rudolph da Vinci comes to your house and is a friend of yours. Aren't you afraid of his writing to the papers to say he's never heard of you? Oh, shame! And to think that you're my tenant."

Maddened though she was at this personal attack on her honour, Susan was still mindful of the promise of secrecy she had given to Nunky. But she felt that a ferret had got her by the throat.

" I'm not responsible for what Ulrica says," she faltered.

" You're party to it," cried Mrs. Mantrip, biting hard. " You allow it to go on, and I have no doubt whatever that you encourage it. It is my privilege to tell you, Miss Leg, that your whole life is a lie, and that from henceforth we are strangers."

The breaking-point had come, and Susan rose to her feet.

" You are speaking to Rudolph da Vinci," she said.

Mrs. Mantrip gave a shrill maniac sort of laugh and rang the bell.

" Am I indeed? " she said. " Such a pleasure! How I enjoyed your last book, Mr. da Vinci. . . . Show Miss Leg out."

" Not quite so fast," said Susan, with a wonderful gesture of contempt which she had invented for Serena. " Before we become total strangers, I shall have one word more to say. I wish to use your telephone."

" It is at your disposal," said Mrs. Mantrip, wondering what the next wriggle would be, " but please be quick."

Susan rang up her own house three doors away.

" Is that Bosanquet? " she said. " Yes, Mademoiselle speaking. . . . Is Mr. Cartwright there? . . . Very well, give him the ledger containing the bound manuscript sheets of *Amor Vincit*, and ask him to bring it in person to Mrs. Mantrip's house, No. 22. At once please: the quicker the better.''

Though Mrs. Mantrip's face remained as bleak as the most forbidding rocks of the Matterhorn, this message made her soul quake. Something within her shrieked to her to fall on her knees and implore Susan's pardon, but the sheer impossibility of that common little woman being He still clung about her. She could not believe it.

They sat in silence till the door-bell rang, looking fixedly at divergent points of the ceiling. Cartwright entered, carrying the ledger.

'' You have met, I think,'' said Susan. '' Nunky, I have had to tell this lady who I am. It couldn't be helped. Please put the ledger before her. She may like to look at it. The manuscript of *Amor Vincit*, she will observe, is in my handwriting, and if she looks inside the cover she will see my name written there with the date and the place, No. 25 Durham Square. Now, Nunky, just say who I am.''

'' You are Rudolph da Vinci, Susanna,'' said Nunky.

No further sublimity was possible, and after a moment's silence, during which Mrs. Mantrip turned the leaves of the manuscript backwards and forwards in a bewildered manner, Susan picked up the ledger and gave it back to Cartwright. '' Carry it for me, will you, Nunky? '' she said. '' Good afternoon, Mrs. Mantrip.''

As they passed the window the stricken lady inside heard above the smart tattoo of the rain on the umbrellas of Rudolph and his publisher, that gay laughter which Susan had cribbed from her own creation, Serena Lomond. The sound mocked her: gay though it was, it represented to her the dirge of hopes that would now never be fulfilled, and of shattered visions. For months she had had as her tenant the author who was the light and lantern of her own secret life, with every opportunity for making a friend of her, and never once had such a possibility entered her head. Instead, when first her misbegotten ingenuity surmised that Susan had a secret life, too, she had made so appallingly wide a shot as to what that secret life was that it would not bear thinking of. But far worse than that was the bleeding remembrance of this last hour. And worst of all was the last moment of that interview when Susan had revealed herself, and, with a shriek of insensate laughter and a speech charged with the utmost that irony could compass, she had rung the bell for her parlourmaid to show out a henceforth stranger . . . Nunky's arrival . . . the ledger containing the marvellous manuscript . . . collapse.

There on the table stood the photograph that had once been her joy and pride, the lodestar of her secret life, now known to be spurious in itself and further invalidated by her own subtle forgery. Half an hour ago she could have obtained ten pounds for it, but now in a spasm of rage and despair, she ripped the frame open and tore it and the letter across and across. It was no easy task, for the cardboard of its mount was thick and stubborn, and even before the work of passionate destruction was over, she perceived that she had made yet one more mistake. She ought, of course, to have sent it back to Susan, declining any sort of payment for it, but (in the third person) saying that she was only too happy to return to her the object of which she wished to repossess herself. That would have been a generous gesture to which Susan could hardly have failed to respond, but now the flames were licking the charred edges of its fragments. She could not even return it with a threatening letter to Miss Mimps, demanding the immediate return of ten pounds, on the grounds that the photograph was not, as Miss Mimps had represented it to be, the picture of Rudolph da Vinci at all, nor was the signature his, nor was the letter. Now the ten pounds had gone, the photograph had gone, and Rudolph da Vinci had gone.

Through the desolating gloom there shone one ray of comfort. She had not yet finished the second and careful perusal of *Amor Vincit*. She went back to her bedroom and lit the gas-fire again.

XIII

NATURE copied Art this winter and, following the lines laid down by the greatest of modern novelists, she provided a good snowstorm on the twenty-second of December and, after discharging and partially thawing it, she decreed a sharp frost. In consequence, a great many people fell down on ice-covered pavements and sustained bruises and fractures, trollies skidded into taxicabs, water-pipes burst and plumbers had to work overtime; but these little unpleasantnesses only affected the minority, and it was evident that Nature intended that all good Christian people should be very hearty and jolly as befitted the season. She had provided all the properties (ice, snow, sun, holly, mistletoe, turkeys, etc.) needed for a Rudolph da Vinci Christmas, and Susan, looking out of her drawing-room window (she had lately put in a central-heating installation which was a wonderful success) and feeling very warm and comfortable, was convinced that Nature had been reading the last chapter of *Heart's Queen*. There was a slight opaqueness gathering in the air this morning, which looked as if a London fog might presently descend on the town, and that would be a dismal trick to play. But Susan did not regret that she had settled to spend Christmas in London instead of going to Brighton, for then she would not have been able to provide such a treat for the Square as it would enjoy on Christmas night.

The festivities were to begin with a dinner at half-past eight. Most of the magnates in the Square were coming: Mr. Salt, the Gandish family, including Black and White, Elizabeth, Lady Eva and her husband (if his X-ray examination showed that he had not yet got cancer), Mr. Mason, and the Vicar. From outside the Square there would flock to her house even more distinguished guests: the Dowager Duchess of Middlesex and her newly-acquired husband, Mr. John Pump (Her Grace, Susan was glad to know, had retained her title, feeling unequal to the shock of so radical a change of name); Lady Rye, the Baroness in her own right, who had just been divorced, and the man who was the primary cause of this passionate incident; Mrs. Bramham, M.P., Mr. Cartwright, Mr. Augustus Bosanquet, and Lady Mackleton (unpaid). Finally, there were coming Miss Mimps (forgiveness could hardly go further) and Mrs. Mantrip (forgiveness succeeded in doing so). In all, as Augustus said, *dix-sept*, or as Ulrica subsequently wrote, " Covers were laid for seventeen."

Mr. Armstrong, M.P., could not come because he was very ill. He had been seized with a severe attack of jaundice, immediately after learning that *Amor Vincit* had sold 120,000 copies on the day of publication. Nunky had sent him this news with a copy of the book, though no others were sent out for review, and Mr. Armstrong had read it. Whether from that cause or not, he had become rapidly worse: his doctor had never seen so serious a case. But to-day he seemed to have turned the corner, and Susan was glad, for she had not meant to kill him.

Among these interesting names there is one the inclusion of which must naturally arouse incredulity and demands a full explanation as to how it came to be there. Stricken as she had been by the frightful disclosure recorded in the last chapter, Mrs. Mantrip had sufficiently rallied next day to call on many of her friends in the Square and proclaimed the stupendous truth. Though it was involved with such personal disaster for her, it was a faint consolation to be the first to know it and to disseminate it. It was inconvenient, to be sure, that everyone remembered that not many weeks ago she had proclaimed that Susan was Ulrica, but this time there could be no doubt that the news was correct. Mr. Cartwright's solemn asseveration as in a creed, " You are Rudolph da Vinci," carried conviction. This was presently confirmed, for Mr. Cartwright now consented to a public announcement in the press that Miss Susan Leg, so well known in the highest social circles for her charming parties, was the great novelist. With such circulation as she had now attained the mystery of R. da V. had served its turn, and, since it was bound to leak out, a torrent was more striking for advertising purposes than dribblings.

Augustus Bosanquet, of course, had made the original proclamation, for the truculent editor who had put the embargo on the names of Rudolph and Susan being mentioned at all by Ulrica in the *Evening Chronicle*, at once removed it in view of the immense interest this revelation must arouse, and his newsboards announced in the largest red type, " Great Literary Mystery Solved." Ulrica's entire column was devoted to it and, locally, the propagandists of the Square eagerly wooed Susan again. She had disappointed them in not being Ulrica, but that was meddling Margaret Mantrip's fault, not hers, and now all they asked of her was to honour their various proceedings in her own person. Miss Susan Leg (alias Rudolph da Vinci) was enough for any of them, and she had promised to present the prizes for the Serpentine Oaks of the Hyde Park Swimming Club on Christmas morning, provided that the course was not too thickly frozen to permit of sport.

Mrs. Mantrip then had had the consolation of

being the first to proclaim the news, but bitter indeed
was her fate, and before long she had been totally
unable to bear it. From the depths of her humiliation
she wrote a letter to Susan containing a larger assort-
ment of abject apologies than had ever been put into
one envelope before. She protested that she made no
excuses and then proceeded to make some beauties.
She reminded Susan that she had spent ten pounds
on the purchase of what she believed to be Rudolph
da Vinci's photograph, so profound was her admiration of the Master, so happy it made her to be able
to look on his supposed features, so strong was
the inspiration he shed over her own literary work.
As to what the real history of that picture was she
made no inquiries. She knew, however, that Miss
Leg did not wish it to remain at large, and she
had herself destroyed it, willingly sacrificing ten
pounds since this would be pleasing in the Master's
sight.

Then as to the forged invocation, " Dear Mrs.
Mantrip," of the letter. The forgery, she confessed,
was hers, and she was very greatly to blame. But
could not Rudolph da Vinci understand (she was sure
he could) what secret romantic joy it gave her thus
fondly to feign that the Master had once written to her ?
The creator of *Heart's Queen* would sympathize
with a forgery that had its rise in adoration. On that
terrible afternoon she had been engaged in her second
(though by no means her last) perusal of *Amor Vincit,*
and might she say that in her opinion the Master had
never created a more moving and beautiful character
than Serena Lomond? Mrs. Mantrip might be wrong,
but surely there was portraiture, delicate, subtle, but
unmistakable in the portrayal of that exquisite creature
(hinted at also, surely, in her initials), just as there was
portraiture biting and justly terrible in the presentment
of the venal critic. The way the latter was handled
reminded her of the methods of Dante. . . . " I could

not rest, dear Miss Leg," she concluded, " without opening my heart to you, and doing all I can—alas, how little—to convince you of the sincerity of my regret. And should you decide to have nothing more to do with me, it will be something to remember that there was a time when, all unknowing, I was privileged to talk with her whose genius I so profoundly revere."

Susan's eyes filled with tears as she read this moving appeal. She rang the bell for Bosanquet, who thought it was for tea and brought it up.

" Oh, Bosanquet," she said, " really a most touching letter from Mrs. Mantrip. So properly expressed, and she's so miserable, poor thing, and says I'm like Dante. Telephone to her, and ask her to come to tea at once."

" After those dreadful things she said to you, miss ? " asked Bosanquet. " Is it wise ? "

" Serena Lomond would have forgiven her," said Susan, " and I shall too. Besides, she recognized Serena Lomond. So ask her cordially and playfully. Say I shan't begin tea till she comes, and I'm so hungry."

There had been an affecting scene. Mrs. Mantrip hurried round, so as not to keep Susan waiting, and Susan, keeping up this pretty playfulness, gobbled several pieces of muffin to show how hungry she was, and there was a brilliant flow of small talk about the weather, and Elizabeth, and dogs in the garden, as if no ruinous storm had ever wrecked the fairer garden of a budding friendship. Then they both ran dry simultaneously. Mrs. Mantrip could think of nothing but her contrition, of which it still choked her to speak, and Susan of nothing but her own magnanimity. Fortunately the alleviating processes of nature came to Mrs. Mantrip's aid; she burst into quantities of tears, and Susan, more magnanimous than ever, comforted her. " There, there ! " she said, patting the penitent on the shoulder. "Don't give it a thought again. Besides, I am to blame a little, too."

"No!" sobbed Mrs. Mantrip. "Never! No!"

"But I am!" said Susan, beginning to talk baby language as Serena sometimes did to Nursie. "Me was naughty girlie to let Bosanquet sign the picky of Augustus. What was other girlie to think, but that it was one of Vinchy-pinchy?"

Mrs. Mantrip recognized Nature copying Art (Nature being Susan and the art hers also), and a watery smile came over her twisted face.

"That noble Serena!" she sobbed. "I recognized who she was instantly. Oh, to think that the original should be being so sweet to me after all I've done! But for years, Miss Leg——"

"No, Susan," interrupted Susan, "or Serena, if you like."

"Oh, may I?" cried Mrs. Mantrip. "How perfectly lovely! For years, Serena, your books have been the secret joy of my heart. I've got them all: I read them over and over again. If I feel sad, I go to them for sympathy; if I feel gay, I go to them for laughter and joy. You make me believe, you always have, in noble aspiration, and if a fairy godmother had given me a wish, my wish would have been to know you. And then when that wish was granted to me, when you told me who you were, all I could do was to tell you that you were a liar and say that we must be strangers henceforth. And oh, to think of my stuck-up pride, keeping my devotion to R. da V. secret, because I had the reputation of being highbrow and because the critics never noticed you! And my saying that I wouldn't come to dinner, and wouldn't lend you a book because my tastes in literature were so different from yours!"

"But how often good comes out of evil, dear," said Susan, quoting from Serena.

"And that's your doing too," squeaked Mrs.

Mantrip. " Nothing but good can come out of you. And to think that I'm really forgiven ! "

Susan kissed her and they held each other's hands, and looked with damp smiles into each other's eyes, until these beautiful gestures of reconciliation and dawning friendship became quite embarrassing to both. They both longed to look elsewhere, and eventually Susan, with an effort, broke the spell and said she was still hungry, and Mrs. Mantrip found that she could eat a little now. Then they talked and they talked, and Susan showed her friend the box of penholders like an entomological specimen-box in which were fixed, each with its label, the pens with which she had written her books. The first was just a common wooden penholder, gnawed at the end; the second was of bone. Then came a series of stylograph and fountain pens, and the last three (those that had inscribed *Rosemary and Rue, Julian Beltravers,* and *Amor Vincit*) were of purple glass, red enamel and silver respectively.

" So silly of me," said Susan, " but when I had finished *Apples of Sodom* I merely happened to keep the pen, that wooden one, with which I had written it. Then the notion struck me that I would get a new pen-holder for each book, and write nothing else with it, and that's how the collection began. Bosanquet is so proud of them; it was he who set them up so neatly in their case. He thinks they might be of some interest some day."

" Thinks ! Might ! Some day ! " ejaculated Mrs. Mantrip. " That's the one I love most, Serena, the silver one which wrote *Amor Vincit*. But then there's the stylograph that wrote *Heart's Queen*. Precious relics ! What will happen to them eventually ? "

Susan considered whether she would not give one to Mrs. Mantrip straight away, but it would spoil the collection; it would be like a set of books with one volume missing. Besides, there was a point where generosity became quixotism.

" I haven't really made up my mind what to do
with them," she said.

" The British Museum, without doubt," said Mrs.
Mantrip. " Otherwise America will get them."

They went down to the pantry. It was in commission again for its domestic uses, since there was no book
now going on, but the gramophone still stood there,
as Susan only needed it when she was writing, and she
intended for the future always to occupy the pantry for
her work.

" I mustn't be a nuisance to my neighbours," she
said. " I should hate to think that while I was so
happy, scribbling away, other people were suffering for
it. And Bosanquet's so kind. He makes shift to do
his work somewhere else when Mademoiselle is busy,
don't you, Bosanquet? "

The reconciliation then, was beautifully complete,
and thus Mrs. Mantrip came to be among Susan's
guests at the Christmas dinner. Food was to be
followed by a tree, and all her guests would receive
handsome and suitable presents. Susan was very busy
for the two preceding days with the purchase of these.
For the Dowager Duchess of Middlesex there was a
copy of the *Peerage*, for Mr. Salt a bathing-costume
in the colours of the Hyde Park Swimming Club, for
Jimmie Mason the *Life of Beethoven*, for Mr. Gandish
the best Badminton racket that money could procure,
for Lady Eva a crystal divining-ball, for Elizabeth a
silver dog-collar of Bully Boy's size, for Miss Mimps a
typewriter which would be a secret reminder of old
days, and for Lady Rye a history of the Cinque Ports.
Susan thought out something useful and suitable for
everybody, but well she knew that none of these
presents would be more highly appreciated than the
gift she had prepared for Mrs. Mantrip. This was a
large photograph of herself signed Rudolph da Vinci
in her own hand. It had been specially taken by
flashlight in the pantry, and there she was at her table,

with her gramophone beside her, busily writing with
the silver pen of *Amor Vincit*. The frame had a
glazed back, and mounted there was a letter from
herself which repeated as near as she could remember
it the forged document which had perished in the
flames. But this letter began " Dearest, darling
Margaret."

Nature unfortunately forgot about the directions for
suitable weather in *Heart's Queen*, and a thick fog
ushered in Christmas Day. But the gallant Susan
arrived at the Serpentine at the appointed hour, and
found six even more gallant gentlemen prepared to con-
test the Serpentine Oaks. Though there were ice-floes
about, the course was happily not frozen over, and
though the starting-post was invisible, a megaphone
proclaimed that the Leanders were off. There was a
most exciting finish, for five of the six racers foamed
up to the winning-post within a few yards of each other.
But there was nothing to be seen of Mr. Salt, and for
the moment it was feared that he must have been
drowned, which would have been a very sad end to
the meeting. But this luckily proved not to be the
case. He had started from scratch, a long way behind
the other competitors, and, having lost his sense of
direction in the fog, had swum nearly across the
Serpentine instead of along it. As he had been
swimming like mad all the time, he began to think that
it was very odd that he did not come into touch with
any of the others, and presently it dawned on him that
he must have been swimming in the wrong direction.
So he turned back and arrived at the shore in time to
stop the Club dragging the water for his body, having
swum at least twice the distance of the Oaks, and being
still as fresh as a daisy. Susan had brought with her
an autographed copy of *Amor Vincit*, as a consolation
prize for some competitor who had not won, but had

acquitted himself nobly, and she gave it to Mr. Salt.
He made a short speech saying that he was sure the
winner was envious of him, and the winner confessed
he was.

Then there were all the Christmas presents to be
arranged. It was impossible to attach such ponderous
objects as a *Peerage*, a typewriter and a *Life of
Beethoven* to a spruce fir, for no sapling tree could
stand such weights, and Susan and Bosanquet stowed
them in a cache behind the tree, from which they would
be brought out and presented to the recipients. She
would have liked Bosanquet to dress up as Father
Christmas, as the Duke did in *Heart's Queen*, but this
Bosanquet respectfully declined to do, for the lesion to
his dignity as a butler would have been irreparable.
Dukes might do as they liked. Besides, he would
be busy concocting the wassail-bowl. Mrs. Mantrip
had found a recipe for this refreshing drink in
Bishop Heber's Journal, where he described his first
Christmas in Calcutta. Spirits and spices were the
powerful and fragrant ingredients of which it was
chiefly compounded, and the new Indian converts
to Christianity appeared to have taken very kindly
to it.

The fog grew thicker during the day, and the Badminton competition for Mr. Gandish's Noel Cup that
afternoon had to be abandoned, since the admirable
electric installation in his court could not pierce it
sufficiently to make play possible. Those of Susan's
guests who came from far arrived at the most divergent
hours, for there was no telling how long it would
take to traverse any given distance. The Dowager
Duchess, for instance, having struck a clearer belt, was
half an hour before the appointed time, while Miss
Mimps, who had struck a thick one, had not arrived
at a quarter to nine, and they sat down to dinner
without her. It was lucky that it was this way round,
for Susan could not have brought herself not to wait

for Her Grace, but cared much less about not waiting for Miss Mimps.

Mimps arrived during fish, and the party was now complete. Never had M. Rouen proved himself more sublime an artist, and Susan was almost sorry that Mr. Armstrong was bright yellow, for he would have enjoyed himself so immensely. But if the dinner was a triumph for M. Rouen, it was an even more glorious occasion for her: a Duchess's legs, not to mention many other highly distinguished limbs, were underneath Susan's table, and Rudolph da Vinci, now openly and officially manifest, beamed on his guests. . . .

It was wonderful to think that scarcely six months had elapsed since she had come to live in the Square, obscure and unknown, without any history or antecedents except those which she was most anxious to suppress, and had been considered a very doubtful acquisition to the high and cultured life of the place. She had been asked to Mrs. Mantrip's luncheon-party to see if she would " do," and she had produced, on the whole, a very poor impression. She had incurred a well-earned unpopularity with her immediate neighbours, owing to the inordinate nuisance she had made of herself with her gramophone and her wireless. She had been misunderstood and misinterpreted, for had not the whole Square at one time believed that, at the most, she was Ulrica ? She had been told by one who, as well as a Duchess, was now among her most fervent admirers, that she wasn't Rudolph da Vinci at all, and that henceforth she was a stranger. Six months ago she had thought herself fortunate to secure the presence of Lady Mackleton at her parties, in order to give them tone, at the price of two guineas a dinner plus taxi-fares, and to-day the best listener in London was more than content to find her own way here through the fog, without any prospect of receiving a cheque to-morrow. Apart from Nunky, who had known all along the splendour of her secret life, and the Bosanquets who

had guessed it, there was only one person present,
Lady Eva, who had had the penetration to perceive
from the first that she had unique and marvellous gifts,
and even she had been a victim of the general delusion
that she was only Ulrica. To-day Lady Eva's occult
intuition had justified itself, and across the grove of
orchids that separated her from her hostess, her eye
was on her, feasting itself on the corn-coloured
halo.

There were too many guests to permit of general
conversation, but talk was brisk and gay. Mr.
Pump was evidently a most amusing gentleman; he
imitated a pig squealing to the admiration of all who
heard him, and his bride insisted on a moment's silence
in order that he might do it again louder. Elizabeth was regaling Augustus with loathsome details
about Sabrina's eczema; Nunky was evidently much
smitten with the charms of Lady Rye; Mrs. Mantrip
was telling Mr. Salt what a beautiful swimmer Papa
used to be, before his asthma made it impossible for
him to bathe; Mr. Gandish was hopeful of getting
Mrs. Bramham, M.P., to induce the Board of Works
to erect a hundred Badminton courts in East London,
and Lady Mackleton was indefatigable in listening to anyone who spoke to her. "They're all
enjoying themselves," thought Susan. "They're
all talking at once, and eating the best dinner in
London."

One or two slight awkwardnesses occurred before
they left the table. The fog, or possibly even the
champagne must have gone to Mimps's head, for in
one of the rare pauses of the loud talk, she had called
out to Susan in her shrill voice, "Well, Susie dear,
this is a pleasant change from those frowzy old days
in the typing-office." But Susie dear gave her so
deadly a glance that the words froze on her lips, and
Bosanquet, to punish her, took her helping of turkey
away before she had finished it. Had she said a

word more, she would certainly not have received her Christmas present. . . . Again, when dinner was over, and Mrs. Mantrip rose to propose their hostess's health, she made an unfortunate slip, in the middle of her beautiful peroration. She said:

"We have all of us, I expect, a secret life unknown to the world, but when, by accident or design, these secret lives of ours come to light, how seldom, alas! does it happen, as in the case of our beloved hostess, that instead of there being discreditable exposures, we stand revealed, as she has done, in a blaze of added glory, of fame, not infamy."

Suddenly she remembered that Lady Rye had only just emerged from the Divorce Court in a blaze of infamy, and leaving an eloquent and moving passage unuttered for fear that there might lurk in it other allusions of an unsuitable sort, she hastily proposed the health of Rudolph da Vinci.

The Christmas-tree followed, and the presents were so great a success that for a time most of the recipients could only attend to their own. The Duchess read all about herself in the *Peerage,* Miss Mimps practised on her typewriter which she pronounced to be a peach, Mr. Salt most humorously put on his bathing-costume over his dress clothes, Mr. Gandish made championlike swipes with his perfectly balanced racket and Mrs. Mantrip gazed and gazed at her photograph. The wassail-bowl reunited them again, and after much pressing Susan was induced to read aloud the last chapter of *Amor Vincit*. But Bishop Heber's recipe was wonderfully potent, and everyone kept dropping off into an uneasy doze, waking with a start and then dozing again, as the interminable recital proceeded. Even the reader herself was very drowsy; she yawned heavily, the book slipped from her hand, and she had a little nap too.

Bosanquet's entry to announce the Duchess's car was like that of the Fairy Prince into an assembly of Sleeping Beauties. . . . How they had all enjoyed that wonderful chapter! "Thank you, Miss Leg."

THE END